Praise for

JOAN JOHNSTON

"Johnston warms your heart and tickles your fancy."
—*New York Daily News*

"Romance devotees will find Johnston lively and well-written, and
her characters perfectly enchanting."
—*Publishers Weekly*

"Joan Johnston continually gives us everything we want...a story that
you wish would never end, and lots of tension and sensuality."
—*Romantic Times BOOKreviews*

"Joan Johnston [creates] unforgettable subplots and characters who
make every fine thread weave into a touching tapestry."
—*Affaire de Coeur*

"Johnston's characters struggle against seriously deranged foes and
face seemingly insurmountable obstacles to true love."
—*Booklist*

"A guaranteed good read."
—*New York Times* bestselling author Heather Graham

JOAN
JOHNSTON
OUTCAST

MIRA®

MIRA

Recycling programs
for this product may
not exist in your area.

ISBN-13: 978-0-7783-2574-1

OUTCAST

Copyright © 2009 by Joan Johnston.

All rights reserved. Except for use in any review, the reproduction or
utilization of this work in whole or in part in any form by any electronic,
mechanical or other means, now known or hereafter invented, including
xerography, photocopying and recording, or in any information storage or
retrieval system, is forbidden without the written permission of the publisher,
MIRA Books, 225 Duncan Mill Road, Don Mills, Ontario, Canada M3B 3K9.

This is a work of fiction. Names, characters, places and incidents are
either the product of the author's imagination or are used fictitiously, and
any resemblance to actual persons, living or dead, business establishments,
events or locales is entirely coincidental.

MIRA and the Star Colophon are trademarks used under license and registered
in Australia, New Zealand, Philippines, United States Patent and Trademark
Office and in other countries.

www.MIRABooks.com

Printed in U.S.A.

For Logan and Meghan

Bright lights in my life
who shine with joy.

Prologue

Ben Benedict's gaze moved restlessly from one potential partner to the next in the Georgetown bar. He wanted a woman. Check that. He wanted sex. Which made him a bastard, he supposed. It was hard to admit that what he really wanted—what he really needed—was to hold another human being close. To feel alive. To forget.

He gritted his teeth as his hands began to tremble. He turned toward the mirror behind the dark, crowded bar and clenched his fists on his knees. He stared down at the glass of McClelland's single malt whiskey in front of him. Alcohol would dull his senses while he was awake, but it wouldn't keep him from dreaming. It sure as hell didn't stop the nightmares.

Ben pictured himself walking along a mountain trail through a fragrant forest of green pines and golden aspen, sunlight streaming through the lush foliage, and felt the tension ease from his body.

"I saw you looking at me. I thought I'd come over and say hello."

He took his time turning to face the pretty young woman who'd slid onto the bar stool next to him. He flattened his now-quiet hands on his jeans and prayed his body would cooperate long enough for him to do the sweet-talking necessary to get her into bed.

She had spiked, light brown hair and long-lashed eyes. Several buttons of her blouse were undone, revealing a hint of enticing cleavage, and her skirt was short and tight, show-ing off very long legs.

Legs that could likely wrap entirely around him.

Ben tried to smile but couldn't manage it. He kept his blue eyes on her and willed her to be the kind of woman he needed tonight. Uninvolved. Unexceptional. Uninhibited.

"You don't have a government job, not with hair down over your collar," she said.

He shivered as she brushed a hand through the black locks that fell over the collar of his white Oxford-cloth shirt, teasing the skin at his nape. It took all his willpower to remain still as she settled her hand on his shoulder.

She tilted her head like a small bird and slowly surveyed him from head to foot, her dark brown eyes telling him she liked his chiseled features, his broad shoulders, his narrow waist and hips. And the way his jeans cupped his sex. Her gaze was almost a physical caress, and his body reacted predictably.

She made a purring sound in her throat before her eyes met his again. "What kind of job does one do in D.C. if one isn't in politics?"

"Does it matter?" he asked, avoiding the question.

She laughed nervously and let her hand drop.

I did something to scare her off. But what? He consciously relaxed his body, modulated his voice to make it less sharp and said, "What do you do?"

She smiled, revealing perfectly capped teeth, and said, "Secretary to an assistant undersecretary who's an assistant secretary to a secretary. If you know what I mean."

He knew he was supposed to laugh. But he couldn't man-age that, either. "Would you like to come to my place?" Sensing her hesitation, he quickly added, "For a nightcap?"

He watched two narrow lines appear above her upturned nose, between her finely tweezed eyebrows.

"You're not a serial killer or anything, are you?"

He made a sound that might have been a snort. "Not hardly."

She surveyed him for another moment, and he did his best to look unthreatening.

"All right," she said, placing her hands on the edge of the polished wooden bar to push herself off the backless stool. "Just let me tell my girlfriend I'm leaving."

He watched her walk over to a high-top table and confer with another woman. He nodded as her friend waved at him. Made himself wait for the woman's return. He felt like bolting, but his need was greater than his fear that if he invited her home, she would discover his secret.

"I live around the corner," he said when she rejoined him. "Mind if we walk?"

"No problem. I told my friend I'd take a cab home."

"Fine." He didn't allow the women he brought home to spend the night. That was far too dangerous. "You ready?"

"Let's go." She slid her arm through his and hugged their bodies close. He could feel the weight of her breast through the arm of his black leather jacket as they left the bar.

He would take the brief escape she offered, the momentary warmth and comfort of another human body. Give pleasure in exchange. And send her back into the night.

1

The shooter aimed carefully and squeezed the trigger. One dead. He squeezed again. A second victim dropped in his tracks. He held his breath and squeezed a third time. As the third victim fell to the ground, he whispered, "Gotcha!"

The teenage boy standing next to him whistled in appreciation. "You're a crazy man with that gun."

Ben Benedict, former military sniper, grinned as he blew off imaginary smoke at the end of his plastic M1911 Colt .45 and shoved the gun back into its plastic holster on the arcade video machine. "That's me. Your average lunatic with a gun. But you notice I won."

The thirteen-year-old playing "House of the Dead" with Ben laughed. "Really, man, you're loco. I've never seen anybody shoot like you. You never miss."

Ben accepted the compliment without bothering to deny the charge of insanity. It was entirely possible the kid was right.

Ben had done his best to hide the nightmares, the night sweats, the daytime flashbacks, the trembling that started without warning and ended just as mysteriously, from his family and his new boss at Immigration and Customs Enforcement, called ICE, the largest branch of the Department of Homeland Security.

As far as Ben knew, none of them suspected his struggle to appear normal since he'd resigned his commission in the army six months ago to become an ICE agent.

"One more game," the kid pleaded.

"It's Wednesday. I know you have homework."

"I can do it later."

Ben shook his head. "I can't stay. My stepmom's giving a prewedding party for my sister Julia and Sergeant Collins tonight. My whole family's supposed to be there. She'll have my head if I'm late."

"I can't believe your sister's gonna marry a cop on Saturday."

"Sergeant Collins is not just another cop. He's my friend," Ben said. Their families owned neighboring plantation homes south of Richmond, Virginia. They'd been best buds until Ben's parents had divorced, and Ben had left Richmond to go live with his father in Chevy Chase. After that, Ben had only seen Waverly when he visited his mother on holidays and vacations.

Waverly Fairchild Collins, III, possessed a notable Virginia pedigree, but his family had been forced to sell most of the land around their plantation home after the Crash in 1929. The Benedicts still owned the vast tract of rich farmland surrounding their estate, The Seasons, where their ancestors had grown tobacco, but which now produced pecans and peaches.

The family gathered at the old plantation house, a white, two-story monstrosity right out of *Gone With the Wind,* on holidays and special occasions.

"That cop might be your friend," Epifanio said. "But to me, he'll always be a sonofabitch."

Ben bit his lip to keep himself from giving the kid a hard time about his language. At least Epifanio had given up using *fuck* every other word.

Ben had met Epifanio five months ago, when his older brother Ricardo had been caught in a joint ICE-MPD sting aimed at gang kids boosting cars in Washington, D.C. for shipment to South America. Sergeant Waverly Collins, head of the Metropolitan Police Department Gang Unit, was the man who'd arrested Ricardo. Epifanio didn't know that Ben, representing ICE, had also been involved in the sting.

ICE was working with the MPD Gang Unit because so

many members of D.C. gangs—the Vatos Locos, Latin Kings, 18th Street gang, and especially MS-13—had once been members of violent gangs south of the border.

Gangs had been named a danger by Homeland Security because so many of their members were illegal aliens. Ben had seen the results of gang violence—the extortion, the theft, the beatings, the senseless death and destruction. The government feared that foreign terrorists might recruit these kids, many of them gangsters without a moral compass, to commit acts of terrorism. Hence the effort to interfere with the gangs' financial survival by eliminating all their sources of income.

Illegal aliens caught in the sting, including Ricardo, were deported back to their homes, usually somewhere in Central or South America.

Upon learning that he was being deported, Ricardo had asked if someone would notify his grandmother. His *abuela* didn't have a phone, so he couldn't call her, and she couldn't read, so a letter wouldn't work.

Ben seemed to be the only one moved by the eighteen-year-old's plea. Despite warnings from Waverly not to get involved, Ben had gone to see Ricardo's grandmother at her run-down apartment in the Columbia Heights neighborhood, a half hour north of his row house in Georgetown.

Mrs. Fuentes was a small, wizened woman with white hair she wore in braids bobby-pinned at the top of her head. She reminded Ben of his maternal grandmother, who'd died in a private plane crash along with his grandfather when he was ten.

Quiet tears had streamed down Mrs. Fuentes's brown, wrinkled face when Ben told her Ricardo's fate. Mrs. Fuentes offered Ben a cup of coffee, which he'd felt obliged to take.

When she had him seated in the tiny living room, where the brown couch was covered with vinyl to protect it, she told him how worried she was that Ricardo's little brother Epifanio—who, thank the Blessed Virgin, had been born to a black father in the United States—would follow in his older brother's footsteps and end up dead on the streets from drugs or gang violence. The 18th Street gang was already pressuring Epifanio to join.

Waverly laughed when Ben told him later how he'd offered to check in on Epifanio now and then and do what he could to keep the kid in school. Waverly warned Ben that he was asking for heartache. He'd told Ben his chances of keeping Epifanio out of the 18th Street gang and off hard drugs—highly addictive crystal meth and crack cocaine—when his brother had been a gang member and a methamphetamines addict, were slim to none.

Despite Waverly's advice, Ben had made a point of seeing the kid at least once a week over the past five months, although he never had told the kid what he really did for a living. Epifanio thought Ben worked in an office in downtown D.C., which Ben did. It just happened to be the ICE office.

It had taken a long time to earn the kid's trust. And there had been setbacks.

Three months ago, Ben had come by one afternoon when Mrs. Fuentes was still at her babysitting job and been concerned when Epifanio didn't answer his knock. He'd stepped inside the unlocked apartment and found Epifanio sitting on his bed, leaning against an interior wall spray-painted with graffiti, his pupils dilated so wide that Ben could have fallen into the kid's eyes.

"What are you on?" he'd demanded, searching around the kid's iron cot for drug paraphernalia. He'd pulled out his cell phone to call 911, afraid the boy might be in danger of OD-ing, but Epifanio had grabbed his wrist and said, "It's only Ecstasy."

"*Only* Ecstasy?" Ecstasy wasn't addictive, but it was still a powerful narcotic. Then he'd had another thought. "Where did you get the money to buy that junk?"

The kid had hung his head.

"Well?"

"I stole the E from a locker at school," he'd mumbled.

Ben had been so mad he could have wrung the kid's neck. "I'm taking you to the emergency room."

"It'll wear off in a couple of hours," Epifanio protested.

Ben had hauled the kid out to his car anyway, taken him to the emergency room and waited with him while the hospital did a blood test. The toxicology report confirmed that the only drug in Epifanio's system was the amphetamines in Ecstasy.

Ben had been standing by, his arms crossed over his chest, when Mrs. Fuentes arrived at Epifanio's hospital bedside, her dark brown eyes huge with fear.

Epifanio had been defiantly silent in response to Ben's disapproval. But when his grandmother sank into the chair beside his bed, crossed herself, closed her eyes and folded her hands in prayer, the kid started to cry.

"I'm sorry, *Abuela,*" he said. "I won't do it again. I promise."

Ben had kept up his visits to the household. And the kid had been true to his word. Two months later, Epifanio was still off drugs, still not part of a gang and still in school. Ben was counting his blessings, but because of constant reminders from Waverly that the good behavior couldn't last, he was taking things one day at a time.

"I'm looking forward to having the sergeant as my brother-in-law," he told the boy.

"I hate cops," Epifanio said, his dark eyes narrowed, his lips pressed flat.

I'm a cop, Ben thought. But he merely met the kid's gaze.

Epifanio made a face as he holstered his own plastic gun. "You might wanta watch yourself when you come around to the neighborhood. I been hearing rumors of something bad goin' down."

"Bad like what?" Ben asked.

Epifanio shrugged. "Just guys lookin' over their shoulders, you know? That sorta creepy feeling you get when something's not right?"

Epifanio might not belong to the 18th Street gang, dubbed

the 1-8 by the MPD, but most of the kids in his neighborhood did. It was impossible for him to avoid them entirely.

As far as anyone in the neighborhood knew, Ben was supposedly a "Big Brother" from the community group Big Brothers and Big Sisters. His ICE connection was a secret. Which was why another ICE agent monitored the activities of the 18th Street gang.

"Thanks for the heads up," Ben said.

Trouble among the gangs hit the streets like ocean waves. Some waves passed without incident. Some devastated everything in their path. He put a hand on Epifanio's shoulder and said, "You be careful out there, too."

"You know I will," Epifanio said with a cheeky grin.

"How about that homework?" Ben said.

The kid grinned. "I ain't got—"

"Don't have—" Ben automatically corrected.

"Any homework," Epifanio finished, his grin widening.

Ben ruffled the boy's short dreads, something he wouldn't have done even a few weeks ago. "Then go read a book."

As they left the Games & More video arcade, Epifanio teasingly flashed Ben the 18th Street gang sign. He laughed when Ben frowned at the display, then sauntered down the street toward home.

Ben stuck his suddenly trembling hands deep in his pockets, clenching them into fists. He could feel his heart pounding in his chest. He had trouble catching his breath.

He felt the searing heat of the desert. The grittiness of the sand at his collar. The stickiness of blood on his hands.

"Hey! You gonna stand there all day? We're late!"

Ben's tongue was stuck to the roof of his mouth. He jerked a nod toward Waverly, who'd pulled his Ford Explorer up to the curb.

"You okay?" Waverly asked, sticking his head out the open window.

Ben forced himself to take a step. Another step. He crossed

behind the car, to give himself time to recover. After all these months, he wasn't going to let this…shit…get the better of him. The incidents were occurring less often. They were less severe. Surely, at some point, they would stop entirely.

By the time he got to the front passenger door of the car his hands were out of his pockets and functioning without a visible tremor. As he slipped into Waverly's Ford he said, "I can't believe you and Julia are letting Patsy throw you a party, especially this close to the wedding."

"Your dad was more of a dad to me than my own. When she suggested it, I didn't want to say no," Waverly replied. "Don't blame me if your stepmother invited your whole family. Julia said just about everybody agreed to come."

Ben groaned. "Everybody? My mom and the senator in the same room with my dad and Patsy?"

"Yep," Waverly said.

Ben groaned. Although his parents had divorced twenty years ago, his mother had never forgiven his father for cheating on her with another woman. His father had never forgiven his mother for her lack of understanding and inability to pardon what he claimed was a single lapse in judgment under extraordinary circumstances.

Both had remarried within a year, and from what Ben could see, both had remarkably successful second marriages. But he was pretty sure his parents had never really stopped loving each other. Otherwise, they wouldn't still be so miserable in each other's presence.

Unfortunately, their continuing attraction made things pretty uncomfortable whenever their respective spouses were in the room. Which meant the party tonight would be a parental minefield, exacerbated by the warfare that went on between the very different children who'd grown up as relatives because of their two second marriages.

Ben was one of thirteen siblings. And nobody was married yet or had produced offspring.

Actually, fourteen siblings. He was forgetting the reason for his parents' divorce, his father's bastard son, Ryan Donovan McKenzie. Ryan was the result of a one-night stand his father had indulged in with a barmaid, Mary Kate McKenzie. His dad had insisted on acknowledging and supporting his illegitimate son, and invited Ryan to every family gathering. The Black Sheep always declined.

"How many of the Fabulous Fourteen have said they're coming?" Ben asked Waverly.

"The senator's three kids by his late wife, one of your three brothers, your stepmom's twins with her ex from Texas and your three half sisters. And, of course, my lovely fiancée. In short, nearly the whole dysfunctional bunch. No surprise, the Black Sheep sent his regrets. Should be a great party."

Ben felt his heart take an extra thump. "I can hardly wait."

2

"How are things with the kid?" Waverly asked as he drove out of the ethnically and economically mixed Columbia Heights neighborhood toward elite Chevy Chase, Maryland, where the party was being held. Columbia Heights was becoming gentrified, forcing out the poor, but right now it was still a blend of the crumbling old and the very new. The distance to Chevy Chase wasn't far in miles, but it might as well have been a trip to the moon, the two worlds were so far apart.

"The kid is fine," Ben said as he reached for the rep-striped tie he'd left in the backseat with a jacket earlier in the day.

"For now."

Ben buttoned up his shirt, slipped the tie around his neck and began to tie it. "I'm optimistic."

"You're naive."

"You're jaded." Ben shoved the Windsor knot up to his throat.

"Maybe so. We'll see."

Ben hesitated, then said, "Epifanio has heard rumblings that something bad is in the works."

"If the kid asks too many questions, they're going to shut him up. Forever," Waverly warned. "Don't push it."

"I didn't ask for information. He volunteered it."

"Someday somebody's going to make the connection between you and ICE and the kid. They'll start to wonder what he's told you. And—" Waverly made a ragged sound as he drew his forefinger across his throat.

"I'm his Big Brother. That's all."

"Yeah. Right," Waverly said.

As the man in charge of the MPD Gang Unit for the past two years, Waverly knew far more about gang behavior than Ben did. If Waverly was worried about Epifanio, Ben knew there was something to worry about.

"Have you heard something I haven't?" he asked.

"Just the same stuff as the kid," Waverly said. "That something is going to happen. Something big."

"What are we talking about here?" Ben asked. "New car theft ring? Counterfeit bills? Drug shipment? Illegal weapons?"

"Terrorism."

Ben mentally reeled. He'd chosen to work on an ICE joint task force with the MPD dismantling gangs in D.C., rather than join the investigative arm of ICE and search out terrorists, precisely because he'd had enough of war. Apparently, this time the war was coming to him.

"Terrorism," he mused. "What does that mean? I have trouble imagining white or black or Hispanic or Asian gangs hijacking planes and flying them into buildings."

"Maybe not. But they can help smuggle dirty bombs or biological weapons across the border from Central or South America. Or learn how to make improvised explosive devices—IEDs—and plant them in big cities across America—Los Angeles, Houston, Miami, Chicago, Detroit, New York—and of course, the District."

"Is that really going to happen?"

"Nobody knows for sure," Waverly said. "But you and I are going to keep a damned close eye on MS."

Mara Salvatrucha 13, called MS by the MPD, was known to be a merciless and violent gang in El Salvador, where it had originated. Its members had brought that arbitrary death-dealing with them when they stole across the border and joined MS gangs formed in the States.

"Are several gangs involved?" Ben asked. "Or only MS?"

"MPD and ICE share info, so I'm sure you know Al Qaeda

had sent lieutenants to El Salvador to recruit members of MS to commit terrorist acts. The presumption is they'll make use of members of MS here in the States to help them, by threatening their families in El Salvador, if necessary. Which is why we're focusing on MS."

Ben hadn't wanted to believe Al Qaeda would be successful in El Salvador. His job was going to change radically if a bunch of hired assassins began infiltrating across the border and joining local MS gangs to cover up their terrorist activities.

"Have you heard anything on the streets about exactly who— or what—Al Qaeda's target might be in D.C.?" Ben asked.

"That, my friend, is the sixty-four-thousand-dollar question. They have a helluva lot of choices." Waverly brought his car to a stop in front of an impressive, two-story Colonial redbrick home with white shutters and a tall, elegant front door.

"We've reached the end of your father's obscenely long driveway—and this conversation," Waverly said. "You know Julia doesn't like me to talk about work around your mother. It upsets her."

Ben got out of the car and dumped his leather jacket in the backseat. He grabbed a navy suit jacket from a hanger on a hook over the window to wear with his khaki trousers. He knew what really upset his mother was the idea of her eighteen-year-old daughter marrying a thirty-year-old cop. Especially since the bride and groom had only met six months ago.

And it wasn't just the age difference, or the short time they'd known each other. His mother blamed him for the fact that in three days Julia would be marrying a man with a dangerous job that could get him killed. Worst of all, the young couple was determined to live on the paltry income of a D.C. cop.

Ben's mother, Abigail Coates Benedict Hamilton, not only had inherited wealth of her own, but a year after she'd divorced Ben's even wealthier father, she'd married a wealthy widower, the senior senator from Virginia, Randolph Cornelius "Ham" Hamilton, III.

Ben's half sister Julia had been born into a life of opulence and privilege. His mother couldn't bear the thought of Julia wanting for anything. She deplored the small apartment that was all Waverly could afford, and which would be her daughter's first home, and had announced she was "devastated" that Julia would be attending Georgetown University instead of her alma mater, Wellesley.

Seeing that Waverly and Julia were in love, Ben had let his mother's complaints roll off his shoulders. The fact he pretty much always fell short of pleasing his mother was something he'd learned to cope with at a very young age. Eight, to be precise.

That was the year his parents divorced. Ben had always wondered who'd come up with the idea to split up the Benedicts' four living sons—Nash, Ben, Carter and Rhett—and give two to each parent.

Nash, who was eleven, and Rhett, who was only a baby, had stayed with his mother. Ben, who'd been a little intimidated by his father, Foster Holloway Benedict, an army officer who'd been awarded the Medal of Honor, had begged to be allowed to stay with his mother in their home in Richmond. But his father had taken him away to live in Chevy Chase, along with his younger brother Carter.

Not that Ben had spent much time with his father once he'd taken up residence in the mansion in Chevy Chase. Within a year of his parents' divorce, his father had married a woman named Patsy Taggart. Patsy had done all the caretaking while his father was off being a soldier. At thirteen, Ben had been sent off to Massachusetts to attend Groton, an Episcopal prep school.

At the time Patsy married his father, she'd had twin two-year-old sons who lived most of the year in Texas with her former husband. But it wasn't long before she was pregnant with Ben's twin sisters Amanda and Bethany. A few years later, Camille had come along. Ben called the girls the ABCs, because their names started with the first letters of the alphabet.

It was hard not to love the ABCs because they so obviously adored him, and he did his best to be a protective and loving big brother.

It had taken a long time before he let Patsy fill the hole left in his heart when his mother had given him away. But his step-mother had been persistent. He loved her now far more than the mother who'd borne him.

Ben had seen the pain in his biological mother's eyes when he'd remained aloof through the years. Diabolically, his parents had arranged for their four sons to spend time together in the same households from time to time—for holidays or vacations—so they wouldn't lose touch with each other.

As it turned out, he and Carter were close. Rhett, no sur-prise, was everybody's friend. Nash was unknowable

Ben had always been in awe of Nash, because when that Solomon-like custody decision was being made, he'd refused to leave their mother. Ben had overheard him tell their father flat out, "I'm not going."

Of course, that meant Ben had been forced to go instead. He didn't blame Nash. Ultimately, his mother had agreed with the decision to send him away.

Ben had never given her another chance to reject him. But he dreaded family gatherings because it dragged up all that ancient history.

He was keenly aware that he'd once again managed to dis-appoint her by introducing Julia to Waverly. Ben felt an ache in his chest. He focused on the peaceful forest scene that helped him quiet the demons. The last thing he wanted was to have an attack now.

He thought of how little any of his family knew about the bad things that had happened to him as a soldier. And how grateful he was that they'd never asked.

Ben intended to keep it that way, which was why he was so careful to conceal the nightmares and all the rest of the crap he was dealing with these days. If his family got an inkling he was having trouble coping with a world not at war, they'd be in his face wanting to help.

He envied the Black Sheep, who had just said no, and his two brothers, who had good excuses to be absent tonight. Carter was serving with the marines in Iraq, and Nash was out of the country doing whatever secret work he did for the president.

"Ben! You're here!" his thirteen-year-old sister Camille squealed as he stepped into the circular domed foyer of his father's Chevy Chase mansion with Waverly on his heels.

"I'm here," he replied, putting a smile on his face and opening his arms to catch Camille as she leapt into them.

"Ben! You came!" his seventeen-year-old sister Bethany said, her long blond curls bouncing as she hurried toward him.

As if he'd had a choice. He hugged Camille before setting her down, then wrapped an arm around Bethany's shoulder.

"Ben! You need a shave!" Bethany's twin sister Amanda said as she wrinkled her nose.

Ben grinned as Amanda put her hands on either side of his bristly face and leaned forward to kiss him on each cheek, in the continental style she must have learned in the exclusive Swiss boarding school she and Bethany attended.

"Girls! Give Ben a chance to get in the door."

His half sisters stepped back to allow their mother to embrace her stepson. His father's second wife wasn't conventionally pretty and she'd never been thin. But Patsy had hazel eyes that warmed to a golden brown every time she smiled.

When he hugged her back, he did it with all the love a son gave to his mother.

"Wave!" a female voice shrieked.

Ben watched a blond streak go flying by and laughed as Julia threw herself into Waverly's open arms in much the same way his youngest half sister had flown into his. Except Julia followed the hug with a long, lascivious kiss.

Ben was pretty sure his mother would have been appalled to see her only daughter behaving like a hoyden. And equally sure that Julia would have found a way to charm her mother out of any rebuke for her behavior.

Ben turned back to his stepmother, urging her and his sisters toward the living room as he said, "I can't believe you got that uppity Swiss school to let the girls come home for a wedding."

"Mom didn't give them any choice," Amanda interjected.

Ben had long ago realized his mother and his stepmother were equally strong women in their own ways. He just saw a softer side to Patsy that his mother didn't possess. Or had never shown to him.

"Where's Dad?" he asked as his stepmother herded everyone toward the living room.

"Reception at the Argentine embassy," Patsy said. "He'll be here later. I mostly wanted to give you kids a chance to catch up with each other before the wedding."

Ben found his youngest brother sitting on the arm of a silk-covered sofa, flirting with one of the caterer's helpers who was passing canapés. Rhett's job was made easier by his incredible good looks. His parents had produced five sons—Darlington, the fourth boy, had died at age four—and with the fifth, his mother had produced a perfect male specimen. At least, every girl who'd ever crossed Rhett's path seemed to think so.

"Welcome, Ben. Hi, there, Waverly," Rhett called as Ben entered the room with his entourage of females and the groom.

Rhett rose and whispered something in the helper's ear that made her duck her head and blush, then crossed to Ben with his hand outstretched. Ben started to shake Rhett's hand, but his younger brother used his grip to pull Ben close. He wrapped his other arm around Ben's neck and gave him a hard hug.

"How the hell are you?" Rhett asked. "You've been slipperier than a fish lately. Where have you been keeping yourself?"

Away from all of you, Ben thought. *So you don't find out the truth about me.* "I've been working," he replied. "How'd you get away from West Point?"

"You know Mom," Rhett said with a grin. "She had a

word with the senator who had a word with the comman-
dant." He opened his arms wide. "And here I am in the middle of the week."

Yes, my two mothers are very much alike, Ben thought.
Both women had no qualms about going around the rules if
the rules didn't suit them. The result of being indecently
wealthy all their lives, he supposed. Patsy's family had land
in Texas swimming in oil.

"Where's Mom?" Ben asked as he searched the enormous
living room and the four hallways leading away from it.

"The senator had some business on the Hill, so she rep-
resented him at a reception at the Argentine embassy
tonight," Rhett replied. "They'll both be here later to toast
the bride and groom."

*Dad and Mom on their own in the same place at the same
time?* He glanced at Patsy, wondering if she was aware that his
mother and father were together tonight at the Argentine
embassy, while she was here. His father who, after nineteen
years of marriage to another woman, still snuck longing glances
at Abby Hamilton whenever he thought no one was looking.

"Hello, Ben."

Ben shook hands with his stepbrother John, the senator's
son. At thirty-seven, John Hamilton was the eldest sibling and
the one most likely to antagonize the Benedict boys. John was
a pacifist and happily defended conscientious objectors. He
was militant in his belief that there were better ways to settle
disputes between countries than to wage wars.

Ben didn't really disagree. But Foster Benedict had retired
from the army as a four-star general. All four Benedict boys had
attended, or in Rhett's case was still attending, a military
academy. And three of the Benedict boys had served honorably,
and in Carter's case was still serving, in the military. Thus, any
conversation with John often descended into controversy.

"You look beat," John said.

Ben was surprised John had noticed—much less commented on—the dark patches under his eyes. Nightmares had been interrupting his sleep, but he wasn't about to confess that to anyone. Instead he said, "Too much carousing."

Which earned him a disdainfully raised eyebrow from his stepbrother. John's two sisters, thirty-four-year-old Augusta and twenty-six-year-old Alexis, who went by the nicknames Gus and Alex, merely waved to Ben from the opposite side of the room, where they sat in comfortable chairs before a cheerfully crackling fire in the redbrick fireplace.

Ben was keeping mental track in his head of everyone he'd greeted. Fourteen siblings minus himself and the three who weren't coming left ten. Camille, Bethany, Amanda, Julia—although she hadn't exactly "greeted" him—Rhett, John, Augusta and Alexis. That left Patsy's twenty-year-old twin sons from her first marriage, who weren't in the living room.

"Where are the twins?" he asked Patsy.

She glanced around the living room and down the various hallways and said, "I'm not really sure."

"They're in the kitchen," Rhett volunteered.

"What are they doing in there?" Patsy asked.

"Josh bet Reese he could—"

"Josh *bet* Reese?" Patsy interrupted. "Those two will be the death of me yet." She turned and hurried toward the kitchen.

"Josh bet Reese what?" Ben asked Rhett.

"That he could swallow a whole egg."

"Without choking to death?" Ben said. "Why didn't you say something to Patsy sooner?"

"Josh shot me a wink. I figured he had some trick up his sleeve," Rhett said with a shrug. "As usual."

"This I gotta see," Ben said, hurrying after a disappearing Patsy.

When Ben got to the kitchen he saw a smug-looking Josh with slimy egg dripping down his chin and an angry Reese counting twenties out of his wallet onto the Mediterranean-tiled kitchen counter.

"What's going on here, Reese?" Patsy demanded. "What is that all over your face, Josh?"

"Egg," Josh said with a grin. "I bet Reese I could swallow a whole egg."

"Looks like you lost," Ben said, giving Reese a comforting pat on the shoulder.

"The sonofabitch cheated!" Reese said as he laid the fifth twenty on the counter. "He broke it up in his mouth and chewed the shell before he swallowed it."

"You did what?" Patsy said to Josh. She whirled on Reese and snapped, "Watch your language, young man!" She glanced at the two middle-aged women preparing food on the other side of the kitchen and said, "There are ladies present."

"Sorry, Mom," Reese said.

"It was just a raw egg, Mom. And a little eggshell," Josh said. "It won't kill me."

Patsy threw up her hands. "I give up. You two are incorrigible. You talk some sense into them, Ben." She turned and stalked back toward the living room.

"How are things on the ranch?" Ben asked with a wry twist of his mouth.

"It's a lot warmer in Texas than it is here," Josh said, grabbing a towel from a rack and wiping the egg off his face. "And there aren't any females around to drive a man crazy."

"Sounds good to me," Ben said, unable to keep from smiling.

"I don't know why Mom keeps insisting we come up here," Reese said. "Why don't you guys come down to the ranch sometime?"

"That might be a little awkward," Ben pointed out, "considering your dad and your two uncles live there."

"Dad wouldn't care," Josh said. "He doesn't have a girlfriend or anything. And Uncle Cain and Uncle Cash are more like older brothers than uncles, they're so much younger than Dad."

"I know the ABCs would like to come visit," Ben said. "They love to go horseback riding."

Josh and Reese exchanged a glance.

"What?" Ben said.

"We heard Mom talking on the phone to your dad tonight," Josh said.

"*Over*heard, you mean?" Ben said with an edge to his voice.

"They were arguing," Reese said in his defense. "It was hard not to hear."

"And?" Ben prodded.

After a pause Reese said, "She was threatening to take the ABCs and head for Texas if he missed this party."

"That was all we heard." Josh shoved Reese in the shoulder. "Because he didn't think we should listen anymore."

It was enough, Ben realized. He couldn't say he hadn't seen friction between Patsy and his father. If he'd noticed those secret looks his father shot his mother, Patsy had likely noticed them, as well. But like all kids, he didn't want his parents to split up. Especially since he liked Patsy a hell of a lot better than he liked his own mother.

"Patsy doesn't know you heard?" Ben asked.

Josh and Reese shook their heads.

"Keep it that way. Maybe things will change."

"Do you really think so?" Josh asked, his eyes bleak. "I think it would kill Dad to have Mom back in Texas at her dad's ranch. It's too close to the Bar-3, you know. Dad would have to see her all the time."

Another man in love with a wife he's lost? Ben wondered. He hoped he never fell in love. The people he knew who'd done it—his father, Patsy, his mother—had only suffered as a result.

"Everything'll settle back down," he told the twins. It was what he wanted to believe. He hoped he was right.

Ben heard a commotion in the living room. He listened for a moment and heard his mother's voice. And his father's. They must have arrived together from the embassy party. He listened for the senator's gruff voice but didn't hear it.

He wondered how Patsy was handling the fact his mother

and father had arrived together. As the perfect hostess she was, he supposed. But she would be hurting. Because his father couldn't keep his eyes off his mother whenever she was in the same room.

Ben's stomach knotted. He forced himself to leave the kitchen. He had to help Patsy by distracting his father.

That shouldn't be too hard. All he'd have to do was mention his job.

3

Ben was exhausted. He sat in his undershorts on the brocade-upholstered couch in his newly furnished four-story row house in Georgetown, his head in his hands. He could see the pink-and-yellow light of dawn through the silk-draped windows. When was this going to end? How long was he going to have these damned nightmares? He'd woken up screaming. And been afraid to go back to sleep.

He rubbed a hand across his bristly face. Thank God he'd been alone. Thank God he'd sent home the woman he'd picked up at a bar last night after he'd left Patsy's party. He didn't remember much about her, except that her body had been a brief haven for his.

He pressed the heels of his hands into his gritty eyes. He'd been seeking escape from more than his own troubles. He'd felt bad for Patsy.

When he'd entered the living room last night, his father had been helping his mother remove her coat. Patsy would have had to be blind to miss the yearning in his eyes. And his step-mother was a woman who saw things very clearly.

Ben had been furious with his father. And frustrated by his inability to change the situation. It was a feeling he'd lived with since he was eight and understood that his father had gotten another woman pregnant, which had caused his mother to ask for a divorce.

But he was no longer a helpless child. He could protect his stepmother. And had, by refocusing his father's attention on himself. "Looks like some kind of gang trouble is going to hit the District soon," he'd said.

"You should have stayed in the army," his father replied. "There you could have done some real good for this country."

"I'm doing good where I am, Dad," he'd said. "The threat is right here in our backyard."

"You were a good soldier. A great soldier."

"I'm a good ICE agent." But it was clear from his father's expression that there was no chance for greatness in that role.

His father snorted. "You spend your days rounding up illegal aliens and deporting them."

"That isn't all I do." But he knew that, in his father's eyes, his work as an ICE agent could never measure up to the contribution he could make to his country as part of the military. His father couldn't understand why he'd resigned his commission after training for a life in the army.

And he wasn't about to tell him the truth.

Luckily, within a few minutes Ham had arrived, everyone shared a toast to the bride and groom, and Ben's mother and the senator left to return to the senator's Georgetown home.

Ben had given Patsy a hard hug before he left. But he hadn't looked her in the face. Because he couldn't bear to see the silent suffering in her eyes.

Ben wondered if Patsy and his father had argued last night. Probably they had. He worried that the day was coming when they wouldn't make up.

Ben shoved his hands through his hair. In order not to stick out as a cop on the street, he was allowed to let his hair grow long. But it was time for a haircut. He needed to get up off the couch and get moving. Get a shower. Eat some breakfast. When was the last time he'd eaten a decent meal? Breakfast yesterday, maybe. He'd had no appetite last night. No wonder his stomach felt like it was gnawing on his insides.

He had to check in with his ICE boss, Tony Pellicano, at nine. Then he wanted to spend some time driving around the

Columbia Heights neighborhood. There were kids from gangs other than the 18th Street crowd who might be able to tell him something more about the storm that was threatening to break over D.C.

A half hour later, after a shower and a bowl of shredded wheat—the banana he'd planned to slice on top had been rotten—Ben was out the door. He loved living in Georgetown, loved the feel of it, the brick and the trees and the sunshine that made it feel so alive, even though most of the row houses had been built more than a century before.

But Georgetown had opted out of having the Metro come through—bringing in the riffraff—so he needed a car to get around. He'd been drunk when he'd left the Hare & Hound last night, so he'd left his car parked on the street near the pub and walked home with his nameless paramour. Which meant he needed to walk back this morning to pick it up.

He found himself gaining ground on a stray dog striding along the brick sidewalk in front of him. The heavily muscled black-and-tan rottweiler was wearing a spiked collar, from which a piece of heavy chain dangled. The dog sniffed a Japanese cherry tree, lifted his leg, then marched on down the sidewalk as though he owned it.

The dog's head turned sharply, and Ben followed the beast's gaze to a bunch of uniformed schoolgirls, laughing and chattering as they made their way down the opposite side of the street.

Ben felt his neck hairs prickle when the rottweiler started across the road toward the girls, disappearing between two parked SUVs.

Ben picked up his pace, afraid the stray might attack the girls, several of whom had begun skipping, seeming to flee the dog. Making themselves prey.

The dog shot out from between the parked cars at exactly the same moment as a Toyota SUV found a break in the morning traffic and barreled past. The driver hit his brakes and laid ten feet of rubber before he slammed into the rottweiler, sending it flying.

The girls screamed.

The dog howled in anguish.

Ben stared in disbelief as the driver glanced back over his shoulder, then laid more rubber as he snaked through traffic to escape the scene.

As Ben approached the rottweiler the injured beast bared its sharp teeth and growled ferociously. The bones in one of the dog's hind legs were sticking through its flesh. The beast tried to rise, then yelped in pain and fell back to the ground. There was no way to get near the animal without getting mauled.

"I'm calling 911!" one of the schoolgirls cried as she began searching through her backpack.

Another girl pointed to a brick building across the street and said, "There's an emergency vet right there on the corner." She focused her teary eyes on Ben and said, "Won't you please take him there, sir? Please?"

Ben glanced at the vet's office across the street, thinking the vet would have some idea how to subdue the dog so he could be moved and treated.

Then the decision was taken out of his hands. One of the schoolgirls bent down and reached out a hand to the growling, slavering beast. Jaws snapping, the animal charged at her.

Ben had no choice but to intervene.

4

"Pregnant? How could she be pregnant?" Annagreit Schuster wasn't often surprised, but the news that her Maine Coon cat, Penelope, was expecting a happy event—was, in fact, in labor—came as a complete shock. Penelope never left the confines of Anna's small, upstairs apartment in a renovated Georgetown brownstone, except to lie in the sun on the second-floor balcony. How could she have gotten pregnant?

Anna eyed the ten-pound, tabby-and-white-striped cat lying on the emergency vet's metal examining table. Then she turned her gaze to the twelve-year-old boy standing beside her, his head hung low. "Henry?" she said. "Is there something you haven't told me?"

"When I first started cat-sitting for you, before I knew better, I left the front door open and Penelope ran out. I found her before you got home, so I didn't see any reason to tell you." He looked up at her with guilt-ridden mud-brown eyes and said, "I'm sorry, Anna."

Anna brushed her hand soothingly across the boy's tight black curls from crown to nape. Henry's widowed mother was a surgical nurse, and she was often gone when Henry got home from school. Since Anna lived across the hall, she'd offered him a job cat-sitting, mostly to keep him from ending up home alone. She'd never seen him looking so forlorn.

"It's all right, Henry. At least Penelope doesn't have a tumor." Which was what Anna had thought when she'd seen

Penelope acting so strangely this morning and felt the cat's lumpy belly under the thick hair that grew on her stomach.

"If you take Penelope home and make her comfortable in a box in the closet, or any quiet place in the house, she should be able to deliver on her own," the vet said.

"Are you sure?" Anna asked anxiously. She knew virtually nothing about birthing babies, human or feline.

"She's going to be more relaxed in familiar surroundings. If you have any concerns at all, give me a call."

Penelope raised her head from the examining table, looked plaintively at Anna and called out to her with the chirping trill distinctive to Maine Coon cats, which didn't meow like other cats.

"Does it hurt?" Henry asked. "For her to have babies, I mean."

Anna looked to the emergency vet, but before he could answer, the examining room door flew open.

"Doc, I need some help here!"

Anna barely had time to register the blood soaking the white T-shirt of the man who'd burst in, and the enormous size of the injured rottweiler in his muscular arms, before Penelope gave a chirp that was more of a shriek and bounded to her feet. Her pregnant body arched, bushy tail held high. Her pretty cat face scrunched into something resembling an alien beast, mouth wide and wicked teeth bared at this sudden threat.

"Get your damned cat off the table, lady!" the man snapped. "So I can lay this dog down." The man's leather coat was wrapped over the animal's hindquarters. As he leaned forward, the coat slid off the dog onto the examining table like a black snake and then dropped onto the floor.

Penelope hissed menacingly.

The dog growled back through his teeth, which Anna saw with horror were still clamped hard into human flesh. The man's forearm was streaming blood from numerous canine tooth puncture wounds where the dog had hold of him.

She grabbed for Penelope, who raked her hand with bared

claws. Anna cried out in pain and astonishment, "Penelope!" She stared at the four distinct lines of blood Penelope's claws had torn in her skin. Penelope had scratched her when she was a kitten, but never once in the five years since.

"Come on, lady," the intruder commanded. "Move the damned cat!"

Anna was more cautious this time, but calling Penelope's name had made the cat aware of her, and Penelope allowed herself to be lifted into Anna's arms.

As soon as Penelope was off the metal table, the man bent over it and laid the dog there. Even then, the dog held on. Anna didn't want to look at the injured animal, but she couldn't help noticing the naked bone protruding through a bloody tear in one of its hind legs.

She noticed Henry was also staring with wide, horrified eyes at the dog's blood and bone. "Come on, Henry," she said gently. "We need to get Penelope home so she can have her babies in peace and quiet."

She shot an admonishing look at the man, but his attention was focused on the dog, whose teeth were still deeply embedded in his arm.

Anna would have liked to stay and help, but she felt Penelope's belly ripple and realized she'd better get her cat back to the comfortable traveling cage in her car and drive the few blocks home before kittens started arriving.

"Henry," she repeated. "Let's go."

"I want to see how the vet gets the dog to let go of the guy's arm," Henry said, his eyes riveted on the scene in front of him.

So do I, Anna thought. But what she said as she backed her way out of the emergency room door was, "Come on, Henry. We need to get Penelope home. And you need to get to school."

Reluctantly, the boy turned and hurried after her.

5

Anna couldn't believe she was back at the emergency room—this time, one for humans. One of the deep scratches on her hand had been seeping all day. She thought it might need a stitch or two. And she needed a tetanus shot.

After she'd left the vet's office with Penelope, she'd called her office and asked the secretary to reschedule her morning patients. Anna was one of four doctors, two men and two women, practicing together in a high-rise in downtown D.C., where they did psychological counseling.

She hadn't wanted to leave Penelope alone to deliver her first litter. The four adorable kittens arrived safe and sound, and in time for Anna to make her afternoon appointments.

She came directly home after her last session of the day because she knew Henry would be on her doorstep the instant he got home from school. She wanted to be there when he arrived, to make sure Penelope didn't take umbrage and claw him if he reached out to pet the kittens.

By the time Henry's mother came home, it was dark out. Anna fixed herself something to eat and watched *Grey's Anatomy,* debating whether to have her injury treated, worried that she might get stuck in an emergency room half the night.

But she knew it was better to deal with problems head-on than to let them slide. So at 10:37 p.m. she'd headed out to a twenty-four-hour urgent care facility not far from the emergency vet's office.

She looked through the glass door of the clinic to see if

there were a lot of people ahead of her and counted a mother with two young boys, a father with a babe in arms, an elderly couple, a young couple with a toddler—and the stranger who'd been bitten earlier in the day by his rottweiler.

He'd changed out of the bloody white T-shirt and khaki pants he'd been wearing. He was dressed now in a short-sleeved gray T-shirt and jeans. The well-worn black leather jacket that had fallen on the examining table this morning had been replaced by a well-worn brown leather bomber jacket, which lay tossed over a nearby orange plastic chair. He had on comfortable-looking brown loafers but no socks, even though the early October evening was chilly.

He was engrossed in a paperback. Not a good sign. How long was the wait, anyway?

Anna wasn't sure whether to say hello to him on her way to the reception desk. He hadn't exactly exuded charm earlier in the day. He sat slumped in his chair. The David Baldacci novel he was reading suggested he didn't want to be bothered by anyone.

He glanced up at her as she passed by. As she opened her mouth to greet him, he frowned and returned his gaze to his book.

Anna would have felt insulted at being dismissed so absolutely, except she knew exactly how he must be feeling. Her day hadn't exactly been a bowl of cherries, either.

Many of Anna's patients were MPD cops, District firemen and U.S. government employees who came to see her because of stress that affected their job performance and personal lives. This afternoon, she'd seen a new patient, a young fireman who'd recently responded to a violent car crash in which a little boy—the same age and with the same hair color as his own son—had been torn limb from limb by the crushing force of metal when the child restraint straps held his body snug in his car seat.

Now the fireman had trouble driving in the car with his son without his throat swelling closed and his breathing becoming erratic. He had nightmares and had wakened his wife crying.

Which made him afraid to go to sleep. He was suffering from sleep deprivation and not functioning well on the job.

Anna had known she was dealing with a classic case of Post-Traumatic Stress Disorder, more commonly called PTSD. She'd been able to give her patient suggestions for how to deal with his condition, but the sad truth was that PTSD was insidious. Even years later, some small, insignificant thing could trigger a physiological and psychological response to the original traumatizing incident.

When Anna checked in with the urgent care receptionist, she learned she might be waiting a long time.

And she didn't have a book.

She took the empty seat farthest from the mother and two rambunctious boys, across from the stranger. Which meant she either had to stare at him or at her feet.

She didn't remember him being so good-looking. She knew he was tall, because she was 5'10" and he'd looked down at her in the vet's office. She knew he was strong, because he'd come in carrying a hundred-pound dog. But she hadn't focused on his face. She found it fascinating.

His cheeks were hollowed and stubbled with dark beard, and the cheekbones looked as though they'd been carved from stone by a loving sculptor. His lips were bowed. They looked soft in comparison to the hard muscle and sinew she saw in the rest of his body. He had black hair, expensively cut. She didn't know how she knew that, but it wasn't a stretch, considering the price of real estate in Georgetown.

He looked up at her as though he'd been aware of her intense perusal and glared.

Anna knew she was supposed to be intimidated into lowering her gaze. But she wasn't. And she didn't.

"How did you get your dog to let go of your arm?" she asked.

"It wasn't my dog."

He returned to his book, as though that was the end of that.

Anna's brow furrowed. "Not your dog? I don't understand."

With obvious irritation, he raised his eyes—an icy blue, like glacier water—to her and said, "I saw the dog get hit by a car. The driver didn't stop."

She waited for further explanation, but when it didn't come she said, "Oh, I see."

"You see what?"

"The dog bit you, even though you were trying to help, because it was hurt and you were a stranger. That was a very kind thing to do."

"I didn't have much choice," he said curtly. "The dog was about to snap at a kid." He made a point of turning the page in his book and started reading again.

She saw the white gauze bandage on his arm was stained with blood. "Henry would never forgive me if I didn't ask."

He looked up, clearly annoyed. "Who's Henry?" Then he said, "Oh, yeah. Your kid."

She smiled and said, "Henry isn't mine any more than the dog was yours."

At his questioning look she said, "Henry lives across the hall. He takes care of Penelope—my cat—in the afternoons."

He made a "get to it" sign by rotating his hand.

"How did you get the dog to let go of your arm?"

"The vet injected him with a drug that put him to sleep. He was going to have to do it anyway to treat his wounds."

"Oh."

"Is there anything else you'd like to know? So I can read in peace?"

"Is the dog all right?" she asked.

"He was when I left."

"You must live nearby."

"Close enough."

"I live a block south and two blocks east. I walked here. Wish I'd worn a coat." Anna pulled her three-quarter-length gray wool sweater more tightly around her. "It was colder out than I thought it would be."

Anna wished she hadn't volunteered the information about where she lived. Especially since the stranger didn't seem at all interested.

Which was when Anna realized that she was.

When was the last time she'd been on a date? Three months ago, at least. And why was that? She had reasonable office hours, and Penelope could easily be left for the evening. Anna had even been asked out a couple of times. She simply hadn't been intrigued enough by any of those men to say yes.

She was intrigued now. And being completely ignored.

She looked for a wedding band and didn't see one. But that didn't mean he wasn't involved with someone. Except, he was so surly, she was sure he would have used that excuse to be rid of her if he could have.

She wanted to know more. She wanted to know him.

"I just thought of something," she said. "Do you have to get rabies shots?"

"Someone who knew the owner must have seen or heard what happened, because the owner showed up at the vet's," the stranger replied. "The dog had been vaccinated."

"That was lucky."

"Lady, nothing about this day has been lucky."

At that moment, the nurse called out, "Mr. Benedict. The doctor can see you now."

Anna watched "Mr. Benedict" close his book and rise to leave without another word. He was churlish. And unfriendly. And morose. Almost rude. She was glad he was gone.

And regretted bitterly that he hadn't been more interested in getting to know her.

6

Anna stepped out of the warmth and bright light of the urgent care facility into the cold night air and gasped as a hulking figure emerged from the darkness. "Good Lord!" she said, putting a hand to her heart as the stranger with the dog bite stepped into the light. "You scared me to death!"

"I stayed to walk you home."

She wasn't far from home, but there was enough crime in Georgetown that it was a thoughtful gesture—if a bit suspect, considering the stranger's off-putting behavior toward her inside.

"Why would you want to do that?" she asked, drawing her sweater tighter around her.

He shrugged. "It's late. It's dark. You're alone."

"All true." But she was pretty sure none of that had anything to do with the reason he'd stayed. She thought it was more likely *he* was alone. And wanted female company. Was she willing to provide it?

"You walked here, too?" she asked.

He nodded.

"All right," she said at last.

Anna shivered with excitement and anticipation as the stranger set a large hand at the small of her back. She was surprised at the visceral reaction she had to his touch.

During the short, silent walk, she debated whether to invite him inside. For coffee. To get to know him better. If she did, he would probably think she was inviting him inside for something else. For sex.

Anna didn't believe in one-night stands. Safe sex was tough enough to manage if you knew your partner. This man was a literal stranger. She knew his last name was Benedict, but that was all.

On the other hand, if she didn't invite him in, she was afraid she'd never see him again. And in that case, she knew she would always regret not knowing how his lips would feel on hers.

"How's your arm?" she said to break the silence that had descended between them.

"I can't feel anything right now. How's your hand?"

She raised her hand to observe the small bandage that covered two neat black stitches. "I'll survive."

That was the extent of their conversation.

She knew nothing more about him when they arrived at the bottom step of the stately brownstone where she lived, which had been broken into four condominium units, than she'd known when he offered to walk her home. Except that he smelled good, a mixture of musk and man. And that she didn't want him to walk out of her life.

"Would you like to come up for some coffee?" she asked.

He shrugged. "Why not?"

Anna used her key to get into the entryway, then took the stranger's large, callused hand and led him to the polished wooden stairs covered by an oriental runner. "I'm one flight up."

She had left a few lamps on, so they were greeted by soft golden light as she unlocked her front door and ushered the stranger into her small living room.

As soon as the door closed, he took her into his arms. His ice-blue eyes looked warm as Caribbean waters when he lowered his head to bring their mouths close.

Anna felt a little off balance because of the speed at which he'd moved, but she realized this was exactly where she wanted to be, that she desperately wanted to taste his lips.

She felt her pulse thrum as he set an arm around her hips and drew her close. Close enough to feel that he was aroused.

And to feel him begin to tremble.

With desire, she thought at first. But when she raised a hand to his nape, it felt slick with sweat. Strange, when they'd been walking in the cold night air.

She leaned back to look into the stranger's face and saw he had his eyes closed. And his jaw clenched.

Oh, God. Oh, no. Not him.

He was exhibiting classic symptoms of PTSD. Anna hoped she was wrong, but she didn't think she was. Her heart swelled with compassion. She put her arms around his shoulders protectively, leaned close to his ear and said, "You're all right. I'm here."

She felt him shudder and knew that whatever he was experiencing had nothing to do with desire.

She lifted a hand to brush a dark lock of hair from his forehead. "We're in my apartment in Georgetown," she murmured. "My Maine Coon cat Penelope has a litter of adorable kittens in a basket in the next room. Your arm might be aching because you just had stitches where a dog bit you earlier today."

She talked to him calmly, as she would have to one of her patients, and gradually felt his trembling stop. When he opened his eyes, he seemed surprised to see her still standing within his embrace.

He abruptly let go of her and took a step back.

Reluctantly, she took another step back herself. "Are you all right?"

He looked away and down. Ashamed, she knew. Upset. Angry with himself.

"Soldier?" she asked. "Cop? Fireman?"

He grimaced, then met her gaze and said gruffly, "Soldier."

"You should get some—"

"I don't need any help." He turned and reached for the doorknob.

She took two quick steps and put her hand over his. She met his startled gaze and said, "I'd like to see you again."

He frowned and said, "I don't think that's a good idea."

Then he was gone.

7

Ben recognized his body's heightened awareness, the thudding heart, the fetid sweat in his armpits, his rapid eye movement scouting the terrain, rigid muscles tightened to the point of pain, ready to explode into action: it was the knowledge of death waiting around the corner.

He had to remind himself he wasn't scouting some war-torn foreign city. He was merely driving his black SUV through the Columbia Heights neighborhood in Washington, D.C.

Nevertheless, he could smell danger in the wind.

"How's your arm?" Waverly asked from the passenger's seat of Ben's SUV.

Ben flinched as he flexed his injured left arm, which was stuck out the window. "Fine."

"Dog bites can get infected easily."

"The doctor shot me up with antibiotics last night."

"Does it hurt?"

"Like a sonofabitch."

"You should be at home taking it easy."

"Not an option. Not after Epifanio called and asked me to meet him. The kid's found out something about whatever's going down on the streets, Waverly. I can feel it in my bones."

"We'll know soon enough." Waverly's eyes, cop's eyes, stayed on the street. Alert. Probing.

Epifanio had borrowed a friend's cell phone and called Ben from the bathroom at school earlier in the afternoon. He'd refused to tell Ben why he had to see him, just ordered, "Get your ass over here, man."

"After school, right?" Ben had asked, to confirm that Epifanio wasn't truant.

"Yeah. On the corner. Like always."

Ben knew which corner Epifanio meant. It was the site of a convenience store near Lincoln Middle School where the 18th Street gang hung out. The kid had sounded anxious and afraid.

"Are you okay?" Ben asked. "Are you safe?"

"Sure," the kid said.

"I can call the police and have them—"

"No cops!"

He'd sounded frightened at the possibility the cops might come for him, panicked almost, so Ben had backed off.

He'd called Waverly as soon as he'd hung up the phone and shared his concern about the boy.

"You want me to have a black-and-white pick him up?" Waverly had asked.

"I think that'll just scare him," Ben said. "Maybe make him run, and get him into another kind of trouble."

"What's your plan?"

"I'm meeting him after school."

"How about if I come along?"

Since Waverly didn't wear a uniform, Ben figured he could easily pass him off as a friend. But if things went south, he might very well need his friend's help.

"You can come, but you're a friend, not a cop, got it?"

Ben eyed the vacant faces of the truants and dropouts walking the streets of the broken-down neighborhood. "Never thought I'd see so many thousand-yard stares in faces so young. Hard to believe they're just kids."

"Kids with guns and knives," Waverly said. "Don't ever underestimate them."

Ben had too recently fought in Iraq and Afghanistan against boy soldiers to discount the danger of a child with a gun. He was very much aware of the savagery bubbling beneath the surface whenever roaming gangs prowled the streets. And he had a gut feeling, an awful premonition he couldn't shake, that Epifanio was in real peril.

As opposed to the phantoms that had plagued Ben last night. He didn't know what had triggered the flashback in the woman's apartment. He just wished it had happened later. After he'd sated himself with her.

She was different somehow from the other women he'd picked up over the past six months. He'd felt poleaxed the instant he'd laid eyes on her in the vet's office yesterday morning. It could have been the oddity of the circumstances. It wasn't every day you met a woman with a dog attached to your arm. But the flare of sexual desire he'd felt was so strong it had spooked him.

Which was why he'd avoided her at the urgent care clinic. The last thing he wanted to do was get emotionally involved. That led to loving. And loving led to pain.

He'd wanted—needed—to put himself inside her. What alarmed him was the equal need he'd felt to hold her in his arms and keep her safe.

Safe from what? What horror had she witnessed that had put that shadowed look in her eyes? He didn't want to know.

In the end, she was the one who'd ended up holding him, keeping him safe. He'd been lucky to beat a hasty retreat without indulging the need he'd felt. Somehow he knew that having her once would not have been enough. Letting her into his life was simply asking for trouble.

Ben turned the corner onto 16th Street NW, just as Lincoln Middle School let out. The Latino, Black and Asian kids had formed into knots that Ben recognized by the gang colors they substituted for their maroon and khaki school uniforms and by their gang hand sign greetings to each other.

He saw a cluster of the brown pants and white T-shirts worn by the 18th Street gang and felt a chill run down his spine.

"I wish he'd given me some clue what he's found out," Ben muttered, his eyes still shifting right, then left, then up to the rearview mirror to check behind him.

"I don't like the feel of this any more than you do," Waverly said.

Ben adjusted the Glock 19 he was wearing in a slide belt holster concealed under his leather jacket, then shifted it back where it had been before he'd adjusted it.

"Why are you so jumpy?" Waverly asked.

Ben glanced at the man who would be his brother-in-law by tomorrow noon, noting his friend's clean-shaven, thirty-year-old face, his calm brown eyes, his not-quite-regulation police haircut. Ben was the same age but felt decades older. He put his eyes back on the street. "Seen too much bad stuff, I guess."

It hadn't taken him more than one war, and a couple of military interventions, to realize he didn't want a career in the army. Yet here he was, a soldier in a different kind of army fighting a different kind of war. His job, once again, was to protect the innocent, who were as difficult to identify in this American landscape as they had been in a foreign setting.

Waverly pointed to an alley on the right, a block down from the neighborhood convenience store where Ben was supposed to meet Epifanio and said, "What's going on over there?"

Ben slowed his SUV to a crawl as he watched the altercation at the entrance to the alley. What Ben saw were two different gangs on the same turf. And neither of them happy about it.

"Looks like the One-Eight pitted against MS guys," Waverly said.

"Not good," Ben muttered.

"You hear about the kid who lost his fingers to a machete in a mall in Virginia? That was MS," Waverly said.

Ben felt his gut tighten. Machetes reminded him of the time he'd spent on a special mission in Somalia. He focused on the kids in the alley to keep his mind from forming images he didn't want to remember.

Suddenly, Waverly cried, "One of them's waving a knife!"

Ben put the SUV in Park and was out the door before he had time to think what he was doing. "Call for backup," he yelled over his shoulder. He heard Waverly shouting agreement behind him, but he didn't pause, just pulled his Glock and headed toward the alley on the run.

As he raced forward he shouted, "Police! Put down the knife! Put it down!"

The boy in danger of being stabbed backed away, trying to escape. And Ben realized who it was.

He saw the look of terror in Epifanio's eyes and felt his gut tighten in fear, which turned to horror as he watched the knife tear into the boy's white T-shirt.

Most of the kids had fled, leaving only the perpetrator and the victim. Ben watched as a boy sporting an MS gang tatt— the number 13 tattooed in black ink on his cheek—eyed him, then reached around and purposely cut Epifanio's throat.

Rich red blood spurted from Epifanio's jugular.

Ben saw the shock in the boy's brown eyes as he collapsed on the asphalt. And then watched the kid with the knife flee down the alley.

Ben felt his throat constrict with emotion, but he didn't stop to offer comfort to the dying boy. As a combat veteran, he knew a good-as-dead man when he saw one. Waverly would do what was necessary till help arrived. There was no saving the kid. But he could catch the killer.

He darted after the boy with the knife, stumbling over debris the kid threw back into his path as he ran along the uneven brick pavement. "Stop, or I'll shoot!"

The youth gave a hoot of hysterical laughter and ran faster.

Ben took a shooting stance and aimed for the kid's leg. But to his surprise, his hands were shaking so badly he couldn't get a good aim. "Damn!"

He shot once into the side brick wall above the boy's head, to see if he could scare the kid into stopping. When the killer kept running, Ben realized he should have known better. These kids had grown up with violence. They heard gunshots every Saturday night and had seen their friends die early deaths. He took his finger off the trigger and raced after the boy.

As the curly-headed, café-au-lait-colored kid ran, he kept pulling up his jeans, which he'd been wearing down around his hips. The shoelaces on his Air Jordans were untied, causing him to trip and lose his balance.

Which was how Ben caught up to him. It was a great open-field tackle against a zigzagging opponent. The kid howled like a banshee, and Ben nearly broke the boy's wrist getting him to drop the bloodstained knife. His knee in the small of the boy's back, he wrestled the kid's hands behind him and slapped on the metal cuffs he kept in a case on the back of his belt.

His chest was heaving, and his heart felt like it might pound out of his chest. He resisted the urge to shake the kid within an inch of his life. Or smash the smirk off his face. Or pick him up and throw him back down and stomp on him. All natural responses when an enemy had killed a friend. All impulses that he'd learned to control in battle.

Ben swore every foul oath he knew. He should have called the cops whether Epifanio wanted him to or not. He should have done something, anything, to make the kid understand the danger of asking questions that might put him at risk. He should have been there the moment school let out.

His mistakes had cost the kid his life.

Ben could feel the shakes coming on, his body's response to seeing a boy he'd grown to care for killed in front of his eyes. His heart squeezed when he realized he was going to have to tell Epifanio's *abuela* that her grandson had met the fate she'd always feared, the fate Ben had been trying so hard to save him from. Ben didn't know if he could bear watching those ancient brown eyes fill with tears of sorrow.

He heard sirens in the distance and realized help was on

the way. He huffed out a breath and hauled the killer to his feet. "Your ass is busted."

"Epifanio ain't goin' to say nothin' to nobody now," the kid shot back.

Ben didn't say another word as he frog-marched the boy back down the alley. He was met halfway to the corner by MPD cops with their guns out, backup he presumed Waverly had called in. He held up his ICE badge and handed over his prisoner.

"How's the kid who was stabbed?" he asked.

"Paramedics are with him now," one of the cops replied.

Ben started running again. Maybe he could get to Epifanio before the boy died. Maybe he could find out what the kid knew that was so important it had gotten him killed.

A moment later he was on one knee in the blood that had pooled around the dying youth. He looked into the eyes of the paramedic kneeling on the other side of the boy, but the woman shook her head.

"Epifanio," Ben said, his voice harsh, his throat aching.

The thirteen-year-old's eyes fluttered open. He reached weakly toward Ben, who grasped his hand.

"Why did he want you dead?" Ben asked. "What is it you know?"

The boy looked at him with anguished eyes. He opened his mouth, but his larynx had been severed, along with his jugular.

"Don't worry," Ben said in a husky voice. "I'll take care of your *abuela*. I'll make sure she's okay. You just rest now."

The boy's eyes had fallen closed, but his bloody hand tightened weakly on Ben's. A dying breath soughed out of his mouth, along with a bubble of blood.

Ben eased his hand free and stumbled to his feet, wiping Epifanio's blood on his jeans. He recognized the familiar meaty smell. The stickiness of it.

Senseless. Stupid. His gaze searched the area. *What a waste!* He wasn't sure what he sought until he saw Waverly standing near the cop car that now held the killer.

His friend saw him coming and met him halfway.

"I've had enough," Ben said. "I quit."

Waverly looked from the kid in the cop car to the dead kid on the ground and said, "You can't quit."

"I sure as hell can," Ben said. "I don't need the hassle. I don't need the—"

"Pain?" Waverly interjected. "I know you don't need the money. But you can't quit, Ben."

"Why the hell not?" he said, stalking toward his SUV.

Waverly kept pace with him. "You're doing good work here. You understand these kids. You understand the violence that threatens them. You want peace in these neighborhoods as much as I do. As we all do."

"There's no such thing as peace. Just intervals without war."

"That doesn't sound like the Ben I know."

"You don't know shit about me," Ben retorted. "I've changed in the years since we were kids playing cops and robbers."

"You're forgetting that I watched you stop squabbles between your parents both before and after their divorce. You learned to negotiate peace between warring factions when you were still in short pants.

"Besides," Waverly said, eyeing Ben. "Only cowards quit."

Ben's face turned chalk white. "I'm not a—"

"No, you're not a coward. You're a man who needs purpose in his life," Waverly continued relentlessly. "Which you've found among these kids. Kids who need someone like you to help them find their way back to the straight and narrow."

Ben said nothing. His throat had swollen closed.

8

"Damn it, Benedict! Did you have to shoot at the kid?" Tony Pellicano, the special agent in charge of the D.C. ICE office, gripped the top of the swivel chair behind his cluttered desk with white-knuckled hands and glared at Ben. "That was the mayor on the phone. He's not happy. I had to explain to him why one of my agents was firing bullets at a fourteen-year-old. What were you thinking?"

Ben stared at his boss with disbelief. "I watched that *kid* cut another kid's throat. And I shot once—over his head. Sir."

Ben's boss smacked his black leather chair as though it was the back of Ben's head, then stalked back and forth behind his desk, waving his hands and ranting. Ben followed his tall, rail-thin boss's constant, agitated movement with his eyes, while his hands gripped the arms of the maroon leather studded chair in which he sat.

"This isn't a war zone," Tony ranted. "We don't shoot first and ask questions later."

Ben felt his heart thudding in his chest, licked at the sweat beaded above his lip, and said, "You don't have to tell me this isn't—"

"You returning vets have the wrong—"

Ben came out of his chair as though he'd been catapulted from it. "The last thing on earth I want to do is kill some kid. I shot over his head to slow him down. I wanted to catch a killer. What's wrong with that?"

Tony stared at him stony-faced and said, "I want you to see a doctor, a psychiatrist who specializes in cases like this."

Ben stood stunned. "What?" If Tony only knew how hard it had been for him to fire his weapon at all, he would realize Ben wasn't going to be a threat to the peace and harmony of D.C. streets. "There's nothing wrong with me, sir," Ben managed to say.

"You shoot, you talk. Those are my rules," Tony said implacably.

"I'm not talking to any shrink."

"Then pass me your credentials and your weapon," Tony said, holding out his hand. "Your choice."

Ben's stomach rolled. He swallowed down bile. If there was one thing he didn't want to do, it was talk to some doctor about killing kids. Especially after what had happened in Afghanistan. But his boss wasn't giving him any choice. He lowered his gaze and said, "Who do I have to see?"

"We've got a psych trauma team on the payroll," Tony said.

"I'll make an appointment."

"I had them called when I heard you'd fired your weapon. They sent over a therapist—Dr. Schuster. She's waiting for you in the conference room."

"Waverly's wedding rehearsal is tonight, and I have paperwork to finish. I don't have time—"

"You don't leave this office until you talk with a doctor. That's an order."

"Fine," Ben said between tight jaws. "Are we done here?"

Tony sighed. "Until today, I've been happy with the way you've been doing your job, Ben. The gang kids like you. You write great reports. You can type. Even better, you can spell. You're responsible. You're respectful. You're reliable. I just can't have a gunslinger working for me."

"I'm not a—"

"Go see Dr. Schuster," Tony interrupted brusquely. "Do it now."

9

Dr. Annagreit Schuster recognized the ICE agent standing in the doorway. He'd yelled at her yesterday morning at the vet's office. He'd ignored her at the urgent care clinic. He'd fallen apart in her arms last night, then walked out of her apartment leaving her unsatisfied.

She noted the wary look in his cold blue eyes as he leaned against the doorway to the conference room. She saw the tension in his bunched shoulders and the anger in his tight jaws and balled fists. She looked for a bandage on his left forearm, but he was wearing a long-sleeved Georgetown University T-shirt that covered it.

He spoke without saying a word: *I don't want to be here. There's nothing you can say or do to help me. I'm fine.*

"Have a seat, Agent Benedict," Anna said, gesturing to one of the comfortable swivel chairs across from her at the center of the oval-shaped, highly polished conference table.

Anna had read in Ben's personnel file that his job was to make friends of the kids in local gangs, in conjunction with similar MPD efforts, in order to direct them away from unlawful activities. He was also tasked with locating and arresting gang members with a possible terrorist agenda—and, of course, deporting illegal aliens who infiltrated the gangs.

It was work with an indisputable humanitarian goal. And numerous possibilities for violence.

"How long is this going to take?" he demanded from the doorway.

"As long as it takes," she replied in an even voice. As with all Federal government clients involved in a shooting, she needed to evaluate how the subject was coping with the traumatic incident and to make a judgment whether he needed immediate or follow-up counseling. Sometimes that took five minutes, sometimes it took much longer.

Anna had firsthand information about this man that didn't come out of his file. She'd seen what she believed was evidence of post-traumatic stress last night. But she wasn't sure she could—or should—use that information against him in this evaluation.

For the first time since he'd left her townhome, Anna was glad their encounter had ended so abruptly. If their relationship had become physical, she could not ethically have treated him. Perhaps it was shaving hairs to say she was emotionally uninvolved, but she very much wanted to help this man.

Anna didn't repeat her request for Benedict to sit. She waited, letting him approach on his own. She shouldn't have been surprised by his caution, considering what she'd learned about Benjamin Preston Benedict from the personnel file she'd been presented with when she'd arrived at the ICE office a half hour ago.

She'd taken one look at Ben Benedict's picture and actually felt a little thrill at the thought of seeing him again. Which she'd immediately quelled. If she wanted to treat Agent Benedict, their relationship had to remain professional.

According to his file, Ben Benedict was a former army major, the veteran of several military campaigns. He'd been trained as a sniper, and he'd employed those skills in Afghanistan and Iraq. He'd apparently been a good soldier. Heroic, in fact. He'd been decorated for his valor with the Distinguished Service Cross, two silver stars and a Purple Heart.

She had her own evidence of his good character. Not many men would have tried to approach an injured rottweiler, let alone succeed in rescuing it. He was obviously a man who'd learned how to survive in life-threatening situations. Part of which was reconnoitering the terrain before venturing into hazardous territory.

Anna observed Ben Benedict, looking for signs of trauma. He hadn't shaved this morning, and his darkly stubbled jawline made his cheekbones even more prominent. She'd known he was tall. His record said he was 6'3". The sweatshirt emphasized his broad shoulders but hid his impressive biceps.

His body was coiled, like a cornered animal facing a threatening foe. But after that first, revealingly apprehensive glance, his blue eyes had become shuttered. As the door slid silently closed behind him, Agent Benedict snagged a chair directly across from her and slumped into it. "You don't look like a doctor."

"No?"

"You look like a model."

Anna managed not to sigh with frustration. She had, in fact, modeled as a young woman. And yes, she was blond and blue-eyed, long-legged, and reputed to be beautiful, if the European magazine covers she'd graced as a teen were any measure. But at twenty-nine, she'd long since put all that behind her.

When she'd first started her practice, she'd briefly explained her modeling past to each inquiring patient. She'd also revealed, to those who'd asked, the nature of the life-altering event that had taken her from modeling to trauma therapy.

But Anna had since learned not to reveal even that much about herself to patients. So she merely said, "Tell me about the shooting."

"I already told my boss. I didn't shoot at the kid. I shot over his head."

"Why was that?"

"What?"

"Why didn't you shoot him?" Anna watched the frown of confusion form on Agent Benedict's very attractive face.

"Why didn't I kill him, you mean?"

Anna heard the edge of rancor in his voice and said, "Yes, that's what I mean."

"I'm not a killer."

"But you wanted to kill him." She made it a statement, to see if he would deny it.

To her surprise he said, "Hell, yes! I watched him kill a kid I've spent the past five months getting to know and like. I wanted to murder the sonofabitch."

"Then why didn't you?"

He huffed out a breath and leaned his broad shoulders across the conference table, moving aggressively into her space. "Look, Miss—whatever your name is—I was a soldier. I've killed men. And women. And—" He cut himself off. "I've killed enough people that I've lost count of— Haven't wanted to count them," he corrected. "I've killed often enough to know what it means to end a life. I don't take that power lightly.

"So I didn't kill the bastard. I caught him, and he'll spend a few years in juvie and be out on the streets to kill again someday."

"You sound angry."

He lurched to his feet. "You're damned right, I'm angry! This is bullshit. Are we done?"

"Yes, we're done."

He shot her the same wary look she'd seen on his face in the doorway. "What happens now?"

"I'll make my report to your boss."

He perched his fists on his hips. "Which is what?"

"You could benefit from further counseling."

"In your opinion," he said with a sneer.

"In my opinion," she said, meeting his gaze with a steady look, even though she felt a frisson of…something…pass between them.

"Would that counseling be with you?"

"I'm available."

"Really?" he said, the sneer becoming a leer.

Anna flushed. She should be immune to the sort of look

she was getting from Agent Benedict. It was a form of attack, when the patient felt defenseless. "ICE makes my services available to anyone who needs them."

"I don't need them," he said flatly. "Are we done?"

"We're done."

He stalked to the door, yanked it open and headed down the hall without looking back.

Anna released a breath she hadn't realized she'd been holding. *That is a dangerous man.* The thought was disconcerting, considering the fact that she'd made up her mind to clear Agent Benedict for duty. However, she would recommend additional counseling.

She realized something else equally upsetting. She still desired him. Still imagined what it might be like to have him hold her in his arms. Still imagined being possessed by him.

Anna sighed. She'd been single too long. Alone too long. Human beings had a physiological need for sex that was as basic as their need for food, water and sleep. A need she realized she would have been happy to fulfill with Ben Benedict.

Unfortunately, if he became her patient, Agent Benedict would be off-limits as a potential sex partner. Anna was glad he'd shown such animosity for her. Sessions with him would have been fraught with inappropriate sexual tension.

Anna felt a fleeting moment of regret for what might have been. If his behavior today was anything to judge by, she wouldn't be seeing Agent Benedict again.

10

"It isn't easy being rich," Ben said.

"Tell that to the next poor man you meet," Waverly replied.

Ben changed gears in his bright red 1963 Jaguar E-Type Roadster and accelerated. He and Waverly had spent an exhausting afternoon filing reports on the gang killing with their respective law-enforcement agencies. Now they were racing to Waverly's wedding rehearsal and dinner at one of the several homes owned by the bride's family, a former plantation called Hamilton Farm southeast of Richmond.

Racing was probably the wrong word for how they'd left D.C. *Crawling* fit better. They'd gotten caught in the crush of traffic on I-95 South close to the city. Ben knew they'd never arrive on time unless he kept his foot on the gas now.

"You're going to get a ticket," Waverly warned.

"You can flash your badge and get me out of it."

"Flash your own badge," Waverly retorted.

"You're changing the subject."

"Which is?"

"Being rich is a curse."

Waverly snorted. "You're not going to get any sympathy from me. I earn a living wage. Period. I'd give my left nut to have a car like this." His hand brushed the black leather interior of the long-nosed, ragtop, six-figure Jag.

"After you marry my sister tomorrow afternoon," Ben said, "you'll be rich enough to afford any car you want."

Waverly frowned. "I don't want Julia's money. If I didn't love her so much, her family connections would have scared me off."

"I had no idea when I introduced the two of you that you'd take one look at each other and go off the deep end. You're not the kind of rich preppie she was used to dating. Which I suppose was the attraction," Ben mused.

"I didn't want to fall in love with her," Waverly said, "for precisely that reason. There's a lifetime of experience separating eighteen and thirty. And I'm a cop. I was afraid she would get tired of me and want to move on."

Ben might have agreed that Waverly was right—that Julia was still a relative babe-in-the-woods—except she'd grown up with a senator for a father and a doyenne of the Washington social scene for a mother. Julia had probably experienced more socially and intellectually in her eighteen years than other women did in their entire lives.

And he knew for a fact that she'd been sexually active since she was fifteen, because she'd come to him for advice when he was home for a few days on leave from the army. He'd told her to wait, but she'd sworn she was in love forever. So he'd told her what he knew about the use of condoms and birth control pills.

Julia had been in love at least twice more, but he suspected she'd had more than two other sexual partners. So she probably had a pretty good idea what she liked in bed and what she was looking for in a man.

Ben had been as worried as Waverly at first that Julia would tire of him. But it hadn't happened. Instead, she'd encouraged Waverly to propose. And he had.

"I guess if anything worries me, it's that this is all happening in such a hurry," Ben said. He eyed his friend and watched as Waverly shifted nervously. "Oh, shit. There's a baby on the way."

Waverly shot him a guilty glance. "We were being careful. The condom broke. But I'm glad she's pregnant."

"What about college? She's already started the fall term at Georgetown."

"She can still go."

"Who's going to take care of the baby?"

"We can get a babysitter."

"You have any idea how much it costs for child care these days? For diapers and baby food? You have a one-bedroom apartment. You're going to need a bigger place."

"We can't afford a bigger place right now, especially with the doctor's bills," Waverly said.

"You're damned lucky Julia has money of her own."

"Julia has agreed to live on my income," Waverly said.

Ben shook his head. "How long do you think that's going to last?"

"The rest of our lives."

"Do you really think Julia can live without all the luxuries she's grown up with? That she'll want her child to grow up without a bedroom of his or her own? Even if Julia were willing, her parents won't be."

"Julia promised me she won't ask her parents to buy her stuff once we're married," Waverly said.

"She won't need to ask. All she'll have to do is mention she needs something and Ham or my mother will get it for her. Which is a moot point, because Julia can buy anything she wants for herself in three years, when she turns twenty-one and inherits the fifty-million-dollar trust fund that's waiting for her."

"Fifty million?" Waverly blurted.

"I thought you knew."

"She told me she had a *little* money coming when she turned twenty-one. I knew your family had money, but... She never said— Damn it all to hell!"

"I wish I'd never introduced the two of you," Ben muttered.

"Don't say that. I love her." Waverly rubbed his palms dry on his tuxedo trousers. "I can't believe this." He stared at

Ben, his eyes wide, as though they were ten thousand feet in the air and Ben had just told him both engines had flamed out.

"See what I mean?" Ben said. "Right now you're thinking, 'Why on earth would you take a regular job when you have that kind of money, Ben?' Tell me I'm wrong."

"You're not wrong," Waverly said. "Why *did* you take a regular job with that kind of money?"

"Just stupid, I guess," Ben said.

After graduation from West Point, Ben had gone into the army. It had seemed romantic and exciting and challenging. It gave him something to do with his life.

Until the day came when he'd realized he couldn't remain a soldier one more hour. That he had to quit.

But he'd lived as a soldier most of his life, in a family full of soldiers, and he'd felt surprisingly lost after he left the military. He'd needed a reason to get out of bed in the morning. He'd needed something useful to do with his life.

No one who needed to work simply to put food on the table or clothes on his back or a roof over his head could understand the utter emptiness—the unnecessariness—of a life where all those things were already provided.

Ben had thought about ridding himself of his wealth. But there were problems with that, too.

Ben grimaced when he heard a wailing siren and saw flashing red-and-blue lights in his rearview mirror. He carefully maneuvered his Jag through a slick pile of burnished leaves on the side of the road. They were less than ten miles from Hamilton Farm. "Don't say it," he said before Waverly could speak.

The Virginia motorcycle cop had a hand on his Glock as he approached the driver's-side window. "License and registration," he said.

Ben handed over his license and registration.

"Show him your badge, Ben," Waverly said irritably. "You'll be in trouble with your boss if you end up with a ticket for speeding."

"What badge is that, sir?" the cop asked.

"Just write the ticket," Ben said.

"What badge is that, sir?" the cop repeated.

Ben shot Waverly a dark look and pulled out his ICE badge. "You should ask him for his badge, too."

The cop eyed Waverly, who said, "I'm MPD."

"The senator's been looking for you," the cop said, as he handed back Ben's license and registration. "I'll give you an escort to The Farm."

The cop pulled his Harley-Davidson out in front of Ben's Jag and turned on his flashing lights and siren.

"Does this happen often?" Waverly asked, his eyes wide with astonishment.

Ben shot his friend a sardonic look. "Get used to it. Like I said. It isn't easy being rich."

He glanced at his friend and saw the dawning realization in Waverly's eyes that when he married into Julia's family, his life would take a drastic turn.

"Does Julia have to take the money?" Waverly said. "Can she turn it down?"

"You can't get rid of my mother's money. Or the senator's money. Neither Julia—nor your child—will ever want for anything if they can help it."

"I intend to support my family myself," Waverly said through tight jaws.

"Good luck telling Julia's parents to butt out of your life," Ben said as they entered the half-mile-long, oak-tree-lined drive along the James River that led to The Farm.

"I plan to do just that," Waverly said. "Tonight."

Ben grinned as the elegant Southern mansion came into view. "This I have to see."

11

"You're late."

"Hello, Ham," Ben said, shaking hands with his mother's second husband.

Randolph Cornelius Hamilton, III, met them in the wild-rose-wallpapered foyer of The Farm with a bourbon in hand. His glazed eyes and slurred voice suggested he'd already had a few.

Waverly cleared his throat nervously and said, "Good evening, Senator. There was an incident—"

Ben watched as Ham waved away his future son-in-law's offered hand. Waverly accepted the dismissal without protest. Ben couldn't imagine Waverly confronting the senator about supporting Julia. But he had a feeling it would liven up the party if he did.

"I know about the kid getting his throat cut," Ham said. "Terrible!" He turned and headed down the oak-pegged central hallway, obviously expecting the two of them to follow.

Ham glanced at Ben over his shoulder and said, "I would think you could have arranged to do your paperwork on Monday. Everyone's been waiting in the parlor for half an hour to go in to dinner."

Ben exchanged a chagrined look with Waverly. The rich and powerful didn't believe that the rules applied to them. Don't want to hang around and do your job? Just leave. It can wait until you're good and ready to do it.

The wedding being held tomorrow at Hamilton Farm,

home to Hamiltons since Virginia was a colony, was the Washington society event of the season. The expected crowd of several hundred included the exceedingly rich and the oh-so-powerful. Julia had acceded to Waverly's request to keep the wedding party small, so there were only four male and four female members of the wedding party.

"I assume that the 'everyone' waiting in the parlor includes Mother," Ben said.

"And your father," the senator added ominously.

Ben grimaced. He'd tried to talk Waverly out of making Foster Benedict part of the wedding festivities. Waverly had argued that since both his parents were dead, he wanted Ben's dad to participate in the wedding as one of his groomsmen.

Even when Ben had pointed out the problems of having both his mother and father under the same roof for an extended period of time, Waverly had remained adamant. Ben could count on one hand the number of times his parents had sat down at the same dinner table in the twenty years since their divorce. This made four.

His mother was a lady in every situation. His father was a former officer and a gentleman. They'd loved each other passionately. Which meant they'd hurt each other horribly.

And the love and the pain were ongoing.

It was like watching an impending train wreck and knowing there was nothing you could do to prevent it. At the same time, you couldn't take your eyes away.

"They're here!" Ham announced as he entered the parlor with Ben and Waverly.

Ben took one look at the tableau—his father on one side of the room, his mother on the other—and could almost feel the tension arcing between them.

The furniture was Victorian, which meant spindly and uncomfortably stuffed with horsehair, and there was little of it in the parlor. The twelve-foot windows were draped elegantly with pale-rose-colored silk, and the walls bore an ivy-patterned rice paper above and forest-green wainscoting below.

The other two groomsmen were standing near a sideboard that held a wide selection of crystal liquor decanters. His mother, his half sister Julia and Julia's three bridesmaids and maid of honor were arranged on the settee and wing chairs. His father and stepmother stood alone near the only apparent warmth in the room—the crackling fire in the white-marble-faced fireplace.

His mother immediately stood, adjusted her expensive, yet elegantly simple, black off-the-shoulder evening gown around her and said, "Shall we go in to dinner?"

"Abigail?" Ham said, holding out his arm to his wife.

Ben's mother crossed and laid her hand on Ham's arm. "Hello, Ben," she said as she moved past him. "I'm so glad you were able to make it."

Ben heard a world of censure in his mother's voice. Apparently, she'd spent more discomfiting time in his father's company than she'd wanted to.

"Julia?" Waverly said, holding out his arm to his fiancée.

Julia crossed to Waverly and tucked her arm around his. "You got here just in time to avoid World War III," Ben heard her murmur as she kissed her fiancé tenderly on the lips.

Ben could understand how Waverly had fallen in love with Julia. She was as beautiful as his mother must have been at the same age. She had perfect teeth that she displayed in a perpetual smile and cornflower-blue eyes that gazed adoringly at his friend pretty much all the time. Her sun-streaked blond hair proved, even more than the healthy glow of her flawless skin, how much time Julia spent outdoors horseback riding and playing tennis and sailing.

Most of all, for a girl who'd been given everything she could want from the day she was born, Julia was surprisingly kind and thoughtful of others.

Ben watched as each of the groomsmen held out an arm

to one of the bridesmaids. Rhett winked at him as he passed by, then turned his charming smile toward the young woman he was escorting.

He looked for his eldest brother, then recalled that Nash was off on some troubleshooting mission for the president and had said he might or might not make it to the wedding tomorrow. Ben thought of Carter, as he often did, now that he was no longer fighting overseas himself, and prayed that his younger brother was safe and well in Iraq.

Ben held out his arm to the maid of honor, one of Julia's very young friends, who lifted her chin proudly as she put her arm through his.

"Hello, Paige," Ben said with a smile meant to melt some of the ice he could see in her eyes and in her spine.

"Hello, Mr. Benedict," the girl replied with frost in her voice.

"Please call me Ben."

"I'm being polite to you for Julia's sake," the girl said haughtily. "But I don't like you. Or your friend."

"If you think Julia's making a mistake marrying Waverly, why did you agree to be her maid of honor?"

"It is when one's friends are being foolish that those friends need one the most."

Despite the speech without contractions, or maybe because of it, Paige Carrington seemed even younger than the nineteen years old Ben knew she was. He felt too old and jaded to be a part of this wedding party, but he'd promised Waverly he'd be his best man. The worst was almost over. He hoped.

Hamilton Farm's exquisite mahogany dining-room table would have seated twenty easily. The wedding party of fourteen was spread out along the length of it. Four tall silver epergnes holding white beeswax candles and layered with pale pink roses made conversation with those sitting across the table difficult, if not impossible.

Ben leaned to his left and whispered to Julia, "Remind

me again why we're having the rehearsal after dinner, instead of before?"

"Archbishop Hostetler is performing another wedding right now," Julia said. "He should be done by the time we're finished with dinner."

Ben wished Waverly were sitting closer. He was at the end of the table on the other side of Julia. Ben could see his friend was uncomfortable with the undeniable evidence of the Hamiltons' wealth—the silver service, the gold-trimmed china and the servile waiters.

He was clearly too nervous to enjoy his food. Ben watched as Waverly's bowl of she-crab soup went back full, then watched Waverly fidget as a uniformed waiter served him orange-glazed pork loin, new potatoes and honeyed peas and carrots.

For the next hour, Waverly tossed back champagne like there was no tomorrow. And Ben was pretty sure he hated the stuff.

Ben kept his gaze focused on Waverly, because he didn't like what he saw when he glanced at his father, who was sitting near the center of the opposite side of the table. It was annoying to watch his father glancing surreptitiously at his mother.

Ben wondered how his stepmother, who was positioned near the head of the table beside Ham, could sit there and ignore his father's disrespectful behavior.

Ben heard laughter at Rhett's end of the table and watched as his mother shot her youngest son an admonishing look. Rhett's grin was unrepentant. He picked up his champagne glass and drank deep as he stared into the eyes of the blushing bridesmaid to his right.

Ben heard Waverly loudly clear his throat. His friend scraped his chair back as he stood, champagne glass in hand. It seemed the groom was about to offer a toast to his bride.

The first words out of Waverly's mouth made it clear Ben was wrong.

12

"Mr.—Senator—and Mrs. Hamilton, I love your daughter," Waverly began. "My goal in life is to make Julia happy. Without using her money." He flushed deeply and added, "I mean, with the money I earn. I mean, I intend to be the one to support my wife."

"Why, you…" Ham spluttered.

"Honey," Julia said to Waverly, "we can talk about this later."

"Insolent puppy!" Ham snarled.

"Let the man have his say," Ben's father interjected.

"No one dictates to me in my own home," Ham said ominously.

"Waverly has a right to speak," Ben's father insisted.

"He has no rights in this house!" Ham said heatedly. "Not where my daughter is concerned. I will be the one—"

Waverly interrupted, "Sir, I only want to make it clear—"

Ham whirled on the groom and said, "If you know what's good for you, young man, you will keep your mouth shut."

"I will not," Waverly said, his face pale.

Ben was surprised at Waverly's stubbornness. At his courage in the face of a very powerful—and unhappy—future father-in-law. He felt the knot growing in his stomach. He watched carefully, alarmed because his father looked agitated enough at Ham for the two of them to come to blows. Ben began figuring the quickest way to get between them if that happened.

Julia had insisted on being seated next to her future husband, and now Ben realized she must have anticipated some sort of confrontation during dinner. She reached out and laid a hand on Waverly's arm, attempting to tug him back into his seat.

It didn't work.

"Julia and I don't need your money," Waverly said to Ham, his brown eyes earnest. "We plan to live a simple, happy, loving, long life together."

Ham's lips became a rigid hyphen.

Ben's glance slid to his mother. Abigail Coates Benedict Hamilton delicately dabbed at the sides of her pink-painted mouth with her napkin. With exquisite grace, she raised her eyes from the antique lace tablecloth and met Waverly's troubled gaze.

"I know you love Julia," she said in a calm, quiet voice. "And that you will do your best to make her happy."

Ben held his breath. *Do your best?* The insinuation was there that Waverly's best wouldn't be nearly good enough.

"What does that mean?" Ben's father demanded.

Ben nearly groaned aloud. Why couldn't his father leave well enough alone?

"Just what I said," his mother replied, her voice even.

"It sounded like you were denigrating the boy."

"The boy?" his mother said, lifting an eyebrow.

Ben watched his father scowl as he corrected, "The young man."

"That certainly was not my intention," his mother said, her voice showing agitation for the first time.

Julia rose abruptly from her chair and stood beside Waverly. She stared with dismay at her mother and said, "Wave will make me happy, Mother." She gazed imploringly at her father and said, "I love him, Daddy."

The bridesmaids and two younger groomsmen lowered their glances nervously. Hands gripped napkins in laps.

Ben felt the muscles tighten in his neck and shoulders, felt his legs tense for action.

"I know you love Waverly, dear," his mother said to Julia. "But—"

"But what, Abby?" his father interrupted. "He's not good enough? Your daughter deserves better?"

"What the hell is your problem?" Ham demanded.

"Honey," his father's second wife implored. "Maybe—"

"Stay out of this, Patsy!" his father snapped.

Ben watched his stepmother's hazel eyes flash. Watched her lips press flat. In his experience, Patsy Taggart Benedict gave as good as she got. She shot a look toward the end of the table, but she held her tongue.

Ben followed Patsy's glance to his mother and saw that her eyes had narrowed. Saw her mouth begin to purse. And felt his stomach roll. His mother had a very long fuse, but the explosions when she blew were dangerous and devastating.

Ben was seven—his younger brother Darling had just died in an accident—when his parents began to fight on a regular basis. He would grab five-year-old Carter and head for the nearest closet, where they would hide until the yelling had stopped.

It had almost always started like this. With a question. And an unsatisfactory answer.

In an effort to avert the calamity he foresaw, Ben rose with his champagne glass in hand and said, "To Julia and Waverly. May they live happily ever after."

His father was quick to join him. "To Julia and Waverly," he echoed as he stood.

He was followed, Ben was surprised to note, by Paige, who rose and said, "To Julia and Waverly."

Chairs scraped on hardwood as the bridesmaids and groomsmen quickly got to their feet. Ben watched tears brim in Julia's beautiful blue eyes as she glanced toward her obdurate father.

Those glistening tears broke the senator's will, and he stood, holding his glass out as he said, "To Julia." And then, reluctantly, "And Waverly."

His mother was last to rise. Her gaze was focused on her daughter as she said, "To the bride and groom. May they live a fairy-tale life…happily ever after."

There were cries of "Here! Here!" as everyone drank.

Waverly swallowed the last of the champagne in his glass and allowed Julia to give him a loving kiss and shove him back into his seat.

The knot remained tight in Ben's stomach until the archbishop arrived, shortly after the pecan pie was served. Everyone happily abandoned the dining-room table for the gazebo on the back lawn, where the wedding would be held. Even though most of the women were wrapped in fur, it was bitterly cold outside, and the rehearsal was brief. Everyone was happy to get back inside.

The bridesmaids meandered upstairs, where they would spend the night talking with the bride. The groomsmen got into their cars and headed to the bachelor party being held at the Benedicts' estate, The Seasons, a mere five miles, as the crow flies, from Hamilton Farm.

The senator and Ben's mother were walking the archbishop out to the foyer when Ben's father stopped him and said, "How about a quick nightcap, son?"

"Dad, I'm hosting the bachelor party."

"I want to talk with you about what happened today in D.C."

"Can we catch up at the party? I need to say good-bye to Patsy, but then I really should be going."

"Patsy's in the parlor. Come on, I'll pour you a drink."

Ben realized his father wasn't going to take no for an answer and nodded his acquiescence. Patsy gave his father a worried look and a kiss on the cheek. "Be careful driving home tonight, Foster," she said.

"I will," his father said. "You be careful driving back, too, honey."

"I will," Patsy replied.

Patsy and his father had come in separate cars because

Foster had been late getting away from the White House. He worked as a special advisor to the president, and lately there always seemed to be some crisis brewing for which his services were required. It worked out all right because now he had a way to get himself home after the bachelor party.

Foster gave Patsy a hug and said, "I'm sorry about earlier tonight."

"I can't believe you let that woman get under your skin. Again."

His father shrugged apologetically.

Patsy shook her head, then turned and gave Ben a hard hug and a quick kiss. "And you. You saved the day. As usual."

"I don't know about that," Ben said.

"Trust me. If you hadn't stood up when you did things might have gotten out of hand."

"Thanks, Patsy," Ben said, uncomfortable being reminded of all the times he'd acted as a peacemaker. And the reason it had been necessary.

"I'm sorry I can't stay and visit longer," Patsy said. "Camille has a school project to finish this weekend. Come see us more often. We miss you."

Ben didn't reply. He felt his stepmother's pain from being second fiddle too much to spend more time with her. And the less opportunity his father had to chide him for leaving the military, the better.

Once Patsy was gone, Ben took the crystal glass of bourbon his father handed him and said, "I was afraid you and the senator were going to end up trading punches."

"Waverly Collins has giant-sized balls," his father said with a chuckle. "I'll say that for him."

"My friend is in love." *And has a baby on the way.* Ben stared at the iced bourbon in his glass, thinking the last thing he needed was more alcohol, then swallowed it down. "And he was drunk, of course."

"How are you doing?" his father said.

"I'm fine." Ben didn't feel like explaining to yet another person, especially his father, why he'd shot at some gang kid. He did his best to steer the conversation in another direction. "It was good of you to defend Waverly tonight."

"I didn't know Ham could turn that shade of purple," his father said wryly. "If it hadn't been for you, things might have gotten ugly. And Julia—"

"Julia has always been able to wrap Ham and Mother around her little finger." Ben saw his father frown at the interruption but continued, "Neither of them is happy with her choice of husband. But neither of them is willing to make her unhappy by saying she can't have the man she wants."

Unfortunately, Foster Benedict wasn't the kind of man who let himself get distracted. He looked into Ben's eyes and said, "Are you all right, son?"

"Why wouldn't I be?" Ben replied.

"I read the report from the mayor's office on that gang killing this afternoon. You actually shot at a fourteen-year-old kid?"

Ben huffed out a frustrated breath. "Dad, he was—" Ben cut himself off as he saw his mother enter the parlor and head in their direction.

Ben watched his father's shoulders tense as his ex-wife stopped in front of him. Ben could smell his mother's perfume, a musky scent she'd worn for as long as he could remember. He'd been surprised as a kid when he'd realized all women didn't smell like that.

"I wondered if you would mind giving President Taylor a message for me," she said to Ben's father.

Ben was surprised at the request. His father had been named a special advisor to President Andrea Taylor shortly after her election eighteen months ago. The president had taken quick advantage of Foster Benedict's military expertise when she had to make decisions about which covert antiterrorist activities to support.

It might have been a perfect job for his father if Ben's

brother Nash hadn't been the man in charge of planning and executing the covert activities authorized by the president. Ben's eldest brother and his father often knocked heads when it came to how an operation should be conducted.

Ben had figured the president would get tired of refereeing and get rid of one, or both, of them.

But his father gave consistently wise advice.

And Nash Benedict was the best at what he did, a sometime assassin who worked directly for the president with unsurpassed skill and daring.

So President Taylor kept them both. Listened to both. And made her own choices.

Abigail Hamilton had been studying to be a surgeon before she'd married Foster Benedict, and her prodigious charitable activities were directed toward medical causes. So Ben wasn't surprised when she said, "Would you please ask Andrea if she would mind meeting with the nurses who work in the Pediatric Oncology Clinic at Georgetown University Hospital before she takes her tour of the children's cancer ward next week? The administrator says the nurses deserve an attagirl. I don't think Andrea will mind, but I need to make sure before we say anything to the nurses."

"Why don't you call her yourself?" his father said.

His mother wrinkled her nose. "There's a new, overly protective executive administrative assistant to the chief of staff. The impertinent female makes it impossible for old friends to talk to the president without telling her exactly what they want first."

And his mother had no intention of doing that, Ben thought with amusement. She intended to put the administrative assistant in her place by using her contacts to go around the woman.

"No problem," his father said. "I'll give you a call after I talk with Andrea on Monday."

Ben saw the trap into which his mother had fallen before she did herself. She'd avoided the administrative assistant, all right, but she'd obliged herself to accept a call from her former husband. Whom she otherwise avoided like three-day-old fish.

Ben saw the momentary hesitation before his mother nodded and said, "Thank you."

She turned her attention to Ben. "Ham told me what happened in Washington today. Are you all right?"

"I'm fine," Ben said, somehow managing not to snap the words at her. "I'd better get going. I'm Waverly's ride to his bachelor party."

"If you need anything…" his father began.

"Dad, I've got everything covered." Ben escaped the room, leaving his parents standing awkwardly across from each other. It served them right, he thought. Any animosity—or attraction—that existed between his divorced parents should have been dealt with a long time ago.

He made a detour to the kitchen hunting for Waverly, then searched each room as he walked toward the front of the house, finding no sign of his friend. He eyed the staircase that led upstairs where the bridesmaids—and the bride?—had disappeared. Surely Waverly hadn't gone up there. Not with the senator breathing fire.

He let out an exasperated breath as he debated where to search next. Where the hell was the groom?

13

Ben caught a glimpse of Waverly standing on the front porch as the archbishop exited the front door. The groom had his arms wrapped around the bride. Ben eased surreptitiously past the senator, who was headed upstairs, and slipped out the front door. "Hey, buddy," he said to his friend. "You ready to go?"

"Ready as I'll ever be," Waverly said, his voice slurred.

"You be good, now, sweetheart," Julia said, standing on tiptoe within her fiancé's embrace to kiss him on the lips.

"Don't worry, honey," Waverly said. "I'm not going to do anything bad."

"It's your bachelor party, Wave. I forgive you in advance for all transgressions," Julia said with a fond smile as she re-arranged the tie on Waverly's tux.

Ben curbed his impatience with effort. The groomsmen had left long ago to join a bunch of Waverly's cop buddies at The Seasons. The family butler and maid were there to direct the caterers, so the bachelor party was doubtless in full swing. Without its host. Or the groom. Whom Ben was having trouble separating from his bride.

Waverly pulled Julia close for a hug. "I'm marrying the most loving, understanding woman in the world."

"Look at those naked floozies all you want," Julia said, returning the hug, then pulling back to meet Waverly's blood-shot brown eyes. "Just be sure you don't touch!"

"Damn, Waverly," Ben said with a shake of his head. "The little woman's already got you on a short leash."

Julia punched Ben in the arm. "You shut up, Benjamin. There's nothing wrong with a groom respecting the wishes of his bride the night before their wedding."

Ben hooked an arm around Julia's neck, and she slugged him hard in the stomach with her fist.

"Let me go, you big bully!" she said with a laugh, wrenching herself free at the same moment Ben released her.

Ben genuinely liked his half sister. She'd attached herself to him every time he and Carter came to visit, following him around like a puppy. When he was a teenager, he'd found her a nuisance, but he'd never failed to pick her up when she'd raised her arms and smiled up at him.

He hoped Julia and Waverly were going to be happy. But he didn't believe in fairy tales. She was too young to understand the problems her money would create for their marriage. And Waverly was too blinded by love to believe they wouldn't live happily ever after.

Julia shoved both hands through her long blond hair, fluffing it, and tugged up the bodice of her strapless pink satin dress. "I'm not a kid anymore, Ben. You have to stop treating me like one."

"No, you're not, Little Bit," Ben said, his voice gruff. "You're about to become a wife."

"And I'm marrying the best man in the world," Julia said with a beatific smile. She turned and grabbed both of Waverly's ears and gave him a smacking kiss on the lips.

"Waverly was a good boy—a pretty good boy—" Ben amended "—at the rehearsal dinner. I watched him jump with alacrity through every hoop Mother and the senator put in front of him."

"Waverly's marrying into a political family. Hoop-jumping is a necessary skill," Julia said.

"And—I'm—damned—good—at—it," Waverly said painstakingly.

Ben heard in Waverly's precise diction just how much liquid courage he'd needed to make it through the rehearsal dinner with Julia's intimidating parents. He still couldn't believe the announcement Waverly had made when he'd stood up, champagne glass in hand. But he admired his friend for it.

Ben was jerked from his rumination by Julia's rough tug on the two ends of his untied bow tie. "Hey!" he said, grabbing her wrists.

"How drunk are you?" she asked.

"I'm sober enough to drive."

"I'm counting on you to take care of Wave tonight," Julia said. "Make sure he gets back here on time for the wedding tomorrow afternoon."

"We won't be leaving The Seasons," Ben said. "If Waverly doesn't show up tomorrow, you can come over and get him."

Julia batted his arm. "Don't tease me, Ben. Keep an eye on Wave for me. Don't let him drink too much."

"It's already too late for that," Ben said, pointing to Waverly, who was slumped against a wide Corinthian column on the front porch, his eyes closed, his mouth hanging open.

"Then take him home and put him to bed," Julia said, shooting a tolerant glance in her future husband's direction.

At the word *bed*, Waverly's eyes opened and he smiled broadly at Julia. "You want to go to bed, sweetheart? I thought you said we should spend tonight apart."

Ben smirked at Julia, lifted an inquiring eyebrow, and was amused by the rosy blush that appeared on his half sister's cheeks.

Julia turned to Waverly and said, "Honey, you're staying with Ben tonight."

"Oh," he said, struggling to focus bleary eyes. "Okay."

"Please get him out of here," Julia said to Ben, "before Mother and Daddy come out here and find him like this."

"Let's go, Waverly." Ben slipped an arm around his friend's shoulders and helped him navigate the front steps.

"Wait!" Julia called out when they reached the redbrick driveway.

Ben half turned with Waverly as Julia tripped down the steps. She held her fiancé's face gently between her palms and gave him a tender kiss on the lips. "Good night, my love," she murmured. "Until tomorrow."

When Waverly reached drunkenly for her, she turned and ran back up the stairs.

"Take it easy, buddy. Tomorrow she'll be your wife, and you can sleep with her every night for the rest of your life."

"Love her so much," Waverly said, staring after Julia.

"Yeah, I know." As he stuffed Waverly into the passenger seat of his Jag, Ben heard a cell phone play the "Hallelujah Chorus."

"That's mine," Waverly said, fumbling in his tux jacket for his phone. He dropped it on the floor at his feet.

As Ben picked it up and handed it to his friend, he said, "You had this on all night? You *do* like living dangerously. If that had rung during dinner—"

"'Lo," Wave said. "Uh-huh. Yeah. A few."

Ben was halfway to The Seasons before the conversation was over. He turned to his friend and said, "Julia wanted to whisper sweet nothings?"

"I have to go back to D.C.," Waverly said slowly and distinctly.

"Have you forgotten about your bachelor party? Friends? Strippers? The works?"

"Screw the party."

Ben stared at his friend. "Who was that on the phone?"

"None of your business."

"Look, if there's some problem—"

"I have to go out for a li'l while," Waverly slurred. "I'll be back. I just have to go do something."

"You shouldn't be driving. If you need to go somewhere, let me take you there."

Waverly shook his head, then put his hands to either side of it and closed his eyes, as though he were dizzy. "Just get me to my car."

One of Waverly's cop friends was supposed to have driven his Ford Explorer to The Seasons.

"I can't let you drive, Waverly. Not in this condition."

"I'll stop and get some coffee. Don't argue with me, Ben. I don't have any choice."

"Then let me drive you where you have to go," Ben insisted.

"You've seen me drive in worse shape."

"When we were stupid kids. Before I promised Julia I'd get you to your wedding in one piece. If you drive drunk—"

"Stow it, Ben."

They'd reached The Seasons, and Ben pulled his Jag in next to Waverly's Ford SUV. "Friends don't let friends drive drunk."

"If you're my friend, you'll let me do this," Waverly said. "I need to settle this before Julia and I take off on our honeymoon."

"There's another woman?" Ben said incredulously. "Is that it?"

"Hell, no! It's gang— It's none of your business."

"What's so important you have to miss your bachelor party to handle it?"

"This can't wait."

Ben put a hand on his friend's arm. "Look, Waverly, I can't let you drive."

Wave pulled free and shoved open the door of the Jag. "I'm not sure when I'll get back. Tell the guys I'll see them at the wedding."

Ben jumped out of his Jag and grabbed for the keys to the Explorer where they'd been left above the visor.

"What do you think you're doing?" Waverly demanded.

"Saving your life," Ben said. "And maybe the lives of other innocent drivers. You're drunk, buddy."

"Give me my keys!"

Waverly grabbed for the keys and Ben deftly stepped aside. Waverly's momentum carried him forward, so he lost his footing and landed on his hands and knees. He came up mad and he came up swinging.

Ben bunched his hand into a fist around the keys and hit Waverly hard in the chin. "Damn it, Waverly!" he shouted as he nursed his stinging knuckles. "What the hell is wrong with you?"

Waverly was out cold.

Ben stuffed Waverly's keys back behind the visor and returned to heft his friend over his shoulder. He hauled Waverly inside, grunting with the strain as he headed up the broad, winding, *Gone With the Wind* staircase. He could hear the shouts and laughter of Waverly's friends coming from the kitchen and parlor.

"Damn you, Waverly," Ben snarled at his unconscious friend. "Julia's going to give me hell if your chin is bruised tomorrow. But I promised her I'd get you to your wedding alive and well. And, by God, that's exactly what I intend to do!"

14

"Wake up, you sonofabitch!"

Ben felt himself falling off the bed and realized the sheet and blanket had been ripped out from under him. He hit the Aubusson carpet on his hands and knees, searching frantically for his XM107 .50 caliber long-range sniper rifle. Which wasn't there.

A breath shuddered out of him as he reminded himself he was no longer in the desert. He was in his bedroom at The Seasons. And he stank with the foul sweat of someone scared shitless.

He'd been dreaming again. The same lousy dream. He looked at his shaking hands, expecting them to be covered with sticky red blood. His fingertips were callused but clean.

"Get up!" Waverly ordered.

Ben sucked in a breath and shoved himself upright enough to see a furious Waverly standing in boxers and a T-shirt on the other side of the bed.

"I told you I had to get back to D.C. last night. Look at this!" Waverly leaned across the bed to shove *The Washington Post* under Ben's nose.

Ben was still hung over—he'd celebrated Waverly's wedding after he'd put the groom to bed—and he struggled to focus his eyes. The headline was hard to miss: "Gang Riot Leaves 3 Dead."

"This is all my fault," Waverly gritted out between tight jaws.

"How could it be your fault?"

Waverly threw the folded paper in Ben's face. "That call

last night was from my confidential informant. My CI told me trouble was brewing between MS and the One-Eight, that a shoot-out was likely. I knew those kids. I could have intervened. Maybe I could have prevented those deaths."

"And maybe not," Ben said, pushing himself to his feet.

"Both gangs will be out for blood now. I need to get to D.C. and find the other boy involved in that shooting—the one still left alive—before the whole city erupts in gang violence."

"Have you forgotten you're getting married at one o'clock? You don't have time to go to D.C. The only place you have time to hit is the shower."

"I should have left you asleep," Waverly snarled as he whirled on his barefoot heel and headed out the door.

Ben crossed the bedroom by the most direct route, vaulting across the high, four-poster bed. He hurried down the hall after Waverly and caught up to him in the bedroom where he'd spent the night.

"You've trained your men to handle exactly this kind of situation. Let them handle it. When you get back from your honeymoon—"

"Shut up, Ben." Waverly riffled through an overnight bag beside the bed and came up with a pair of jeans and a long-sleeved soccer shirt, which he pulled on. He grabbed socks and a pair of Nikes and stuffed his feet in them. Then he added his shoulder holster and Glock and palmed his MPD badge into his pocket.

"If you drive to D.C. now you're going to be late to your wedding," Ben warned. "I promised Julia I'd get you there on time. Which means talking you out of this insanity."

For a moment, Waverly looked troubled. Then he zipped and snapped his jeans. "Julia will understand."

"Julia will be hurt if you leave her standing at the altar," Ben said implacably. "And my mother and the senator will likely forbid you to see her ever again."

Ben watched Waverly hesitate for an instant before he bent

and tied the laces on his shoes. He realized his friend was going, and that if he didn't want to be left behind, he'd better get himself dressed.

"Aren't you going to shave? Or brush your teeth?" Ben said when Waverly headed for the bedroom door.

Without a word, Waverly turned around and headed for the bathroom. He struggled to unwrap one of the plastic-packaged toothbrushes on the counter.

As Waverly was reaching for the toothpaste, Ben raced back to his bedroom. He yanked on jeans and a T-shirt, then threw on a V-neck gray cashmere sweater. He shoved his bare feet into comfortable brown loafers, grabbed a soft brown leather bomber jacket, stuck his 9mm Glock in the back of his jeans and bounded out the door.

Waverly was already at the bottom of the stairs.

"Hey!" he shouted. "I'm coming with you."

Waverly didn't answer, just kept moving.

Ben retrieved a Kevlar bulletproof vest he kept in the trunk of his Jaguar as Waverly gunned the Ford engine. Ben jerked open the passenger's door, threw the protective vest into the backseat, and jumped into the SUV. "How about hitting a drive-thru for a cup of coffee?"

Waverly shot Ben an irritated look, but when they got to the first town, he drove through a McDonald's.

"I was thinking Starbucks," Ben said. When Waverly scowled, he added, "But coffee is coffee."

As Ben sipped his coffee he said, "How about giving Julia a call?"

"I'm hoping—planning—to get back in time for the wedding. I don't want to worry her unnecessarily."

Ben looked at his watch. It was 7:02 a.m. The round-trip drive alone would take four hours. There was a chance they'd be back in time to change into their morning coats and show up on time at a one o'clock wedding. If they weren't delayed. If nothing went wrong. "It's your neck," he muttered.

He doubted Waverly heard him, because his friend was on the phone with Harry Saunders, the MPD sergeant who was supposed to replace him as head of the Gang Unit while he was gone for his two-week honeymoon in Tahiti. When that call was done, Waverly contacted every other member of the unit on the job to find out how the search was going for the 1-8 shooter still at large.

Ben only heard one side of the conversation, but it appeared a member of MS and a member of the 1-8 had gotten into an altercation over a girl at a dance at the Latin American Youth Center.

"What do you know about the girl?" Ben asked Waverly between calls.

"I noticed her hanging around with one of the MS guys for the first time last week. I couldn't find her on any previous gang database. She's got long, straight black hair and light gray eyes."

Waverly shot Ben a quick glance. "She's a looker. She speaks English but with an accent. My CI thought her name was Patricia—Trisha—Reynolds. He thought she was attending school here in D.C., but he wasn't sure where.

"I found four girls named Patricia Reynolds enrolled in District schools," Waverly continued, "but none of them fit the description he gave me. I haven't been able to find out where this girl is living. She looks fifteen, maybe sixteen. Could be older, could be younger, I don't know."

Waverly explained that his CI had called after the gang members had been thrown out of the center for fighting over the girl. From insults that had been flung, it was clear they'd planned to settle things later. His CI had told him when and where the gangs were going to meet.

"But I never got there."

Ben heard what Waverly didn't say. That because he hadn't been there to intervene, three kids—two from MS and one from the 1-8—had ended up dead.

After they'd been driving through the green, gold and russet countryside for another fifteen minutes without any sound except the tires on macadam, Ben said, "What makes you think you could have talked those kids out of shooting each other?"

Waverly was silent so long, Ben figured his friend wasn't going to answer him.

At last he said, "A guy in MS and one of the One-Eight already had a row over the girl last week. Just threats. I was there, and I was able to talk some sense into them."

"You were a long way from Columbia Heights last night. Wouldn't it have made more sense to call someone else on the Gang Unit and let them handle it? Why did it have to be you?"

"I've worked hard to get these kids to trust me," Waverly said. "They'd do for me what they might not do for anyone else. I figured I could talk the two boys out of fighting. Especially over a girl that may not be interested in either one of them."

"You don't think she is?"

Waverly frowned. "I don't know. Silvio seemed to think—"

"Silvio?"

Waverly hesitated, then said, "Silvio's my confidential informant in MS. I picked him up for grand theft auto and found out he's illegal. So long as he keeps me informed on MS activities, he doesn't get deported back to El Salvador.

I called him after I got back to the office yesterday afternoon to see if he might know why Epifanio was killed. I heard you tell your boss that the killer said he'd cut Epifanio's throat to shut him up."

"And?"

"Silvio said he didn't know anything, but he'd ask around." Waverly glanced at Ben and said, "You can see why I didn't want him picked up along with everybody else last night. If he gets in any more trouble, his ass is out of here."

"What is it you hope to accomplish with this race to D.C.?"

"Somebody has to stop both gangs from retaliating."

"You think they'll listen to you when blood's already been spilled?" Ben said doubtfully.

Waverly grimaced. "I have to try."

"Who're you planning to see first?"

"The One-Eight. They hang at Moe's on Saturday mornings."

Ben realized that the moment he showed up at Moe's with Waverly, the 1-8 would make him as a cop. Not that it mattered, now that Epifanio was dead. "You think the One-Eight will be there, after what happened last night?" Ben asked.

"I know they're there, because of what happened last night. Besides, I've had guys from the unit watching them."

They pulled into the parking lot at Moe's at 9:05 a.m. The instant Waverly stepped out of the car, he was approached by two MPD officers from the Gang Unit who'd been surveilling Moe's, a combination restaurant and sports bar with lots of TVs and video games that was open pretty much all the time.

Ben put on his Kevlar vest as Waverly and the two cops spoke in low tones on the other side of the car. He noticed Waverly hadn't moved to collect his vest from the rear of the SUV, so he did it himself. He carted the protective vest over to his friend and interrupted his conversation to say, "Put this on."

Waverly tried to brush the vest aside, but Ben said, "I'm not going back to Virginia and tell Julia you got shot on your wedding day. Now put the damned thing on."

Waverly took the vest from Ben and put it on as he finished conferring with the cops who'd been watching the gang. Ben heard him tell the cops to wait outside, that he'd let them know if he needed them.

When he and Waverly stepped inside the dimly lit sports bar, Ben saw that the billiard tables and computer games had been abandoned in favor of a series of booths where the 18th Street gang was bunched. They were talking loud and looking mean.

Ben searched for weapons in the crowd but didn't see any. Which didn't mean they weren't carrying concealed. He watched Waverly approach the gang fearlessly. Carelessly,

Ben thought. He took a step closer to his friend and watched his back. Ben recognized several of the kids.

"How are you doing, Juan?" Waverly asked the leader of the gang, who was sitting at the center of the crowd.

"How do you think?" Juan Alvarez shot back. "We're mad. And we're going to get even!" He crossed his arms at the wrists and stuck both forefingers high in the air in the 1-8 gang sign. The rest of the gang did the same, a guttural shout issuing from their throats.

Ben felt the hairs rise on his neck. Maybe Waverly's trip hadn't been so dumb after all. These kids reminded him of hungry wolves determined to make a kill. He deferred to Waverly's greater experience and kept his mouth shut and his eyes open.

The leader of the 1-8 turned to Ben and said, "Didn't figure you for no cop."

Ben didn't reply. The bold letters on his Kevlar vest answered for him.

"We had an agreement," Waverly said to Juan. "You promised if there was ever any violence, you'd give me twenty-four hours to find the guilty parties and put their asses away before you went after them yourselves."

The crowd murmured and Ben realized that the relative peace among the gangs in D.C. over the past several years had been bought with a lot of promises. Now Waverly was going to have to put up or shut up.

"Twenty-four hours from when they were shot," Juan said, making it a definitive statement, rather than a question.

Ben did the math and realized that nearly twelve of Waverly's twenty-four hours were already gone. No wonder he'd been in a hurry to get to D.C. this morning.

"That was the deal," Waverly said. "How about it? Will you keep your promise?"

Ben could see there were several boys—and girls—who wanted a chance to kick ass. But he knew Juan Alvarez had been around long enough to see how a gang war could escalate. His younger sister had been an innocent victim of a gang drive-by shooting.

"You got twelve hours," the kid told Waverly.

"MS has the same deal," Waverly said. "So I gotta ask. Who did the shooting on your side?"

"Raul and Frankie," Juan said bitterly.

"And they're both dead," Waverly said. "What about the MS guys who shot them?"

"One of them is dead, but Pedro Gonzalez got away clean. For twelve more hours, anyway."

Ben felt a chill of foreboding run down his spine. Pedro Gonzalez wasn't just any MS gangster. He was the younger brother of Jorge Gonzalez, the guy at the top of the MS chain of command.

That little fact didn't seem to phase Waverly. They were going hunting for an MS killer. And they had twelve hours to find him.

Unless they wanted to get back to Hamilton Farm in time for Waverly's wedding. That was scheduled to start three hours and forty-two minutes from now.

15

Ben knew that killing a man, even an enemy, wasn't easy. Soldiers had to be carefully taught to take human life. Nevertheless, a lot of soldiers couldn't—or wouldn't—kill, even with their lives on the line. But they would kill to save their buddies. They would kill to keep their friends alive.

So he understood how the gang shootings might have gotten out of hand. And how volatile the situation was now.

"I suppose you know where MS is hanging out this morning, too," Ben said as they once again drove through the streets of Columbia Heights.

"I wish I did," Waverly said bitterly.

"You don't?"

Waverly shook his head. "I know where they usually hang out. But nobody in my unit has seen hide nor hair of them since last night."

"Then we're done here," Ben said. "You've got your promise from the One-Eight to stay put for a while. Call your chief and tell her she's got twelve hours to find the killer. Then we can head back to Virginia and get you married."

"I might know where to find Pedro Gonzalez."

"Then call your boss and tell her where to look."

"I'd rather do this myself."

Ben stared at his friend. "I don't know whether you're being stubborn or just plain stupid. What's going on here, Waverly? Do you want to marry my sister, or not?"

"None of this would have happened if I hadn't gotten drunk last night. I can't just walk away. I need to finish this."

Ben knew better than to try to talk Waverly out of his guilt. But he didn't want Julia left waiting at the altar, either. "If you're determined to go off on this wild-goose chase, call Julia and tell her you're going to be late."

"Not yet."

"The groomsmen have likely noticed we're gone," Ben said. "They're going to start making inquiries."

"Let them."

"How about if I call my dad? He can run interference for you with my mother."

"Not yet," Waverly said.

Ben glanced at his watch. Three hours and seven minutes. And counting.

To his surprise, Waverly pulled in behind Lincoln Middle School. "What are we doing here on a Saturday morning? There's no school in session."

"I caught Pedro in the maintenance shed behind the school a week ago making out with a girl. He'd picked the lock." He shrugged. "It's worth a look. If he isn't hiding there…" He sighed and glanced at his watch. "I may have to let someone else clean up my mess."

Waverly turned off the ignition and left the car. Ben followed him to a 14'x14' maintenance shack. He squinted his eyes against the glare of the morning sun off the shiny waffled metal. He saw the padlock was undone. And heard the low murmur of voices inside.

Ben grabbed Waverly's arm as his friend reached for the door handle and said in a low voice, "If you think there's a killer in there, we need to call for backup."

"My wedding starts in three hours and four minutes," Waverly whispered back. "I've got a two-hour drive to get there and I need to shower and shave and change my clothes. I don't have time to wait."

"This is crazy," Ben said.

Waverly looked him in the eye and said, "We can handle this."

Ben understood Waverly's reasoning, even if he didn't agree with it. If what they were facing was a single kid with a gun, the two of them were probably enough firepower to subdue him. They could always call for backup if things went south. Besides, he could see from Waverly's grim, white-faced expression that he wasn't going to talk him out of it.

"Watch yourself," Ben said. "Julia is too young to be a widow before she's a wife."

At that moment, someone shoved open the door to the shack. The first kid out saw the two of them and shouted over his shoulder, "Pedro, it's the cops!"

As Ben and Waverly backed up, their guns pulled and held in a shooting stance, MS gang members swarmed from the shack like angry wasps.

"Let them go," Waverly said tightly as he took a step back. "We only want Pedro."

Ben's eyes followed the boys as they fled to make sure no one decided to turn around and take a shot at them from behind.

"Pedro, drop your gun and come out with your hands over your head," Waverly shouted.

Ben was holding his breath, praying the kid would give up, when he heard a male and female voice arguing. He glanced at Waverly, and they took up positions backed up on either side of the open door.

"*Pinché, puercos!*" the boy inside yelled back. "You come in here and somebody's gonna die."

They heard a female cry of pain.

Ben shot another look at Waverly, then focused on the black space that led into the shack. Neither of them had counted on Pedro having a hostage.

"Who's in there with you?" Waverly called out.

"I got a girl in here," Pedro replied.

Ben could hear muffled noises from the girl, as Pedro shouted, "Go away! Or I swear I'll kill her."

Ben heard the girl scream in pain and reached for his phone to call for backup. Before he could get it out of his pocket, Waverly had breached the doorway.

"You stupid sonofabitch," Ben muttered. He heard a shot ping off metal as he quickly followed Waverly inside. He slid behind a stack of fertilizer bags and waited for his eyes to adjust to the dim interior, which was lit by flickering fluorescent tubes running along the center of the pitched metal roof.

He saw Waverly crouched on the other side of the doorway behind a riding lawn mower and whispered, "Are you all right?"

"I'm good," Waverly whispered back.

Ben could hear a girl crying toward the back of the shack, hidden by a stack of cardboard boxes. He consciously controlled his breathing, but he could feel the hair prickle on the back of his neck. He had a flashback, a vision of himself standing over a bloody body, the sun beating on his back. He realized he was dripping with sweat. He shook his head and made himself focus on the present.

The kid on the other side of the shed had already killed once. He had nothing to lose by killing again. The boy had to be desperate, knowing what was waiting for him if he was caught.

"There's no reason anybody else has to get hurt," Waverly said. "Let the girl go."

The boy stood up, holding a gun to the head of a petite, honey-skinned girl with long, straight black hair. His other arm was clasped around her slender waist. She was beautiful, Ben realized. Was she the one the two boys had fought over?

"I'm leaving here," Pedro said, "and she's going with me."

The girl's light gray eyes were wide with fright, and blood streamed from her temple.

Ben looked down at his hands and realized they were trembling. Again. He tightened his two-handed hold on his Glock in an attempt to steady his nerves and fight off his PTSD.

He shot a quick look around the corrugated metal walls of the shed, at the various metal tools hanging there from which a bullet could ricochet. This was the worst possible site for a gunfight.

Ben was glad he'd insisted Waverly put on a protective vest. Now if he could just get him to keep his head down. Ben heard sirens in the distance and hoped someone had responded to the shots by calling the police.

"In another minute, a whole lot of cops are going to be here," Waverly said to the kid. "Let's settle this between us now."

The boy took a step forward with the girl. "I'm leavin'. And you're not gonna stop me."

Ben flashed again on the desert. He was sighting through the Leupold 16X scope on his XM107 .50 caliber sniper rifle at a target five hundred meters away. He'd been a last-minute substitute for a sniper who'd gotten appendicitis, sent to kill whoever came to pick up a load of munitions stolen from an army dump in Afghanistan. He'd already pulled the trigger when a kid stepped in front of his intended target. He heard a scream.

Ben realized the scream he heard was happening now, not in the past. He saw the girl across the shed suddenly slump and wasn't sure whether she'd actually fainted or whether she'd faked it. The result was the same. She became a dead weight the slender El Salvadoran boy couldn't carry. When he was forced to drop her, he lost his shield.

And Ben shot him in the shoulder of his gun arm.

Ben saw the startled look on Waverly's face as the kid stumbled backward onto the ground, but he'd seen the shot and taken it, shooting to wound, so the boy would live to learn from his mistakes. He kept his eyes on the pistol the boy had dropped when he was shot.

And realized the kid was reaching for it.

"Keep your head down!" he yelled at Waverly. "Don't do it," he warned the kid.

The boy swore as he grabbed the weapon and shot off two more rounds in Ben's direction.

Ben grunted with pain when the first bullet grazed the top of his shoulder, ripping through his gray cashmere sweater. His flesh stung, and he could feel something wet and warm dripping down his back. He ducked behind the fertilizer bags and heard the second bullet ricochet off something metal behind him.

"I'm hit!" Waverly cried, grabbing his hip at a spot below his Kevlar vest.

"See what you made me do!" the kid yelled as he struggled to his feet, waving the gun and ducking behind cover as he made his way around the edge of the maintenance shack toward the door.

Ben followed the kid's progress with his Glock. "Drop the gun."

The kid aimed and fired at Ben.

And Ben shot back.

He felt his heart flutter in his chest, aware that this bullet had done more than wound. It was a choice of kill or be killed, but he still felt sick to his stomach. He held himself on a tight leash as he approached the shooter to make sure he was no longer a threat.

Ben's gut wrenched as he looked down at the unlined face of the youth staring back at him with vacant eyes. He grunted at the pain in his shoulder as he bent to retrieve the boy's gun. Better to get it out of the way. With his luck, the girl would wake up and decide she wanted to avenge the boy's death. Stranger things had happened.

"Is he dead?" Waverly called.

"Yeah."

"Shit."

Ben gagged and fought the urge to vomit. He leaned a hand against the corrugated wall and took several deep breaths. He staggered over to the girl and saw she was still out cold. There was a bloody gash across her temple where the boy had apparently struck her with his gun. He had to swallow again because his stomach was threatening to erupt.

Ben could feel the sweat trickling down the center of his back. And blood crawling slowly down his shoulder. His body was trembling uncontrollably. He didn't want Waverly to see him like this.

Suck it up, soldier, he muttered to himself. *You've seen death before.* That was a big part of his problem. He'd left the army so he wouldn't have to kill again. Ben stuck his Glock in the back of his jeans, stuck the boy's Beretta in his jacket pocket, then clenched and unclenched his hands a couple of times, which seemed to help.

"Ben? What's going on?"

"Just checking to make sure the girl's okay."

"Is she?"

"Looks all right. Just knocked out." He headed back across the shed to Waverly and asked, "How bad are you hurt?"

"Ricochet hit my leg." Waverly was on the ground on his side, leaning up on an elbow, the other hand clasped near his hip.

Ben yanked off his jacket, knelt and slipped it over Waverly's shoulders to keep him warm. Then he wrapped Waverly's hand more firmly around his bleeding leg. "Hold tight. I'm going to call for help."

When he reached Waverly's Ford Explorer, he keyed the police radio inside and said, "Shots fired. Officer down. Officer needs assistance." He identified himself and asked for backup and paramedics. He gave the school's address when asked and the location of the maintenance shed.

"Send the coroner, homicide—whoever you'd send to an officer-involved shooting," Ben said to the dispatcher. "There's also a dead murder suspect and an injured hostage."

Ben forced himself to remain calm and patient, answering the dispatcher's questions, knowing that his information was important to get the right kind of help in a hurry. He asked the dispatcher to contact his boss at ICE and tell him what was going on.

The dispatcher wanted more information, but Ben left the radio hanging and ran back to the shed. Waverly and Julia were going to have to postpone the wedding because of Waverly's wound. His mother was going to be pissed as hell. Julia probably wasn't going to be too happy, either.

To his surprise and dismay, a large pool of blood was spreading out on the cement floor around his friend, who was now lying flat.

"What the hell's going on, Waverly? I thought you said you weren't hurt bad."

Waverly gave him a look that Ben had seen in other men's faces. Dying men's faces. "I think that ricochet must have cut my femoral artery," he said with a shrug and a rueful shake of his head.

"Where the hell are the paramedics?" Ben yelled. The sirens he'd heard earlier must not have been coming their way. "I need something to use as a tourniquet." He wasn't wearing a belt and neither was Waverly. He ran to the dead kid, but his beltless pants were hanging halfway down his butt.

Ben found one on the girl. He was unbuckling her belt when she came to and grabbed his arm in a surprisingly strong grip. His dog-bitten arm. Ben yelped and grabbed her wrist to keep her from hurting him further. "I need—"

"Get away from me!" she cried. "Help! Rape! Someone help me!" She screamed and kicked out at him, contorting her body to escape his grasp, writhing like a snake.

"I need your belt," Ben tried explaining. "I'm not going to hurt you." But she was too scared to listen and making too much noise to hear him.

He held her tight in one arm while he unbuckled her belt and began pulling it free from the loops of her jeans with the other. Her teeth clamped onto his injured arm. He yowled in agony as he freed the belt. He tried once more to reason with her, but when she kicked for his balls, he clipped her on the chin just hard enough to daze her.

Ben laid her gently on the concrete floor. "I just wanted your belt, goddamn it! I wasn't going to hurt you." He cradled his dog-bitten arm, which was bleeding again through his sweater, as he ran back to Waverly with the belt.

He was shocked at how white his friend was. He knelt in the blood that surrounded Waverly and slipped the belt around the top of Waverly's thigh.

He was just cinching the belt tight when the girl slipped up behind him, grabbed his Glock from the back of his jeans and aimed it at him.

She stood facing him, her teeth bared in a feral snarl. "You tried to rape me."

He met her gaze and said, "He's bleeding out. Just let me tighten your belt on his leg."

"You're a bad man." She was holding the Glock with both hands, the barrel aimed at his chest like she knew how to use it. And her hands were steady.

"I only wanted your belt. See?" he said, finally notching the black studded leather belt in the last hole around Waverly's leg. "I needed a tourniquet."

He'd barely finished speaking when he lunged at the girl, grabbing her arm to shove the gun away from his face. It went off, exploding a fluorescent tube and showering shards of glass onto their heads.

She was struggling in his arms, beating on his chest with her fists, when he heard a harsh voice say, "Let the girl go!"

Ben heard the command and turned, but the instant he did, one of the several MPD officers in the doorway yelled, "Drop your weapon! Down on your knees! Hands behind your head."

Ben knew it would save time to drop his gun and assume the position, so he did.

As soon as she was free, the girl hit him hard in the eye with her balled fist and yelled, "He tried to rape me!"

Two of the cops shoved him flat on the floor and one leaned his knee painfully into Ben's back while the other cuffed his hands high behind him. "I'm with ICE," he managed to say as his cheek was pressed to the gritty concrete floor. He felt broken glass from the fluorescent tube dig into his cheek.

"My badge is in my pocket. My partner's been shot. I wanted her belt to use as a tourniquet."

"Watch out!" one of the cops yelled. "The girl's grabbed his gun. She's running!"

Ben could hear sounds of a chase, but he knew, after all the flack his incident had caused yesterday, nobody was going to shoot at her. Unless they were fleet enough to catch her, she was gone. With his Glock.

He could hear sirens, but they were still a long way off.

The cops returned, huffing. One rolled him over and found his badge. "He's ICE, like he said."

"Hey, aren't you the guy who shot at that kid yesterday? I was there. You're Benedict, right?"

"Yeah. That's me."

The cop glanced at the dead boy, a bullet hole between his eyes, and said, "Looks like your aim improved."

"The wounded man's with MPD," Ben said as they yanked him onto his feet. "How is he?"

"He don't look so good," one of the cops said, gesturing to Waverly.

Ben rubbed his wrists as he hurried to Waverly's side. More police had shown up. There was no way to get close without stepping in Waverly's blood. He clamped his teeth and knelt in the growing red pool. "Find out where the hell the paramedics are," he growled at the police standing around him.

The cement floor was slanted and the blood flowing from Waverly's hip had run down into his short brown hair. Ben fought the flashback that threatened to overwhelm him—of another time, another victim.

He swallowed hard as he lifted Waverly's bloody head

into his lap. "Hey, buddy," he croaked. He had to clear his throat to ask, "How's it going?"

"Tell Julia I love her," Waverly said in a calm, quiet voice. "I'll always love her."

"You can tell her yourself. She's going to be mad that she has to postpone the wedding, but she'll get over it."

Ben willed Waverly to live. "You hang on," he said. "Help is on the way." He turned to one of the cops standing nearby and raged, "Where the hell are the paramedics?"

"They ran a red and had an accident. They're sending another ambulance."

Ben turned back to Waverly and wondered just how long it took a man to bleed out if you cut his femoral artery.

"I want you to make me a promise," Waverly said in a faint voice. His eyes no longer seemed to focus on Ben, but at some point in the distance.

Ben thought of the last promise he'd made to Julia. That he'd get Waverly to his wedding on time. He leaned close and rasped, "Anything."

"Promise me you won't quit."

"What?"

"I know you. You're going to use this as an excuse to turn your back on these kids. I'm telling you, don't do it. I'm asking you not to quit."

"This is not the time—"

Waverly grabbed his wrist and said, "Promise me, Ben."

Ben felt like howling. Instead, he reached down and took Waverly's hand in his. His friend's hand was cold and he barely had a grip. "Okay. Fine. I promise I won't quit, you jackass. Now you've got to fight. You've got to hang on. Or Julia's going to kill me."

Waverly smiled as his eyes slid closed.

16

Twenty-year-old Aisha Kamal cried bitterly. Pedro Gonzalez, the MS-13 gang member who had been her only contact with Al Qaeda in America, was dead. Everything was ruined. Now she would never be able to avenge the destruction of her family in Afghanistan.

Through eyes blurred by tears, Aisha looked around the tiny bedroom she shared with two "sisters" and one "brother." It was one of only four rooms occupied by the El Salvadoran family with whom she had lived for the past month as their niece, Trisha Reynaldo.

Mrs. Reynaldo had a younger sister in El Salvador who was being held hostage by MS to ensure the Reynaldos' cooperation in housing Aisha and keeping her true identity secret while she was on this mission for Al Qaeda.

Every sacrifice Aisha had made to come to Washington, D.C., to live as a hated American had been for nothing. On her own, she could never hope to wreak the devastation on the infidels that had been promised by Al Qaeda when they recruited her in Afghanistan.

She had good reason to kill every American she could.

Seven years ago, when she was only thirteen, the Americans had bombed supposedly Taliban targets in Charikar, eleven kilometers—seven American miles—northwest of Bagram Air Base, and reduced her home to rubble. Her father Labib and her older brother Hussein had been crushed to death.

Two years later, when she was fifteen, the Americans had

arrested her husband Jamal. He had been tortured and sent to prison in faraway Guantánamo for supposedly plotting to blow up petrol stored at Bagram. He had not been heard from since.

Nine months, one week and three days ago, when she was nineteen, an American soldier had shot and killed her ten-year-old brother Basim.

Aisha had watched as her brother's right shoulder and chest disappeared in a red mist. Had seen the shocked surprise on his face as his body slumped onto the cobbles in the marketplace like a slaughtered sheep.

Tears had sprung from her eyes, and she had angrily wiped them away beneath her burka as she hurried to Basim's crumpled body. She had warned her brother not to get involved with Abdul—that Abdul was a fool. But Basim had been swollen with hatred of the Americans, like a tick ready to burst. He had agreed to hide a portion of the confiscated Russian munitions stolen from the Americans.

When none of her entreaties had swayed her younger brother from his course, she had followed him to the market-place, hoping that she could somehow protect him.

Instead, she had seen Abdul run away. And watched Basim die a sudden, brutal death.

Aisha had no memory of how she had done what she had done next. Even now, she marveled at her daring. She had known the Americans would come soon to confirm their kill. If Allah was merciful, her brother's assassin would be among them. Aisha had rooted through the canvas bag of munitions Abdul had abandoned on the ground and found a Russian grenade.

She had waited until she saw the armored vehicle race into the square and the two men spill out. Then she had pulled the pin and laid it in Basim's lifeless hand.

And walked away.

She found cover behind a sturdy mud-and-straw pillar, then turned to memorize the features of the assassin, still carrying the big rifle he had used to destroy her brother, as he walked toward Basim's body. The stark blue eyes and black hair. The straight nose and sharp cheekbones. The drawn, thin-lipped mouth.

Soon he would be dead. But she would never forget his face.

But the assassin's instincts had been sharp, his reflexes even sharper. He had seen the grenade and called a warning to his friend. She had not seen what happened next because she had hidden her face from the blast.

As dirt and body parts fell to the ground, she had walked back into the square to see his dead body with her own eyes, to praise Allah for granting her revenge. And realized that while the grenade had shredded the body of his fellow soldier, the assassin had merely been dazed by the concussion.

She stood staring down at his bloodied face, raging inside because she could see he had suffered only a few small cuts. She sought for some way to kill him, but she had no weapon, and he was quickly recovering his senses.

She reached down and grabbed one of the two metal discs hanging from a chain around his neck. She yanked it free, knowing that it identified him, knowing that someday, somehow, she would find him and finish what she had started.

She was hiding again behind the pillar when he rose like an avenging monster from the bloody carnage left by the grenade, roaring with rage. He had shot his gun into the sky until it was empty, scaring away everyone in the marketplace.

Aisha had watched as he dropped his weapon and sank to his knees beside the body of the other American.

In that moment, her brother's murderer had been vulnerable. She could have killed him with a rock, he was so oblivious to everything around her. But fear had held her in place, rooted to the ground like the grapevines her father had grown once upon a time.

The assassin must have called for help, because soon a helicopter hovered overhead. And the moment when she could have killed him was gone.

Her mother had mourned the death of the last male in her family until she died of starvation. Aisha had stood at her mother's graveside feeling desolate and desperate. She had become a female without the protection of a male relative, or any means of survival.

Two weeks later, her brother's friend Hamed, who belonged to Hezbe Islami Gulbuddin, a fundamentalist faction of the mujahideen with ties to Al Qaeda, had sent his sister to speak with her.

"Hamed needs your help," the girl had said.

"The help of a woman?" Aisha asked dubiously.

"They need someone who speaks English to carry out a mission in the United States."

"I only speak a little," she said. But the truth was, the missionary who had come to Charikar had taught her a great deal, because her gray eyes and long black hair reminded him of his daughter.

"You will have a chance to kill many Americans," Hamed had promised when he spoke to her at last. "But you will have to leave Charikar and may never see your home again."

Aisha had spread her hands wide and said, "What is there left here for me?"

Within a month, Al Qaeda had smuggled her into El Salvador. There she worked with operatives in hiding who were associated with Mara Salvatrucha, or MS, as they were called. They had taught her how to handle weapons, including the one she must deliver to kill the Americans. They had taught her more English words and American customs. She had learned not to feel self-conscious around men without the burka she had worn in public ever since she had become a woman.

Aisha had been a very good student because she had realized that when she went to America, she might have another chance to meet the assassin who had killed Basim.

She reached up to clutch the American soldier's dog tag

she wore on a ball chain around her neck. She had memorized the information contained on the tag.

BENEDICT
BENJAMIN P.
229 58 3751
APOS
EPISCOPALIAN

She would be happy to finish the blood feud he had begun in Charikar.

With the help of MS, she had made her way into the United States through the border at Brownsville, Texas, hitchhiked to Corpus Christi, then caught a Greyhound bus to Washington, D.C.

She possessed a forged green card that showed her age as fourteen. She was gracefully slender, barely five feet tall, with petal-soft, honey-toned skin and features delicate enough to easily pass for someone six years younger than she was. Mrs. Reynaldo had taken her to Lincoln Middle School when she arrived and enrolled her in the eighth grade. Becoming a middle-school student had effectively hidden her real age and identity.

It had also made it possible for her to meet easily with Pedro Gonzalez, a member of MS who actually was fourteen and a student at Lincoln Middle School.

This past week, Pedro had finally given Aisha the message from Al Qaeda she had been waiting for. In ten days, she would be given a weapon to be used against high-ranking Americans attending a private party in Georgetown.

Unfortunately, Pedro had not yet told her where she was supposed to retrieve the weapon. And now Pedro was dead.

Stupid boy! He did not know she was twenty, and she could not tell him. He had been jealous of her talking to a boy from the 18th Street gang she knew from school. Talking between unrelated males and females was allowed in America, she had been taught. Nor were women mere chattel. They did not have to listen to and obey men. So she had told Pedro to go away, that she would speak with whomever she pleased.

She rued her foolhardy defiance. She should have known Pedro would react as a jealous fool. Had not her husband beaten her when she had innocently raised her eyes to his friend all those years ago?

Pedro had killed the boy she had spoken with and another boy who had come to his aid. And they had shot Pedro's friend.

Today, the cop had killed Pedro. The cop whose face had looked so familiar as she fought with him. Whose blue eyes had reminded her so much of the soldier who had killed her younger brother.

Then the other policeman had said his name: BENEDICT.

She saw the letters as they appeared on his dog tag. As she had felt them stamped in the cold metal with her fingertips so many times. And realized that she was looking at the man who had killed her brother. Aisha had hoped and prayed she would meet Basim's assassin when she came to America. Oh, how she had prayed! She had never really expected her prayers to be answered.

But Allah was merciful. With tragedy had come a miracle.

She had wanted to kill BENEDICT with his own gun but realized that if she did, he would be the only American she would be allowed to kill. The other policemen in the shed would catch her and put her in prison and she would not be able to complete her mission. And she had been determined to kill as many Americans as she could to avenge her family.

She had seen BENEDICT's anguish as he tried to stem the bleeding from his friend's wound. And realized suddenly that she could have vengeance even more satisfying than his death. She could make sure he suffered as she had suffered. She could kill those he loved. And let him live.

Aisha felt the cold steel under her pillow. She had the assassin's Glock. She had been trained to use it, along with other weapons. Now that there was no more chance of completing her mission for Al Qaeda, she would focus on what could be accomplished.

Revenge for Basim's death.

Aisha heard tapping on her bedroom windowpane. "Aisha," a voice called quietly.

Aisha sat up and wiped her eyes. She got out of bed, slid open the cracked window and stared in surprise at Silvio Delgado. He was even shorter than she was, with a round face, spiked black hair, a boy's mustache and large brown eyes. Like Pedro, he was a member of MS. "What are you doing here?"

"I'm here to help you complete your mission."

Aisha's eyes narrowed. "Pedro never said anything about you."

"Of course not. That way, if you were ever arrested, you wouldn't be able to say anything to the cops."

"I thought because Pedro was killed—"

"Your friend Khalid in El Salvador thought of everything," Silvio interrupted. "I'm here to help you."

"Where is the weapon? Where do I pick it up?"

"I'll get it. And bring it to you when it's safe. There are too many cops nosing around right now. And those ICE guys, like the one who killed Pedro, are bad news."

"I'm going to kill him myself, with great pleasure, before I do what I have to do."

"You need to focus on your mission," Silvio said. "That's the best way to make the Americans suffer."

"Of course," Aisha said. Except, there was one American who would be suffering the torments of the damned over the next ten days, as he lost one loved one after another. On the day she became a martyr, she would make sure that BENEDICT left this earth with her. She would go to Paradise, while the infidel spent all eternity in Hell.

"I'll be in touch," Silvio said as he disappeared into the darkness outside her window.

Aisha lay back down on her bed and stared at the plastered

ceiling. She could hear the mother of the house trying to shush her crying baby, while two of her supposed siblings quarreled in front of the loud TV in the living room. She shut out the sounds, so she could concentrate.

The assassin was bound to come looking for her. After all, she had stolen his weapon. When he found her, she would make a friend of him. And then kill someone he loved and make him watch. As she had watched her father and her brothers and her mother die.

When his heart was shattered as hers had been, she would kill him. And have her revenge. She stuck her hand under the pillow and pulled out the gun she had stolen from Basim's killer. The gun she would use to shoot him between those cold blue American eyes.

17

"I just have a scratch on my shoulder," Ben said. "I don't need to be in the hospital."

"You blacked out," his boss replied, pacing the length of Ben's hospital bed. "That's a symptom of something." Tony grasped the foot rail with both hands and made eye contact with Ben. "The cops on the scene said you stood up when the paramedics arrived and just keeled over. You were lucky you didn't hit your head on that concrete floor and end up with a concussion. Thank God they caught you on the way down."

"Look, I'm fine," Ben said, working to keep his voice unemotional. "I'd lost some blood from the wound in my shoulder. It made me light-headed. That's all it was. I want to go home." He had to get out of here. He needed to be alone.

"Give yourself some time," Tony said in a quiet voice. "You've lost a friend."

Waverly is dead. Tony said he'd been pronounced dead when he arrived at the hospital. The truth of it was still sinking in. Ben felt a tremor roll through his body. He didn't want to break down in front of his boss.

How can I ever console Julia?

"I want to go home," he repeated. He castigated himself for not stopping his friend from going into that shed. Hell, for not stopping his friend from leaving The Seasons. He'd kept Waverly from driving drunk last night. Why hadn't he confiscated his keys this morning?

"You're staying right where you are until you're cleared

by the doctors—including Dr. Schuster," his boss said. "You shot at a kid yesterday and killed one today. You watched your sister's fiancé die in your arms on his wedding day. I doubt very much you're okay."

Tony hesitated, then added, "And if you are okay after all that, then there really is something wrong with you."

Ben said nothing. He'd told Waverly he wanted to quit. But work was the only thing that had given his life meaning—and held off the demons—since he'd left the army. Without it, he wasn't sure what he would do.

"What you've been through is enough to rattle anyone," Tony continued. "Besides, you have to take some time off while we investigate the shooting."

"It was a good shooting."

"I'm sure it was. It appears you followed protocol and did everything you could to avoid killing the boy. Still, there are procedures to be followed after an incident like this."

"I don't need to see a shrink," Ben said sullenly.

"I'm not going to argue with you, Agent Benedict. Dr. Schuster is outside. She'll see you after you've talked with your family. You'll keep talking to her until she's satisfied that you're okay and gives me the word that you can come back to work."

"I'm okay right now," Ben said, fighting to keep the quiver from his voice.

"Sure you are," Tony said. "Shall I send your family in? They've been waiting here for hours to see you."

Ben was startled. "Hours? How long was I out?" He looked for the gold Mariner's Rolex his father had given him upon his graduation from West Point, but it was gone from his wrist. There was no clock in the room. He glanced at the window, but the blinds were drawn. "What time is it?"

"About 6:00 p.m."

Ben felt a chill run down his spine. That was nearly the entire day gone. "Has my family been here the whole time?"

"They came right from the wedding. Didn't even change

their clothes. They're dressed in morning coats and fancy dresses. The bride is still in her wedding gown. Or she was the last time I saw her."

Ben felt acid in his throat.

"You don't have to see them, if you'd rather not."

Ben shrank from the thought of explaining to Julia how he'd allowed Waverly to get shot—let alone die—when he'd promised her he'd make sure her fiancé got to their wedding on time.

The last person he wanted to see right now was Julia. Or his mother and the senator. Or his father and stepmother and the ABCs. Or Rhett, with his warped sense of humor, for that matter. But if he was going to convince Tony he was okay, he'd have to see them all.

"Okay," he said. "Send them in."

18

Ben's jaws were clamped so tight a muscle jerked in his cheek. His hands were balled into fists under the sheet, bracing for the attack he expected from the senator and his mother. But the only person who entered the room after Tony Pellicano left was Julia.

"Hello, Ben," she said.

Ben saw the mascara clumped around her eyes and the dried tears on her cheeks. It hurt to see her wearing her wedding gown, a simple white strapless dress with a beaded bodice that fit to her tiny waist, then flowed down to her feet and trailed behind her. Her long blond hair was upswept as though to hold a veil, but the veil was missing. As he watched, tears welled in her beautiful blue eyes and spilled over.

"Oh, God, Julia. I am so sorry." The words were wrenched from somewhere deep inside him.

"You promised, Ben," she said in a small voice.

"I know. I—" He couldn't breathe.

Suddenly she was beating his chest with her fists and screaming, "You promised you promised you promised!"

He wrapped his arms around her and pulled her up onto the bed with him. He held her tight along the length of him, as she collapsed into sobs.

His throat ached and his nose burned. He gritted his teeth, determined not to cry.

"He's gone, Ben," Julia cried. "Wave is gone!"

"I know, Little Bit. I know."

He didn't know how long she wept against his shoulder, but at last she sighed deeply and said in a quiet voice, "Mother won't let me see him. She says I shouldn't have to see my dead fiancé on my wedding day."

"Maybe she's right."

She raised her head to look into his eyes and said fiercely, "I need to see him, Ben." She laid her cheek back against his chest and murmured, "To believe he's really gone."

"Then you will," Ben said. "I'll talk to Dad, and he'll take care of it. I'd go with you myself, but I'm stuck here for a while."

"Thank you, Ben."

"I am so sorry, Julia," he said again. "This was all my fault."

She pulled herself free of his embrace and slid off the bed to face him, her arms crossed protectively across her breasts. "Yes, it is your fault."

Ben cringed inwardly.

"You should have known better than to let him go anywhere this morning."

He didn't make excuses. He'd learned in the military that excuses didn't matter. What mattered was what you did—or did not—do.

"I knew going in that one day Wave might be…hurt." She cleared her throat and met his gaze. "Wave told me you know that I'm pregnant. And you still let him get killed."

"Julia, I—"

"Now our son will never know his father. He'll be a bastard."

She burst into tears again, and Ben slid his feet over the edge of the bed and pulled her, struggling, into his embrace.

"Don't, Julia. Don't do this to yourself."

"You're the one who did this, Ben," she said, shoving against his shoulders to be free, making him gasp as she brushed against his gunshot wound. "You could have stopped him. And you didn't."

Ben hugged her tight, offering what comfort he could, which seemed too little in light of all she'd lost.

"How am I ever going to tell Mother and Daddy the truth?" she murmured as she collapsed against him.

"Do you want me to tell them?" He held his breath, as he waited for her answer.

She took a step back, freeing herself from his embrace. "No. I need to do it." A breath soughed out of her. "They're going to be hurt. And disappointed in me."

"You were in love. That should be explanation enough."

"You'd better get back in bed, so I can let everyone in here." She shoved at his hip, and he slid his feet back under the covers. She tucked the sheet in tightly around him. "Everyone wants to see with their own eyes that you're okay."

She stepped closer, frowning as she grazed his scraped and discolored face with her fingertips. "You are okay, aren't you?"

"I wish it had been me, Julia," he blurted.

She remained silent for a long time, staring at her hand, which had dropped and was smoothing the tucked-in sheet. "I know it's a horrible thing to say. I know it isn't nice or kind." She looked into his eyes and said, "But I wish it had been you, too."

Then she fled from the room.

While he was still reeling, the senator and his mother entered, along with his father and stepmother and Rhett. He saw Amanda, Bethany and Camille standing huddled together outside before the door closed. His mother glanced worriedly at him, searching his bruised face, which he worked desperately to keep impassive, then turned and hurried after Julia.

"The ABCs have been scared to death," Rhett said as he plopped himself on the foot of the hospital bed. "You don't look so bad."

"How are you, son?" his father asked, his arm around Patsy, who had a tissue stuffed against her mouth and nose. Her eyes were red-rimmed.

Seeing Patsy in tears made his insides cramp. He managed to croak, "I'm fine, Dad."

"What the hell were the two of you thinking?" the senator

demanded. "What kind of idiot gets involved in a shoot-out the day of his wedding? I knew that sonofabitch was wrong for my daughter, but—"

Ben's fist shot out and caught the senator on the chin, sending the older man reeling. "You lousy bastard! How dare you!"

"Ben! No!" Patsy cried.

Ben struggled to get out of bed, to continue his attack, but he was trapped by the tucked-in sheet. He wouldn't have gotten far, because both Rhett and his father got in his way. When Rhett's fingers dug into the wound on his shoulder, he wrenched away and cried out in pain.

"Damn it, Ben," Rhett said, releasing him. "Settle down!"

His father wrapped him up in his arms and Ben pressed his face against his father's chest, breathing deeply, struggling not to sob aloud.

"Get out of here, Ham," he heard his father say in a harsh voice. "And stay the hell away from Ben."

"He hit me!" Ham said, laboring to his feet, shrugging off Rhett's offer of help.

"If he hadn't, I would have," his father said. "Now get out of here."

The senator left.

Ben realized, when his breathing quieted, that Patsy and Rhett were gone, too. He lifted his head from his father's chest and scooted back on the bed, keeping his eyes lowered.

"You okay now?" his father said as he took a step back.

Ben took a shuddering breath. "I've been better."

"I know you did everything you could to save Waverly."

Ben swallowed over the painful knot in his throat as he met his father's gaze. He wanted to explain to someone what had happened. "It was a freak accident, Dad. A ricochet that hit his femoral artery. The paramedics got delayed and he bled out."

"While you held him in your arms," his father said quietly.

Ben lowered his gaze again and nodded. A tear slid down his cheek and he quickly swiped it away.

"I hope you're going to take a little time off."

"I'm going to—" Ben had been about to say *quit* but remembered at the last second the promise he'd made to Waverly. His chest physically ached where his heart should be.

I can't quit. I promised Waverly I wouldn't quit. So I'm stuck doing a job I don't think I can do. Someday soon somebody's gonna catch me trembling like an old woman, figure out what a mess I am, and put me in the loony bin.

"I guess I'll have to be away from the job a few days to let this shoulder heal," Ben said at last.

"Do you think you'll be well enough to attend the funeral?"

"I'll be there," Ben said determinedly. "Dad, I promised Julia she can see Waverly. I told her you'd arrange it. Will you?"

"Her mother doesn't think it's a good idea."

"Julia wants to see his body," Ben said. "So she'll know he's really dead. I think she should. If you can't arrange it, then I will."

"I'll take care of it," his father said.

"Thanks, Dad." He could feel the tears brimming in his eyes again and blinked to hold them back.

There was a knock on the door and Dr. Schuster stuck her head inside. "Oh. I thought you were alone."

"Get out," Ben snarled, appalled at being caught at such a vulnerable moment by this woman, of all people.

"I was just leaving," his father said.

Ben resisted the urge to grab his father's hand, to keep him at his side. He shot a venomous look at Anna Schuster and saw her recoil before she stood back to allow his father to leave.

She entered and let the hospital door close behind her. "Well, Agent Benedict," she said as she crossed the room to his bed. "We meet again."

19

Anna focused on Agent Benedict's eyes, because they were the window to a man's soul. And found them barred by a blue steel wall. She was looking for emotions that would reveal how he was coping with the traumatic events of the morning. For shock. For guilt and shame. For grief, of course. And anger. But Ben Benedict was keeping his feelings strictly to himself.

Not a good sign.

In a gentle voice she said, "Tell me, Agent Benedict, are you more angry with yourself right now? Or your friend?"

"What?"

He looked shocked now, Anna thought. "Are you feeling guilty for being alive? Do you believe you should have been able to save your friend?"

"Who the hell do you think you are?"

"Someone who wants to help," Anna said, keeping her distance from his hospital bed, giving him the space to vent, or to come apart at the seams, if that was what he chose to do. "Are you going to answer my questions?"

"No."

"Because the answer is yes?"

Ben Benedict glared at her from menacing blue eyes. "Don't push it, lady."

She moved toward him, increasing the emotional threat, watching with wary eyes for the danger she saw in his coiled body. "My name is Dr. Schuster. Or Anna, if you'd prefer."

"Look, lady," Ben said nastily, "I may have to talk to you, but I don't have to do it now. Get out."

"From the reports I read, your friend's death was an unfortunate accident. He was wearing a vest, but the bullet caught him below that. The ambulance was delayed by an accident en route. You put a tourniquet on his wound, but since his femoral artery was involved, that wasn't enough to keep him from bleeding out."

Ben gave her a mulish look and remained silent.

"I understand your friend—"

"His name was Waverly," Ben snapped.

"Your friend Waverly was supposed to be married earlier today. That you were his best man. And his bride was your sister."

Anna watched Ben Benedict jerk at every statement pronouncing the enormity of the loss he'd just suffered. For which she suspected he was blaming himself. And they hadn't even gotten to the young man Agent Benedict had shot and killed.

"I'm very sorry for your loss," she said.

"You can go to hell."

"I'll be seeing you every day for the next week here in the hospital."

"I'm getting out of here today."

"I don't think—"

Grabbing the pristine white sheet with both fists, he ripped it away from his bare legs and shoved them over the edge of the bed. "I'm not wearing anything under this hospital gown, so unless you want to get an eyeful, you better get out."

"It's nothing I haven't seen before," Anna said in a neutral voice. But her heart was thumping hard in her chest.

He wavered, looking dizzy, when he finally stood on his bare feet. When she reached out to steady him, he shoved her hand away and said, "You'll get out of here, if you know what's good for you."

He began yanking on the hospital gown, which was held

together by narrow strings at his neck and back that gave way to his strength. He pressed his lips tight, she believed to keep from yelping when the rending cotton put pressure on the bandage on his right shoulder.

He hesitated for an instant, meeting her gaze and giving her a last chance to retreat, then wrenched the gown away from his body and threw it onto the floor.

Leaving him naked.

He smirked at her, expecting her to protect her modesty by turning her back, or turning tail and fleeing the room.

Annagreit Schuster was made of sterner stuff. She'd treated a great many men who were suffering the way this one was now. But she couldn't help looking at his body.

Agent Benedict had the iron-hard physique of a man who'd fought for a living, broad-shouldered and virile. His flesh bore scars—gunshot and shrapnel wounds—from combat. As her gaze slid down his muscular frame, she saw a physical response to her perusal she hadn't expected. And which was entirely unwelcome.

She forced her gaze back to his scratched and bruised face. His eyes gleamed with triumph. And with malice. She fought to quiet her racing heart, but her voice was breathless when she spoke. "You should get back in bed."

"Want to join me?" he said, leering unpleasantly.

"Sex won't solve your problems, Ben. You need time to deal with the pain of what happened today. To grieve. To—"

"Shut up," he said.

"—forgive yourself."

He grabbed her arms and shook her. "I said shut up!"

She put her hands to his stubbled cheeks, keeping her gaze focused on his eyes, fighting the hysterical urge to scratch and claw her way free. She realized she had underestimated the enormity of his anguish. Underestimated his desire to repress it. And his inability to do so.

She saw a flicker of agony in his eyes before they were

shuttered again. He was fighting for his sanity. Seeking relief for his tormented soul.

She stopped resisting his hold and became pliant and receiving. She heard the despairing sound he made as his mouth came down hard on hers.

His arms surrounded her like iron bands, as he pulled her tight against naked muscle and sinew. She welcomed the thrust of his tongue as he sought connection with another human being.

Even while she was feeling aroused by the masculine chest against which her breasts were crushed, Anna's mind was frantically searching for a way out for both of them.

He yanked her silk blouse out of her skirt and shoved it up, making a sound in his throat as his hands slid up her naked back.

Anna realized she was in serious trouble. And it was all her own fault. She knew the hazards inherent in her job, but she'd gotten complacent, because she'd always been able to control the situation in the past.

Agent Benedict had managed to fool her about the depth of his suffering. And they were both about to pay for her mistake.

20

"I guess the rumors were wrong. You look fine to me."

Ben's head popped up from where he was pressing kisses to Anna's throat beneath her ear. "How the hell did you get here?" he rasped, gaping at the intruder.

Anna jerked free of his embrace, staring with alarm at the intimidating man standing in the doorway dressed in jungle cammies and black jump boots.

She'd thought Ben Benedict was physically perfect. This man was a larger-than-life version of Ben. He was taller, even more broad-shouldered, with sharp cheekbones and hollowed cheeks, piercing blue eyes and very unmilitary black hair that hung over both brow and collar.

"I wasn't expecting you," Ben said.

The man in the doorway lifted an eyebrow, curved his lips into a smile and shot Anna a wink. "Sorry to interrupt."

Anna pushed a hand through her mussed hair, then realized her blouse was hanging half in and half out of her skirt and hurriedly began tucking it back in.

She was relieved when the stranger turned his gaze back to Ben and said, "I heard you had some trouble today. I stopped by to see how you are." His blue eyes twinkled as he said, "I see you're just fine."

Ben grimaced. "I thought you were off somewhere playing soldier."

"I thought I'd find you in bed." The tall man glanced at Anna and said, "I suppose I almost did."

Anna flushed to the roots of her blond hair. "I'll leave the two of you to talk."

"You're not going to introduce me to your girl?" the man said, stopping Anna in her tracks.

"She's not my girl," Ben said with a snarl. "She's my shrink."

The big man chuckled. "Well, well."

Anna was embarrassed, but she figured the best defense was a good offense. She approached the grinning man and asked, "Who are you?"

He jerked a thumb in Ben's direction. "I'm his big brother. Nash Benedict, at your service, ma'am." He gave her a brief, somehow courtly bow from the waist. "Do you have a name?"

"Annagreit Schuster. Anna. Dr. Schuster," she said, flustered by the intensity of his gaze. It was bad enough to get caught as she had, but much worse to know the imposing man was a member of Ben's family. "We were… I was… That is…"

"Don't mind me, Doctor," Nash said. "Looked to me like whatever therapy you were applying was doing the job."

"This isn't what it looked like," Anna protested.

"Sure as hell wasn't," Ben said, seeming to realize at last that he was naked. He crossed to the narrow closet on the opposite side of the bed, apparently in search of something to put on. He pulled out his boxers, bloody jeans and brown loafers. "Damn. They must have cut my sweater and T-shirt off in the emergency room."

He began dressing, seemingly oblivious to Anna's presence.

Ben's older brother unbuttoned his camouflage shirt and pulled it off, then stripped off an army green T-shirt and pitched it to Ben, before putting his shirt back on.

Anna narrowly avoided gasping when she looked from one brother's impressive bare chest to the other. She wanted to leave, but it would have felt too much like an ignominious retreat. So she stayed. And took advantage of the opportunity to say to Ben, "You shouldn't be leaving the hospital."

"Butt out," he snapped, not even looking in her direction.

She turned to his older brother and said, "He isn't in any shape to leave the hospital. Uh—" She glanced at Nash Benedict's uniform shirt, looking for some military insignia so she would know how to address him. But there was none.

Anna wanted to ask what he was doing in a military uniform with no rank on his collar, but realized that was none of her business. "What should I call you?" she said at last.

"Call me Nash," he said.

"Very well, Nash. Your brother needs time to process everything that happened to him yesterday and this morning. He can't go back to work until I clear him to be on the job. Which means he needs to be somewhere I can find him, to see him daily for therapy."

Nash's lips twitched and one dark brow rose in speculation. Anna knew he was imagining the form her "therapy" might take. She flushed again, aware that her light-skinned complexion was revealing her discomfort by displaying two rosy blotches on her cheeks.

"Tell you what I'll do, Dr. Schuster," Nash said. "I'll give Ben a ride to his place in Georgetown. I assume you have the address?"

Anna nodded. She knew more about Ben Benedict from his personnel file than he could imagine.

"I'll sit on him there until Monday morning," Nash said. "How does that sound?"

Ben shot his brother a frown, but he didn't argue with him.

Anna figured that was the best deal she was going to get, so she took it. "I want him at my office for therapy Monday at nine."

"If that's where you want him, that's where he'll be," Nash assured her.

Dressed at last, Ben turned to her and said, "I want a different doctor."

Anna stared at him aghast. It was certainly the patient's prerogative to choose his physician. Considering what had just happened, she ought to be glad Ben was asking to work with someone else. But she felt to blame for today's awkward kissing incident. And she knew she could help him, if he would only give her the chance.

She bluffed and said, "You're assigned to me, Agent Benedict. You don't get to pick and choose. I'm your doctor, like it or not."

"I don't like it."

"Hey, little brother," Nash said. "Give her a chance. Seems to me the two of you have a few things in common."

"Yeah, I guess we do," Ben said, staring at her as though he were seeing her naked. Which he almost had.

Anna fought the flush. And lost. "I'll see you Monday morning, nine o'clock sharp, my office."

She turned her back on the two grinning male faces and pulled open Ben's hospital-room door, keeping her shoulders back and her chin up. She thought she'd made a pretty good, maybe even dignified, exit. Until she heard the male laughter as the door closed behind her.

21

Abigail Hamilton stared at the young man lying dead on the metal table in the frigid hospital morgue, a white plastic sheet folded down to reveal his bloodless face and marblelike shoulders, and felt her eyes begin to water.

Her daughter pulled free of her protective embrace and crossed to stand beside the corpse. "He looks cold," Julia said in a little girl's voice. She brushed a lock of Waverly Collins's short brown hair back from his unblemished face and said, "It isn't fair, Mother."

"I know. I'm so sorry, honey."

Abby hadn't shed a tear when the awful news came, nearly a half hour after the wedding was scheduled to start—with the groom and the best man missing—that her daughter's fiancé was dead. In the weeks leading up to Julia's wedding, Abby had fought a sense of foreboding.

She'd told herself her misgivings were the result of the speed with which Julia's courtship had proceeded. She firmly believed her daughter was too young to marry, that Julia couldn't possibly know her prospective groom well enough to commit to a lifetime with him. And Waverly Collins, Metropolitan Police Department sergeant, was far from the kind of man Abby had imagined her only daughter marrying.

As Abby watched her devastated daughter grieve, she struggled with her feelings of relief, and the guilt she felt because of that relief. Julia was obviously in terrible pain.

Abby consoled herself with the belief that even greater pain—when the marriage fell apart, perhaps when children were involved—had been averted.

She would never have admitted as much to anyone. Even to Ham, whom she knew was as unhappy with Julia's choice of husband as she had been.

Julia draped her body across Waverly's chest, but she didn't make a sound. She was cried out, Abby suspected, at least for the moment. Too deeply sad to feel anything except a bottomless well of loss.

Abby knew what it felt like to believe your world had ended. What it felt like to lose someone you loved more than your own life. She also knew what it felt like to be angry with the person you loved because he'd caused the disaster that had left you so devastated.

In ways Abby had never expected, the death of this young man brought back vivid memories of what it had been like when Foster Benedict broke her heart a little more than twenty years ago. When she had experienced the death of her marriage. And had tried to kill her love for him.

Unsuccessfully.

The ache in her chest was so sharp she stifled a gasp. No, life wasn't fair. She should still be married to Foster Benedict. She should have forgiven his transgression. He'd begged long enough and hard enough to be forgiven.

Amazing how, in hindsight, what Foster had done was not so dreadful. He was human. He should have been allowed one lapse in judgment.

But at that moment in time they were grieving the loss of their fourth son, Darlington Hawkins Benedict. Darlington had lived up to his name and been a darling boy of four, with dark curls and bright gray eyes, when he fell from a tree he'd climbed and broke his neck.

She'd been pregnant with Rhett. And hormonal. And unable to console Foster. Or to countenance his act of betrayal with another woman, who'd offered him physical solace, which had resulted in such terrible consequences for her and Foster.

And for that woman, who bore a child out of wedlock.

How unfortunate that Foster's one indiscretion should result in a pregnancy. That he should want to do the honorable thing and acknowledge his illegitimate child. And support the little boy, Ryan Donovan McKenzie, who was born to a too-sympathetic Irish waitress named Mary Kate McKenzie.

Abby suddenly sobbed. She attempted to stop the sound with her hands, but Julia's head came up, and their eyes locked.

"Oh, Mother," she cried. "I can't bear it!"

Abby closed the distance between them and grabbed her daughter with all the desperation she felt. "I know you don't believe me, Julia. But you will survive this. You will love again."

Not as deeply. Never as carelessly. You will remember this pain and guard your heart. But you will love again.

Abby kept her bleak thoughts to herself. There would be time enough later to tell her daughter about the challenges she would face loving again, when another man asked her to share his life.

"Have you finished saying good-bye to Waverly?" she asked.

Julia glanced once more at the still form on the cold metal table and said, "I thought this would help. It only hurts more."

Abby held her daughter tight. Time would ease her pain. But based on her own experience, she feared Julia might never heal completely. Abby still bore a gaping wound where Foster Benedict had been cut out of her life. It had scabbed over many times. But it didn't take much to tear off the scab so she bled again.

To survive, she'd kept the flames of resentment alive. Yes, she should have forgiven her adulterous husband twenty years ago. But ultimately, Foster was responsible for the betrayal that had torn their lives apart.

Whether from a sixth sense that gave her an awareness of him, a recognition of his smell, or just an animal instinct for self-preservation, Abby realized suddenly that Foster had entered the room. She stiffened and raised her head to meet his gaze.

He looked exhausted. *He's getting older,* she thought. Hair that had once been black was threaded with silver, and there were deep crow's-feet around his eyes. He'd just turned fifty-six, but his jawline was firm and his chin still jutted as though he was ready to fight the world.

"I wanted to make sure you were both all right," he said.

"We're fine," Abby said to cut off any further offer of comfort. She didn't need Foster in her life. She didn't want him reminding her what was missing from her marriage to Ham.

"Nash showed up. He arrived at The Farm for the wedding reception and heard what happened. He promised to keep an eye on Ben when he leaves the hospital."

"*When* he leaves?" Abby said. "I thought Ben was supposed to be in the hospital at least overnight."

Foster shook his head. "He only has a scratch. Unless they tie him to the bed, he'll be gone within the hour. I asked Nash to stick with him for the next day or so, to make sure he's okay."

Foster had known how much she would worry about Ben, and had done something to assuage her concern. As he always had when they were a young couple and she worried about her boys.

He put a hand on Julia's shoulder and said, "I'm sorry, sweetie. He was a good man."

"Thank you," Julia said, her eyes bright with unshed tears.

"We should get home," Abby said brusquely. "We left things at The Farm in a terrible mess."

"I stayed after you guys took off this afternoon and asked the caterers to clean up the mess. Everything should be cleared away by the time you get home."

Abby nearly swore aloud. Removing all evidence of the aborted wedding was the kind of considerate detail Ham would never have bothered to handle. Thoughtfulness had always been second nature to Foster. Except that one time when he had slipped. And broken her heart.

"You didn't need to do that," she said.

"I knew you'd all be too busy to think about it. I hope you don't mind."

Abby felt a pang of longing for what she'd lost. She swallowed hard and said, "Thank you, Foster."

"Anything else I can do?" he asked. "For either of you?"

Go away. Stay away. Get completely out of my life.

Something she realized wasn't possible when they shared four sons.

"You've done enough," Abby said. And bit her lip when it came out sounding bitter, instead of grateful.

She saw the blaze of rancor in his steel-gray eyes before he masked it. She could hardly blame Foster for being frustrated with her. But it was hard to pretend that everything was all right between them when it wasn't.

She still loved him. And hated him for ruining their lives.

"Good-bye, Foster," she said. Without the wedding activities to bring them together, and with Ben expected to recover quickly, it was unlikely their paths would cross again anytime soon.

She saw the longing in his eyes. And ignored it. He was married to Patsy. She was married to Ham. There was no going back.

22

"I'm sure you have better things to do than babysit me," Ben said as he dropped his keys on the writing table inside the door to his turn-of-the-century row house in Georgetown.

"Nothing I'd rather be doing." Nash stalked around the divided rooms on the main floor—living room with wood-carved fireplace, banquet-size formal dining room, modern kitchen with a glass-walled breakfast bar leading to a private garden—like a wild animal searching out predators in a new den. "I'm sorry I missed the housewarming. This is nice."

"You don't have to hang around," Ben said, staying near the leaded-glass vestibule to let Nash back out. "Really, I'm okay."

"Trying to get rid of me?" Nash asked, his hip cocked, his hands propped on his waist.

Ben's mouth quirked. Trust Nash to get to the meat of the matter. "Yeah, I am."

Nash laughed. "Too bad. I'm posted here for the next thirty-six hours. What's upstairs?" he asked, peering up the L-shaped, wood-paneled staircase.

"More of the same," Ben said.

"Got a housekeeper? Girlfriend? Anybody likely to be up there?"

It took Ben a moment to realize that Nash was trying to determine whether they were alone. "My housekeeper has a key. But she isn't working today. Unless someone broke in while I was at the hospital, we're alone. Look, I figure Mother sent you to make sure I'm okay, so—"

"Nope. Dad did."

Ben raised a brow in surprise. Not surprised that his father had asked Nash to ride herd on him. Surprised that Nash, who got along with his father like two wildcats in a burlap sack, had agreed. "How long are you planning to play big brother?"

Nash turned, and Ben watched with amazement as his brother transformed before his eyes into the leader of a fierce band of special forces soldiers that he was. "I'm not here just to keep an eye on you, Ben. I came with an assignment for you."

Ben frowned in confusion. "What are you talking about?"

Nash headed into the living room. "Those look like comfortable chairs. How about we take a load off? We need to talk."

Ben realized he was feeling a little light-headed and wondered if Nash could possibly have realized that fact when he'd suggested they sit down. He closed the front door and followed his brother.

Nash dropped into one of the two large wing chairs that faced the large fireplace and put his feet up on the solid, petit-point stool—his mother's housewarming gift—in front of him.

Ben felt cold. He flipped the switch, igniting a flickering gas fire, before he slid into the other chair. He eyed Nash askance, waiting for him to speak, wishing that the heat from the fire could warm the block of ice inside him.

Ben knew his brother did covert work for the president, although Nash had never shared the details of a single mission. He couldn't imagine what his brother had in mind. Ben had turned his back on soldiering. Quit for good. So what could Nash possibly want him to do?

"I came straight back here from El Salvador because of what I found out there," Nash said.

"Do I need some sort of secret clearance to hear about this?" Ben asked.

"I decide who has the need to know," Nash said. "Can I trust you to keep your mouth shut?"

Ben nodded. "Of course."

"It turns out you're in a perfect position, working with the MPD Gang Unit, to do this job."

"What do D.C. gangs have to do with top secret stuff?" Ben asked.

"We've been watching a high-ranking Al Qaeda leader living in El Salvador, Abdul-Majeed Zayed. I've confirmed that he's paying MS-13 gang members in the States to work for Al Qaeda. We caught MS in Los Angeles buying up garage door openers."

"Sonofabitch," Ben said. Garage door openers were commonly used by Al Qaeda to remotely set off explosives.

"So we know he's teaching them how to make bombs. This morning, while you were out cold, an IED exploded on Michigan Avenue in Chicago."

Ben couldn't believe Tony hadn't said something to him about the bomb. He must really have expected him to be out of commission for a while. Hadn't Waverly warned him that such attacks were a possibility? "How can you be sure who's responsible so soon after the attack?"

"ICE and local police departments have been watching MS all over the country. They'd been surveilling the boy who set off the bomb in Chicago. He disappeared off the grid a couple of hours before the IED was detonated. We found enough remains to confirm it was him. Guess he didn't have a remote detonator. Or decided he'd rather be a martyr."

"What does that attack have to do with me?"

"We think Al Qaeda has sent someone from El Salvador to D.C. with a weapon of mass destruction."

Ben sucked in a deep breath and let it out. "A dirty bomb?"

"We're not sure what kind of weapon to expect," Nash said. "It might be something biological. Whatever it is, the plan is to take out the country's leaders. All of whom are in D.C. for that Israeli-Syrian peace summit."

"I'd like to help," Ben said. "There's just one hitch. I can't go back to work until the lady doctor says I can."

"That's all been fixed," Nash said.

"You mean I don't have to go see her on Monday?"

"You absolutely have to go see her on Monday."

"I don't understand," Ben said.

"It's been fixed with your boss that you can go back to work on Monday *on the condition* that you continue to see Dr. Schuster every day until she says you're okay."

"That's blackmail."

"I thought you liked the lady."

"I like her looks. Hell, she's a knockout. That doesn't mean I like having her probing around inside my head."

"I suppose there are other parts you'd rather have her probing," Nash said with a chuckle.

Ben found himself imagining Anna naked and realized that he liked what he saw way too much. So he said, "What else can you tell me about the danger we're facing here in D.C.?"

Nash shrugged. "Nothing. I'm heading back to El Salvador Monday to see what I can find out. Meanwhile, I need someone I can trust to figure out who in MS—or hanging around with MS gang members—might be assigned to deliver the weapon to its target. We need to know what type of weapon they're using and what, exactly, their target is.

"I need you to be another set of eyes here in D.C. This person-of-interest would likely be someone who's shown up in D.C. during the past three months. Probably a new member of MS."

Ben thought immediately of the pretty girl Waverly had mentioned, Trisha Reynolds. According to Waverly, she wasn't enrolled in any school in the D.C. area. She wasn't on the list of gang members kept by the MPD Gang Unit, which made her a new face.

She'd had no gang tats that Ben had seen, so maybe she didn't belong to a gang. But she'd sparked a war between the 1-8 and MS. So maybe she did.

"I might know someone who fits the bill," Ben said.

"Who is it?"

"The girl who gave me this," Ben said, holding out his arm to reveal a perfect set of human teeth marks across a row of black stitches. "And this." He pointed to his black eye.

Nash grimaced. "Ouch. Our subject isn't likely to be female. But don't rule her out."

"What do I do with her when I find her?"

"You think you can?"

Ben nodded. "You want me to arrest her?"

Nash shook his head. "Just monitor her movements. See who she meets with. Keep an eye out for anyone who looks or acts suspicious."

"Then what?" Ben asked.

"If we're watching closely enough, someone in MS will let us know when and where the weapon is being delivered, so we can intercept it."

"I can do that." Ben's throat felt raw, the result of continually swallowing down the pain of Waverly's death. And the sorrow at being forced to kill again.

"I was only at The Farm this morning for a few minutes," Nash said, "and things were pretty chaotic. But I didn't see Morgan Hunter. Wasn't she invited to the wedding?"

Ben was surprised to hear Nash ask about Carter's girlfriend. Ben knew Julia had asked Morgan to be a bridesmaid, but she'd declined, since there was no formal understanding between her and Carter, and she barely knew Julia.

"Sure, Morgan was invited," Ben said. "Why do you ask?"

"I promised Carter I'd keep an eye on her while he's overseas."

"How's that been going?" Ben asked. "Keeping an eye on Morgan?"

"I've come around a few times to the fire station to visit with her after she's done with her shift. Taken her out to dinner a couple of times. Sailing once. She's easy to talk to, laughs a lot."

"Sounds like you might like her yourself," Ben said.

Nash kept his gaze focused on the fire.

Ben didn't think Nash was going to reply to the disturbing suggestion that he had a thing for their brother's girlfriend.

At last he said, "She loves him. And he loves her."

And that settles that, Ben thought.

"You better get some rest," Nash said.

"Goddamn it, I'm fine," Ben snapped.

"You got shot. Your friend got killed. And you killed a kid. Go to bed. Get some rest. There'll be plenty to do when you wake up."

"What are you going to do?"

"I'm going to sit right here. In case you need me."

Ben met his brother's steady gaze and realized that Nash likely knew about—probably had experienced himself—the nightmares that haunted a man after a traumatic day like today.

Ben was glad Nash was there. Grateful for the offer of comfort. Aware that having his brother right downstairs, within shouting distance, might keep the demons away.

"Good night," Ben said. "Will I see you in the morning?"

"I'll be right here."

23

Ben was still in bed late Sunday morning when his cell phone rang. He looked at the caller ID, which told him it wasn't someone in his family. He almost let the call go to voice mail. But he realized it might be one of the several kids, others like Epifanio he was trying to keep out of gangs, to whom he'd given his number, telling them to call if they were ever in trouble.

He flipped open the phone and said, "Hello."

"Agent Benedict, this is Anna Schuster."

An image of her naked flashed so quickly before his eyes that he sucked in a breath. He was hard as a rock in two seconds flat. Which made him furious. He had enough trouble in his life without adding a woman who could make him feel so much so fast. "What the hell do you want now?" he said ungraciously.

Silence. Then Anna said, "My vet called me yesterday afternoon about the rottweiler you left there on Friday morning."

"I told you, it isn't my dog."

"I know that," she said. "But the owner doesn't want him, and the vet said if he can't find someone to take Rocky—that's the dog's name—he's going to have to put him down on Monday."

"I don't want a dog," Ben said. He got along just fine without having a dog with a wagging tail—or a woman with a smile on her face, for that matter—greeting him at the door every time he got home.

"Here's the problem," Anna continued as though he hadn't

spoken. "Rocky bit you. Which the vet would have to report to a pound or anyplace else where the dog might go to be adopted. And once they hear the dog has bitten someone, there goes Rocky's chances of getting adopted."

"It's not my problem," Ben said stubbornly. "What happened to the owner? Why doesn't he take the dog?"

"The vet had to amputate Rocky's hind leg. The bones were shattered. The owner said he doesn't want a crippled dog."

"What makes you think I'd want a crippled dog?" Ben challenged. "Especially one that viciously bit me."

"You're Rocky's only hope."

The silence stretched on the phone until Ben finally said, "Why don't you take the dog?"

"I have a cat. And four brand-new kittens."

"Crippled or whole, I don't want a dog," Ben said. It wasn't his responsibility to save someone else's dog.

"All right," Anna said with a sigh. "If you change your mind, here's the vet's number."

She recited it, and because he had a pen and paper handy, Ben wrote it down.

"The vet said he would euthanize Rocky on Monday, sometime after noon, so you've got until then to decide."

"I've already decided," Ben said.

"Good morning, Agent Benedict," the doctor said.

She'd hung up before he could express his own feelings about the kind of morning he wished on her, after laying that kind of guilt trip on him. Why was the dog his problem? He was sorry the animal was going to be put down, but he wasn't home enough to take care of a dog.

Ben snapped his phone closed and dropped it on the end table, then settled back down on his bed. "Damn it," he muttered. "I don't want a dog."

24

Anna wouldn't have bet money that Ben Benedict would show up at her office on Monday morning at 9:00 a.m. for therapy. But she was there waiting, in case he did. Harrison, Parker, Johnson & Schuster, P.A., was in a high-rise bordering Washington's infamous Needle Park, prowled at night by junkies, and directly across the park from the government building that housed the ICE offices.

She'd had a long conversation with her mentor, Ike Harrison, the senior partner in the practice, earlier that morning. She told him what had transpired so far between her and Ben, from the incident in her apartment to the incident in the hospital, and asked whether he thought she should pass Ben Benedict off to one of the other psychiatrists in their group.

"Sounds to me like you're emotionally involved with the patient," Ike had said, puffing on a sweet-smelling tobacco as he put a match to the bowl of his pipe.

"The incident at the hospital was more physical than emotional," Anna had argued. "And nothing happened, really, in my apartment. I think I can maintain my professional distance with Agent Benedict. And I want to help him."

"Why?" Ike had asked.

She shrugged. "He needs help."

Ike had chuckled. "They all need help. What makes this patient any different from the others you've treated?"

Anna fought the flush that threatened. She'd consulted Ike precisely because she was afraid she cared too much about

Ben Benedict. But she also thought she knew best how to help him. "If I'm the one treating him, I'll be able to monitor his progress. And sleep more soundly at night."

"It's up to you what you do. But it's a fine line, Anna. Be sure you don't cross it. Don't let your empathy tempt you into a personal—by which I mean sexual—relationship with Benedict."

"I would never—"

He cut her off with a wave of his hand. "I know you wouldn't. Nevertheless, I will remind you that the professional sanctions—and the criminal penalties—for unethical behavior toward a patient are very serious. A misstep could cost you your career. In a worst-case scenario, you could end up in prison."

"I know."

Anna was glad she'd spoken with Ike. He'd reminded her that no matter how attracted she was to Ben Benedict, if she wanted to help him, she had to do it within the strict ethical guidelines provided by the American Psychiatric Association. She'd come out of Ike's office down the hall ready to be Dr. Schuster to Ben Benedict—and nothing more.

As she stared out the window, she wondered if Ben had contacted the vet and adopted the dog. That was another example of how their relationship hadn't been strictly doctor-patient. She should have let the vet call Agent Benedict. But she'd believed she would do a better job of convincing him to rescue the rottweiler. Anna owned a cat instead of a dog herself because her professional hours kept her away from home for long hours during the day. But that didn't mean she didn't love dogs.

She and her twin sister Lisele had gotten a cocker spaniel puppy for Christmas when they were six. They'd named her Queenie. She and Lisele had been as inseparable from Queenie as they had been from each other growing up in Vermont.

Queenie was dead now. So was Lisele. But some of Anna's happiest memories of her sister involved the two of them tossing a tennis ball to each other in the backyard—in thigh-deep snow, in fragrant spring grass, in rustling piles of fall leaves—laughing hilariously as Queenie leapt higher and higher to intercept it.

At exactly 9:00 a.m. Ben Benedict rang the buzzer to let her know he'd arrived in the outer office. She started to check her appearance in the mirror across from the couch, then smiled ruefully and headed for the door.

"Good morning, Agent Benedict," she said as she let him in.

He nodded curtly. "Morning."

Nothing good about it, Anna saw from his expression. "Have a seat," she said, gesturing him into the sun-bright room.

"Surprised to see me?" he asked, taking in Anna's modern, glass-walled office.

"Frankly, yes," she said. "But I'm glad to see you."

He turned and eyed her up and down. "I must say, you're a sight for sore eyes, Doc."

Anna ignored the remark. "You can sit on the couch, or lie down, whichever would be more comfortable."

"I'll sit." Benedict frowned at the knobby-weave couch, then plopped down on the end of it farthest from the chair where Anna usually sat, a healthy potted ficus at her shoulder. He eyed the box of Kleenex on the table beside the couch and glowered.

Getting him to cry would be therapeutically helpful. But Anna wasn't counting on Agent Benedict letting down the walls that protected him from pain anytime soon.

"Well, Doc. What's on the menu today?"

He was taking charge, she saw. To obviate the fact that she was the one in control of the session.

"Before we get started," she said, "I want to ask what you decided about the dog."

Ben made a disgusted sound in his throat. "I told you Sunday morning I don't want a dog. My mind hasn't changed."

"I'm sorry to hear that."

She waited, but he neither defended nor explained his

decision. Well, she'd done her best for the animal. It was time to see what she could do for the man.

"I guess we should get started," she said, tugging her skirt down over her knees. "Tell me, Agent Benedict, how did you sleep last night?"

She saw a flicker of panic in his eyes before he said, "Like Rip Fucking van Winkle."

"That's not what your brother said."

Ben looked as though he'd been struck with an ax. "What?"

"Nash called this morning. He mentioned you had a nightmare last night."

"I've told you. I've told him. I've told anybody and everybody who'll listen. I'm fine!"

Anna remained silent long enough for Agent Benedict to fidget. Then she said, "Tell me about your nightmare."

"That's none of your business."

But of course, it was. It was her job to discover his reactions to the recent trauma and reaffirm to him that, whatever they were, they were normal.

She picked up her notepad and pen and settled into her high-backed swivel chair, crossing her legs comfortably. "Was the nightmare about your friend's death? Or was it related to an event during your military service?"

Benedict shot her a baleful glare. "What difference does it make?"

Anna didn't rise to the bait. She simply waited, pen in hand, purposefully keeping her toe, at the end of a pointy-toed patent leather high heel, perfectly still.

"Awfully dressed up today, aren't you?" he said at last, avoiding the question.

He was giving her a thorough perusal, from her upswept blond hair to her long-sleeved white V-necked silk blouse, to the belted black pencil skirt that ended just above her knees. Anna resisted the urge to tug it down.

His gaze kept moving down the length of her very long

legs—shaved last night, no nylons—to her very long feet, about which she was self-conscious. She felt her body flush as though he'd stroked her. *Watch yourself,* she warned. But before she could stop herself, she'd returned his attack.

"You forgot to shave," she said coolly.

He brushed a hand across the several-days' growth of dark beard that covered his cheeks and chin. "I'm sure you know I can't go back to work until I spend this hour with you. I can shave when we're done here."

Anna frowned. "You're going back to work today?"

"You bet. You must have been told. I'm back on the job."

"Nobody's told me anything," Anna said, struggling to keep her voice even. "I was under the impression that I was responsible for clearing you to return to work."

"Things have changed, Doc," he said, his eyes gleaming with satisfaction.

"Would you mind explaining?"

"I've got an assignment that takes priority over this bullshit counseling."

"It isn't bullshit," Anna retorted. She forced herself to take a deep breath before she continued, "Post-traumatic stress can be debilitating if it's not treated. You need—"

He interrupted her again. "I'm going to come here every day. And then I'm going to work."

"You need time to process what's happened to you this past week."

"I've done all the processing I'm going to do," Benedict said, undressing her with his eyes as he spoke.

Anna felt nettled by both his verbal response and the lazy-lidded look in his eyes. "We'll see about that," she muttered.

He sat forward. "What did you say?"

She started to say "Nothing," but replied, "I don't think you should be working yet."

"Good thing you're not the one making that decision."

Anna realized an argument was a waste of time. She

needed to help Ben Benedict as much as she could while he was here. When he was gone, she would advise Tony Pellicano in no uncertain terms that Agent Benedict had no business being out on the streets of D.C. carrying a gun.

"Tell me what happened on Saturday," Anna said.

"Why bother? It's done and over."

"Humor me."

He snorted. "Waverly woke up pissed as hell because of the gang deaths in D.C."

"Why was he mad?"

"He'd gotten a call the night before from some kid warning him there was going to be trouble. But he was drunk and I wouldn't let him drive."

"That seems like a sound decision."

"I had to knock him out to keep him from going," Benedict said. "When he woke up the next morning, he blamed himself for the deaths of those three kids who got shot."

"Was he to blame?" Anna asked.

"Of course not. But he ended up dead, anyway."

"Your loss must be especially sad because your friend—"

"Waverly," he interjected.

"Waverly," she repeated smoothly, "was supposed to be married on Saturday to your sister."

"Half sister. Julia. She's eighteen. But you probably know that, too," he said resentfully.

"How is Julia coping?"

"I don't have the faintest idea."

"You haven't talked to her?"

He hesitated, then said, "I spoke to her at the hospital."

"And?"

Anna watched as Benedict swallowed hard, then said, "She blames me for Waverly's death."

"Do you think you're to blame?"

He picked at a loose string on his faded jeans. "I promised her I'd get Waverly to their wedding on time. I didn't."

"I see. So you should have stopped him from going to D.C.?"

"He must have known he was going to be late—maybe even miss—his own wedding," Benedict mused. "He was still determined to go." He added in a quiet voice, "Yes, I should have stopped him."

"Could you have stopped him?"

"Not without knocking him out again," he said flatly.

"So it was his choice to go."

"Yeah," Benedict admitted grudgingly.

"What happened when you arrived in D.C.?"

"We checked in with the One-Eight."

Anna lifted an inquiring brow. "The One-Eight?"

"Short for the 18th Street gang. They agreed to hold off on any further violence for twelve hours. To give us a chance to find the shooter from MS—that's the Mara Salvatrucha Thirteen gang—who'd killed two of the One-Eight."

"And you found the shooter?"

"Yeah. That was the guy I put down."

"Put down?" Anna said gently.

"Like a rabid animal," Benedict confirmed. "I gave him a chance to put down his gun. But he was never going to stop killing until somebody killed him. My only regret is that I didn't stop him with my first shot."

"You did something wrong?"

"I gave the fucker a chance to live, instead of shooting him dead when I had the chance," Benedict said viciously. "He took two more shots at me and Waverly after I hit him the first time. He grazed me. And killed Waverly."

"You sound very angry."

"Damned straight I'm angry! Waverly never should have died. Things might have turned out different if—"

Anna watched tears brim in his eyes. "If?" she prodded.

"If I hadn't let him go to D.C. in the first place. If he'd settled for talking to the One-Eight that morning and headed back to Virginia to get married. If I hadn't let him go into that maintenance shack. If I'd shot that killer dead when I had the chance. If the ambulance hadn't gotten in a wreck. If—If—If! I had a lot of chances to keep Waverly alive."

"It sounds like Waverly made a few of those choices."

"He didn't have the experience with war that I have. I know what kids with guns can do," he ranted.

"They start out innocent, but they get infected with the vitriol that adults spill around them, so some ten-year-old gets talked into tossing a grenade. I learned my lesson in Somalia. And Iraq. And Afghanistan.

"Those infected kids look at you with big, childlike eyes, but if you hold out a friendly hand, you're liable to end up with it blown off," he said, his voice harsh with anger and pain. "I've seen how the really bad guys out there in the world turn kids into weapons. How they convince them that the afterlife is better than this one, so they'll be willing to blow themselves up and take a lot of other innocent lives along with them.

"I should've considered the possibility that that fourteen-year-old boy would rather fight to the death than be taken alive. I should've been ready for it."

The feral glow in Ben Benedict's blue eyes was frightening. Anna was sure he had no idea that tears were streaming down his cheeks.

She stayed very still. It was apparent that he was reliving an earlier trauma. One that still haunted him.

Anna was suddenly certain that this wasn't the first time Ben Benedict had killed a child. And lived to regret it.

25

The moment Ben Benedict was out the door, Anna called his ICE boss.

"Good morning, Dr. Schuster," Tony Pellicano said. "What can I do for you?"

"You can get Agent Benedict off the streets."

Anna heard silence on the other end of the line. At last Tony said, "I can't do that."

"Why not?" she demanded.

"There are matters of national security that require him to be on the job."

"Are you telling me that Ben Benedict is the only man who can save the country from whatever this threat is? That there isn't another ICE agent out there who's qualified to take over?"

"Benedict is the best—"

This time Anna interrupted. "I believe Agent Benedict is suffering from post-traumatic stress not only as a result of what happened Saturday but also as a result of his military service."

"Benedict had all the psychological tests we require to become an ICE agent," Tony said. "And passed them all with flying colors."

"Then he's managed to fool you, because he isn't well. I suspect he wasn't well when he came to work for you."

"You're the one who cleared him to go back to work after the incident on Friday," Tony countered.

"I recommended additional therapy," she reminded him. "And Saturday hadn't happened yet."

Tony sighed. "We need him."

"What's so important that you'd put a man in a fragile state of mental health out on the streets of D.C. with a gun?"

"I can't tell you that."

"This man is a time bomb," Anna said. "He could explode at any moment."

"That's your opinion," Tony said.

"That's what you pay me for!" Anna shot back. "What's the point of requiring counseling if you're not going to respect my evaluation of the patient?"

"Agent Benedict is needed on the streets. As long as he sees you every day, that's the way it's going to be."

"But he needs time—"

"Good-bye, Dr. Schuster."

Anna found herself listening to a dial tone on her landline. She slumped back into her chair. She'd done what she could. No one could blame her later if Ben Benedict self-destructed as a result of some additional stress while working on the streets of D.C.

She leaned her head back against her chair, closed her eyes and thought of her sister. Lisele had killed herself after a trauma. She had convinced Anna she was all right. And then slit her wrists.

Anna had become a psychiatrist, specializing in trauma therapy, to help others heal from traumatic events. She knew she could help Ben Benedict deal with his guilt and shame and anger and fear. But there was simply no telling what cracks would appear in his tightly controlled facade if he was involved in another violent incident.

Anna chewed on a hangnail. It was a bad habit she'd broken herself of long ago, which reoccurred when she was under stress. She ought to let it go. Ethically, she'd done everything she could to protect her patient.

But it wasn't enough.

She'd held this man in her arms while he trembled. She'd

tasted the desperation in his kiss. And she'd seen his tears. How could she turn her back on him? He needed someone to take care of him, especially because he was so determined not to take care of himself.

She wasn't going to believe his protestations, as she had Lisele's. She knew better. This man was in terrible trouble. She couldn't simply turn her back on him and walk away.

Anna sat up. There was more than one way to skin a cat. If she couldn't get Benedict's boss to take him off the streets, maybe she could appeal to his family.

Anna realized that if she went over Tony's head and contacted Ben Benedict's father, ICE might terminate her psychiatric group's contract with them. Not to mention the ethical considerations of such behavior. She had to believe Agent Benedict was a threat "to himself or others" to take the step she was about to take.

Anna thought she could argue the point successfully. But she was still walking on thin ice contacting his father—the contact in case of emergency named in his personnel file—to express her concern. No number was listed for Foster Benedict, but she knew from reports she'd heard on CNN that he worked at the White House as a special advisor to the president.

She wondered for a moment why she was so willing to take such a risk for a man who'd made a point of insulting her every time they met. A man who disparaged the help she'd offered.

Then she remembered that frisson of *something* that had passed between them the first time they'd met. And the frisson of *something* she'd felt when his eyes had lingered on her this morning.

It shouldn't make a difference that she was attracted to Agent Benedict. Especially when he was her patient. But the truth was, it did. She wasn't willing to let the chips fall where they may. She wanted Ben Benedict to have the best possible chance to recover for entirely selfish reasons. Because once he was well, they could explore that *something* and see where it led.

Anna reached for the phone again and dialed information. "I'd like the number for the White House."

26

Abigail Hamilton tried calling her ex-husband on his cell phone, but the call went directly to voice mail. She pursed her lips, then dialed the number he'd given her to reach him at the White House. She ended up talking to the same troublesome executive administrative assistant to the president's chief of staff with whom she'd crossed swords the previous week.

"This is Abigail Hamilton, Miss Harrison," she said, identifying herself. "I'd like to speak with Foster Benedict."

"Mr. Benedict is in a meeting with the president, Mrs. Hamilton. May I take a message?"

"Please let Foster know it's an emergency, and I must speak with him as soon as possible. I'm at home."

"Of course, Mrs. Hamilton."

Abby hung up the phone, stuck her elbow on her antique Sheraton desk in her bedroom at The Farm, dropped her chin into her palm, and waited. She was certain that Foster would call her back the moment he got her message, because she had never called him in the past unless it was an emergency that dealt with one of their sons.

Abby didn't mean to scare Foster. She knew he would immediately think the worst. With Carter serving in Iraq, she held her breath every time the doorbell rang, even though notification of Carter being wounded or killed in action would likely go to Foster first, since Carter had grown up in Foster's household.

But one of their children was in trouble. And she needed Foster's help.

Less than sixty seconds later, the phone rang. "Has something happened to Carter?" Foster asked immediately.

"No. It's—"

"Thank God!"

"It's Ben," Abby said. "I've just received a very disturbing phone call from his trauma therapist, Dr. Annagreit Schuster. She tried calling you, but she couldn't get through, so she called me."

"What are you talking about?" Foster said.

"Did you know our son is already back at work?"

Abby felt the hesitation on the other end of the line and said incredulously, "You knew?"

"He's needed, Abby. It's a matter of national security."

"How could Ben's work with gangs in D.C. have anything to do with national security?"

"I can't tell you that."

"Damn it, Foster! I can't believe you're allowing our son to go back into a threatening situation when his doctor says he's suffering from post-traumatic stress."

"He's required to have therapy every day in order to report to work," Foster explained.

"What if he's involved in another incident?" Abby said. "One that pushes him over the brink? Dr. Schuster seems to think that it wouldn't take much for Ben to break."

"Dr. Schuster overstepped her bounds when she brought you into this. If Ben weren't able to work, he wouldn't be working."

"And you're making this judgment based on what?"

"Nash's evaluation of his brother."

Abby scoffed. "When did Nash become a psychiatrist?"

"Nash has to evaluate men in the field all the time. He told me he thinks Ben can handle the job he's been assigned."

"And you're satisfied with that?"

"Ben's a grown man, capable of making decisions for himself. And he wants to work." Foster paused, then added, "He's stronger than you think, Abby."

"Ben's human. He's not invulnerable to PTSD. If he's suffering as badly as Dr. Schuster thinks he is, he shouldn't be working. Our son is in trouble, Foster. I'm asking you to help him. Please."

Abby waited impatiently for Foster's response. She knew he liked to digest information before speaking. But the silence on the other end of the line irked her all the same.

"What is it you want me to do, Abby?"

"Get Ben excused from this assignment, whatever it is."

"I can't do that."

"Why not?"

"All I can say is that it's a matter of national security, and Ben is in a unique position to be able to help resolve it."

Abby tried to imagine what problem involving gangs in D.C. could rise to the level of "national security." And thought of the bomb that had recently exploded in Chicago. The one the government and CNN and MSNBC and ABC and CBS said was some sort of gas-line explosion, but which Fox News—currently on the opposite side of the political fence from the president—had speculated was a terrorist attack.

"Is there another bomb out there, Foster?" The nation's terrorist threat condition was still "orange," despite the bombing in Chicago. "Is there a bomb threat in the District? And some kid in a gang knows where the bomb is?"

Foster remained silent, and Abby took that as confirmation that her guess was on the mark. "Are you telling me our son is out on the streets of D.C. hunting for some suicide bomber?"

"I don't want you worrying about Ben," Foster said.

"How can I not worry?" Abby said. "Dr. Schuster said—"

"Dr. Schuster had no business contacting you," Foster retorted.

"I'm glad she did! And you will not retaliate against her for letting me know that my son is in trouble and that no one around him seems to care. Do you hear me, Foster?"

"You're shouting, so yes, I can hear you."

Abby seethed. She lowered the volume of her speech, but not its intensity. "You need to do something to help Ben, Foster. Because if he does fall apart, I'm going to blame you."

Abby slammed down the phone, feeling helpless. She knew better than to appeal to Ben to take himself out of the fray. He was a soldier. A soldier fought until he could fight no more. Post-traumatic stress was the modern name for what had once been called shell shock. But a modern name made it no less horrifying for the men who suffered from it, or for the families who loved those tortured men.

Abby put a hand to her chest, which ached with love for her son. It hadn't been easy allowing Foster to take two of her children to live in another home. She'd been suffering from postpartum depression at the time, and she'd barely been able to take care of herself and Rhett. So she'd agreed to send Ben and Carter to live with their father.

She wouldn't even have kept Nash, except at twelve years old, Nash knew what had happened to cause the rift between his parents and he'd refused to go with his father.

As with the prodigal son in the Bible, the children who were gone from her life were all the more precious to her. Abby was determined not to let Ben become a casualty of the War on Terror. If Foster wouldn't help, she'd find someone who would.

Abby picked up the phone and began dialing.

27

Ben didn't bother heading home to shave after he left Annagreit Schuster's office. There was no need, because he didn't plan to check in with his boss before he hit the streets. There was a chance Tony would agree with Dr. Schuster that he wasn't well enough to work and tell him to go home.

Ben had no intention of sitting on his hands waiting for someone else to do his job. He figured it was better to ask forgiveness than permission. So he headed straight for Columbia Heights. He intended to find the girl who'd stolen his Glock.

Ben was driving Waverly's Ford Explorer, which MPD had brought to his Georgetown home after Waverly's death. He wasn't sure who'd made that decision, but he was grateful to have the police radio so that he could hear what was happening around the District, and which he could use to call for backup if he ran into trouble.

Ben had been told that Harry Saunders would be taking over as the sergeant in charge of the MPD Gang Unit, so he would be working with Harry from now on.

But not today. Waverly wasn't even buried yet. It was too soon to shake hands with a new MPD partner. Ben knew that doing any sort of investigating in Columbia Heights on his own was dumb, risky even. But he was sick and tired of everyone thinking there was something wrong with him, that he couldn't handle himself. Damn it, he was fine!

He drove up one street and down another looking for MS gang truants he could interrogate. It would be icing on the cake if he could make contact with Waverly's CI, who apparently knew Trisha Reynolds.

Ben was searching for anyone wearing MS colors, the blue and white from the El Salvadoran flag. Or someone sporting one of the many MS-13 gang markings, including an MS, a 13, or dice, crossbones or daggers.

At last he saw a boy who looked promising—he had an MS tattooed on his cheek—and abruptly pulled Waverly's Explorer to the curb.

The kid took one look at him and ran.

Ben gave chase. Every time his foot hit the sidewalk, his eye throbbed where the girl had hit him. When he threw himself out lengthwise and tackled the kid, he felt the stitches tear on his shoulder.

"Get the fuck off me!" the kid shouted as Ben snapped cuffs on him and yanked him to his feet. "You got nothin' on me."

"All I want to do is talk," Ben said. "Give me any more lip, and I'll take you in and we'll just see what we've got on you."

The kid shut up. He had an adolescent mustache that emphasized his youth. Ben realized that a week ago he'd wanted to help kids like this. Right now, all he felt like doing was punching this kid in the mouth. He reined in his anger. It wasn't going to help matters if he let his grief and frustration get the better of him.

"I'm looking for the girl who caused the shoot-out," Ben said. "Goes by the name Trisha Reynolds."

"Don't know who you're talkin' about," the kid replied.

"Don't lie to me." Ben lifted the kid's hands, which were cuffed behind him, putting pressure on the boy's shoulder joints.

"Ow! What's your problem?"

"My problem is I can't find the girl."

The kid squinted his eyes as he stared at Ben. "Why you want the girl? Not her fault those cops started shooting in that shed."

"The kid shot first," Ben said through tight jaws.

The boy's eyes went wide. "You one of the cops who shot Pedro?"

Ben didn't confirm or deny the statement.

"Jorge's looking for you. He's gonna make you pay for killing his little brother. You better get your ass out of here while you still can."

"Where can I find the girl?" Ben repeated.

The kid twisted his lips and let out a shrill whistle. "You're in some deep shit now."

Ben felt the hairs prickle on the back of his neck. His muscles tensed for flight, like an animal that suddenly senses it has become prey.

Ben had known he was on shaky ground coming to this neighborhood without backup. He'd taken what precautions he could. After he'd left the doctor's office, he'd stuck his personal weapon, a Colt .45 semiautomatic, in the back of his jeans and put on his bulletproof vest under his Georgetown University sweatshirt. Which wasn't going to do him much good if he got slammed in the head with a 2x4.

He realized just how foolish he'd been when rough-looking young men wearing blue and white, and sporting MS and crossbone tatts on their faces and necks, appeared from various points along the street. From alleys. From storefronts. From parked cars. From ramshackle row houses.

Before he knew it, Ben was trapped.

"Hey, Silvio," the boy leading the surrounding press of gang kids said.

Ben eyed the boy he'd cuffed. It seemed he'd accidentally stumbled on Waverly's CI.

"What's happening?" the gang leader asked.

"He's mad 'cause I won't tell him where to find Trisha Reynaldo," Silvio replied.

Ben heard the difference between the name he'd used for the girl, Trisha *Reynolds,* and the name Silvio had used, Trisha *Reynaldo.* He wondered if Silvio had given Waverly the wrong information, or whether Waverly had recorded the name incorrectly. At least now he had another name to search in school records.

Jorge met Ben's gaze with dark, menacing eyes. "Why you lookin' for Trisha?"

"That's between me and the girl."

One of the MS gang members pointed at Ben and said, "I saw him at the shed. He's one of the cops who shot Pedro."

Jorge's eyes narrowed to dangerous slits. "That true?"

Ben wasn't sure when he'd reached for the Colt .45. He just looked down and saw it was in his hand. All the kids except Jorge backed up a step. "I came here looking for a girl named Trisha Reynolds," Ben said. "I'm not looking for trouble."

"Don't matter," Jorge said. "You're a dead man anyway."

Ben hooked his hand around Silvio's arm and started in the direction of Waverly's Explorer. He'd taken two cautious steps sideways when an ancient white Thunderbird loaded with truant kids from the 1-8 cruised past. They threw catcalls at the MS gang from their open windows.

MS returned the insults, flipping birds and gang signs at their rivals. The battered car suddenly stopped in the middle of the street, all four doors opened and six rough-looking males stepped out onto the pavement.

Ben felt a shiver of fear run down his spine.

He realized that Pedro's older brother was still watching him like a hawk, even though the rest of the MS gang had been distracted by the 1-8 intrusion. A dog yelped as though it had been kicked. A baby wailed in distress. On some conscious level Ben heard both gangs shouting names at each other. But he was certain the greatest danger lay right in front of him.

"I'm leaving," he told the MS leader. "And I'm taking my prisoner with me."

He kept his gun on Jorge as he backed toward his car with Silvio in tow.

But he never made it.

28

The knife appeared in Jorge's hand an instant before Ben heard the first police siren.

The El Salvadoran jerked his head toward the sound.

Ben watched as Jorge nervously turned the switchblade in his hand, clearly trying to decide whether he had time to begin and end his fight with Ben before the cops showed up.

He turned back to Ben, scowled and said, "Another time, gringo."

In another moment, both ends of the street were blocked as cop cars screeched to a halt. The insults abruptly ended as the gang kids abandoned their attack on each other to flee from their common enemy.

The MS gang melted back into the landscape. The 1-8 members scrambled into the ancient Thunderbird and laid down rubber making a K-turn as they headed down a narrow alley halfway between the police barricades at either end of the street.

For Ben, everything was moving in slow motion. He couldn't believe rescue had arrived in the nick of time. He stared, disbelieving, at his boss, who was striding down the street toward him.

"Fuck!" Silvio said as he tried to jerk free and run.

Ben tightened his hold on the kid's arm until he yelled in pain.

"Let him go, Ben," Tony said quietly.

Ben suddenly realized Tony was approaching cautiously,

that he had his hands out in front of him, as though to keep Ben calm. Ben started to say, "This wasn't my fault."

But his tongue was stuck to the roof of his mouth.

"Let the kid go," Tony repeated.

Ben was reluctant to release his prisoner until he realized there were MPD officers moving down the street, their weapons unholstered, even though there wasn't a single gang kid in sight.

It suddenly occurred to him that their guns were out because *his* gun was out. That they considered *him* the threat.

"I'm not—" He cleared his throat and tried again. "I'm not going to shoot anyone, Tony," he said. "I just got myself into a situation where I…"

Ben recognized the looks in the eyes of the cops who were slowly closing in on him. They were afraid of him. Afraid of what he'd do. Kill the kid, maybe? Kill himself? Shoot at them? He was perfectly sane. Perfectly rational. And he resented the implication—the look in their eyes—that said he wasn't.

"It doesn't matter," Tony said, holding out his hand. "I'll take your weapon."

As though this was all a bad nightmare, Ben placed the grip of his Colt in Tony's hand. Tony handed the weapon to an ICE agent standing nearby whom Ben knew. The man lowered his gaze when Ben tried to meet it.

"And your creds," Tony said.

"What?"

"Hand over your credentials, Ben."

Ben glared at the ICE agent, who took a step closer to Tony, as though Tony might need backup to retrieve Ben's credentials. Ben pulled out the leather wallet containing his badge and identification and slapped it in Tony's hand. "There. Are you happy?"

"Nothing about this makes me happy." He stuck the leather folder in his jacket pocket, then passed Silvio off to Harry Saunders.

"What are you doing?" Ben demanded.

"Taking the kid in, of course."

"He was Waverly's CI."

"Which is why we have to take him in," Tony said. "We don't want MS getting suspicious. We'll let him go in a couple of hours."

"I want to talk to him," Ben said.

"You're not talking to anyone," Tony said. "You're going home."

Silvio shot a shit-eating grin at Ben before he was shoved inside the backseat of a waiting MPD black-and-white.

Harry Saunders talked quietly to Tony, who said, "Thanks. I appreciate the help."

Ben watched as the MPD cops headed back to their cars, shooting an occasional glance back at him over their shoulders. He felt resentful and let the ones who eyed him see it.

"Looks like your doctor was right," Tony said.

"What?"

"You're a disaster waiting to happen. You nearly incited a riot. We're lucky there aren't a dozen dead kids littering the streets right now."

"How did you know to come looking for me?" Ben asked.

"We've been hunting you all morning," Tony said.

"What for?"

"To tell you you're off the job—"

"What the hell?"

"—until you're cleared by Dr. Schuster."

Ben stared at his boss for a moment, until the second half of what he'd said sank in. "Since when?"

"Since Senator Hamilton confronted the president and tore her a new asshole for demanding the services of an agent who was, according to the doctor treating him for PTSD, a 'ticking bomb.'"

"You've got to be kidding."

"I told Dr. Schuster this morning that you were needed on the street, but it seems she didn't agree. Apparently, she kept making phone calls until she found someone who'd back her up."

"Sonofabitch!"

"I'm sorry, Ben. You're going to have to take some time off."

"Tell me at least that you fired her ass, that she's off the job."

Tony shook his head. "Got orders about that, too. Until she, personally, clears you for duty, you don't come back to work. I can't fire her. And neither can you."

"We'll see about that," Ben muttered.

"Go home, Ben. Get some rest."

Ben left Tony standing in the middle of the street. He intended to have a nice, long talk with Annagreit Schuster. He was done fooling around. There would be no need to *fire* her. If she was smart, the woman would quit on the spot.

29

Ben realized how lucky he was that his boss had trusted him to head home. Especially when he had an entirely different destination in mind. He got back into Waverly's SUV and drove straight for Annagreit Schuster's office.

When his cell phone rang, he was tempted to ignore it. He checked the caller ID, saw it was Julia and reluctantly answered the call.

"Hi, Little Bit. What's up?"

"I want to go there, Ben."

"Where is that?"

"To the place where Wave died."

"Aw, Julia," Ben said. "What good is that going to do?"

"I'm having trouble believing this is all real. That some fourteen-year-old boy shot Wave. I want to see where it all happened."

"Julia, this is crazy."

"Yes, I know. I'm feeling a little crazy right now. Humor me."

Ben knew just how Julia felt. Getting relieved of his badge and his gun had been unreal. He was having trouble himself taking in everything that had happened over the past few days. He doubted that seeing bloodstains on the concrete floor of a metal shed was going to help his sister, but he understood her need to do *something* to deal with her feelings of grief. "Where are you?"

"I'm at Georgetown University Hospital with Mother. She's here setting up some charity event. Can you come get me?"

"I'm working," he lied.

"No, you're not. Mother called Daddy and he called the president and you've got a week off or something. I guess I'm not the only one who's gone over the bend."

Ben swore and shook his head in disbelief. "For crying out loud, Julia. How many people know about this?" Ben felt a rush of humiliation. He had a pretty good idea of who'd contacted his mother, and he had more than a few things to say to that busybody shrink. Annagreit Schuster wouldn't be in such a hurry the next time to stick her nose in where it didn't belong.

Meanwhile, he wasn't going to let anyone—not his boss or his mother or his therapist or the president of the United States—stop him from finding the girl and retrieving his Glock.

"Ben? Will you come get me?"

"Sure. Why not?" He'd take Julia to Lincoln Middle School this afternoon where he could also do a little investigating of his own, then go see the good doctor at home tonight. That way, nobody would get in his way when he gave Annagreit Schuster a piece of his—according to her—malfunctioning mind.

He had a new last name for the girl who'd stolen his Glock: Reynaldo. And Lincoln Middle School, where both Epifanio and Pedro had attended classes, wasn't a bad place to start looking for her.

The school had both a magnetometer to relieve kids of metal weapons at the doorway, and a cop walking the halls, so taking Julia there during school hours should be safe.

Julia was waiting on the street in front of the hospital. Ben stopped at the curb long enough to pick her up. She was wearing a navy pea jacket and classic gray wool slacks with black boots. Her neck was wrapped in several layers of white knit scarf. Her golden blond hair shone in the sun. Her face looked ethereally beautiful, but her blue eyes were pools of pain.

"Thanks, Ben," she said as she hopped inside Waverly's Ford and buckled her seat belt. She pulled off her gloves and ran her fingertips over the worn leather seat, then clasped the gloves in her lap and caught her lower lip in her teeth.

Ben realized she was trying not to cry. "You must have spent a lot of time on that leather seat with Waverly behind the wheel."

She nodded and hiccupped to stifle a sob. She tried to smile but failed. "More time on the leather couch in Wave's apartment, actually."

"Have you told Mother about the baby?"

She shook her head. "I've been thinking the best thing might be to ask to travel around Europe by myself for a couple of months. Mother wanted me to do that this past summer, but I didn't want to leave Wave. I can go somewhere and have the baby."

"What purpose will that serve? You're going to have to tell Mother about the baby sooner or later."

"Not if I don't keep it."

Ben stared at his sister in horror. "*It?* That's Wave's kid you're talking about. Your own flesh and blood. You couldn't have loved him very much if you're willing to give away the last living part of him."

Julia started to cry and Ben pulled to the curb. He reached for his sister and pulled her into his arms as her body heaved with sobs. "You don't have to make any decisions right now," he said. "Give yourself a little time."

"Time is the one thing I don't have," Julia said. "I'm already two months gone. I'll be showing soon. I won't be able to hide the truth from Mother."

"Would it be so bad if she found out? You were in love. You got pregnant. It happens."

"She'd want me to keep the baby," Julia blurted.

Ben dropped his arms and sat back to stare at her. Her chin was tucked and her eyes were down. "Why don't you want to keep this baby, Julia?"

"I'm not ready to raise a child all by myself."

"Other women your age do it all the time."

"I'm not *other women.*"

"No, you've got the advantage of having the money to hire a nanny. You'll have all the help and support you need. So why don't you want to keep Wave's baby?"

She swallowed hard. "It might not be his."

Ben bit his tongue to keep from lashing out at her. "So you were duping him into marrying you to give some other man's bastard a name?"

In a voice so quiet he had to strain to hear her, Julia said, "I was raped."

Ben stared at her in patent disbelief. "You mean you couldn't get some old boyfriend to back off?"

She stared up at him with stark eyes. "No. I mean a man held a knife to my throat and raped me."

"Where? When? Did you recognize him? Could you describe him?" Ben realized he was reacting like a cop and stopped himself to ask the more important questions, "Are you all right? Did you get checked out at a hospital?"

"If you mean did I have evidence of the rape collected at a hospital, the answer is no. It happened on campus. I stayed late one night at the GU library. I was attacked in the tiered parking lot where I'd left my car. He came up behind me." She shrugged helplessly, hopelessly. "I never saw him."

"So you never reported it?" Ben said, unable to keep the disapproval from his voice.

"I couldn't bear for anyone to know," Julia said in an agonized voice. "I never thought anyone would have to know."

Ben reached for Julia again but she jerked away.

"Don't touch me! I feel just the way I thought I'd feel if I ever told anyone the truth. Dirty. I need a shower."

Ben shook his head. "You can't wash this away, Julia. You have to deal with it."

"How? By telling the world I've been raped? No thank you!"

"You need to tell the police, at least. If there's a rapist on the Georgetown University campus, we need to find him."

"No one else has reported being raped on campus over the past six months. I've checked."

"That doesn't mean another girl has been raped and kept it to herself like you. Or been raped on another campus."

Julia moaned. "It's too late now. Besides, I never saw him. I don't know what he looks like."

But when the baby was born, they'd have his DNA, Ben thought. He'd be able to run it through the federal database of DNA from known felons and see if he got a hit.

Unless the baby was Wave's.

Ben slid back to his side of the seat and started the engine. Before he put the SUV in gear he said, "Is there a chance this child is Wave's?"

Julia nodded. "Please don't tell Mother about…anything."

"I think you should tell her everything. But I won't. And I'm here if you need to talk."

Julia turned to stare out the window at the gradually deteriorating urban landscape as they left Georgetown and drove northeast through the District.

Ben pulled into a visitor's spot in the parking lot at Lincoln Middle School. "I need to go inside to check out something with the school registrar. Do you want to come with me? The shed is around back. I'll show it to you first, if you want."

She pulled on her gloves one at a time and said, "Later, I think. After you talk to the registrar."

"Everyone must be at lunch," Julia said as they passed several empty classrooms.

"Hold it right there."

Ben turned to find an armed, uniformed MPD officer in the school hallway. At the same instant he realized he had no official government credentials to flash in the registrar's office when he asked for information about Trisha Reynaldo. They'd been confiscated by his boss, along with his weapon.

He recognized the cop as a former member of the MPD

Gang Unit who'd been assigned to patrol the halls of Lincoln Middle School. "Hi, Charlie. What's up?"

"What are you doing here, Ben? Who's that with you?"

"This is my sister, Julia Hamilton."

"Waverly's fiancée?" he asked.

"Yes," Julia answered.

He nodded to her and said, "I'm real sorry about what happened to Wave, Miss. He was one of the good guys."

Ben had held his breath waiting for Charlie to make some remark about him being forced off the job earlier in the day. But it seemed Charlie hadn't heard yet. Maybe he could finesse getting the information he wanted from the registrar.

"Hey, you there! What are you doing in here?"

Ben took one look at the man dressed like his seventh grade history teacher in a loud tie and corduroy jacket and automatically reached for his ICE credentials, but, of course, they weren't there. "Damn," he muttered.

The teacher's tight frown was stuck on his face like chewing gum on the underside of a desk.

"I'm seeking information about a girl I think might be one of your students," Ben said.

"You can't be here during school hours if you're not a parent or legal guardian," the teacher replied by rote.

Ben was waiting for the teacher to ask for his badge, when Charlie said, "He's okay. Agent Benedict works for Immigration and Customs Enforcement."

There was a disturbance at the other end of the hall and Charlie said, "Gotta go to work. Yell if you need me."

"Thanks, Charlie." Ben turned back to the teacher, who seemed to accept his authority to be there. "I'm looking for a girl named Trisha Reynaldo. I wanted to check with your registrar—"

"I know Trisha. She's in my homeroom."

Ben couldn't believe his luck. "Where is she now?"

"She's in the cafeteria having lunch." The teacher shoved

a hand through his hair, leaving the top of his head momentarily bald, before he brushed it back into place. "Why do you want to talk with her?"

Ben wasn't about to tell this man the girl had stolen his Glock. "That's classified." Ben held his breath to see if the teacher would challenge him. But apparently, in this age of terrorist threats, people were more willing to cede the government the right to keep secrets. "Is there somewhere I could talk with her in private?" Ben asked.

The teacher straightened his tie. "Of course. I'll have her go to the principal's office."

Ben didn't want to take a chance that the principal would ask him for credentials. "I'd rather speak with her somewhere we can talk without other kids seeing us."

The teacher looked at him with suspicious eyes, then turned to Julia, who smiled at him.

"Who are you?" he asked her.

"She's with me," Ben said to keep Julia from admitting she had no governmental authority to be in the school, either.

That seemed to satisfy the man. "I'll escort Trisha to my homeroom." He pointed to a door with a window in it across the hall. "The room's empty right now. Will that do?"

"That'll be fine," Ben said. "We'll wait for the two of you there."

Ben turned to Julia and said, "This is the girl I think might have stolen my gun yesterday. With the screening they do at the front door, she wouldn't have brought it to school with her, but I don't know how she'll react when she sees me. I don't suppose you'd consider waiting for me in the car?"

"Not a chance."

"Then sit quietly out of the way and don't say a word," Ben instructed as he opened the classroom door.

As Ben played out Trisha's potential reactions in his mind, he realized this wasn't the smartest thing he'd ever done. If she made any kind of a fuss, which was a distinct possibility, he didn't have credentials to explain his presence here. He figured the chances were slim to none the girl was going to have his Glock with her at school, but the simple fact was, he didn't have a weapon to protect against that one in a million chance that she did.

What was it he hoped to accomplish with this meeting?

He should have simply called Tony when he confirmed the girl was here. But Tony would have told him he had no business investigating when he was on suspension. That he should have gone home and stayed there.

Ben balled his hands into fighting fists. He wasn't about to go home like a whipped cur with his tail between his legs. He had a job to do, with or without credentials. Nash was counting on him. Somewhere out there Al Qaeda was waiting to attack, using some kid with a bomb as their messenger of death. This girl might be the link that would lead him to that kid and that bomb.

30

Aisha saw her homeroom teacher, Mr. Garvey, walking purposefully between the rows of cafeteria tables and wondered who was in trouble. Mr. Garvey—everybody called him Mr. Gravy, because there was usually a food stain on his colorful tie—stopped right in front of her.

"Come with me, Trisha," he said.

Aisha felt her blood run cold. His voice sounded serious. Ominous. She had the assassin's gun hidden in her backpack. She'd overheard a kid in the 1-8 saying that the magnetometer wasn't working right and figured the gun was safer with her than hidden in her bedroom. "What do you want me for?" she asked the teacher.

"You'll find out soon enough."

Aisha's eyes darted toward the fire door on the opposite side of the cafeteria. If she bolted, Mr. Garvey would surely shout for help, and one of the numerous teachers in the cafeteria would likely catch her before she escaped.

Maybe what Mr. Garvey wanted had nothing to do with the Glock in her backpack. Maybe he wanted to ask about the bruised cut over her right eye.

Maybe the entire Al Qaeda plot had been discovered, and she was about to share her husband's fate: to be taken to some secret location where she would be tortured and then disappear.

"I'm not finished with my lunch," she said, amazed at how normal her voice sounded, considering how terrified she felt.

"You can finish it later. Leave your tray there."

Apparently, whatever Mr. Garvey wanted with her wasn't going to take very long. "All right," she said as she rose.

Mr. Garvey stepped back as she slipped her backpack over one shoulder, then led her in the direction from which he'd come.

"Where are we going?" she asked, hop-skipping to catch up and walk beside him.

"Homeroom."

Aisha eased out a breath of air she hadn't realized she'd been holding. She wasn't going to the principal's office. So maybe nobody knew she had the gun. Maybe she'd messed up on her history pop quiz. Maybe she was going to be named hall monitor. Maybe—

Aisha stopped dead in the doorway to her homeroom when she saw her brother's assassin leaning against Mr. Garvey's desk. He turned when she appeared and put his fisted hands on his hips. She whirled and would have fled, except Mr. Garvey's considerable bulk was blocking the doorway.

"Let me out of here," she said, using her shoulder to try and shove him aside, upset by the terror she heard in her voice.

"These people want to talk with you, Trisha," Mr. Garvey said in an inexorable voice, his meaty hands on her shoulders turning her back around.

"Come in, Trisha," the assassin said. "We don't mean you any harm. I'm Agent Benedict, with Immigration and Customs Enforcement." His eyes shifted to Mr. Garvey as he added, "An investigative arm of Homeland Security."

Aisha had blanched at the word *immigration*. She'd been told her papers were good. But what if they were flawed somehow. She couldn't afford to get detained and deported. She was a key player in what was to come.

The assassin focused his gaze back on her, his blue eyes two dangerous daggers that pierced her to the heart, and said, "I'd like to have my gun back."

"You didn't say anything about a weapon," Mr. Garvey protested.

Aisha watched, wide-eyed, as the slender blond woman who'd been sitting in a student desk near the side wall joined the assassin. Aisha swallowed to force saliva down her painfully pinched throat.

If only she could come away from this encounter without raising suspicion of her true intent. She was determined to cause the deaths of as many Americans as Allah allowed with the terrible weapon that would be put in her hands. She did not want to be discovered now, before her mission was completed.

Maybe all the assassin wanted was his gun back, and once he got it, he would go away and leave her to plot her revenge.

Aisha slid the ratty backpack off her shoulder and held it out to the assassin. "Your gun is in there. I am sorry I took it. I was scared. I did not know what to do with it, so I kept it."

Her brother's killer took the backpack, unzipped it and began carefully rummaging through it.

Aisha had forgotten about Mr. Garvey, who came up behind her. "You brought a gun to school, Trisha?"

"I'm glad she did," Basim's killer said. "The sooner I get my Glock back, the better."

The assassin retrieved his gun and set the backpack down, out of Aisha's reach. He removed the clip, checked to see whether a round had been chambered—it had—then slid the nine-millimeter Glock into the back of his jeans under his leather jacket.

"You can expect to be expelled for this, young lady," Mr. Garvey said. "At the very least!"

"I told you this visit was classified," the assassin said in a steely voice. "Which means every part of this visit must remain secret. Including the fact that this young woman had my weapon in her possession."

"But we have a zero-tolerance policy," Mr. Garvey protested.

The young blond woman stepped forward, smiling at Aisha's

homeroom teacher. Aisha realized, even though she was sure Mr. Garvey did not, that he was being walked backward out of the room. The woman admonished her teacher not to say anything to anyone before the door clicked closed in his face.

Aisha did not know whether to feel safer with Mr. Garvey gone or not. "Who are you?" she asked the woman.

"I'm his sister, Julia," the woman said with a gesture toward Basim's assassin.

Aisha tried to still the joy that made her body tremble at this announcement. Here was someone the assassin loved. Someone he would surely grieve if she were to die. Aisha sent a prayer to Allah for sending this blessing, this opportunity to wreak terrible vengeance upon the man who had shot Basim.

Every day she had run her fingers over the name pressed into the metal dog tag, saying a prayer and asking Allah to help her find him. She would repay the assassin as Allah willed it—an eye for an eye. BENEDICT had killed her brother while she watched. She would find a way to kill his sister while he watched.

She glanced from one face to the other. They were not alike, these two, except for those ice-blue eyes. The woman's hair was blond, while BENEDICT's was black. She was short, while he was tall. But she could see they liked each other. And BENEDICT's eyes slid to the girl often with concern.

"Now what?" Julia asked as she crossed the room to join her brother.

"I have some questions for Trisha." He gestured to one of the student desks and said, "Have a seat, please."

"You're scaring her," Aisha heard the young woman whisper.

BENEDICT grimaced, then said, "I just want to ask you a few questions, Trisha. Then you can leave."

That sounded too good to be true, but Aisha lowered herself into the desk closest to where she stood—and to the door. "What do you want to know?" she asked in her accented English.

BENEDICT leaned his hips back against the teacher's desk, while his sister sat down in a student desk not far from her.

"What's your full name?" the assassin asked.

"Trisha Reynaldo."

"Where do you live?"

Aisha gave the Reynaldos' address.

"How long have you been living in America?"

"My cousin invited me to come live with her a year ago, when my mother died," Aisha said, reciting the background facts she'd been taught and had carefully memorized. "I finally came to the United States one month ago. I have a green card, which is pink, actually."

"You're from El Salvador?" Agent Benedict asked.

Aisha nodded.

"What's your connection to MS?"

"I have no connection to any gang," Aisha replied calmly, although her heart thumped erratically in her chest.

BENEDICT raised a skeptical brow. "Yet three gang members are dead, apparently fighting over you."

Aisha felt her cheeks burn as though she'd been standing too long in the Afghani sun. "I only wanted to watch the others dance. I had no intention of dancing myself. I did not know Pedro liked me, or that he would object if another boy asked me to dance. I did not know they would fight."

"What were you doing in that shed on Saturday morning with Pedro?" BENEDICT asked.

"Pedro would not let me go home. He threatened me with his gun. His friends tried to make him let me go. But he would not."

The assassin rubbed a hand across the nape of his neck, then shook his head. "Did you know a boy named Epifanio Fuentes? He went to school here. He was killed on Friday."

Aisha wasn't sure whether to admit she knew Epifanio or not. But a lie might be discovered and lead the assassin to question the truth of what else she had said. She nodded. "We had English class together."

"Do you know any reason why anyone would want to kill him?"

Aisha shrugged. "I did not know him well. We sat across from each other."

That was how Epifanio had overheard her talking with Pedro and saw the note Pedro had tried to hand her, which had fallen on the floor. How he'd become suspicious. He'd actually confronted Aisha and asked her what the note meant.

Don't worry, the device will be here in time for the party.

It had been foolish of Pedro to put such a message in writing. Especially foolish to use a word like *device,* which had piqued Epifanio's curiosity.

It had been Aisha who'd urged Pedro to silence Epifanio. She'd grown up in a violent world, where death was an everyday occurrence. So she was surprised at Pedro's reluctance to kill the boy, who might ruin everything if he opened his mouth about what he'd seen.

"It'll cause problems if we kill him," he'd argued. "He's tight with the One-Eight. The cops are going to ask what he did to get his throat cut, which might lead them to us."

But she'd been adamant. "What will Al Qaeda say when our mission fails because a curious boy saw a note that you wrote?"

Pedro had made up an excuse why Epifanio had to be killed that had nothing to do with Al Qaeda. He'd told a boastful member of MS that Epifanio had been dissing him and the rest of the gang, and the only thing to do was to shut his mouth.

Men—boys—were so easy to manipulate, Aisha thought.

Aisha realized that if she wanted to kill the girl and make her brother watch, she would need to take advantage of this opportunity to befriend them.

"It is hard not to belong to a gang," she said. "But I do not want to join."

"I can help you with that," BENEDICT said.

"*We* can help you with that," the girl chimed in.

The assassin looked askance at his sister. Clearly he did not want her involved.

"I want to help," Julia said to her brother.

"You have no idea what you're getting into," he replied.

The assassin's sister turned to Aisha and said, "If you like, we could spend time together away from here, away from the gangs."

"Doing what?" BENEDICT said to his sister, clearly upset, his eyes narrowed and his jaw tight.

The girl turned to Aisha and said, "What would you like to do, Trisha?"

Aisha smiled her most American smile and said, "Shop."

31

"I want to see where Wave died," Julia said as they left the school.

Ben had been hoping Julia would be distracted by their talk with Trisha Reynaldo and the plan to meet with the girl to go shopping on Saturday, and forget about looking at the maintenance shed.

"The building's probably locked," he said.

She shook her head. "I assume the door has been sealed by the police and the area blocked off by crime-scene tape. Which we can get around."

She'd learned a lot about police procedures from Waverly in just six months, Ben mused. "There's nothing to see, Julia. Except dried blood on a concrete floor. Just don't come crying to me if you have nightmares."

"It's too late for that," she murmured as she followed him to the shed.

Ben saw that someone had already broken the police seal. Kids most likely. He held the yellow crime-scene tape out of the way so Julia could step inside.

He heard her gasp as he stepped in behind her.

"Oh, God, Ben!" She turned and lurched into his arms, hiding her face against his chest. "He lost so much blood!"

He'd watched Waverly bleed out, so he should have been ready for the size of the brown stain on the cement, which spread far beyond the taped outline of where Waverly's body had lain. He'd had some inkling of how awful it would be to come back here. How it would look. How it would smell.

But he hadn't known his knees would nearly buckle. He held tight to Julia, drawing needed comfort from her. She burrowed closer to him, making one grieving mass out of two suffering beings.

He didn't know how long they stood like that, but he was grateful that she didn't expect him to speak. His throat ached with the effort to contain his emotions.

He didn't want to feel so much. Had been trying for months not to feel at all. And failing miserably. He'd seen death before many times, even lost close friends, and coped just fine. But the walls he'd built as a soldier to protect himself seemed to be crumbling. And there wasn't a damned thing he could do about it.

Julia looked up at him with tortured eyes. "Why, Ben? Why did this have to happen? Wave and I missed a whole lifetime together. I can't bear it."

"Shh. Shh," he said, cupping her head and pulling her close to calm her. He felt her tremble in his arms.

"Thank God I have my big brother to get me through this," she murmured, gripping him more tightly. "Promise me you'll take care of yourself, Ben. Promise me you'll stay safe."

Tears stung his eyes and he blinked them back. Maybe the damned doctor was right. Maybe he should go home and stay there. Look at him. Scratch a little and feelings spilled out. But looking back on the events of Saturday morning, he didn't know what he could have done differently.

"Are we done here?" he asked Julia at last.

She took a step back and nodded.

When they got back to the car he said, "Julia, you have to take care of yourself. You have a child to think about."

She stared out the window. "A child that might not be his."

"The child is innocent, no matter who the father is."

She turned to glare at him. "I know that."

"I'm trying to help."

"Well, you're not!"

They were halfway back to Georgetown University Hospital before he spoke again. "I wish you'd reconsider this shopping trip with Trisha Reynaldo. I'm not sure it's safe for you to be hanging out with her."

"Why not?"

"She sparked a gang war all by herself."

"You're being paranoid," Julia accused.

"Contact with anyone even loosely tied to a D.C. gang is dangerous," he cautioned.

"We're going to an upscale mall," Julia said.

"Where are you picking her up?"

"She said she'd meet me in the Lincoln Middle School parking lot. She said it's not far from where she lives."

"Why do you care about this girl? What's in it for you?"

"I suppose it's a way of staying close to Waverly. I knew so little about his work. But I know he cared a lot about the kids he saw every day."

"The best way you can help is to stay out of the way."

"Too late. Besides, what could go wrong?"

"Nothing, if I'm there, too," he said.

"We won't be able to enjoy ourselves if you're standing around asking 'Are you done yet?'"

Ben had no comeback, because the truth was, he didn't have the patience to shop by himself, let alone with two women. After talking with the girl, he had no concrete reason to believe that Trisha Reynaldo was a danger to his sister or anyone else. But it couldn't hurt to check in on the two of them. "How about meeting up for lunch?"

Julia grimaced. "You're being overprotective."

"In light of recent events, I think you can cut me some slack."

Julia sighed. "All right. We're going to Tysons Corner. I'll give you a call to let you know where we've decided to eat."

"Sounds good." Before the weekend, he would do a little

more research into Trisha Reynaldo's background and find out for himself whether she had closer ties to one of the D.C. gangs than she was admitting.

When Julia's cell phone rang, she pulled it out of her purse, looked at the caller ID and said, "Uh-oh."

"Mother?" Ben guessed.

"Hello, Mother," Julia said, answering the call. "I'm with Ben. We went for a ride. We're on our way back to the hospital now." Julia looked at the street signs on the corner they were passing. "In fact, we're right around the corner. I'll come up— You don't need— Fine."

Julia slid her phone closed. "She's been worried sick, wondering where I am. She's meeting us out front. She wants to talk to you."

"Great. You escape for an hour and I'm in the doghouse."

"Thank you for taking me there," Julia said.

"She doesn't look happy," Ben said, as he caught sight of his mother walking to the curb. He pulled up in front of her and said to Julia, "Don't forget. Call me on Saturday."

"I will," Julia promised.

As Julia opened the car door his mother said, "Go wait for me inside, honey. I want to talk to Ben alone." She slipped into the passenger's seat and closed the door before she turned to Ben and said, "What do you think you're doing?"

"I took Julia for a ride."

"You're not supposed to be on the streets doing anything. You're supposed to be home resting."

Ben stared at his mother in disbelief. "Are you kidding?"

"Your doctor said—"

"That damned woman had no right to say anything to anyone," Ben interrupted. "Least of all *you*."

"I'm glad she did," his mother retorted. "If you're in trouble, I want to help."

"I can take care of myself. I don't appreciate your interference."

"I'm your mother."

"Patsy's my mother!" he blurted. Ben was immediately sorry when he saw the hurt look in his mother's eyes. Of course he was more emotionally connected to the mother who'd raised him. But he still loved the mother who'd borne him.

And resented her for giving him away.

She'd made a choice. So he'd made a choice. To love Patsy more, so it wouldn't hurt so much that he wasn't one of the sons his mother had kept when she'd divorced his father.

Nash and Rhett were the favored sons. He and Carter had been farmed out to his father. He'd heard all the rational reasons why his parents had torn their family down the middle and each taken half. But it didn't make him feel any less rejected.

"If you won't take care of yourself," his mother said quietly, "those who love you are going to step in to help. Including me."

Before he could respond, she opened the car door, stepped out and closed the door quietly behind her.

Ben slammed a fist on the dash. "That damned doctor!"

It was time to give her a piece of his—demented? deluded? deranged?—mind.

32

Finding a spot to park on the street in Georgetown was tough, and Ben ended up so far from Anna Schuster's apartment, that his route walking back took him right past the vet's office. Which reminded him of Rocky the rottweiler. He glanced at his watch. Four o'clock. The dog was probably already dead.

Ben kept walking.

That dog doesn't deserve to die. Being crippled doesn't make him worthless. After all, he still has a tail to wag.

Ben turned and trotted back to the door of the vet's office. He still didn't want a dog. But if he rescued the rottweiler, he could at least buy some time to find the animal a good home.

"Oh, you came," the doctor said with a relieved smile. "She said you would."

"What?"

"Dr. Schuster. I called her when the noon deadline came to euthanize the dog, and she said I should wait, because you would come. And you did."

Ben gritted his teeth.

"The bill is $952.35."

"What?"

"She said you'd pay with a credit card."

Without a word, Ben pulled out his wallet and handed the vet his American Express card.

The vet shot Ben a rueful grin. "I don't take American Express."

He put the black card away and pulled out a Visa. "Will this one do?"

The vet handed the card to his pretty assistant and said, "Come on back with me to the kennel. I have some instructions to give you for Rocky's care."

"I'm not ready to take the dog home today," Ben said.

"She said you'd say that, too," the vet said with a smile.

Ben managed not to snarl.

"I have everything you need—food, dog bed, collar, leash, antibiotics—all ready for you to take home."

"What about the dog?" Ben said. "Maybe Rocky's not ready to leave here yet. I mean, he's had major surgery, right? As I understand it, he had a rear leg amputated."

"Rocky's making a remarkable recovery." The vet began walking down a row of cages. "Dogs can manage very well on three legs. Rocky was on his feet the day after surgery and he's doing great. You will have to bring him back in about a week to have the stitches out."

"I just…I'm not really ready…" Ben realized that if he told the truth, that he didn't want the dog, the vet might decide to euthanize Rocky after all. "Could you just keep him for tonight?"

"Anna said you'd say that, too," the vet said with a laugh. "Bringing a pet into your home is a little like screwing up the courage to swim in an icy, spring-fed pond. Some folks like to dip in a toe. With a pet, you kind of have to dive right in."

"Yeah, well." Ben had always considered himself a "dive right in" kind of guy. But his head was whirling. What had he gotten himself into? Check that. What had Anna gotten him into?

"Was there anything else Dr. Schuster told you?" Ben asked sarcastically.

"She said you were a good guy and that you'd take good care of the dog."

They'd reached the large cage where Rocky was penned. The dog was standing with his nose pressed against the wire mesh like a condemned prisoner. The instant he saw Ben, his damned tail started wagging.

Ben turned to the vet and said, "I'll take him with me."

33

By five o'clock Ben was leaning against the brick wall of Annagreit Schuster's brownstone, hidden by the early evening shadows, waiting to confront the doctor.

He'd left the vet's office, walked back to his car and driven it around back to the kennel to pick up Rocky and all the paraphernalia the vet had provided.

The dog immediately curled himself up in the bed Ben put in the back of the SUV. Ben had planned to take the dog home and return to confront Anna, but he changed his mind when he drove by a parking space within a block of her front door.

He'd left the windows cracked so the cool evening air could reach the dog and headed for Anna's front porch.

He had a few home truths to tell her.

Ben watched the young boy he'd met at the vet's office with Anna arrive at Anna's brownstone surrounded by older boys whom Ben knew, from their colors and gang tatts, were members of the 1-8. He wondered if the doctor knew her cat-sitter was running with a gang—and what the 1-8 was doing in Georgetown.

"Hello, Henry," he said as the gang turned the corner and walked out of sight. "Didn't know you were in the One-Eight."

Henry was so startled he stumbled on the stairs. Ben reached out and caught his arm to keep him from falling. Recognition flashed across the boy's pimpled face. He glanced over his shoulder and looked relieved that the other boys were no longer in sight. "I'm not in the One-Eight."

"But you'd like to be?"

Henry shrugged. "I like having someone to talk to when no one's around. Don't tell Anna. She'll tell my mother."

"How old are you, Henry?"

"I'll be thirteen on December tenth."

"What are those boys doing in this neighborhood?"

Henry flushed. "Nothing."

Ben raised an eyebrow. "This isn't their usual territory."

"They're entitled to be here same as anyone else," Henry blustered.

Ben kept his gaze focused on the kid's eyes until Henry admitted, "They're looking for some guys in MS they followed here from Columbia Heights."

Ben felt his gut tighten. This was exactly the sort of gang activity Nash had told him to be watching for.

Henry's chest puffed out as he continued, "My friends—" he jerked a thumb in the direction of the boys whose company he'd left "—have been following MS trying to figure out what they're doing. So they can fuck it up."

Ben saw the flush on Henry's downy cheeks that showed just how uncomfortable the boy was using foul language. Henry was the sort of kid who could easily get sucked into a gang. Alone too much, no parents around. Full of adolescent hormones and wanting so badly to be, or at least act, grown up. Needing the approval and company of other equally abandoned boys.

Ben had way too much trouble on his plate already, but he found he couldn't ignore Henry's situation. "You know what a One-Eight initiation is like, Henry?"

The boy's eyes look troubled. "Sort of."

"You hurt anyone yet or been hurt yourself?" Ben knew that beatings—giving and receiving them—were often part of a gang initiation. "Used drugs? Stolen anything? Killed anyone?"

Henry's brown eyes opened wide enough to expose the whites. "I wouldn't do that!"

"That's what gangs do, Henry. They hurt people. They rob and steal. They do drugs. You want to be a part of all that?"

Ben saw the kid struggle between the desire to belong and his conscience, which told him there was *right* and *wrong*. And what Ben was describing was *wrong*.

"They're nice to me," the kid said softly.

"Yeah," Ben agreed, laying a hand on Henry's shoulder. "But they're not nice." So long as the boy was useful to them, they would hide their true colors. "Have they talked about what MS is doing in Georgetown? Do they know?"

The kid ducked out from under Ben's hand and turned to look at him suspiciously. "Why do you want to know?"

"My job is keeping the peace between the gangs in D.C."

"You're a cop?" Henry said incredulously. "Where's your badge? And your uniform?"

Since his ICE credentials had been confiscated, he was forced to improvise, "I'm undercover. You know what that is?"

Henry snorted. "Of course. I watch TV, you know. *CSI, NCIS, Law and Order.*"

"Okay. So you understand why I wouldn't carry a badge with me. Believe me when I tell you, gang kids haunting the alleys in Georgetown are up to no good. If you know anything, you need to spill it."

"I'm no snitch," Henry said.

"Never said you were. But if you have information that could help keep the peace here in the District, I need to know it."

The toe of Henry's high-tops traced a crack in the brick porch. "MS is waiting for a package of some kind. It's supposed to be delivered to a house in Georgetown." He looked up at Ben. "The One-Eight plans to intercept it. That's all I know. Really."

It might not have seemed like much to Henry. But Ben had some inkling what that package might be. An *improvised explosive device.* What a surprise for the 1-8 if they did intercept it! At least MS knew what they were handling and would be careful. It would be a disaster if the 1-8 intercepted an irradiated IED—or one with a biotoxin attached—without knowing what they had.

He needed to tell his boss what he'd learned, so he could pass it on to the head of DHS, with whom Nash was coordinating.

Except he wasn't supposed to be on the job. He'd surely be shut out of whatever search went on in Georgetown. And if the gangs knew they were being watched, wouldn't they change their drop point? Which meant ICE and the MPD would have to start all over again looking for the "package."

Ben wondered why the bomb was being delivered to Georgetown, when MS mostly haunted Columbia Heights. Maybe that was the whole point. No one expected MS activity in Georgetown, so no one would be looking for trouble there.

Ben lived in Georgetown, and he hadn't noticed anything out of the ordinary. Hadn't seen any gang activity at all. MS and the 1-8 should have stood out like the Beverly Hillbillies at a French embassy reception. Obviously, they were taking some pains not to get noticed. He wondered how long an MS presence in Georgetown would have gone undetected if he hadn't seen Henry with the 1-8.

"Ben? Agent Benedict? Is that you?"

Ben turned to find Annagreit Schuster standing at the bottom of the brownstone steps looking up at him in disbelief.

"What are you doing here?" she asked. "Are you all right?"

Ben winced as Henry gripped his dog-bit arm. He saw the kid's eyes pleading with him: *Don't rat me out.* Ben turned back to the doctor and said, "I came to see you."

He heard Henry release a whoosh of air. The kid shot the doctor a carefree grin and said, "Hi, Anna. I was just going upstairs to do my homework."

Before Ben could stop him, Henry disappeared into the lobby of the building. Ben caught the door before it closed and held it for Dr. Schuster.

She stared at him as she crossed past him and asked again, "Are you all right?"

"I'd rather not discuss my business out here in the hall, Doc."

"Of course," she said, heading up the single flight of stairs to her apartment.

Ben had been nursing his anger all day, determined to vent it the moment he laid eyes on Annagreit Schuster. But he'd gotten distracted by the kid, and the doctor had caught him off guard. Instead of the lambasting he'd intended to give her, he was following her up the stairs, admiring her fanny and her long legs.

She was flustered enough to need two tries to get the key in the lock. Which was some small consolation.

Once they got inside, she dropped a small paper bag of groceries on the kitchen counter, along with her purse and a soft brown leather briefcase. She smoothed her hands down the front of her skirt twice before she turned to face him.

"I'm surprised to see you here."

"You got me taken off the job," he said, stepping into the narrow space between the refrigerator and the kitchen counter, blocking her escape.

"I think we'd be more comfortable in the living room," she said, taking a step forward.

"I'm happy right where I am," he said, refusing to back away. He could see she was wary, uncertain how violent he might get. He wasn't entirely certain himself.

She lifted her chin and stuck her hands on her hips. "Why are you here, Agent Benedict?"

"I would think that's obvious."

He waited for her to speak. To admit her insufferable interference in his life—for his own good, of course.

But she was as good at the game as he was. She never lost eye contact. And never said a word.

"I came here to tell you to butt out of my business," he said at last, with a quirk of his lips that acknowledged her willingness to wait him out.

"I wish I could, Agent Benedict. I don't think that's possible now. Not after what transpired today in Columbia Heights. So the sooner we get started, the sooner you'll get better and the sooner you can get back to work."

"That isn't what's going to happen."

She tilted her head as though she hadn't heard him right. "You do understand that you can't go back to work until I agree you're well enough to go back to work."

"What you don't seem to understand, Doc, is that I don't need to be *on* the job to *do* the job."

She took a step into his space. "You can't go back on the streets in the condition you're in. I won't let you."

"With all due respect, Doc, you can't stop me."

He watched the wheels turn as she considered what to do next.

"All right," she said. "If you insist on being involved in whatever national emergency is so important that you think you're indispensable, I'll go with you."

"What?"

"I'll approve you for duty, but only if I ride along with you and your new partner."

"Don't make me laugh."

"That way I'll be there to help if…if I'm needed." She was talking fast, keeping her intense blue gaze focused on his.

He could feel her touching him even though her hands remained by her sides. He fought against a shudder of physical—sexual—awareness. She was using the attraction he felt for her to worm her way inside his defenses. She wanted inside his head, and he was determined not to let her in there.

"I'm here," she said. "Use me."

Ben felt a surge of anger at her presumption. "I've only got one use for a woman in my life right now, Doc."

She considered that for even less time and said, "Fine."

Ben couldn't believe what he'd heard. "You understand what I'm saying?"

She flushed. "Yes."

He stared at her through narrowed eyes. "Put up or shut up, Doc."

Annagreit Schuster reached up and began unbuttoning her white silk blouse.

34

There was a line doctors didn't cross. Anna was far beyond it, in uncharted territory.

She probably should have excused herself from Agent Benedict's case the moment she realized they'd met previously. Certainly, she should have bowed out after she'd interfered to get him taken off the streets, instead of allowing his mother to talk her into staying on the job.

What she was about to do was, by every ethical standard she knew, flat wrong. Nevertheless, she was going to make love to Ben Benedict.

Have sex, Anna. You're going to have sex with a patient.

"You chickening out, Doc?"

Anna realized she'd stopped with only three buttons undone. "I wish you would believe I only have your best interests at heart. You should be in therapy, not—"

He stopped her speech with a kiss. She'd expected it to be brutal. It was. He was reestablishing the control he needed to feel between them.

She was pliant. Yielding. Surrendering to his power.

The kiss became invasive, his tongue plundering her mouth. She gave in to her feelings of desire for him and raked her hands through his hair, feeling the silky texture, then tugged his shirt out of his jeans to reach for warm, masculine flesh.

His hands made short work of her blouse. She heard the last two buttons pinging off the stove as he ripped the delicate fabric off her shoulders. He unclipped her bra with one hand

and made a guttural sound in his throat as he cupped the weight of her small breast before laving it with his tongue.

She nipped his earlobe and heard him grunt with pleasure. Her hand slid inside the back of his jeans but there wasn't enough room to do what she wanted to do. She made a frustrated sound as he scooped her up in his arms.

It was a small apartment and he found the bedroom without any trouble. But the bed wasn't empty.

"Sonofabitch!"

Penelope had arranged herself and her four kittens in a nest she'd made in the middle of Anna's bed using the top sheet and the bedspread. The mother cat took great exception to Ben Benedict's intrusion. She arched her back and fluffed her tail and hissed like a spitting cobra.

Ben's military survival instincts were still strong, because he reversed course out of the room and kicked the bedroom door shut while Penelope was still in mid-leap.

Anna saw he was laughing before his mouth captured hers more urgently than before. He turned and backed her against her closed bedroom door, yanked up her pencil skirt and groaned when he realized she was wearing a thong. He broke the fragile string across her hips, then unzipped his jeans. He lifted one of her legs and rested it on his hip, uttering a raw sound of need as he thrust himself inside her.

Anna gasped.

Ben Benedict froze. He was deep inside her, but he didn't move a hair, didn't move a muscle. Except to throb inside her.

She realized her nails had dug into his shoulders. She was trembling. With desire.

"Don't stop," she whispered. "Please don't stop."

35

Ben buried his face against Anna's neck as he moved inside her. She smelled like gardenias. One of his hands was braced flat against the cool painted door to give him leverage, while the other kept Anna's leg tight against his hip. He was lost in a well of sensation.

He felt the pleasure-pain when her nails raked his flesh. The softness of her naked breasts and the thrust of her pebbled nipples against his hairy chest. The snugness and the heat and the wetness of her.

He turned his head and sucked on her neck, then kissed the shell of her ear. He searched blindly for her mouth and found it. Tasted her. She welcomed his tongue into her mouth and returned the favor, mimicking the sex act.

And sent him over the edge.

His body tightened and he arched his head back as he sought release. He heard her growl in her throat and felt her convulsing around him.

He cried out as he spilled his seed inside her.

The next thing Ben was aware of was the soft murmur of a comforting female voice and gentle fingertips brushing the damp hair from his forehead. He took a shuddering breath and lifted his head from a petal-soft shoulder to look into Anna-greit Schuster's sated blue eyes.

"I gotta say, Doc. I like your—"

She put her fingertips to his lips. "Don't say anything. I know I have no business doing this with you. But…"

"But what?" he said, levering himself upright and separating their bodies. He turned away and tucked himself back into his jeans and zipped them up. He could hear the rustle of silk as she pulled her pencil skirt back down.

When he turned, she'd wrapped the edges of her torn blouse around her and had her arms crossed protectively over her nearly bare breasts.

"Little late, Doc. The horse is already out of the barn."

He watched a muscle jerk in her cheek as she uncrossed her arms and let the blouse fall open. His body pulsed in response to the sight of her nipples peaked beneath the fragile white silk.

"You are so beautiful," he said reverently as he reached to brush aside the silk and cup one of her perfect, pink-tipped breasts in his palm.

He heard her inhale sharply and met her gaze. Her irises were huge. He felt his body harden as though he hadn't just had the most fulfilling sex of his life.

"Heaven help me," he rasped. "I want you again."

She tried to step back, but her back was already against the door. She lifted her chin and said, "We need to talk."

He retreated a step and snarled, "That the price of a fuck, Doc? A little therapy?"

She opened her mouth—he was sure to swear at him—but closed it before saying anything. He watched her swallow as though it hurt, then say, "I wanted you. You wanted me. We're both adults. And I'm not your doctor anymore."

He frowned. "Then what was all that about wanting to talk?"

"I wanted to say that if we do that again we need to use protection. I'm not on the pill."

"Oh."

"Yeah," she said. "And I wanted to ask whether you've been tested lately. For sexually transmitted diseases."

He grinned. "You are a constant surprise, Doc."

"And," she persisted, "I wanted to ask you to call me Anna. Because—"

"—you're not my doctor anymore. I get it, Doc. I mean, Anna. I'll make sure I've got protection next time. Usually I'm more careful. As far as I know, I don't have any STDs."

She shoved a hand through her tousled blond curls. "I should have stopped you until we could get some protection." She closed her eyes and pressed her fingertips to her temples. "I don't know why I didn't."

"Is this a bad time or something?" he asked.

"For what?" she said, looking slightly dazed as she opened her eyes to stare up at him.

"I mean, are you ovulating?"

Her eyes sparkled, and she put her hands over her mouth to stop a surprised giggle. "I can't believe you asked me that."

"What? I shouldn't know about female ovulation?"

"Honestly? It's a little strange hearing you discuss it," she said, laughing.

"Patsy was a very thorough stepmother," he said, chuckling. "We'll take precautions next time."

She stopped laughing abruptly and looked into his eyes. "I guess that means there's going to be a next time."

"I sure as hell hope so. So long as we can agree you aren't going to pick my brain before, during or after sex."

She frowned and said, "Pick your brain?"

"You know what I mean."

"I need a shower," she said, turning and reaching for the bedroom doorknob. She glanced over her shoulder and said, "I'd ask you to join me, but I don't want to upset Penelope."

He imagined her in the shower and liked what he saw. "I'm willing to make friends with your cat."

"Call for some takeout. There are menus in the drawer by the phone in the kitchen. We can have dinner together and figure out how we're going to find whoever it is you're hunting for."

He'd already turned toward the kitchen when she reappeared in the bedroom doorway. "Can you stay for the night?"

"Afraid I'm going to cut and run?"

"It crossed my mind."

"I don't have a change of clothes."

"I can wash your clothes and dry them so you have something clean to wear in the morning."

"You mean sleep naked?" he said, putting a hand against his chest in feigned shock.

"You have a problem with that?"

"Not at all. Which makes me really sorry I can't stay. I have some things I need to do at home."

She looked into his eyes and said, "I think that's just an excuse. I think you're scared that if you fall asleep here, you might have a nightmare." She took a step toward him. "And that I'll freak out when you wake up screaming."

He grimaced. Damn it. She was right about that, too.

"I won't be surprised if you have a nightmare," she said. "It's a symptom of PTSD. And I promise I won't freak out if it happens."

But she hadn't heard him shriek in a darkened room. Seen him soaked with sweat and stinking with fear. He sometimes scared himself. "You have no idea—" he began savagely.

"I think I do," she interrupted. "The situation may not even arise. But if it does, I can handle it."

"You say that now. What happens when I wake up screaming?"

She crossed to him and put a palm on his chest as she looked up into his eyes. "I'll be there to tell you everything's okay and to reassure you that it's only a dream."

He hesitated. He wanted to believe her. He'd been alone for a very long time. He wouldn't mind sleeping next to her, waking up next to her. The thought was very tempting.

And very frightening.

"Okay, Doc. We'll give it a try. But I think I'll go get us some takeout while you're in the shower."

"Do you have to leave? Can't you call out?"

"If you must know, I have a rottweiler in the car. I have to take my dog home and put him to bed."

She dropped her towel and walked right into his arms, giving him a hard hug and a kiss. "I knew you wouldn't let Rocky die," she whispered in his ear. "Hurry back. I'll be waiting for you."

Ben took the stairs two at a time. If he hurried, he should be able to get Rocky settled in his new home before Anna got out of the shower.

36

Ben woke to the sound of screaming. But it wasn't his own. The wail of agony was coming from Annagreit Schuster. She was sitting upright in bed, eyes wide open. But she wasn't awake.

"Anna! Wake up!" Ben struggled to free himself from the tangled sheets, then grasped her shoulders and shook her. "Wake up, Anna!"

The wailing continued, louder and more terrifying.

Ben grasped her chin and forced her face toward his. He stared into her eyes, barely lit by the soft yellow glow from a night-light, and spoke softly but urgently. "Anna, look at me. *Look at me.* It's all over. It's done."

He heard a strangled sound as the wailing abruptly stopped. She stared at him another few moments before her eyes showed recognition. And humiliation.

"Oh, my God," she whispered. She jerked free of his grasp and put her hands up to hide her face, her breathing erratic.

"So, Doc," he said softly. "It seems we both have our dirty little secrets."

Ben realized he knew nothing about the woman he'd made love to twice last night. He'd noticed that haunted look in her eyes at the vet's office. But she was young and beautiful and he'd presumed her trouble was something like an unhappy romantic breakup. He'd never imagined she suffered nightmares.

Just like him.

"I don't know about you, Doc, but I find this ironic. I'm the one who's supposed to have PTSD, and you're the one who had the nightmare. Care to explain?"

37

Anna knew she owed Ben Benedict an answer. She just wasn't sure how much to tell him. She tried for a smile but it wobbled away. "You can see I do know what you've been going through."

He was sitting on his side of the bed with the sheet draped over his lap, leaning back against a pillow propped against the headboard. She was sitting on her side, holding the sheet to her breasts, exposing her naked back to him, her legs hanging over the edge of the bed.

Penelope was making anxious Maine Coon cat chirping noises from her basket in the corner.

Anna took the sheet with her, pulling it free of the mattress as she crossed the room to comfort the cat, leaving Ben groping for a blanket to stave off the chill night air. "It's all right, Penelope," she murmured. "I'm sorry for waking you up."

She sat beside the cat's basket with her back against a bookcase, the sheet draped around her, stroking Penelope's fur, calming herself as she quieted the cat.

"I'm waiting," Ben said when she remained silent.

Anna lifted her chin and said, "I'll show you mine if you show me yours."

Ben snickered. "Right. You first."

"My twin sister committed suicide."

"Recently?" he asked.

"When I was nineteen."

"How long ago was that?"

"I'm twenty-nine."

"And you're still having nightmares ten years later?" he said incredulously. "Why haven't you gotten some counseling, if you believe in it so much? Physician, heal thyself. Isn't that how the saying goes?"

Anna shoved a hand through her tumbled hair, unable to meet his gaze. "I rarely have nightmares anymore. I don't know what sparked this one. Unless it's meeting you." *And having unprotected sex. At a time of the month when I might get pregnant.*

"Sex with me gave you nightmares?"

Anna laughed softly and shook her head. "Sex with you was a dream come true."

"Then how about coming back to bed?"

"In a while," she promised. She was quiet for a few minutes, simply stroking the cat, then said, "It happened when my sister and I were sophomores at Boston College. We were both studying literature. Lisele wanted to write the great American novel." She smiled ruefully and added, "I was going to be a famous investigative reporter."

"I can see you doing that. You've got that bulldog, grab-on-and-don't-let-go attitude down cold."

"My sister and I were very close," Anna continued, ignoring his jibe, "because we were all alone in the world."

Ben snorted. "I'll be glad to loan you some of my relatives."

"You don't know how lucky you are," she said. "Our parents died in a car accident when we were six. Lisele and I were raised by a maiden aunt who died the summer of our freshman year from a heart attack. Then there were just the two of us."

She hesitated, then said, "Until Lisele met this boy named Paul."

"You were jealous. You broke them up and she killed herself."

"Who's telling this story?"

He carefully scratched the area around the stitches on his arm as he said, "I'm listening."

"It doesn't make me sound like a nice person, but yes, I was terribly jealous. Lisele spent all her time with Paul. I felt left out. I wanted her to go with me to see Madonna in New York, but she wanted to spend that weekend with Paul."

Anna saw Ben open his mouth and glared at him. He mimed zipping his lips with his fingers and she continued, "Lisele agreed to drive with me to New York to see her perform. We had a wonderful time, as I knew we would. But we drove straight back to Boston after the concert because Lisele wanted to spend Sunday with Paul. We were both tired."

Anna was no longer in her bedroom with Ben. She was back on the winding two-lane highway, the pines that framed the road still gray, rather than green, in the faint predawn light. She was making fun of the outrageous costumes Madonna had worn during her concert to keep Lisele awake.

"Lisele must have dozed off for a moment. Our Saturn struck a pregnant woman walking beside the road."

Anna realized she was breathing hard and struggled to calm her heartbeat. And her mind. She took a deep breath and let it out.

"That's enough," Ben said. He crossed the room and lifted her, naked, into his arms.

She grabbed for the sheet and dragged it behind her as he crossed the room.

"I don't need to hear any more," he said as he set her gently on the bed. He lay down beside her and pulled her into his arms, tugging the sheet over both of them to keep off the chill.

Anna met his gaze across the few inches that separated their faces and said, "I need to tell you the rest."

He used a fingertip to brush the hair from her brow. "All right. Go ahead."

She focused on his face, the dark eyebrows, the rough stubble of beard, the soft, bowed lips, determined to explain what had happened that fateful morning without visualizing it in her mind.

"The scene of the accident was…gruesome." She swallowed hard. "It took a long time for help to get to us. The mother lived, but she needed a hysterectomy. The seven-month-old baby in her womb—her first child—died."

She put a hand on his heart, needing to feel warm flesh. "My sister was never able to forgive herself."

"I don't get it," Ben said, playing with a blond curl that had fallen over her breast. "She's the one who was driving the car. Why are you having the nightmares?"

Anna started to tell the whole truth. And settled for half of it. "After the accident, I suspected she was feeling terrible guilt, but I did nothing. She told me she was fine and I believed her. I was happy when she broke up with Paul." She hesitated, then said, "I was the one who found her after she'd slit her wrists in the bathtub."

The flesh prickled on Anna's arms and her insides fluttered as she remembered opening the bathroom door in their tiny Boston apartment. "The water was…so red…with blood. It was too late to do anything. At the funeral, Paul told me she was pregnant with their child. That she didn't think she deserved to have a child when the woman she'd struck couldn't."

Ben hugged Anna tight and she laid her cheek against his chest, accepting the physical comfort he offered.

"Is that why you became a doctor?" he asked. "To save others when you couldn't save your sister."

She nodded.

"It doesn't look like the cure worked, Doc. You're still having nightmares."

"You can learn to deal with PTSD," she said. "Unfortunately, you can't erase the memories that caused it. Sometimes…"

"Sometimes they catch up to you," Ben said quietly.

"I've told you my sad story," she said. "Now it's your turn."

"I'm not interested in talking right now." Ben's callused hand slid down her belly as he trailed kisses across her cheek.

Anna realized talking could wait. She groaned as his fingers caressed soft flesh and raised her chin to give him better access to her throat.

38

Ben couldn't remember the last time he'd slept with a woman spooned against him. Of course, he wasn't exactly sleeping. Neither was Anna. They were both drowsy and sated after extraordinarily satisfying sex, but he had no desire to sleep. It was when he was most relaxed that he was most vulnerable to the nightmares.

"It'll help to talk," she murmured. "Besides, we had a deal."

I'll show you mine if you show me yours.

Somehow it was easier talking because she wasn't facing him. He snugged his arm around her waist to keep her from turning around and said, "I killed a kid. In Afghanistan." He felt vulnerable admitting even that much of the truth.

"Were you in battle when this happened?" she asked.

"Not exactly."

"But you were in a war zone."

"Yeah."

"Was it an accident?"

"Yeah."

"And yet, you blame yourself for the death of the child."

"I blame myself because a boy is dead and I killed him." It was no excuse to say it was an accident.

She pulled his arm free and turned over to face him. "Why did this death hit you so hard?"

He lay back on the pillow and put an arm behind his head, staring at the ceiling. "How the hell do I know?"

She leaned up on one elbow, so she could see his face. "I understand there are innocents killed in wartime more often than civilians want to believe. Had that happened to you before? Killing a civilian in combat? I believe it's called collateral damage."

"Yeah." It had happened more than once in the past. He hadn't always been the one who'd caused the death, but more often than he liked to remember, he'd been part of a squad that had dealt accidental death to innocents.

She sat up cross-legged. "So what made this boy's death different?"

He sat up and shoved his way back against the headboard. "I told you I don't know."

She waited him out.

"I don't," he insisted.

"Perhaps we need to figure that out," she said softly.

He noticed she'd used *we* and realized she'd slipped into therapist mode. He couldn't say he was sorry. He felt better just admitting as much as he had to someone safe. Someone who hadn't judged or excused or sympathized or done anything but listen.

But he also felt exposed, because she'd somehow managed to get inside his head and pry out information that he hadn't wanted to share.

He was tired of talking. Staying here hadn't been about talking. She was here. And she was willing. For the moment.

Ben moved the sheet out of the way and lifted her onto his lap, spreading her legs on either side of him. She laid her hands on his shoulders, being careful to avoid the bandage from his gunshot wound.

"I've got a head game for you, Doc. That is, if you wanna play."

She kissed his cheek with a feather touch that sent a shiver down his spine. "I'm in."

He reached down to touch and realized she was wet and

ready. He grabbed her hips and drove himself inside her, his voice guttural as he said, "I'm in, too."

"What are the rules?" she murmured.

"Whoever stays mum the longest wins." He felt her shiver as he kissed her throat. "Oh, God," he groaned as she lifted herself off him and slid back down again.

"You lose," she whispered.

Ben laughed as he slid his hand to the tiny bud between her thighs. "Wanna play again?"

39

Anna woke when Ben's elbow hit her ribs. They'd made wonderful, exhausting love and then dozed off. If she wasn't mistaken, Ben's efforts to control his PTSD symptoms this evening had come to an end.

He was sound asleep, thrashing in bed, the sheets wrapped tightly around him. With help from the night-light, she was able to avoid being hurt as he lashed out with his fists and feet. She glanced at the digital clock and saw it was 3:22 a.m. Time enough, after he'd fallen asleep, to begin to dream.

And for him to relive the trauma—in his case, several traumas, she believed—that made his existence, awake and asleep, a living hell.

She sat up carefully and quietly, not wanting to wake him yet. She felt like a surgeon holding a scalpel over an unconscious patient whose life was in her hands. Her efforts to heal would be equally life-altering and had to be accomplished with equal precision and attention to detail.

Ben's denial of his problem, and everyone's willingness to believe him when he said he was fine, had made it difficult to help him with therapy in her office. But like him, she didn't have to be *on* the job to *do* the job. Ben seemed willing to let her help. And she was determined not to let him fall through the cracks.

Anna hadn't looked too closely at her motives for becoming personally involved in her patient's life. She knew better than to try to rescue someone with PTSD. The individual had to heal himself. But there was something about this man that made her want to go the extra mile.

There was a great deal about Ben Benedict to admire besides his good looks. He had medals to prove his courage in battle, but she'd seen his valor for herself when he'd saved Rocky, despite the wounds the dog had given him. He not only had compassion for his friend who'd died doing his duty, but he'd done his best not to end the life of the boy who'd killed him.

Anna had seen at the hospital that Ben loved his family and was determined to be strong for them. And despite his protestations, he'd rescued a crippled animal when no one else wanted it. Tonight she'd learned he was a tender and passionate lover.

Was it any wonder she'd thrown out the rule book and followed her heart? This was a man worth knowing. A man worth saving. And maybe, one day, a man worth loving.

The problem was, as things currently stood, the man in her bed wasn't capable of loving her back. Ben would need to heal himself before he could love her. Which was why she wanted him to deal with his trauma sooner, rather than later.

To complicate matters, Anna wasn't sure how much time she was going to have with Ben before he bolted from her apartment—and her life. Which made every moment precious in terms of helping him to heal.

Recovery from PTSD was a long and torturous process. Her first goal was to make sure Ben perceived her home—and her embrace—as a place where he could feel safe, a haven from the unpredictable danger he lived with day-to-day on the streets.

Her next goal was to help him acknowledge his awful memories and mourn them, rather than reliving those traumatic events over and over in his dreams and waking life.

If he stuck around long enough, she was certain she could help him with the final necessary element in his PTSD recovery. He would need to transform his feelings of helplessness during an attack into empowerment. And, what might be most difficult for Ben, give up his need for isolation in favor of more social connections.

Three little steps. It sounded simple. It was anything but.

Ben groaned and shoved against the covers that bound him.

"Ben," Anna said quietly from her side of the bed. "I'm here. You're all right."

He made a guttural sound in his throat.

Anna debated whether to touch him and decided it was worth the risk. She put a firm hand on his shoulder.

He knocked it off with a loud, "No!"

"Ben," she said more loudly, rubbing her tingling wrist. "Wake up."

He sat bolt upright with a cry. She watched him shudder before his shoulders drooped. He swiped the back of his hand across his mouth and said, "God. That was awful."

"Do you want to talk about it?"

"No."

"All right."

He held his hands out in front of him and stared at them. "There's always so much blood."

"Yours?" she asked.

"No."

She didn't ask whose blood it was. She waited for him to tell her.

"It's the kid's blood on my hands. Which is crazy," he said. "Because I never touched him."

"Which kid is that?"

He hesitated, then said, "The nine- or ten-year-old I shot nine months ago in Afghanistan. I shouldn't even have been there. It was some lieutenant's assignment, but he got sick. I was told to terminate whoever showed up to accept some stolen munitions. The kid stepped in front of my target at the last instant and got killed instead."

"There was a lot of blood when he was shot?" Anna asked.

"Yeah. Even with that horrendous wound, he must not

have been dead, because he was still pumping blood into his chest cavity when I got to him. What was left of it, anyway."

"Was anyone there with you. Any other soldiers?"

"My spotter."

"Did he make it out okay?"

Ben turned aside. Very softly he said, "No."

"That must have been hard for you. I'm sorry—"

"*Sorry*'s an easy word to say, Doc," he said harshly. "It doesn't do much good when a man doesn't come home to his family."

"You went to see your spotter's family when you got home?"

He nodded. "Dan's wife was inconsolable. The kids were too young to know what was happening, just scared because their mom was crying so hard."

"And you felt guilty for being alive when your friend was dead?"

He turned harrowed eyes on her. "I felt guilty because I was glad it was him and not me."

Anna had heard other soldiers make the same observation. "That sounds like a normal human reaction."

"If you say so."

"Tell me more about the boy who died."

"He was in the wrong place at the wrong time."

"Any chance he was involved with the stolen munitions?" Anna asked.

"He probably was. Even so, he didn't deserve to die."

"You told me you never touched the boy, right?"

Ben nodded.

"So when you remember this child in your dreams, why are your hands always covered in blood?"

"I have no fucking idea!" he snarled.

The ferocity of his reply suggested to Anna that the answer to that question was significant. And that he'd blocked it because it was so painful. She got up from the bed and pulled off the T-shirt she'd worn to bed, then shoved the male boxers she was wearing down over her ankles, leaving her naked.

"I'm not sure what you're doing," Ben said with the beginning of a grin, "but I like the direction this is going."

She came around the foot of the bed and reached out a hand to him. "Time for a shower."

He flushed, but didn't deny the need for it. The sheets where he lay were damp with fetid sweat. He struggled to untangle himself, swearing under his breath, then dropped his feet over the edge of the bed and stood before her naked, which was how he'd gone to bed.

Aside from his minor wounds, his body looked healthy and powerful, with no inkling of the struggle she knew was going on inside his head. He ignored her hand and scooped her up into his arms, making her laugh in surprise and delight.

Penelope rose and circled her kittens anxiously. Ben turned to the cat and said, "Go back to sleep, Penelope. Unless you'd like to join us."

Penelope sat back down in the basket that contained her kittens.

Ben turned with Anna held snug in his arms and headed for the shower.

40

Anna lathered her hands with gardenia-scented soap and began washing away the layer of sweat that covered Ben's chest and shoulders.

He sniffed at the soap as he took it from her and said, "Smells like you."

"It's my favorite."

As she moved her soapy hands over his body, she measured the breadth of his shoulders, his trim waist, the corded muscle over bone. "You're really fit," she said.

"I'm a soldier—was a soldier," he corrected immediately.

She played with the black curls on his chest, hearing his breath catch as she scratched a fingernail across his budded nipple. She ran her hand down between his legs and said, "This needs washing, too."

She was paying close attention to what she was doing, watching the transformation of his body with awe and pleasure, when he slid a finger inside her.

She looked up in surprise, which was when he captured her mouth with his. His mouth was tender, coaxing, and Anna responded to his need and fed her own.

She had never had sex in the shower. There were myriad sensations to enjoy. The spray of warm water on her body. The avid look in his eyes as he spread her legs, so he could reach her better with his hand. The feel of his mouth at her throat as the passion built between them.

He knew where to touch her with his thumb to heighten her

arousal. In a moment he would be inside her—which was when she realized she had no protection against pregnancy. A condom would have been difficult to manage in the shower anyway.

She never should have let this go so far. She smoothed her hand over Ben's wet hair and said, "Ben, we need to stop."

"Uh," he grunted, apparently lost in a well of pleasure.

"I don't want to have unprotected sex again. Please, stop."

He wasn't so far gone that he didn't hear her. He lifted his head and looked at her with lambent eyes. She saw the flare of frustration in his eyes when he remembered that they'd used up the condoms she had on hand.

He moved her out of the spray of water, then sank to his knees. And placed his mouth at the juncture of her thighs.

She gripped his hair, thinking to pull him back to his feet, but his tongue was doing something that nearly made her knees buckle. "Oh," was all she could manage.

He slipped one of her legs up over his shoulder, spreading her thighs wide so she felt vulnerable and exposed.

Which she was. To his mouth. And his hands. And the gentle lave of his tongue and the nip of his teeth.

She leaned back against the tile wall and let him have his way with her. She could feel the orgasm building inside her, sending spirals of feeling through her legs and belly and up through her body to the back of her nose. She opened her mouth wide to groan deep in her throat with the exquisite pleasure of it.

As the orgasm crested, she was left quivering. She looked down and realized her fingernails had made grooved marks in Ben's left shoulder. He lifted her leg down and held her waist to keep her steady as he rose to his feet and pulled her into his arms.

Her breasts were nestled against his chest, and she could feel his arousal. She reached down to touch, but he caught her hands and wrapped them around his waist and said, "That was for you. I can wait."

She looked up at him, leaned up on tiptoe and kissed him slowly and tenderly, lingering over the touch of lips and tongues. "That was…lovely. Thank you, Ben."

She could feel his smile against her mouth as he said, "The pleasure was entirely mine."

She shivered suddenly, as the last of the hot water disappeared and the shower turned cold.

"We'd better get out of here," he said, quickly rinsing the two of them off one more time and shutting off the water. "And see if we can get some sleep. We have a busy day tomorrow."

It took her a moment to realize what he'd said. "We? Does that mean you're going to let me ride along with you?"

"I thought that was what you wanted," he said as he wrapped her in a towel and began to rub her dry.

"It is."

"I only have one favor to ask."

"What's that?" She was ready to do anything to accommodate him.

He shot her a rueful glance and said, "Remind me to stop at a drugstore at the end of the day."

41

Anna was surprised when, as they were finishing their break-fast of scrambled eggs and bacon, Ben said, "I have a funeral to attend today."

"I thought Waverly was being buried tomorrow."

"He is. Epifanio is being laid to rest this morning."

It only took a moment for Anna to figure out who Epifanio was. "The boy who died on Friday? The one whose murderer you caught?"

"I spent five months getting to know that kid. It was awful having to tell his *abuela* he was dead. Especially when he was turning his life around."

"You must have cared a great deal for him."

Ben nodded.

Anna surmised that Ben had nodded because he couldn't speak. The PTSD would keep his emotions right on the surface. She marveled again at how good he was at concealing his feelings and keeping his condition hidden from his family.

"May I go with you?"

She could see he was torn between having her support and giving her the chance to see him in what was sure to be an emotional situation.

"All right," he said at last. "I need to make a quick trip home to change my clothes, feed Rocky and arrange for the housekeeper to let him out in the backyard to run."

While Ben was gone, Anna called Ike and told him she

needed someone in the practice to cover her patients for the rest of the week.

"Are you all right, Anna?" he asked in a concerned voice.

"I just need some personal time."

"Anna, does this personal time have anything to do with Agent Benedict?"

She opened her mouth to lie to him, but the truth came pouring out. "ICE is requiring a medical release from me for Ben to go back to work. Everyone seems to agree he needs to be on the job to deal with a matter of national security. I decided that the best way to monitor his behavior is to ride along with him and his partner."

"Agent Benedict is your patient, Anna. There are lines—"

"Once I clear him for duty, he'll no longer be my patient."

After another weighty pause Ike said, "Then under what authority are you monitoring his behavior? Wouldn't it be better to assign another doctor to his case?"

"He's dangerously vulnerable, Ike. I can help him. I know I can. I just need to spend time with him, more time than I would have in one-hour sessions in my office."

"You know better than to get personally involved with a patient, Anna. I strongly recommend that you refer Agent Benedict to another doctor. I'd also like the chance to talk some sense into you. I've got a free hour this afternoon at two. Can you come in?"

"I know you have my best interests at heart, Ike. But this is a special case. It requires special treatment."

"Anna, listen to yourself."

"I am listening to myself, Ike. I'm listening to my heart. And it tells me this is the right thing to do."

"Come see me, Anna. Let's talk."

"I'm going to be spending the day with Agent Benedict. I promise I'll keep in touch while I'm out of the office, in case one of my patients is in crisis and needs to see me personally."

"Anna, I have to warn you, if I discover you've committed a breach of ethics, I'll have to report you to the American Psychiatric Association. Your license to practice may be at risk. Think long and hard before you continue on this path."

Anna was shaking when she hung up the phone. She didn't like seeing her actions through Ike's eyes. She was breaking all the rules that had been set up to maintain the line between doctor and patient, which were intended for the good of both parties.

But breaking the rules just didn't seem to matter where Ben Benedict was concerned—which should have been her first warning that she was walking down a slippery slope.

Anna hurried to dress in a long-sleeved, black A-line dress, black tights and short high-heeled boots. Before she had time to really consider what Ike had said, Ben showed up at her front door clean shaven and wearing a tailored black wool-and-silk suit and a gray wool overcoat.

He smiled, and she actually felt butterflies in her stomach.

"Ready?" he asked.

They decided to take her car, which was parked closer than his. As they walked the two blocks to her Mercedes, Anna asked, "Can Epifanio's family afford to have him buried?" If not, the District would arrange an indigent burial.

"His only local relative is his grandmother, Mrs. Fuentes," Ben replied. "The funeral mass is being held at Our Lady Mother Catholic Church. An anonymous donation provided the funds for a casket and a nearby cemetery plot, so Epifanio's *abuela* can visit his grave."

Anna was imagining how much a burial plot within the District would cost. And realizing just how close Ben must have gotten to the boy. "An anonymous donation?" she said, raising a brow in question. Ben's wealth was also a part of his personnel file.

"Yeah," he said almost belligerently. "Anonymous."

When they reached her sedan, Anna handed Ben the keys. It was a subtle statement, but a powerful one: I trust you with my life.

Anna first started seeing signs of Ben's nerves on the drive to the church. He kept wiping his right palm on his suit pants.

"Are you sure you want to attend Epifanio's funeral?" she asked.

"I owe the kid that much," he said. "Besides, some of the One-Eight members who were friends with Epifanio's older brother Ricardo will show up for the mass. Epifanio's *abuela* is having a funeral reception at her home after the interment, and I'll have a chance to question them in a neutral setting."

Epifanio's funeral was being held in a tiny church made of redbrick painted white, which was wedged between two tall, considerably newer buildings in a run-down residential section of Columbia Heights.

A pitifully small group of people, young males and old women, sat scattered in long, dark wooden pews carved with graffiti. A stained-glass window of Jesus, one of whose out-stretched hands had been replaced by a piece of plywood, rose behind the altar.

Epifanio's *abuela* sat alone in the left front pew wearing a gray, faux-fur-collared coat over a plain black wool dress, to ward off the chill in the barely heated church. Because Ben had chosen to sit directly behind her, and because she was so tiny, Anna was able to make out the silver braids pinned atop her head that were covered by a black lace mantilla. Anna's eyes were drawn to the rhinestone clasp at the old woman's nape attached to a strand of plastic pearls.

During the lengthy Catholic funeral mass, Ben reached for Anna's hand and gripped it tightly. She glanced in his direction and saw his bleak eyes were focused on Epifanio's grandmother, who was sobbing quietly into a white, lace-edged handkerchief.

Anna squeezed Ben's hand in reassurance, and when he looked in her direction, she met his gaze, offering silent solace.

Outside the church after the mass, the wind was blustery, the temperature just above freezing. Storm clouds had gathered, but the frigid rain that threatened never fell. The "anonymous donor" had provided a black limousine to drive Mrs. Fuentes to the cemetery. Anna and Ben followed in Anna's car.

At Epifanio's graveside, where a dozen folding white wooden chairs had been covered by a green tent awning in case of inclement weather, Ben let go of Anna's hand long enough to approach Mrs. Fuentes, to speak softly to her and give her a hug.

He turned and surveyed the crowd through narrowed eyes before he took Anna's hand once again and headed back to her car.

She bit her tongue just as she was about to ask, "How are you doing?" He'd been holding on to her hand for dear life for the past hour and a half. But he'd survived the funeral of a child he cared about, consoled the child's grandmother, and was now on his way to do his job at a funeral reception.

He was fine.

"I'm a wreck," Ben said, huffing out a breath of air as he started up Anna's car.

"Funerals are never easy," Anna said. And he had another one to attend tomorrow. What surprised her was his admission that he wasn't handling Epifanio's death as well as he wished. "Want to skip the reception?"

He shook his head. "I need to talk to the One-Eight."

"Maybe I could help. What is it, exactly, that you're trying to find out?"

He glanced sideways at her and said, "I can't tell you that."

She frowned. "What's the big secret?"

"I'm not at liberty to say."

She laughed. "That sounds like something from a spy movie. What could the government possibly want with a bunch of gang kids? I know," she said. "They're trafficking in really big guns. Rockets, probably. Something like that. Am I right?"

"Leave it alone, Doc."

But Anna couldn't leave it alone. "Is that why you had to stay on the job? Why your boss wanted to keep you working when you should have taken a break? There's some terrorist threat here in D.C.?"

He didn't answer.

"Oh, my God," she said, staring at him in horror. "That's it."

"You ask the questions and answer them, too," he said sardonically.

"But I'm right, aren't I?" She crossed her arms and smiled smugly. "I know I'm right." Her smile disappeared. If she was right, it also meant that Ben Benedict was likely to be the victim of even more trauma, because a bunch of terrorists weren't going down without a fight.

"Why are you doing this, Ben? ICE or whoever is involved in finding these terrorists could surely handle the situation without you. Can't you let this go? Can't you let someone else save the world?"

"It's not the world I'm worried about," he said quietly. "It's my friends and family right here in D.C."

Anna sucked in a long, slow breath of air. He'd as much as confirmed that there was a threat to the nation's capital. "What kind of danger are we in? Is it a dirty bomb?"

He grimaced. "Does it matter what kind of weapon gets used? There are lots of ways to exterminate a population."

Anna shuddered.

"We're here," he said as he pulled into a narrow driveway bordered by chain link fence.

Epifanio's grandmother had an apartment in a small frame house peeling flakes of a color green that was so ugly it had likely been bought on sale. The house faced an alley behind a renovated brownstone. "I wish I'd had the chance to know your grandson," Anna said as she and Ben greeted Mrs. Fuentes.

The woman said something in Spanish, and Anna turned to Ben to translate for her.

"She said that you're beautiful. That I should hold you

close and keep you safe," he said as he ushered her farther into the room.

Anna flushed.

Ben had hold of her hand again as he headed into a small space that served as living room, dining room and kitchen. Anna could see a hallway that led to what she supposed must be the bedrooms.

Ben walked right up to a tall, thin boy with brown skin, a black mustache and goatee and piercing brown eyes and said, "Hello, Juan." Ben and the boy he'd greeted exchanged an elaborate handshake.

"Who's your lady friend?" the boy asked, creating a gun with a thumb and forefinger and shooting it in Anna's direction.

"She's a nice lady, so be nice to her," Ben said. "Anna, this is Juan Alvarez, leader of the One-Eight."

Anna couldn't extend her right hand because Ben was still holding it, so she smiled and said, "Hello, Juan. It's nice to meet you."

"Too bad 'bout your cop friend," Juan said. "Don't like cops, but he was okay."

"Thank you," Ben grated out. "Likewise about Epifanio."

Juan shrugged. "Life, man."

Anna could feel the tension in Ben's hand and arm, see it in his shoulders. His upper lip was damp with sweat. She watched as he licked his lips. "Would you like to get something to eat or drink?" she asked, lifting her chin toward the selection of casseroles and desserts in plastic and aluminum containers on the kitchen table.

"Not for me." He turned back to Juan and said, "I hear the One-Eight has been moving around Georgetown."

"You got good ears," Juan replied. "What else you hear?"

"That you're planning to intercept a package being brought in for MS."

"Could be. You got a problem with that?"

"I do if the package is what I think it is," Ben said.

"You know what's coming?" Juan asked. "How 'bout telling me? Drugs? Guns? Counterfeit stuff? What?"

"Nothing that harmless," Ben said.

The boy's eyes widened. "No kidding?"

"You find out where that package is headed, you don't follow it, you call me. Okay?"

"Why should I?" Juan asked.

"You want to be around to see that baby you started in your girlfriend get born and grow up, you call me," Ben said firmly.

"I ain't afraid of those MS dudes," Juan said, jutting his chest out.

"It isn't MS you need to worry about. It's the package they're bringing here." He held up a hand to keep the gang leader from speculating further about the contents of the package. "You're the man, Juan. Take care of yourself. Call me."

"I'll think about it," Juan replied as a very pregnant girl slid her arm through his.

"Hi, Norma," Ben said. "How soon is that baby due?"

"Any day, Mr. Benedict. Me and Juan are getting married. Wanna come to the wedding on Saturday?"

Anna felt Ben's muscles tighten. Felt his hand trembling in hers.

"I wish we could," Anna said. "But we've already made other plans. Thank you so much for asking."

Before Ben could speak, while he was still caught in whatever flashback or memory or moment of indecision that was plaguing him, Anna dragged him toward the front door, where she waved good-bye to Epifanio's grandmother.

By the time they got to her car, Ben was fine again.

"You didn't have to do that," he snapped as he slid behind the wheel. "I would have been fine in a moment or two."

"It seemed to me you'd accomplished what you came here to do," she said as she buckled her seat belt. "I thought maybe we should spend the rest of the day doing something fun."

"Like what?" he asked.

"How about the Smithsonian? Or the Lincoln Memorial?"

"How about the streets of Georgetown?"

Anna sighed. She knew if they went to Georgetown, he would spend the day looking for signs of activity by MS or the 1-8. She was going to have her work cut out for her getting him to relax. "All right. We'll do a walking tour."

"Perfect," he said.

Anna kept him walking and talking—and even got him to laugh once—on the streets of Georgetown.

But he was distracted, and finally said he had to get home to check on Rocky. "I also have a eulogy to write for Waverly's funeral tomorrow."

Anna was disappointed. It seemed Ben was planning to drop her off at her townhome and go home by himself.

Then his eyes flared with an avidity that made her body tremble in anticipation. He grasped her hand and headed for the car. "And I need to make a stop at the drugstore."

42

Anna was surprised to see Rocky standing on three legs waiting for Ben at his front door, tongue lolling and tail wagging. She watched as Ben bent to scratch the animal behind the ears. "Hello, boy," Ben said.

Ben's home was stunning. His four-story row house in Georgetown was impossibly expensive and impeccably decorated. Anna felt breathless as she followed Ben and his dog into the modern kitchen with the groceries they'd purchased on the way home.

"I'm glad you saved Rocky," she said, watching as Ben carefully lifted Rocky's bandage and checked his stitches.

"I'm not keeping him," Ben said flatly. "He's here till I can find him a good home. Luckily my housekeeper likes dogs. He doesn't need more exercise than he gets in the backyard until those stitches come out next week."

He still seemed awfully concerned, Anna thought, about a dog he wasn't going to keep.

Ben began pulling out the steaks he'd bought to grill for them. She'd wondered why he'd bought three and watched with amazement as he got out a knife and cut the third steak into chunks. He put the chopped-up New York strip in a bowl with dry dog food and set the bowl on the kitchen floor.

"No wonder he was wagging his tail when you showed up," Anna said with a laugh.

"He'd wag his tail at me if I was an ax murderer," Ben replied gruffly. "Dogs aren't picky about who they love."

"And people are?"

He eyed her askance. "Forget the therapy, Doc. Let's just have a nice meal and go to bed. It's been a long day."

Anna didn't need Ben to answer her question. She was pretty sure she already knew the answer. What woman had rejected him, she wondered? She was jealous of the woman he'd loved and angry at her for leaving Ben so wounded.

"You must have been very much in love with her," she said quietly.

He frowned in confusion and replied, "The only woman I ever loved was Mary Jane Harlow, my senior year in high school. Soldiers don't have time for love."

Just sex, Anna thought when Ben didn't say it. Could a high school sweetheart have wounded him this badly? She bit back a gasp as she suddenly realized who had rejected him.

His mother.

Anna had read in Ben's personnel file that he was one of five boys born to his mother. After his parents' divorce, he and his younger brother Carter had gone to live with his father. The fourth son, Darlington—a classic Southern name, she'd thought—had died when he was four years old.

Anna couldn't imagine how any mother could give up two of her children, much less how she could decide which two she was sending away. But Abigail Benedict Hamilton had sent two of her children to live with their father. And Ben had been one of them.

He must have felt abandoned and rejected. He must have been hurt terribly. And because he'd spent that first year away in a bachelor household, he wouldn't have been encouraged to express his grief and resentment. She suspected exactly the opposite had happened. He would have bottled all those feelings up inside.

And become the lonely man he was.

As she watched Ben move efficiently around the kitchen, Anna realized this splendid man was more wounded than she'd imagined. She guessed he'd kept himself aloof because he feared that whoever he loved might abandon him, as his mother had done so long ago.

Anna wanted to hold this outcast in her arms and tell him he was a lovable human being. That his mother had been sorely tried when she'd made her decision to send him away, and that it had nothing to do with him as a worthwhile human being. But she knew he wasn't ready to hear the words.

So she settled for a tender embrace.

Anna stepped in front of Ben and put her arms around his waist and leaned her head against his chest so she could hear the beat of his heart.

"What is this all about?" he said, smiling down at her.

She waited for him to realize for himself that she only wanted to hold him and be held in return.

A moment later, he dropped the boxes of food in his hands onto the counter and folded his arms around her.

43

Anna was driving. But no matter how hard she tried to turn the wheel, she couldn't steer the car. She was heading straight for a pregnant woman who stared back at her with wide, frightened eyes. Anna turned to Lisele and shouted, "Do something! Help me stop the car! No no no no no no no no no no!"

"Wake up, damn it!"

Anna was being shaken hard as she awoke. She sagged against Ben's naked chest and swallowed back a sob. His arms surrounded her trembling body as they sat huddled together in the center of his king-size bed.

Rocky was whining beside the bed.

"Go lie down," Ben told the dog. He waited until Rocky was settled in his bed in the corner of the bedroom before he turned his attention back to Anna. "Your turn to do some talking, Doc," he said brusquely. "What the hell was that all about? I thought you told me your sister was driving the car."

"She was."

"So why did I just hear you yell for someone to help *you* stop the car?"

"I'd rather not say," she mumbled.

"Oh, no, you don't," he said, lifting her chin with a forefinger and forcing her to look at him. "I get little enough sleep as it is. If I've got to deal with my demons, you have to deal with yours. I'm getting tired of waking up in the middle of the night. Spill it, Doc."

She scooted away from him and sat cross-legged on her side of the bed. "All right! In my dream, I'm driving the car, the one in the accident with Lisele. I try to steer away from the pregnant woman, but the wheel won't move. I ask Lisele to help me, but she just stares at me with this sad look in her eyes."

"So were you driving, or not?"

"She was driving."

"So why are you driving in your dream?"

She shrugged helplessly. "I guess that's my way of trying to make things turn out differently."

"Doesn't work, does it?" Ben said.

"I've always felt to blame for what happened. For the accident, I mean."

"How was the accident your fault?" Ben asked.

Anna took a deep breath and felt her way slowly through what she said next, trying to be as honest with Ben as she wanted him to be with her. "I probably should have gone to the concert by myself. That way I could have stayed over. Lisele would have spent the weekend with Paul. And everyone would still be alive today."

She gasped and put her hands up to cover her mouth. "Oh, God."

"You okay?"

"I don't think I've ever considered my dream quite that way before." She met his gaze and said quietly, "Thank you, Ben."

"You're welcome, Doc," he said as he picked her up and settled her in his lap. "Now would you mind explaining it to me?"

"Don't you see?" she said. "In my dream, I'm the one driving because I should have been alone that night. I should have let my sister stay home with Paul. I should have let her go her own way. If I hadn't been so jealous—so selfish—she might still be with me today."

"Are you okay with all that now?" Ben asked.

Anna pushed Ben back prone in his bed and laid her head on his chest, trying to absorb what she'd just learned about her own PTSD. "I will be okay, once I forgive myself. Again. Let's go back to sleep. We both need our rest."

But once she was snuggled up next to him, rest was the last thing on Anna's mind. She lay stiff in Ben's embrace, until he leaned down and nudged her lips with his own.

"I don't want to keep you up," she murmured.

"Oh, I'm up all right," he said with a chuckle. He reached into the top drawer of the end table and handed her a condom. "Care to help me out?"

Anna laughed softly as she slipped the condom on him, then reached down to guide Ben Benedict to a warm, safe place, far from the dangerous world outside the door.

44

Anna woke the day of Waverly Collins's funeral feeling relaxed and refreshed. She hadn't suffered another nightmare after they'd gone to sleep the second time. One look at Ben told her he hadn't been as lucky.

He was lying in bed staring at the ceiling, one hand behind his head, the other scratching his lean belly. There were dark circles under his red-rimmed eyes.

How amazing that a man so wounded himself should be the one to help her see the truth about her own demons. She might have the same terrible nightmare in the future, but when she awoke, she would remind herself that there was nothing wrong in having asked Lisele to come with her.

But she would also acknowledge that she should have allowed her sister to decline when she learned of Lisele's plans on Sunday with Paul. Insisting that Lisele come with her had resulted in a tragedy, but it was time to forgive herself for being human and for wanting to keep her twin close for as long as she could.

And she owed her revelation to a grouchy man who'd had his sleep interrupted.

Anna wanted to return the favor. She wanted to help Ben figure out why he had blood on his hands in his nightmare when he looked down on the body of the boy he'd killed in Afghanistan. The blood on his hands meant something. The question was *what?*

It could simply represent guilt. Lady Macbeth never could

get the blood off her hands, no matter how often she washed them. But Ben was a soldier. He'd killed before. So there had to be something more to his dream.

Maybe some of his spotter's blood had splattered on him when he'd been killed. Maybe that was where the blood on his hands—and the guilt—had come from.

Or maybe it wasn't the boy's death in Afghanistan that was troubling Ben at all. Maybe it was the death of some other child in some other war.

The death of some other child.

Anna felt gooseflesh prickle her arms. She glanced at Ben, wondering if she should ask the question that had suddenly come to mind. Wondering if she was right, and if so, whether Ben was ready to confront what might be the true source of his dream.

"Why didn't you wake me?" she asked as she leaned over his body, her chin on his chest, to trace the dark circle under one of his eyes with the pad of her thumb.

"I figured one of us might as well get some sleep," he said, caressing the line of her jaw.

"Was it the same nightmare?" She sat up, holding the sheet to her naked body under her arms.

He rubbed his eyes with his fists as he sat up across from her, leaning back against the wooden headboard, the sheet slipping down to his naked hips. "Yeah."

"Ben, I have a question. It might sound a little strange, but humor me."

"Go for it, Doc."

"How old were you when your younger brother died?"

"That's history," he said abruptly.

"What happened to humoring me?" she said with a coaxing smile, reaching out to lay a hand on his thigh. He shifted away under the sheet and she knew he was avoiding her touch because she'd hit on a very touchy subject. "How old were you when he died?" she asked again.

"Seven," he said abruptly.

"And Darlington was four, is that right?"

Ben nodded.

"How did he die?"

"Is this really necessary?"

Anna nodded.

"He fell from a tree and broke his neck."

Anna frowned. That didn't sound like the sort of death that resulted in a lot of blood. Or any blood, necessarily. "Were you there when it happened?"

He hesitated so long, she thought he wasn't going to answer her. At last he said, "I was the one who told Mother that Darling was dead. She was in the kitchen peeling potatoes for dinner. We were going to have meat loaf and mashed potatoes, my favorite meal. We didn't end up eating anything. I went to bed hungry that night."

"When you found him, what made you think your brother was dead?" Anna asked, bringing Ben back to the subject she wanted him to discuss.

"There was so much blood, I—" He cut himself off and stared at her. He held his hands out in front of him, palms up. "There was so much blood," he repeated, frowning. "I got it all over my hands."

"Where did the blood come from?" Anna asked quietly.

He looked confused for a moment as he stared at his hands. Then he met her gaze and said, "There was an eight-inch-high spiked iron railing around the tree. We'd just moved into the house. Mother had already caught me climbing that oak, and she warned me to stay out of that tree. She was afraid I'd fall and get impaled on one of those spikes."

Anna waited for him to say more, to finish the story, but he didn't. "Is that what happened to Darlington?"

"I told Darling not to follow me," he said angrily. "I told him he was too little to be climbing so high. But he didn't listen. And he fell."

His brow furrowed as if he were in pain, and he leaned forward and put his hands to his ears.

Anna stopped herself just in time from reaching out. Or from saying anything. Ben didn't need comfort right now. He needed the space to think. And remember.

"He screamed when he fell," he said as though the words were torn from him. Ben looked at her in wonder. "That must be the scream I keep hearing in my nightmare. The sound stopped so suddenly, it was like someone clicked off a loud TV."

He stayed silent for so long, Anna prompted, "But you were still up in the tree?"

"I couldn't move. I was frozen."

Anna imagined a dark-haired, blue-eyed, seven-year-old boy up a tree, trembling, crying, probably in shock. He didn't tell her those things, but she knew he was remembering them, or something very similar. Knowing his brother had fallen, was lying hurt on the ground, knowing he was frozen in the branches above, must have been terrifying.

"When I finally got down to Darling, I saw that two of the spikes had poked through his shoulder near his neck."

He huffed out an anxious breath. "I tried to pull him off, but he was stuck." The look in his eyes was stark as he remembered and evaluated as an adult the events that had happened when he was a child.

"I don't know if Darling's neck was broken when he fell," he said bitterly, "or if I killed him trying to get him off those goddamned spikes."

He opened his hands again and stared at them. "The blood...got all over my hands. Darling's eyes were wide open, but no matter how much I shouted his name, he didn't answer me."

Darling! Wake up! Darling, be okay, please! Anna heard Ben's childish cries in her imagination and felt a shiver run down her spine.

Ben rubbed his hands over his face and made a sound of frustration in his throat. "Why is this bothering me now?"

"Only you know the answer to that," Anna said.

He twisted his lips ruefully. "You think so?"

Anna surmised that the child he'd killed in Afghanistan had reminded him of the brother whose death he felt he'd caused so many years ago. She waited to be sure he'd made the connection for himself.

A moment later, Anna heard a gurgling sound and realized Ben was strangling a sob. He turned his head away from her and she watched his Adam's apple bob up and down as he swallowed back the tears. And the pain. He swiped a hand across his eyes and let it drop onto the sheet.

Anna stayed very quiet and very still, letting Ben deal with his feelings and his memories. When he appeared to have his emotions under control, she said, "Did your mother blame you for the accident?"

"She never knew the truth," he blurted. His face flamed as he met Anna's gaze. "I never told her I was climbing the tree and Darling followed me up. I let her think he'd been climbing on his own and that I'd found him like that."

A single tear streamed down his cheek.

"And your parents were so devastated themselves, they had little time to question you more closely. Or to help you deal with your grief. And your guilt."

"All I know is that things went downhill pretty damn fast after that. Mother was pregnant with Rhett and she went so crazy the doctors thought she was going to lose the baby. How could I tell her the truth? She would have hated me."

Anna had another sudden realization. "How soon after Darlington's death did your parents divorce?"

"Within a year."

Which meant that, soon after the accident for which he blamed himself, his mother had sent him away, Anna realized.

"She got rid of me," Ben said dully. "As fast as she could."

"Oh, Ben," Anna said, her heart going out to him. "I'm sure it wasn't like that."

"Kill the messenger," he said. "I can see how that expression got started. After I told Mother what happened to Darling, she couldn't stand to look at me." He met Anna's gaze with pain-filled eyes and snarled, "I guess seeing me reminded her that her precious Darling was dead."

"Is that an accurate memory?" Anna asked. "Could you have imagined your mother's rejection, because you felt guilty? Is it possible *you* were the one who couldn't face *her?*"

Ben was silent.

Anna reached out a hand but he pulled away from her touch.

He kept his gaze turned away from her as he asked, "Do I need to tell them the truth? Is that what's going to heal me?"

"Only you can decide that," Anna said. "Are you afraid of what your parents will think?"

"If there's one thing my father preached to my brothers and me our whole lives, it was the importance of truth. And honor. This is a lie so big…"

"That he might reject you, too?"

"You don't pull your punches, do you, Doc?"

"I want you well."

His lip curled cynically. "And telling the truth will help me get well?"

"It might clear your conscience," Anna said. "It might also stir up unhappy memories for you and your family. You have to be the judge of what's best."

"What purpose would it serve to tell them the truth now?" Ben asked belligerently. "I kept silent about something pretty damned important. How the hell am I supposed to judge what's best for my mother and father at this point in time?"

"Maybe the only person who needed to know the truth is you," Anna said. "Maybe it's enough that you forgive yourself."

"I'll think about it, Doc," he said. "But not right now. Right now, I've got a funeral to attend."

He left the bed and headed for the shower.

Anna watched him go. She didn't follow him, guessing that he needed time alone. He would want to grieve. And think. And decide what was best to do.

But now that Ben knew the true source of his nightmares, he could begin to heal.

45

Ben couldn't seem to make his feet move. He stood at the entrance to the National Cathedral, a historic and breathtakingly beautiful white stone edifice. Inside he knew he would find elaborately carved wooden benches and stunning stained-glass windows. It was an exquisite setting for such a tragic occasion.

He'd spent the past hour at home rereading his eulogy and preparing himself to bury his best friend. But all the while, he'd been wondering whether he ought to use this occasion to take his parents aside and admit the truth of what had happened more than two decades ago.

On the other hand, what possible difference could it make now if he confessed his part in Darling's death?

In his mind's eye, he watched as his mother knelt by Darling's lifeless body.

"Was he like this when you found him?" she'd asked as she tenderly brushed a lock of dark hair off Darling's perfect brow.

"Yes," he'd managed to gasp.

She'd grabbed Ben's hands, where Darling's blood was still red, but increasingly sticky. "Why is there blood all over your hands, Ben? What did you do?"

Maybe she'd known the truth, or guessed it. Maybe that was why she'd sent him away.

He was jerked from his thoughts when Anna took his hand. She looked at him with concern in her eyes. "Are you ready to go inside?"

"As ready as I'll ever be." Ben looked around at the sea of

blue uniforms that surrounded them. Cops really did do it right. Every cop in the District who could be here today was. Lives should be remembered. Deaths should be solemnized.

Ben was distracted when Anna reached up to rearrange his dark blue tie, more as a way to get close and look into his eyes, he thought, than because his tie needed adjustment.

"You okay?" she asked.

He'd been saying it for days. He thought it was more true now than ever before. "I'm fine." Although he wasn't sure how he was going to handle seeing Julia, or whether he would make it through the Episcopal service without breaking down. Which he didn't want to do. Not in front of his parents. Not when he'd just decided he was going to tell them about Darling.

Anna reached down and laced her fingers through his. "Shall we go in?"

As they entered the nave of the cathedral, a policeman with a list on a clipboard checked for Ben's name and said, "First pew, left-hand side, sir. Your name, ma'am?"

Anna started beside him. "Oh. Annagreit Schuster."

The policeman looked. And looked again. "I don't see it here."

"She's with me," Ben said.

"I'm sorry, sir, there's no seating left for visitors."

Ben tightened his grip on Anna's hand. He needed her. He couldn't do this alone. "She's not a visitor. She's with me."

"Sir, I can't allow—"

"You must be Dr. Schuster," he heard his mother say from behind him.

He turned with Anna and found his mother and the senator standing in the nave. She was wearing a simple black A-line sheath, black gloves and a small black hat with black net that covered half her face. Her skin looked ghostly white behind the black net, but she appeared composed.

"Yes, I'm Dr. Schuster," Anna answered, easing her hand from Ben's to take his mother's outstretched hand.

"I'm Ben's mother. Please call me Abby." She turned to the senator and said, "This is Julia's father."

"Good afternoon, Senator Hamilton," Anna said.

The senator didn't offer his hand, merely nodded without speaking.

"It's so nice to meet you at last," his mother said to Anna. She turned to the policeman with the clipboard and said, "My son and his guest will be sitting in the pew with us."

"Yes, ma'am," the policeman replied.

"Where's Julia?" Ben asked, looking past Ham's shoulder toward the empty nave. He saw distress in his mother's eyes. "She broke down in the car. She asked for a few moments to compose herself but she insisted we come ahead. She should be along soon."

"Maybe I should go talk to her," Ben said.

"She asked to be alone," Ham retorted.

His mother had already slid her arm through Anna's. "Please sit by me, Dr. Schuster," his mother said, guiding Anna away from Ben down the center aisle.

Ben started back out the door to find Julia, but his sleeve got caught on something. He turned and found Ham Hamilton holding a handful of navy blue wool.

"Let her alone," the senator said.

"I just want to make sure she's all right."

"She was fine before you interfered in her life and brought that *cop* sniffing around," Ham said angrily.

"That *cop* was my *best friend,*" Ben said, keeping his voice quiet, because every sound seemed to be amplified in the high ceiling. "Waverly loved Julia. And she loved him."

"I know that! Why the hell do you think she's so broken up? She thought the sun rose and set on that boy. Then the sonofa-bitch went and got himself killed. And you didn't stop him."

"Let go of me, Ham." Ben stared into the senator's eyes until the older man let him go. Ben felt suffocated by the stone walls. He had to get outside into the sunlight.

As he searched for the senator's limousine, Ben told himself Ham was wrong. He wasn't to blame for Julia's despair. There wasn't much he could have done to stop Waverly. And he wasn't responsible for his friend's death.

But you might have killed your little brother. Was his neck really broken when he fell? Or was it only cracked? What if you broke his neck yanking on him, trying to get him free of those spikes?

It wasn't until he was years older that Ben had realized how important it was not to move someone with a neck injury. He hadn't understood that as a child. He'd only wanted to get Darling free of the metal spikes, so he could carry him inside to his mother, who would make him well.

Somewhere along the line Ben had figured out that if Darling had died immediately, he wouldn't have bled so much. Which meant even if his neck was compromised when he fell, he likely wasn't dead when Ben reached him. That Ben very well might have killed him.

He remembered more of his conversation with his mother all those years ago.

"What did you do, Ben?" his mother had cried as she stared at the way Darling's neck hung at an odd angle. "His neck is broken!"

"I didn't do anything!" he'd retorted. "He's the one who climbed the tree. He's the one who fell!"

"You're his older brother. You're supposed to watch out for him. You're supposed to take care of him!"

Ben closed his eyes and felt a tear squeeze from between his lids. It hurt to remember his mother's accusations. He'd forgotten them. Or rather, forced them from his mind. Especially when she'd given him away to his father so soon after the accident.

Are you remembering things correctly? Anna had asked him. *Are you sure she couldn't bear to look at you, that it wasn't you who couldn't bear to look at her?*

He'd had his chances that fateful day to admit the truth. It would have been so easy to add a word or two here or there and say, *I was climbing the tree and...* But he hadn't. Maybe because his mother seemed so ready to blame him for Darling's death. All she would have needed were those six words to condemn him.

In the end, it hadn't mattered. She'd dumped him with his father, removing him from her sight. And her heart.

Or maybe not. Maybe that was what he should ask his mother. Maybe that was the question that needed to be answered all these years later. *Did you stop loving me when Darling died?*

And what did that matter, all these years later? He had a stepmother and a father who loved him and whom he loved. He hardly saw his mother these days. He didn't need her love.

But he did want to stop the nightmares. So maybe these old demons had to be confronted. Maybe it was time to ask, and deal with whatever answer his mother gave him.

He saw the senator's chauffeur standing by a limousine parked not far from the front of the church. "Hello, Stanley. Is Julia still inside the car?"

"Yes, sir," Stanley replied.

"Are the doors locked?"

"No, sir."

"I can get it," he said to forestall the chauffeur from opening the limo's back door. He stepped inside and closed the door after him. He scooted across the bench seat so he was sitting beside Julia and slipped an arm around her shoulder.

"Hey, Little Bit. You ready to come inside?"

It was all he could do to finish his greeting. Julia looked appalling. All the light and joy seemed to have drained out of her. He pulled her tight against him and rocked her in his arms. "It's going to be all right. You're going to get through this."

He didn't know whom he was trying to convince, himself or her.

"I know," she said in a surprisingly calm voice. "I'm ready to go inside now."

"I'm not," he admitted, with an aborted attempt at a smile.

She looked up at him and said, "I want to honor Wave's memory by being as brave as he would expect me to be. That means I have to go inside and listen to people tell me what a wonderful man he was and not break down. I can do that," she said, "because I loved Wave, and I owe him that."

Ben figured he owed his friend no less. "All right," he said, taking her hand in his. "Let's go bury a good man."

And heaven help them both.

46

Ben had been stoic throughout Waverly's funeral. Anna hadn't seen a tear, nor so much as a trembling finger. He'd cleared his throat a couple of times during the beautiful eulogy he'd given for his friend, so she knew he was struggling to cope with his grief. But he'd never lost his composure.

He'd comforted his sister and his mother after Waverly was put into the ground, but he'd never asked to be comforted.

Anna knew better. He was suffering terribly. She watched as everyone in his family, from his father and stepmother on down to his youngest sister, leaned on him. She was astounded, really, at how strong he was—even though she knew it wouldn't take much for that tower of strength to crumble.

She'd helped Ben to understand the source of his nightmares, but that had created a whole other set of problems. She didn't like the detached, dispassionate face she'd seen on him today. It wasn't natural.

"You should have cried," she said as they entered his row house after the funeral.

"What good would that have done?" He reached down to pat Rocky's head, and when the dog lifted his nose, scratched under his chin. "Waverly is dead and gone."

"He was your friend. Your sister's fiancé. He will be missed."

"Yes, he will."

"You men and your damned stoicism," she said angrily. Anna froze, suddenly aware that Rocky's fur had hackled at her tone of voice.

Ben put a hand on the dog's back to calm him. "What's wrong with stoicism?"

"Just cry, for heaven's sake," she said irritably. "Tears don't make you less of a man."

"I can't," he said, swallowing hard.

"Why not?"

"Because if I start, I'm not sure I can stop."

It was a stark admission of vulnerability. One she hadn't expected. "Oh, Ben."

She put her arms around him and held him, giving him the support he wouldn't ask for.

But he didn't cry.

That night, Anna soothed him when he awoke trembling and afraid, tears streaming down his face, and held him as he slept afterward. Apparently, understanding hadn't stopped the nightmares.

She was afraid she was fighting a losing battle. Ben was too used to hiding his trauma, too used to pretending he wasn't in terrible pain. Every time she tried to get behind the shield he held out to keep the world away, she felt like she was butting her head against a stone wall.

Meanwhile, the world wasn't standing still. Ben seemed determined to stay involved in resolving the threatened attack on the District. Anna was deathly afraid that a crisis would come before Ben was ready to deal with it. And that the next trauma would be the one that finally sent him over the edge.

47

The day after Waverly's funeral, Ben had gone back to work driving the streets with Harry Saunders. Anna had come with them. When Harry eyed her suspiciously in the rearview mirror, she'd smiled sweetly back at him.

She'd been a silent witness to his and Harry's futile efforts to find out what kind of weapon was being delivered to MS by Al Qaeda. Information seemed to be in scarce supply. He and Harry spent all day Thursday talking with gang kids—the 1-8, MS, Vatos Locos, Latin Kings—to discover the scuttlebutt.

"Something goin' down, for sure," Ben heard again from the 1-8. "We're gonna mess it up good, though."

"MS got a big deal goin'," he heard from the Latin Kings. "Stay outta the way, if you wanta keep livin', is what I heard."

"Bad stuff happenin'. Bad, bad stuff," he heard from the Vatos Locos.

"Don't know nothin'," Silvio had told him, when he and Harry managed to corner Waverly's CI, who was a member of MS and should have had some information on what Al Qaeda was sending and when it would be delivered.

"That's funny," Ben said. "Everybody else seems to think MS has something coming in. Something big. Something dangerous."

Silvio had glanced around to make sure they weren't being watched and admitted, "Maybe something's coming. Just not sure what, you know."

Ben and Anna spent Thursday night at her townhome.

She'd encouraged him to bring Rocky with him. He hadn't been at all surprised when Penelope arched her back and hissed at the sight of the rottweiler.

What did surprise him was the way Rocky stood poised two short feet from Penelope's basket, his eyes riveted on the cat and her kittens, long after she'd stopped spitting at him and laid back down to nurse her babies.

Ben set Rocky's sleeping pallet down in the living room, as far away from Penelope as he could put it. But when he and Anna woke up Friday morning, Rocky was lying next to the basket containing Penelope and her kittens, his nose on his front paws.

"He's watching over them," Anna said.

"He's just waiting for the chance to swallow those kittens whole," Ben said.

As Ben watched in amusement, Penelope left her mewing, week-old kittens in the basket and stalked right past the rott-weiler, tail held high, as though he didn't exist. Rocky never twitched a muscle.

Maybe Anna was right, he thought. Maybe the dog needed something to take care of, something to watch over. Something to give his life purpose.

As Anna's presence gave his life form and substance.

Ben realized that he both loved and dreaded spending his nights with Anna. When he was with her, she prodded at the raw feelings he kept hidden, urging him to pour them out. She never let up asking questions. She never let up demanding answers.

Afterward, he always sought comfort in her body. And he always found it.

His daytime tremors had stopped. And he'd only had two nightmares since Anna had helped him to remember his part in Darling's death. He hadn't even been screaming when he'd woken up last night, just frantic and confused and sweating and hyperventilating.

She'd leaned close murmuring something—he couldn't

remember what—that had lowered his heart rate and calmed his breathing. She'd gotten him up and into the shower to wash off the stinking smell of fear and rewarded him by soaping his body top to bottom, focusing on the special parts in between. Then she'd dropped to her knees and given him a little extra comfort that had left him trembling.

After she'd gently patted him dry with a soft, fluffy towel, the way girls patted themselves dry, she'd taken him back to bed and held his naked body close to hers for the rest of the night.

Damn it, he felt better now than he had in a long, long while.

The woman was starting to convince him that he wasn't guilty of anything more than being human. He'd been a child when he'd lied to his mother. He might even have misinterpreted her subsequent actions, although he hadn't found the courage yet to confront her and find out the truth.

Anna never mentioned Waverly's death. Or the death of the boy he'd shot to save Waverly's life. Or even the kid he'd accidentally killed in Afghanistan. Sometimes he wondered why. Mostly, he was grateful she didn't.

Ben threw his keys on Anna's dresser and rubbed the back of his neck to ease the tension of another day spent worrying and wondering, with no answers forthcoming.

"Are we still meeting Julia and that girl, Trisha Reynaldo, for lunch tomorrow at Tysons Corner?" Anna called to him from the bathroom, where she was applying some sort of cream to her face to remove her makeup.

"As far as I know," Ben said. "Julia's going to call and let me know which restaurant they end up at."

Anna came into the room, still smoothing cream on her face. It was a feminine ritual he found fascinating.

"Would you mind if I drive separately?" she asked. "I need to stop by my office."

"On Saturday morning?"

"I haven't been at work all week. I need to take care of some details."

"No problem. I'll leave a message on your phone where we're supposed to meet them."

He crossed to Anna and slid his arms around her waist, nuzzling the skin beneath her ear and getting a whiff of something sweet and fruity. "Is that stuff the reason your skin is so beautiful?"

"You've got cold cream on your nose," she said, laughing as she tried to wipe it off with the dry edge of her hand.

"You are so beautiful, Anna," he said, kissing her eyebrow and tasting the bitter cream on her face.

"That stuff's not meant to be ingested," Anna teased as she wiped a small bit of cream from his lip and only ended up smearing it more. "Let me wipe this off and—"

"I can't wait," he said, pulling free the towel she had wrapped around her naked body and using it to gently wipe away the cream that covered her face and neck. "I need you."

He dropped the towel. And lifted her into his arms.

"I need you, too," she whispered. Her eyes locked onto his as he lowered her onto the bed.

He freed himself from his clothing, reached for a condom, then thrust into the welcoming warmth of her. He was frightened for a moment by the intensity of his feelings.

He felt her cool hand on his nape as her tongue slipped into his mouth. She tasted good. She wrapped her legs around his waist and arched her body into his as he reached for the tiny bud that he knew would quickly send her over the edge.

She moaned as her body spasmed, and he made a guttural sound as he spent himself inside her. He pulled her close, his breathing still erratic, his heart pounding.

She lay with her head tucked beneath his chin, her hand across his chest. He felt sated and happy. It was a unique and satisfying experience.

It felt like he was home at last.

48

Ike had discovered what Anna had done with Ben Benedict's records and wanted an explanation. Which was why she'd agreed to meet him in his office early Saturday morning. He expected her to justify her reasons for clearing Ben Benedict for duty as an ICE agent and then closing his file.

She had no idea what she was going to tell him.

"You're looking well, Anna," Ike said as she entered his office and sat in the leather chair across from his desk.

"Don't light that," she said as he held a match to the bowl of a meerschaum pipe.

"You never minded my pipe before," he said, puffing as he put fire to the tobacco.

"The truth is, I don't mind the smell. But the smoke isn't good for either one of us."

He unceremoniously dumped the pipe contents into a red-glazed pottery ashtray that looked like it had been made by a child. "Very well, my dear. Since you've kept me from my smoke, let's get right to the point. What's going on between you and Ben Benedict?"

"I don't see where that's relevant, since he's no longer a patient here."

"Are you telling me he's well? That he's showing no further signs of PTSD?"

Anna stared into Ike's heavily jowled face and couldn't lie. "No. I'm not saying he's well. But he's much better."

"Anna," Ike admonished. "If the man is sick, why did you close his file?"

"You know PTSD can show up a quarter century after the inciting event with the right catalyst. It's not something you can really cure. You just help the patient learn to deal with the trauma when the symptoms occur."

"And in one session in your office you taught him all he needs to know?" Ike said cynically.

"He was already doing some of the right things to help himself. I've just made a few more suggestions. He's having fewer nightmares, and he's not having attacks at all during the day."

"How do you know all this about a man who's no longer your patient?" Ike asked.

Anna took a deep breath and let it out. She wanted to say she and Ben were friends. But that wasn't precisely true. She wanted to say they were lovers. But no words of love had been exchanged. So she admitted, "We're sleeping together."

She didn't meet Ike's gaze right away. When she did, she saw his wrinkled brow was furrowed. He was chewing thoughtfully on the stem of his empty pipe.

"What am I going to do with you?"

"Are you going to report me to the APA?" Anna held her breath, waiting to hear that her career as a psychiatrist was in jeopardy.

"If I don't report you, I'm the one behaving unethically. But…" He took the pipe from his mouth and poked a metal tool around in the bowl, freeing the last of the unburned tobacco, which he dumped into the ashtray.

"But?" Anna prodded.

"I've worked with you for two years, Anna, and I've never seen you behave in any way unprofessionally. The amazing thing to me is that you haven't taken a great deal of trouble to hide your unorthodox treatment—as opposed to your un-ethical behavior, which, of course, I would have to report to the APA—with this man. Which suggests to me that you have serious feelings for him."

"I care about Ben, of course, but—"

He held up a hand to cut her off. "Take a good look at your actions, Anna. They'll tell you a great deal about exactly how you feel. Now, are you coming back to work on Monday?"

Anna realized that Ike expected her to stop babysitting Ben and resume treating her other patients, which made perfect sense, if Ben was as mentally healthy as she'd described him.

"I'm worried about what might happen to Ben if he's involved in another trauma," she said. Something that was a distinct possibility.

"None of us can predict the future, Anna. You have to trust Ben to reach out for more help if he needs it. So, will I see you Monday?"

"I'll be here."

49

On his way inside from one of the many parking lots that surrounded Tysons Corner, a popular suburban mall in McLean, Virginia, Ben heard a female voice at his elbow say, "Fancy meeting you here."

He turned and smiled at Anna. "I thought you had some business at the office this morning, Doc."

She smiled back and said, "It didn't take long to straighten out the problem. I can't believe I ran into you. I was going to do some shopping of my own before we meet the girls for lunch. Have you spoken with your sister?"

"Julia picked Trisha up around nine-thirty this morning and they've been shopping ever since."

"It was nice of Julia to offer to do this," Anna said.

"Julia told me she needed something to take her mind off Waverly." Ben snorted. "I just don't understand why you women think shopping is fun."

Anna laughed and Ben felt his heartbeat ratchet up at the happy sound. He supposed one of the results of feeling better himself was enjoying Anna's company more.

"Girls like pretty things because boys like to see girls wearing pretty things," Anna explained. "Where exactly are we supposed to meet the girls for lunch?"

"Trisha picked the Five Guys hamburger joint in the food court on the third floor."

Ben found Julia and Trisha sitting at a table at Five Guys with a pile of shelled peanuts and two Cokes on the table in front of them. The floor around them was stacked with brimful shopping bags.

He started toward their table and heard Anna's high heels clicking on the floor behind him.

"Hi, Ben!" Julia said, jumping up to hug him.

She looked almost happy, Ben thought, not at all like a woman in mourning. "I see you had a successful day shopping."

"You can say that again." Julia started picking up packages. "We've decided we'd rather have pizza than a hamburger. There's a California Pizza Kitchen on the first floor near Nordstrom's. We can drop our packages off at the car on the way."

"Need some help carrying any of those?" Ben asked.

"Yes, please," Julia said, handing him several items.

Ben collected parcels until he had both hands full.

Trisha looked at him and said, "Can you hold one more?"

"Sure," he said. He rearranged what he was holding so she could slide another package under his arm. "Where to?" he asked Julia.

"My car's out this way, Parking Terrace C."

"Hello, Dr. Schuster," Julia said, walking beside Anna. "It's nice to see you again under less trying circumstances. I understand you've been riding with Ben and…" She paused, swallowed, then continued, "Waverly's replacement. This is my new friend, Trisha Reynaldo."

"Please, call me Anna," Anna said with a smile. "It's so nice to meet you, Trisha."

Ben noticed that Trisha had switched her backpack to the opposite shoulder at the same moment Anna held out her hand to be shaken and missed making the physical connection. Anna dropped her hand onto the girl's shoulder instead.

Ben followed behind the three women, listening to their friendly chatter without focusing on what they were saying. He was just glad to see that Julia and Trisha had gotten along, that Julia didn't look as devastated as she had Wednesday at the funeral, and that there were no members of either the 1-8 or MS hanging around them.

As they walked farther and farther away from the mall entrance, Ben asked, "Where are you parked, Julia? New Mexico?"

Julia laughed. "Trisha suggested that I park on the outside edge of the terrace."

Ben wondered why, but didn't ask because his attention was focused on the large package Trisha had put under his arm, which kept threatening to slide out of his grasp.

Julia answered his question when she continued, "So the car would stay warm in the sun."

Julia opened the trunk and dropped a bag inside, then stepped aside so Ben could relieve himself of his packages.

He saw movement in his peripheral vision and instinctively turned to check it out. His breath caught in his chest when he saw a boy standing between two parked cars with a gun in his hand. Ben was poised to reach for his service weapon as the boy pointed the gun at him and yelled, "Keep your nose out of where it doesn't belong!"

Julia screamed and threw a package at the boy.

He turned and shot her in the heart.

Instead of the instant response Ben imagined in his head, his body moved so slowly he felt like he was walking through chest-deep water. He was reacting, but he was getting nowhere fast. He saw everything in slow motion.

Julia stared at him in shock, then looked down at her chest, then back up at him again, before her eyes rolled up in her head and she crumpled to the pavement like a rag doll.

His gaze shot to the boy, an MS tatt visible on his neck as the wind caught the hood of his sweatshirt and pulled it off his head. The kid backed up a few paces, staring down at Julia, then up at Ben. He grinned ghoulishly before he ducked and disappeared in the shiny maze of cars.

The rest of the packages tumbled from Ben's grasp as he

grabbed for his Glock. But his slow, clumsy fingers wouldn't cooperate, and he dropped the weapon as it came free of the holster. He scrambled to retrieve it from under the rear of the car, then rose to give chase.

But Anna grabbed his arm. "Julia needs help!"

It was as though the deep water slowing him down froze in a millisecond. Ben couldn't move. Not a twitch. Not a muscle. He stared down at Julia, noting abstractedly the location and size of the small entrance wound. If the bullet hadn't hit her exactly in the heart, it surely hadn't missed by much.

Trisha was kneeling beside Julia, but she was looking intently up at him with those exotic gray eyes. He was confused by the expression on her face. It seemed almost... exultant. He had an instant of déjà vu and shook his head to clear it.

He should have paid attention when everyone said he needed a break from work. He should have stayed home in bed, instead of asking stupid questions of goddamn gangs. He should have known better than to let MS know that he was onto them.

He'd gotten his sister killed. Just as he'd lured his brother to his death.

Anna placed her hands on either side of his face, forcing him to focus on her, and said quietly, "I need your help to save Julia."

The ice shattered.

He pulled free and dropped to one knee beside Julia, feeling for the pulse at her throat. He found it, thready and slow. "Thank God," he whispered. He put his palm over the wound and applied pressure to stanch the flow of blood.

And watched the blood cover his hands. Again.

"A woman's been shot," he heard Anna say into her cell phone. "I need paramedics at the outside edge of Terrace C parking at Tysons Corner." She bent close to him and asked, "What can I do to help?"

"Call my mother. Use my cell phone. It's in my coat pocket. She's number six on my speed dial. Tell her..."

"What do I tell her?" Anna asked.

Tell her I killed my sister. Just like I killed my brother.

"Tell her Julia's been hurt," he said through tight jaws, as his body began to tremble uncontrollably. "Ask her which hospital she wants her to be taken to by the paramedics."

He heard Anna speaking calmly and quietly into the phone, explaining the situation to his mother and giving her the awful news that Julia had been shot in the chest. He could hear his mother's frantic voice from where he knelt.

"She says to go to Georgetown University Hospital," Anna said as she flipped his phone closed and dropped it back into his jacket pocket. "She'll meet us there."

He realized Julia's chest felt different under his hand. It wasn't moving. He checked with an obviously shaking hand for her pulse. He bent his head close to see if he could feel her breath on his cheek. And felt nothing.

Her heart was no longer beating.

50

Abigail Hamilton was already in her black Lexus sedan on the way to Georgetown University Hospital when she realized she hadn't contacted Ham. She kept swiping at the tears that were blurring her vision. The last thing she wanted to do was have an accident.

Unbelievable. Unbelievable. Unbelievable.

She activated her car speakerphone, searched for a number and called it. When the call was answered she sobbed, collected herself, and said, "Foster?"

"What's happened, Abby? Are you all right?"

When Ben was in the hospital, Foster had given her an emergency number where he could be reached any time of the day or night. He'd told her to call if she was ever in trouble and needed him. She opened her mouth to tell him what had happened, but another sob came out instead.

"Where are you, Abby?" he asked, his voice quiet and sure. "Let me come to you."

She wanted the comfort he was offering. She wanted his arms around her, keeping her safe. But she was married to another man.

"Abby, please, talk to me. What's wrong?"

"Julia's been shot."

"Which hospital has she been taken to?" Foster asked. "I'll meet you there."

"No. Don't come to the hospital." Ham would be there.

Except she hadn't called him yet.

"Which hospital, Abby?" Foster demanded.

She choked back a frightened wail and said, "Georgetown University."

"How is she?"

"I don't know!" she cried. "Ben's doctor, Anna Schuster, was the one who called me. She said Julia spent the morning shopping with some girl from Lincoln Middle School. She and the girl met up for lunch with Ben and the doctor.

"When they got to Julia's car with their packages someone shot Julia. Dr. Schuster couldn't—or wouldn't—tell me anything about Julia's condition. Just that she was shot in the chest, and she'd called the paramedics."

"Is Ben okay?"

"I never thought to ask. I just presumed… He must be okay. He was taking care of Julia." She swallowed over the painful lump in her throat and said, "I can't lose my only daughter. I can't!"

"I'm on my way, Abby. Hold on, sweetheart. Where are you now?"

"I'm nearly there. Hurry, Foster. Please hurry!"

The brakes squealed as Abby stopped near the emergency room. She could hear the wail of a siren as she ran toward the hospital door.

"Please let them be bringing my baby," she said. "And please, God, let her be all right."

51

"**I** killed my sister."

Anna was on her knees beside Ben. His eyes were crazed with guilt and grief. This was exactly what she'd feared. He seemed to be hanging on to control by a thread.

He was giving Julia CPR, talking breathlessly as he pumped on her no-longer-beating heart, then blew precious air into her lungs. "I might as well have taken a gun and shot her myself."

"Stop it, Ben," Anna said, gripping his arm, holding on tight to stop him from teetering over the edge. "Listen to me," she said urgently. "You aren't responsible for what happened here."

He stopped CPR and turned on her in a rage. "The kid who shot her was MS."

"So someone in a gang shot Julia. How are you responsible for that?"

"You heard what he said. 'Keep your nose out of where it doesn't belong!' Do you have any idea what I've been doing the past few days? Do you?"

Of course she did. She'd been with him every day as he'd questioned kids about what trouble MS was brewing. And every night she'd made love with a man frustrated that he hadn't learned anything new.

He shook her so hard her head flopped on her neck. Anna could feel him slipping away. "Ben, please—"

"I've been asking questions," he said inexorably. "Trying

to uncover a terrorist plot involving MS. This is their way of telling me to butt the hell out."

"Then why shoot Julia?" she said as she pulled free and took over CPR on Julia. "Why not simply kill you?"

He shoved his bloody hands through his hair, leaving it standing on end. It was plain he hadn't thought of that. Maybe because he was too agitated to be thinking clearly.

"Julia threw that package to distract the shooter, to save me."

"To watch the one you love die hurts more than dying yourself."

Both Anna and Ben turned to the source of the voice that had spoken. Trisha was standing near Julia's Lexus. The girl's sweater was spattered with blowback from Julia's gunshot wound. Her gray eyes were bright with unshed tears.

What the girl had said was true, Anna knew. It had been devastating for Anna to see her sister lying dead and know she'd had a part in the tragedy. How much worse it must be for Ben, who'd watched a child he'd mentored, then his best friend, and now his sister, all become victims of violence within the same week.

"They made a mistake leaving me alive," Ben said as he stared down at Julia. "A big mistake."

Anna heard the sirens and hoped they arrived soon enough for her to stop the meltdown she saw happening before her eyes. But she couldn't stop CPR on Julia.

"What is it you plan to do?" she asked breathlessly.

"I'm going to find that kid. And—" He cut himself off. "I'm going to find that kid."

The paramedics arrived with a screech of tires and the wail of a dying siren. They took over CPR from Anna, who pushed herself onto her feet and hurried to Ben, who was staring down at Anna as the paramedics hooked up an IV and called for instructions from the hospital.

"She's pregnant, if that makes a difference," Ben said.

"We need to go!" one of the paramedics said.

Anna held on to Ben as they watched Julia being transferred from the ground to a gurney and then loaded into the back of the ambulance.

"I'm going with her," Ben said, attempting to step up into the back of the ambulance.

"Sorry, sir, no room," the paramedic said, as he put a hand to Ben's chest in a way so practiced that he must have done it with a hundred grieving relatives. He quickly closed the door, shutting Ben out.

Ben pounded on the metal panel with his fist. "Open the fucking door!"

"Ben, come on," Anna said, grabbing his arm as the ambulance screamed away. "We can follow in my car."

But he didn't move. He stared at the retreating ambulance as though his feet had rooted in the ground. She realized he couldn't hear her. His eyes were glazed. He'd gone somewhere else in his head. Somewhere away from this tragedy.

52

Aisha's eyes had filled with tears of joy. The assassin's grief was a salve for the hurt she had suffered at his hands. And she had discovered important information. He believed someone in MS was involved in a terrorist plot. He was hunting for her without knowing she was the one he sought. She could not take the chance he would discover the truth. He must die soon.

Before she killed him, she wanted him to suffer more, to suffer as she had suffered. To feel the loss of one person he cared for after another until everyone was gone. The scales were not yet close to even. He had lost a friend. And a sister.

Aisha had seen how the assassin looked at the woman he had brought with him today. She would die next.

53

Foster wasn't surprised that Abby had sent the paramedics to Georgetown University Hospital, since she knew all the administrators there. She'd called him again, frantic when she'd discovered that no one she knew was working on Saturday. When he arrived, she was in the waiting room with the rest of the families anxious for news of their loved one's condition.

"How's Julia?" he asked. It was a sign of how upset she was that Abby threw herself into his arms. Foster held her close, something he hadn't done in more years than he liked to count, only sorry for the reason she had turned to him at last.

Her eyes were liquid as she looked up at him. "They won't tell me anything. I've tried calling Ben to find out what condition she was in when the paramedics picked her up, but he isn't answering his phone. And he hasn't arrived at the hospital yet.

"I called Anna Schuster and she told me Ben wasn't with her, that they'd taken separate cars so she could take the girl Julia was shopping with home. Anna seemed worried that Ben hasn't turned up at the hospital, because he left directly from the mall to come here."

"Let me see what I can find out," Foster said. Before he took more than a step away from Abby, a harried-looking doctor appeared.

"Mrs. Hamilton?"

Foster tried to judge from the look on the doctor's face whether or not Abby's daughter was alive. The doctor's hair was sweaty and flattened as though he'd pulled off a surgical cap, and a surgical mask had been pulled down and hung from the ties at the back of his neck, revealing a gray-bearded, grizzled, exhausted visage. The dark brown eyes were devoid of any emotion.

"How is my daughter?" Abby asked. "How's Julia?"

"Your daughter had no heartbeat when the paramedics put her in the ambulance," the doctor began.

The keening moan that came from Abby's throat sent a shiver down Foster's spine. She turned and grabbed him around the neck, her mouth near his ear, so he winced as she shrieked, "Our baby! Our one little girl, Foster. Julia's dead!"

Foster thought she'd come unhinged. Julia was Ham's daughter. He and Abby had produced five sons.

"Mr. Hamilton—" the doctor began.

"I'm Foster Benedict, a friend of the family," Foster said, over Abby's agonized wails.

"If you can calm Mrs. Hamilton, the news is good," the doctor said. "Her daughter is alive. She was revived by the paramedics en route. The small caliber bullet missed her heart. She survived the surgery to remove the bullet and repair the damage and is in intensive care. But I won't candy-coat it. Her condition is serious."

"Serious. What does that mean, exactly?" Foster asked.

"Her wound is critical, but her vital signs are stable."

"Which means?" Foster prompted again, barely keeping the irritation from his voice.

"We have to wait and see how her body responds to the surgery," the doctor said. "We'll know more in the morning. I'll send a nurse to let Mrs. Hamilton know when she can see her daughter."

"Thank you, Doctor," Foster said.

Once the doctor was gone, Foster took Abby's head between his two hands and forced her chin up so he could look into her shattered, tear-filled blue eyes. "Abby, listen to me. Julia is alive."

She'd gone somewhere inside her head and stared at him without seeming to register what he'd said.

He grabbed her shoulders and gave her a shake. "Abby, did you hear me? Julia is alive."

Her nails dug in as she grabbed his arms. Her eyes showed wary hope. "Don't lie to me, Foster. Please don't lie to me."

"The bullet missed her heart. The paramedics revived her. She survived the surgery to repair the damage and she's in the ICU."

"I want to see her. Please, I want to see our—*my*—baby," she quickly corrected herself.

There it was again, that odd "slip." If it was a slip. He tried to meet Abby's gaze, but she'd lowered it. She'd taken a step back and was gripping her body with her arms as though if she didn't, she'd fly apart.

"That's twice, Abby," he said softly. "Twice you've said Julia is *our* baby."

He waited for her to speak. The damnation was in her silence.

He did the math. It was possible. They'd been together one time after their divorce. A violent quarrel that had ended in desperate sex. Just before she'd married Ham. While he was dating Patsy.

"Oh, God, Abby," he whispered, reaching out and grasping her arms so tight he saw her flinch. "We have a daughter?"

Abby wasn't looking at him. She was looking at something over his shoulder, her eyes wide and frightened.

He turned and saw Patsy standing there. Close enough to have heard everything.

54

Foster found Patsy in the hospital chapel. She was alone. He'd called and asked Patsy to come to the hospital because he'd been worried about how his son would cope with this additional trauma, on top of everything else that had happened to him this week. He'd hoped she would be able to comfort Ben. Only Ben had never shown up.

He came down the center aisle and sat in the second pew beside her. "I didn't know."

She was turning her engagement ring, a four-carat emerald-cut diamond, around and around with the thumb of her ring hand. It was a nervous habit that seemed ominous under the circumstances.

At last she looked him in the eye and said, "You know how I feel about fidelity. It was the bedrock of our relationship. You said you'd learned the consequences of cheating and you would never, ever, betray another woman."

Foster's heart was beating hard. "I never meant to hurt you, Patsy."

"Shut up!" she said. "Just shut up. Don't you dare try to excuse yourself."

"I wasn't going to do that."

"No? Why should I believe you're telling me the truth now? Now that I've discovered our entire marriage began with a lie. That while you were engaged to me, you were fucking your ex-wife."

"Patsy, I—"

She knocked his hand off her arm. "Don't you *dare* say you love me! You might like me. You might even enjoy my body. You might admire and appreciate my abilities as a hostess and a mother. But you don't love me, Foster," she said, tears streaming from her eyes. She swiped the arm of her cotton blouse against her runny nose, something he'd never seen her do in all the years he'd known her.

"You never loved me," she accused, eyes narrowed, teeth bared. "You've never loved any woman but Abby!"

Foster's throat ached because everything she said was true. He could deny it, but she would know he was lying. "What do you want me to do, Patsy?"

She shoved her hands roughly through her short-cropped hair and stared at the ceiling to avoid looking at him. "I'm leaving you, Foster."

He was surprised. Shocked. But he didn't doubt she would do what she said. Her body was taut and her hazel eyes looked dangerous, leonine. She was itching for a fight, ready to scratch and claw. He would have provoked her to it, but he knew she would only feel worse afterward. The Patsy he knew didn't have a violent bone in her body.

As he met her gaze, her palm flew out and slapped his face hard enough to turn his head. She left a bloody scrape where her engagement ring was turned around on her finger.

"I'm not going to apologize for that," she said angrily. "You deserve that and more." She turned her body toward him and said, "Why did you marry me, Foster? Why didn't you just wait her out? Surely you realize Abby would have come crawling back to you, if you'd been free."

He didn't explain himself, didn't defend himself. There was no defense that would soothe Patsy's hurt or appease the terrible harm he'd done.

"I didn't know about Julia," he said again. "Having sex with Abby was… It was a desperate act that—"

"Had terrible consequences," she said bitterly. "I hate you,

Foster. I'm furious with you and right now I hate you. I'm taking Camille and we're going to my father's ranch in Texas. When Amanda and Bethany are done with the school term, I'll have them come to me. If they want to visit you at Christmas, we'll make arrangements."

"How will you explain moving to Texas to the girls?" he asked.

"I'll lie for you, if that's what you're asking. I'll tell them my father has been ill—he has been, by the way—and that I want to spend time with him."

He was still reeling from Abby's confession that Julia was his daughter. Reeling from Patsy's vehement rejection of him. "Do you want a divorce?"

"I…" She looked up at the ceiling again and pressed her hands together under her quivering chin. "I don't know. Right now, I'm so angry and so hurt, I never want to see you again." She lowered her chin and met his gaze and said, "The problem is, even though you never truly loved me, I love—loved—you. I gave you my heart, Foster. And you've trampled it underfoot."

"Pasty, please, you're upset. Give us time—"

"I'm leaving on the first plane out of here tomorrow morning. Don't try to stop me. Between now and then, don't come anywhere near me. Now, if you don't mind, I'd like to pray for Julia's recovery. And for our son, who must be suffering the torments of the damned. And don't dare pretend that Ben isn't as much mine as he is yours. I love him as though he were my own blood and bone."

He searched for something to say that would ease the pain he saw in his wife's eyes. But she closed her eyes and bent her head, shutting him out.

When Foster stood, his knees very nearly collapsed. He stiffened them and walked from the chapel. He'd tried to be a good husband. He'd known the mistake he'd made even as he spoke his vows to Patsy. But he'd spoken those vows, so he'd kept them—the letter of them, if not the spirit.

He felt like hell. His wife of nineteen years was leaving him. His family was once more being torn asunder. And his son was out there somewhere suffering alone.

He couldn't help wondering—and fearing—how Ben would handle one more jagged tear in the fabric of his world.

55

Ben woke up in a hospital bed. The room was bare. No flowers. No water pitcher. And he was thirsty. His mouth tasted foul. How had he gotten here?

His arm itched. He grimaced as he tried to rise and irritated his shoulder. His eyes were swollen. And his throat was sore.

It felt like he'd swallowed a batch of razor blades. He wondered what that was all about. Had he had some kind of surgery with a tube down his throat? He blinked his eyes and found them crusty from sleep. He gingerly worked his aching jaw. Why did his head hurt so much? Had he been shot?

Ben flashed on a pool of blood. Flashed on the dead kid in Afghanistan, whose face changed to that of his brother Darling. Flashed on the gang kid with the bullet hole between his eyes—whose face changed to that of his brother Darling. He felt his throat constrict until it ached.

There was something awful lurking in the shadows of his mind. Something awful he didn't want to see.

He tried to shove himself upright, planning to hunt down some water in the bathroom. And stared at his hands in shock. They were bound in leather restraints attached to the rail of the hospital bed. As were his feet. A band bound his body to the bed at mid-chest.

"What the hell?" he croaked.

"You're awake. At last."

Ben looked up, startled to see Anna rise from a chair in the shadows by a wire-covered window. "Why the hell am I tied down?" he demanded. "Did you do this to me?"

"I arranged to have you brought here last night. And I approved the restraints." She looked down at her hands and admitted, "I lied and told them I was your doctor."

"Which you're not!" He struggled to remember what had happened to put him here.

Anna pressed her hands to her eye sockets. "I don't know why I keep breaking the rules with you."

When she lowered her hands, he eyed the dark bruises of fatigue under her eyes, the mussed hair, the wrinkled, blood-stained clothes. "You look like hell warmed over, Doc."

She put both hands up to tuck wayward blond curls behind her ears. "I've been here ever since you were admitted." She glanced over her shoulder. "That chair doesn't make a very good bed."

Ben glanced at the overcast sky through the steel mesh cage on the windows. *All night? What the hell was going on? What had he done to end up here?* Then he remembered what he'd been trying so hard to forget.

He squeezed his eyes closed, but it did nothing to halt the vision of Julia lying on the cold pavement in the parking lot of a suburban mall, surrounded by a growing pool of sticky red blood. "Oh, God, no."

He saw an image of himself jumping into his car at Tysons Corner, speeding to the hospital. He'd called the hospital on the way and identified himself as an ICE agent investigating the shooting of Julia Hamilton, because he thought that was the surest way to get information on his sister's condition. He'd asked how she was doing.

And been told she'd flatlined in the ambulance.

He'd snapped the phone closed, feeling panicked. His mother would never forgive him now. First Darling, and now Julia. He couldn't face his family. Or his boss. He'd choked when he should have acted, and Julia had been shot and killed.

He'd wanted to crawl into a hole and die.

He remembered gasping for breath, afraid he would suffocate. He'd jerked the car to a stop on the side of the road and pressed his shaking hands to the sides of his head, which was pounding so hard he thought it might explode.

He'd tried all the usual means he'd used in the past to get himself under control, to calm himself. But nothing worked. His whole body was shivering as though he'd been left naked on an Arctic ice floe. He'd forced himself to look around, to try and get hold of his splintering psyche. And realized he was parked near a familiar bar in Georgetown.

Where he'd proceeded to drink himself into the oblivion that promised peace.

He struggled to re-create the events at the bar. And remembered how Anna, frantic and frightened, had found him in the early evening, when he'd already had a great deal to drink. How he'd confided his feelings of fury and frustration. Of desperation and hopelessness. And how she'd betrayed him.

He hadn't given a second thought to the two MPD officers who'd come into the pub and stood at his shoulder. After confirming his identity, and that of Dr. Schuster—the doctor who'd called them—they took him into custody *for his own good*.

He hadn't gone willingly. Drunk as he was, he'd fought them.

"You bitch!" he'd shouted at Anna as the cops manhandled him. "You interfering bitch!"

They'd brought him to this hospital against his will for psychiatric observation because Dr. Schuster had told them he was a threat to himself and others. He couldn't remember every nasty thing he'd said to her, but the wary look in her eyes told him she hadn't forgotten.

He remembered swinging wildly at the cops and getting in a few licks. He didn't remember anything after that.

He flopped back down on the pillow and stared at the ceiling. "So," he said in a dull voice. "Am I officially nuts?"

"You're suffering from post-traumatic stress. You have been for quite some time, I believe. You've been coping with your PTSD well enough to function effectively. But seeing Julia get shot caused you to…become symptomatic."

Ben suddenly knew why his throat hurt so bad. He didn't know how long he'd been in the men's room when Anna found him standing at the sink raging. Banging his head against the broken mirror until blood streamed from cuts on his head and his hands.

No wonder his head hurt. He reached up and felt the stitches through his right eyebrow. He spread his hands and saw minor cuts and stitches along the edge of his left hand.

She'd spoken soothing words, promising to take care of him, to ease his pain.

And this was how she'd done it. By putting him in a god-damned hospital and having him restrained.

He would never forgive her.

He stared at the doctor through narrowed eyes and watched her cross her arms protectively over her chest.

"How about removing these things?" he said, rattling the restraints attached to the hospital rails.

"How are you feeling?" Anna asked as she approached his bed.

"Surely you can come up with something more original than that, Doc," Ben said, struggling against the strap that held him prone. He winced when he felt the new scabs on his forehead flare, which made him flash on Julia again.

He felt angry and frustrated and sad, but worst of all, powerless. "Get these damned things off me!"

He looked up and found Anna's face pensive. He realized if he wanted the straps off he was going to have to pretend not to be as angry as he was. "I'm calm. I'll stay calm. Just let me sit up."

"All right." She reached for the buckle and undid the strap that kept him prone. Then she put an arm around his shoulders and helped him to sit up. He barely stopped himself from jerking free of her touch.

"Can we get rid of these?" He rattled the hand restraints again.

"I'd like to talk to you first."

Ben took hope from the way she'd phrased her sentence. The assumption being, if he acted rationally, she'd let him loose. Once he was free, he could get the hell away from her. And stay the hell away from her. And everyone else.

"All right," he agreed.

"Your family would like to see you."

"No!" The single word of denial sounded frenzied and frightened to his ears. Which he was sure wasn't the "correct" response under the circumstances. But he couldn't face them, not yet. He met Anna's gaze and explained, "Would you want to see your family if you'd killed your sister?"

Ben heard the edge in his voice and realized a molten vat of anger was simmering beneath the surface, waiting to boil over. Keeping it hidden was going to be difficult but was entirely necessary if he wanted out of here. "I don't know what to say to them. Not after I stood right there with my thumb up my ass while Julia was shot and killed."

"Julia isn't dead."

Ben felt his heart skip a beat. He thought he must have heard Anna wrong, because he so badly wanted to believe her. "What did you say?"

"Julia is alive."

"I saw her die with my own eyes," he countered. "The hospital confirmed she flatlined in the ambulance."

"The paramedics brought her back. Twice. She was in serious condition in the ICU overnight. This morning, the doctor says her condition is fair. She's stable and responding to treatment."

"But she's going to be okay?"

"She isn't completely out of danger, but she's young and she's strong. The prognosis is good."

"I want to see her. Right now." He jerked against the restraints, testing their strength.

"I'm not sure that's a good idea."

"Why not?" He felt belligerent and knew he sounded that way, which he realized wasn't helping him.

"We need to make sure you're okay first."

"I'll be okay when I see Julia," he said in a hard voice. He yanked on the restraints and managed to hurt both his dog-bitten arm and his stitched shoulder.

"Tell me what you're feeling right now," Anna said.

"You're lucky my hands are tied," he snarled.

"Why is that?"

He was trying to control the rage, the frustration, the grief, his feelings of powerlessness and helplessness. Because he knew they were all symptoms of PTSD. He wasn't ignorant of his condition. He'd learned what he could about post-traumatic stress so he could heal himself. And it had worked—for a while, anyway.

What he wanted right now was to feel normal. What he felt was panicked. He was afraid he wouldn't be able to convince Anna to let him out of here.

Assuming she had the authority to set him free. "I don't belong here," he said, controlling the emotions that threatened to erupt and give him away. "I need to find the kid who shot Julia. And MS and the One-Eight are going to clash over that package MS is bringing in. I need to be there to stop them."

"I'm sure ICE and the MPD can handle both those situations without you."

"I haven't told my boss everything about what's going on in Georgetown." He hadn't told anyone what Henry had said about the 1-8. He'd simply acted on the information with Harry Saunders.

"Should I have your boss come here?" Anna asked.

Have his boss see him tied up like some loony? "I'd rather talk to Tony in his office."

"I'm not sure you're ready to leave the hospital."

"What if I go home to recuperate?"

"Would you stay at home?" she asked skeptically.

Well, he'd never thought she was stupid. "You're welcome to come with me and stand guard, if that's what it takes to get out of here." Much good it would do her.

He would never trust her with his innermost thoughts again. Not after what she'd done to him last night. When he got out of here, he was going back to work—without her.

Having something to do was what had kept him sane over the past six months. And there was a great deal still to be done. Like questioning the 1-8 and MS about whatever weapon was about to be unleashed on Washington, D.C., and finding the boy who'd shot Julia and asking him what he knew.

The look on Anna's face said she didn't trust him. She was right to be wary. He was certain he could get around whatever measures she put in place to keep track of him once he was out of here.

"I'll get better a lot faster at home than I will tied up here," he said. "Besides, I need to take care of my dog."

"Your dog is fine. Henry's taking care of Penelope and Rocky at my place." Anna ruffled her hair with both hands, then tried to smooth it back down. She pursed her lips and sighed. Finally she said, "I'll make arrangements for your release from the hospital. But I want your promise you'll go straight home—and you'll stay there."

Ben didn't want to make a promise he wasn't going to keep. "I want to see Julia first."

She stood by his right hand, ready to release him. "Do I have your word?"

"How long is this house arrest supposed to last?"

Anna met his gaze and said seriously, "You were in bad shape yesterday. You're human, Ben. You need to give yourself time to process everything that's happened this week."

Which meant she wasn't going to give him the okay to do

anything for a very long time. "I'm feeling a lot better already, knowing Julia's alive. I just want to see her with my own eyes, Doc."

For some reason, she didn't insist on getting his promise that he'd stay home before she began unbuckling the cuffs at his wrists. Was she scared he'd have another meltdown? That wasn't going to happen. He'd been as far down as he intended to go.

From here on out, he was going to do his job. And stay the hell away from Dr. Annagreit Schuster.

56

"How is she?" Ben asked from the doorway to Julia's room.

"She's doing very well," the ICU nurse said quietly.

Ben was dressed in green hospital scrubs Anna had gotten for him, since his clothes were stained with Julia's blood and he hadn't wanted to wait for clean clothes to be brought to him from home.

Anna had gone to administration to arrange for his release from the hospital. She'd asked him to wait in his room for her return. But he was done taking orders from her.

Besides, he had to see with his own eyes that Julia was alive and well.

On the other side of Julia's hospital bed, Ben saw someone sitting next to his sister, her face half-hidden by the bedrails.

"Who's that?" he asked the nurse.

"Oh, that's her friend, the one who was with her when she was shot. The patient's mother okayed the visit."

"What is she doing?" Ben asked.

The nurse turned her attention from Ben to Julia. "What are you doing? Stop that! Stop!"

Ben saw the startled look on Trisha Reynaldo's face as she stood up. And then the flash of hate that hardened her features. He felt a growing horror as he realized the girl had hold of the wires connected to Julia's life support. Apparently, she was trying to disconnect them. Trisha Reynaldo was no innocent. Which meant her connection to the boy in MS who'd taken her hostage was suspect. And that made her dangerous.

He processed all that information in a nanosecond and reacted with equal speed.

As he took a step toward Julia's bed, Trisha held up the medical tube she was threatening to pull free, holding him in place. She bared her teeth and snarled, "Assassin! You killed my brother in the market square. Americans killed my father, my brothers, my mother. You put my husband in prison. Soon I will have vengeance. And join my family in Paradise."

Ben suddenly recalled the exultant look on Trisha's face that had so confused him when Julia was shot. And realized why he'd found her eyes so compelling—and familiar.

He'd never seen the face behind the burka of the Afghani girl who'd leaned over to steal his dog tag in the market square. But he'd never forgotten those stunning gray eyes. It seemed impossible that this was the same girl. But it seemed she was.

Trisha shot him a look of loathing, then yanked the tube free of the machinery.

As Ben charged around the foot of the bed, she leapt past his outstretched grasp and clambered across the top of the bed, heading in the other direction.

As she raced to the door, she yelled back, "I will kill your woman. Then I will kill you and every American I can!"

Before he could change direction to intercept her, Trisha Reynaldo—or whoever she was—had knocked the nurse down and sprinted out the door.

Ben started after her, then heard the loud warning beeps on the monitors attached to Julia's heart. "What the hell did she do?" he yelled at the nurse. "Get over here and fix this."

But the nurse had hit her head against the door jamb when Trisha shoved past her and lay stunned on the floor.

At that moment, Anna showed up in the doorway. "When the elevator opened, I saw Trisha racing down the hall toward the stairs like the hounds of hell were after her. What did you say to her? What's going on?"

Ben had crossed to Julia's bed and was analyzing the medical machinery, trying to figure out how to reconnect it. "Trisha Reynaldo did something to disable Julia's life support."

Ben watched as Anna quickly crossed the room, took a look at the machinery, then reattached the oxygen tube that was helping Julia to breathe. The monitors quieted and all that remained was the steady *beep, beep, beep* of Julia's heart.

A long gust of air shuddered out of him. "Thank you."

Ben's mind was racing, trying to put together all the facts Trisha Reynaldo—clearly that was not her real name—had given him.

She'd called him *assassin*. Ben felt a chill run down his spine. The Afghani girl's quest for vengeance, her threat to kill "every American I can," suggested she was involved with the "package" being delivered to D.C. Which meant the threat everyone feared was very real. And perhaps imminent.

Ben turned and saw Anna staring at him with concern in her eyes. He felt his heart take an extra thump. The Afghani's threat against "his woman" had to be dealt with. Anna would need protection.

A host of hospital personnel had arrived at the door in response to the emergency signal sent to the nurses' station by the heart monitor and were helping the injured nurse to her feet.

Ben turned to the nearest nurse and said, "Call hospital security." He gave her a quick description of Trisha Reynaldo, explained what she'd done, and said, "I don't know if she's armed, but she's definitely dangerous."

He turned to Anna and said, "Do you have your cell phone with you?"

"What's going on?" Anna asked as she handed him her cell phone. "Why would Trisha do such a thing?"

Ben punched in a number and when the phone was answered said, "Harry, I think Trisha Reynaldo is an Al Qaeda operative. She just tried to disconnect Julia's life support. She screamed a lot of things at me when I tried to apprehend her, including the fact that she's hoping to kill a lot of Americans. She knows me—and I recognize her—from Afghanistan."

Ben listened as Harry told him he'd arrange for MPD to put out a BOLO—be on the lookout—for Trisha Reynaldo, and send cops to the Reynaldo home to watch for her.

"She also made a threat against Anna Schuster," Ben said. "You'll need to assign someone to watch Anna's townhome 24-7 until Trisha Reynaldo is picked up."

"Will do," Harry said.

"Watch your six," Ben said before he disconnected the call. It was a military expression that meant "watch your back."

He turned and found Anna at his back. Worried about him. Watching out for him. He was still mad at her for putting him in the hospital, still determined to keep his distance, but he didn't want her hurt on his watch.

He turned away from her probing gaze and punched in his boss's number.

"I thought you were in the hospital," Tony said when he picked up the call.

"I'm no longer a patient," Ben said as he eyed Anna sideways. "I came to check on Julia and found Trisha Reynaldo in her room trying to disconnect Julia's life support. The girl accused me of killing her brother in Afghanistan. I remember her—I remember some girl—standing over me after a grenade exploded and killed my spotter. Trisha—I'm presuming that's not her real name—said Americans had killed her father, her brothers and her mother. And arrested her husband."

"Her *husband?*" Tony said dubiously.

"Afghan girls marry young, but I suspect she's older than she's portrayed herself to us. She might be the Al Qaeda agent we've been trying to locate. At least, she made it clear she has plans to kill a lot of Americans. I've already called Harry and given him a heads-up."

"I suppose it's a waste of breath to tell you to go back to bed," Tony said.

"I know what this girl looks like. I know who she hangs out with. I know where she lives."

"I'll send some agents to run surveillance along with MPD at the Reynaldo house and Lincoln Middle School, in case she returns to either location, but I'm not optimistic she'll be that stupid," Tony said. "Is Dr. Schuster there with you?"

Ben eyed Anna, who was chewing on a hangnail, and said, "She's here."

"Give her the phone."

Ben watched as Anna listened, then he heard her say, "I think he'll be okay." Then she clicked her phone closed. "I told him—"

"I heard what you told him."

He crossed to Julia's side and brushed the hair back from her parchment-white forehead with a trembling hand. "I'm sorry, Julia. I didn't know."

An authoritative male voice said, "There are cops all over the hospital. They said there was a threat to a patient on this floor."

Ben turned to find his father entering Julia's room with his mother.

Ben looked past them and said, "Did you see Trisha Reynaldo on your way up here?"

"No," his mother said. "Why?"

"She tried to kill Julia."

57

Ben was sitting at the same conference table where he'd first met Annagreit Schuster. But she wasn't in the room. The chairs were filled with a variety of governmental officials, including his father, in his role as special advisor to the president. They were there to plan how best to deal with the imminent terrorist threat to the capital.

For once, Ben's boss wasn't pacing. The ICE Special Agent in Charge was leaning against a window ledge, holding a can of Sprite, one foot crossed over the other at the ankle, the toe of his shoe jerking nervously.

The deputy director of the Department of Homeland Security had arranged this Monday afternoon meeting at the ICE offices, because it was a discreet location. Rumors abounded about Al Qaeda threats in the capital, and they didn't want to give credence to the public fear being mongered by television news commentators.

To avoid panic in an already shaky financial environment, the public had been told that the bomb in Chicago was a gas explosion. A similar IED attack in San Francisco had been foiled.

This small summit was a response to new information Nash Benedict had picked up in El Salvador about what form the next attack would likely take, together with Trisha Reynaldo's threat on her way out of Julia's hospital room.

"The president asked me to be here to collect the most up-to-date information about a possible terrorist attack," Foster said from his seat at the center of the oval table facing the door.

Foster turned to Ben and said, "First, I'd like to know why you never reported your suspicions about Trisha Reynaldo."

"That's just it," Ben said from his seat on the opposite side of the table. "The girl wasn't particularly suspicious. Even though she was held hostage by a member of MS, she seemed to be someone who was simply in the wrong place at the wrong time."

Foster turned to Tony and asked, "Have you figured out who she is?"

"The green card was phony," Tony replied. "More than that we don't know. Under questioning, the Reynaldo family admitted they were forced to take her in by MS, who kidnapped Mrs. Reynaldo's sister, who's still living in El Salvador." He turned to Ben and said, "You think you saw the girl in Afghanistan?"

"At the hospital she called me 'assassin.' Said I'd killed her brother. I saw her eyes—I realize now they were hers— when I was lying dazed in the square after someone set off a Russian grenade."

"So you're positively identifying the girl as being Afghani?" his father asked.

"As positive as that sort of ID can be," Ben said.

His father turned to Nash, who was leaning against the wall near the door. "You think she's an Al Qaeda operative?"

"We think Al Qaeda recruited her," Nash said. "You don't have to look far for a motive. Based on what she said to Ben, her family was killed by Americans. She wants revenge, and it appears Al Qaeda is going to help her get it."

"She's apparently got a hard-on for Ben and every Benedict in Washington," Tony said.

Ben could still hear the girl's shrill voice in his ear. "Unfortunately, it's not just me and mine," he pointed out. "She seems committed to killing as many Americans as she can."

Foster gestured to the three people sitting on Ben's side of the table. "Meet Major Harmon Rankle from USAMRIID and Dr. Jennifer Esperanza from the CDC's Coordinating Office for Terrorism Preparedness and Emergency Response. Last, but certainly not least, this is Carla Gordon, who's responsible for the District's Department of Health Bioterrorism Hospital Preparedness Program."

USAMRIID, Ben knew, was the U.S. Army Medical Research Institute of Infectious Diseases at Fort Detrick, Maryland.

Tony took over the rest of the introductions and said, "This is Peter McGovern, Deputy Director of Homeland Security, Captain Olivia Wilson, Chief of the Metropolitan Police Department and Sergeant Harry Saunders, who replaced Waverly Collins as head of the MPD Gang Unit.

Nods of acknowledgment were exchanged around the room.

Foster turned to Nash and said, "Tell everyone what form your team thinks this Al Qaeda attack on the District is going to take."

"We believe it's bioterrorism," Nash said.

"Which means what?" Tony asked.

"A biological weapon aimed at high-ranking government officials," Nash replied.

"Shit," Tony said, standing and pacing a few steps before returning to lean against the window ledge. "Are you talking about something dumped into the drinking water? Something in an envelope delivered to the Capitol or the White House? A missile with a biological warhead? What?"

"From the information I have," the USAMRIID major interjected, "we're looking at an aerosol-borne cocktail of two or more biological agents."

"Type A agents," the CDC doctor added, "which is to say, both lethal and contagious."

Ben hissed in a breath. "Two? *Or more?* That sounds like overkill."

"It'll do the job, all right," Nash said.

"How did you figure that out?" Tony asked the two doctors. "I mean, that cocktail business."

To Ben's surprise, Nash answered the question. "We found evidence in a laboratory in El Salvador of a number of lethal infectious diseases, together with silica, which is used as an excipient in the weaponization of biological agents."

"Whoa," Tony interrupted. "An exipent?"

"Excipient," Nash corrected. "Silica keeps the biological agent stable until it can be delivered as a weapon. We found traces of silica attached to both anthrax and plague."

Tony had just taken a sip of Sprite and it came spewing back out. "Plague?"

"Anthrax *and* plague," Nash said.

"Any signs of anthrax or plague on the BioWatch network?" Tony asked.

The BioWatch system, which consisted of biohazard sensors set to detect eight of the most common bioweapons, had been implemented by Homeland Security in more than thirty cities, including Washington, D.C.

"Nothing has shown up on BioWatch anywhere in the country," the deputy director of Homeland Security replied.

"How bad is this cocktail?" Tony asked, turning to Jennifer Esperanza.

The CDC doctor explained, "Inhalation anthrax is ninety to a hundred percent lethal if symptoms occur before treatment starts. Plague can be treated—if you know you've got it. Mortality is one hundred percent if you don't get treatment before symptoms show up."

"Not to mention the expense of cleaning up the anthrax spores afterward," the MPD captain said. "I'm not sure what the latest figure is, but we're talking nearly a hundred million just to decontaminate the few buildings we cleaned up after the attack in 2001."

Tony frowned and turned to Nash. "How did you figure that out, that it's both anthrax *and* plague?"

Nash hesitated, then said, "We dug up bodies from a mass grave near that abandoned lab in the jungle, men and women—and children—they'd apparently experimented on, and sent samples to USAMRIID."

Nash turned to the USAMRIID major who continued, "We did tests on the tissue samples. Preliminary results showed the victims were infected with both diseases."

"I thought there was a vaccine for anthrax," Tony said, "and that most of the guys in Washington who are targets of biological warfare have taken it."

"Doesn't help them with the pneumonic plague," Nash pointed out.

"Pneumonic?" Tony asked.

"Attacks the lungs and respiratory system," the CDC doctor replied. "Both anthrax and plague show symptoms in two to three days. Both attack the respiratory system."

The deputy director of Homeland Security said, "We have to figure out where and how this lethal biological cocktail is being delivered and intercept it before it reaches its intended target. We're presuming that it won't only be District citizens who are at risk, that this attack will involve surrounding states."

Ben saw his father put his hands together as though in prayer beneath his chin as the deputy director continued, "For obvious reasons, we don't want to contact officials in those states until we're absolutely sure of the facts—and the dangers—involved."

"You're playing a risky game of Russian roulette," the CDC doctor warned. "My advice—and I'm just short of insisting on this—is that a warning be issued."

"That's likely to create a mass exodus from the Eastern seaboard," Foster said, "with a corresponding disruption of markets and business."

"Would you rather see millions dead?" the CDC doctor shot back.

Ben wondered whether his father would recommend to the president that she forbid the CDC from issuing its warning. Or whether, under the circumstances, the CDC would issue the warning and deal with the fallout later.

"Do we have any idea how big or small this bioweapon is, or how it's being transported?" Tony asked Nash. "Or even who the specific target might be?"

Nash shook his head. "It doesn't need to be large. The bioweapon, or several small bioweapons, could fit in a backpack. And our southern borders from California to Texas are a sieve for people on foot."

"We can step up inspections of vehicles and patrols for illegals on foot at the border," Tony said.

"We can inspect," Nash replied. "Doesn't mean we're going to find the car or truck carrying what we're trying to interdict. And there's no way to watch the entire border for someone on foot."

"You're telling me you don't think we can stop this weapon coming in," Tony concluded.

"That's right," Nash said.

"So how do we limit casualties?" Tony asked.

"We quarantine when the first cases show up," the CDC doctor said.

"Is that going to work?" the deputy director of DHS asked.

"If we don't quarantine, the plague will spread exponentially from person to person. Which is why, I presume, they added it to the anthrax," the USAMRIID major replied.

"What constitutes a lethal dose of anthrax?" Ben asked.

The CDC doctor met Ben's gaze and said, "Just ten thousand spores, less than one-millionth of a gram. An infection is invariably fatal within five days to a week after exposure.

"I'll give you a scary scenario," she continued. "It's football season, right? Stadiums full of happy, shrieking fans, not a few of whom are senators and congressmen and high-ranking government officials.

"A hundred kilograms of anthrax—that's just 220 pounds—released in aerosol form from a low-flying aircraft over Washington, D.C., on a clear, calm night, could eventually kill one to three million people. If it's done right, they would never even know they'd been infected."

"Oh, shit," Tony said.

"Oh, shit, is right," Nash said.

"Is that how you think this cocktail will be delivered?" Tony asked Nash, still looking shell-shocked. "Someone steals—or simply rents—a small airplane and sprays an aerosol bioweapon, like some crop duster, on an unsuspecting public?"

"We don't have a clue," Nash replied. "It could just as easily be delivered through grenades or rocket warheads or an IED. Any and every possibility has to be considered."

"Sounds to me like the smart thing would be to evacuate the government from the District," Tony said to the president's advisor, scrubbing a hand across a chin that revealed a shadow of beard, despite having been shaved that morning.

Ben saw that his father was already shaking his head. "It would be impossible to conceal a mass evacuation like that," Foster said. "The last thing we want to do is create panic in the general public, for the reasons I've already stated."

Foster picked up a pencil and ran it through his hands as he added, "The chance exists that the weapon has already been released. Creating panic would only spread the disease."

"What Trisha said—that she *plans* to kill—made it sound like she hasn't yet done whatever she's come to do," Ben said.

"In which case, we need to be especially vigilant over the next few days or weeks to prevent this attack," the deputy director said. "We need to blanket this city with cops and agents, both ICE and FBI, until we find that girl and anyone else connected with this Al Qaeda plot."

"You have any idea how many social gatherings there are of government officials in this city?" Tony said. "Embassy parties, private parties, fund-raising parties. How are we supposed to provide protection at those events against a bio-terrorism attack? Especially when we don't know who the specific targets are or when the attack will come?"

"I think the more urgent question is whether some of this biological weapon has already been delivered," Nash said.

"You think someone besides the Afghani girl may be involved?" Foster asked.

"I don't know. I think we need to keep an eye on cases of influenza at local hospitals." He turned to the D.C. Department of Health Bioterrorism rep and asked, "Have you seen anything suspicious in local hospitals? Clusters of the same illness, for instance."

"The problem is," the DOH rep said, "that local doctors haven't been alerted to watch for specific symptoms. And unfortunately for us, in the beginning stages of the disease, both anthrax and plague have symptoms that could be compared to an ordinary cold."

"What, *exactly*, are the symptoms of this cocktail?" Ben asked, figuring he might need to know if he ended up being inadvertently exposed.

"Anthrax causes fever, fatigue, an unproductive cough and maybe some mild chest discomfort the first couple of days," the CDC doctor replied. "Symptoms so mild you'd be likely to ignore them. If you do, you're dead. Because what comes next is complete respiratory failure."

"I'm feeling a little sick myself right now," Tony murmured.

The room was quiet as the people responsible for getting the word out to the public of the danger that existed—when the time came—digested the enormity of the problem they were facing.

Ben could see the fine line they walked between the disaster that might occur if they didn't find the weapon before it was delivered, or misjudged the exact time to inform the public what was going on and the disease took hold in the population and began to spread.

"We do know one person who's likely involved with the weapon," Ben said quietly. When he had everyone's attention, he continued, "Trisha said she was coming after me. What if I make myself an easy target? That could flush her out."

"You're not going anywhere except back to the hospital," Tony said. "The only reason you're here right now is that you've interacted with this girl up close and personal. We've got a picture of her from her green card application."

"I've been released from the hospital," Ben said. "I'm ready to go back to work. Sir."

"You just had a major meltdown," Tony said.

Ben flushed, avoiding the glances of the doctors and MPD officers in the room. "That happened when I thought my sister had been killed," he pointed out. "Which turned out not to be the case. I've been working closely every day the past week with Dr. Schuster." Ben hoped Tony never found out just how closely.

"So now you're cured?" Tony said sarcastically.

"Not cured. Just functional again. As I have been since I started work here six months ago."

Tony pursed his lips and glanced at Ben's father. "Your call, sir. Do we use him? Or not?"

Ben's father met his gaze and said, "We don't seem to have much choice. He's the one who's spent time with the girl and knows what she looks like. And she's our best lead to the bioweapon."

At that moment, Tony's cell phone rang. He swore and reached toward the holder at his waist to retrieve it.

The doctor from the CDC reached into her briefcase and pulled out a phone that was buzzing quietly.

Nash reached into the pocket of his cammies and pulled out a phone that was apparently vibrating.

As all three looked at their phones to see who'd called, Ben said softly, "It's started."

58

"That was the ICE Special Agent in Charge of the Greater Southwest Region in Fort Worth, Texas," Tony said after all three had finished speaking on their phones. "There's been an incident."

The Deputy Director of Homeland Security swore under his breath.

"I told him to contact the FBI." Tony glanced at Jennifer Esperanza. "And that I would contact the appropriate person at the CDC."

Ben understood interservice rivalry from his days in the military. Now that ICE had become a huge investigative arm of Homeland Security, they were naturally territorial about their responsibility for the safety of the nation. Ben knew the situation was dire when his boss immediately sought help from the FBI.

"What happened?" Foster asked.

"An ICE agent found what he thought were two dead illegals on our side of the border three days ago near Brownsville, Texas," Tony said. "One was still alive. He had him transported to the McAllen Medical Center, the designated trauma center in Hidalgo County.

"The man died the same day he was admitted to the hospital. The two agents and the medical caretakers who handled him, and the medical examiner who did the autopsy on him, are all seriously ill." Tony made a gesture to the CDC doctor, who seemed anxious to speak.

"McAllen Medical Center has reported a rash of respiratory illness to the CDC," she said. "On my advice, a doctor on my staff in Atlanta will tell them to treat for anthrax and plague—and begin quarantine procedures."

"How are we going to keep that quiet?" the deputy director demanded.

"Would you rather I let those people die?" the CDC doctor retorted. "It may already be too late to save them. But there will be more cases who'll have a chance to live."

"We need to keep the press from getting hold of this," the deputy director said. "I don't want to create a national panic."

"The press you can keep quiet," Ben said. "You're not going to stop infected persons from telling their friends and neighbors what's going on via the phone and Internet. The cat is out of the bag, sir."

"We can keep those in the hospital quiet," Foster said, thinking aloud. "They'll be quarantined. And the CDC can muffle the medical caretakers. Can't you, Dr. Esperanza?"

"I would think we need to tell the public we're under attack," Jennifer Esperanza said angrily. "And make sure they get to a hospital for treatment if they fall ill."

"How widespread is the contamination at this point?" Foster asked her.

"We know the hospital and government workers are infected," Dr. Esperanza replied. "In all probability their families have been infected. And the friends of their families. We're going to need to move fast to save lives. We're going to have to issue a warning to the public."

Ben saw the deputy director was already shaking his head.

"If there are additional couriers with this bioweapon, I don't want to alert them that we know they're on the way," he said.

"Meanwhile, Americans may be—will be—dying," Dr. Esperanza said heatedly.

"What about at least sending a warning to local hospitals in Texas?" the D.C. DOH Bioterrorism rep asked.

"How many of those friends of friends will have gotten on a plane in the past twenty-four hours," Ben interjected. "The bioweapon might already have gone national. Or international."

The deputy director glared at him.

Tony turned to the deputy director and said, "At least we have our first clue to how this stuff is coming into the country. Agents went back and searched the site where the illegals were found and a backpack was recovered. Inside was a small fire extinguisher—full of biotoxin."

"Something that small—a single fire extinguisher—sounds containable," the USAMRIID major said. "Maybe that weapon was intended for D.C. Maybe it never got here."

"And maybe it's one of many sent all over the country," Foster said.

"It sounds to me like we're going to have to remove every fire extinguisher in every public building in the city," the MPD chief said.

"Major Rankle could be right," Foster mused. "The infection in South Texas could have been meant for us and never got here."

"We have to assume that Al Qaeda would anticipate an accident like the one that occurred and duplicate their efforts to get these bioweapons into the country," Nash said. "If their couriers were at the Texas border three days ago, they've had time to get across the country on a bus or train or hitchhiking, or in a car they've stolen or bought.

"Based on those assumptions, we can expect them to release their bioweapons in D.C. any day now," Nash finished.

"Won't the BioWatch sniffers detect this cocktail when or if it's released?" Tony asked.

"Depends on whether Al Qaeda releases their bioweapon near enough to one of the sniffers for it to get picked up," the police chief explained.

"I guess you're saying we're lucky we had this early warning," Foster said.

Nash shrugged. "The deaths in Texas are tragic, but on the

whole, that tragic incident may have saved lives." He gestured to Jennifer Esperanza. "Based on what the doc here said, it isn't going to take a lot of this bioweapon to do a lot of damage. All you'd need to do is set a small office fire. If you've substituted a bioweapon for the fire extinguisher hanging on the wall—" He spread his hands wide.

"At least we aren't looking at a stadium full of infected people," the USAMRIID major said.

"I wouldn't count on that being the case," Nash replied. "Just because there may be smaller canisters of this weapon out there, doesn't mean Al Qaeda hasn't made arrangements for larger quantities to be shipped into the country."

"This is our worst nightmare coming true," Dr. Esperanza said. "How are we going to find these couriers and stop this attack? We have no idea how many of them have come across the border."

"But we know where some of them are headed," Nash said. "There's definitely an MS connection to Al Qaeda in El Salvador. And we believe they're using MS gang members here in D.C. to deliver a weapon of some kind."

Ben watched as Tony exchanged a long glance with the MPD chief. He felt the hair on his arms turn to gooseflesh as they both turned their attention to him.

"I think that original idea of Ben's has some merit," Tony said at last. "We need a sacrificial goat to lure this girl into the open." He focused his gaze on Ben. "And you're it."

59

The first person Ben saw when he left the conference room was Anna Schuster. He walked up to her and demanded, "What the hell are you doing here? It isn't safe for you to be running around on your own."

"I've been told MPD officers will be posted at my townhome around the clock," Anna said. "I'm here to talk with you and your boss before I head home."

"I don't have anything to say to you," Ben said, stopping outside Tony's door.

Her face flushed and her blue eyes sparked with anger, but her voice was level when she spoke. "I could have kept you in the hospital up to seventy-two hours for observation. You got out after twenty-four because I thought you were going home to rest and recuperate. Instead, you're back at work."

"I need to be on the job."

"Fine. I want you to check in with me every four hours."

"The hell I will."

"You will, or you'll go back to the hospital," Anna said through tight jaws.

"Fuck."

Anna knocked on the edge of the ICE SAC's open door and entered when he called out to her.

Ben leaned against the doorway. With everything that had happened, he figured Tony was going to agree to Anna's demand that he check in with her every four hours. He resented giving that much control to a woman he couldn't trust not to yank him off the streets. Yes, he'd gone a little nuts when he'd thought Julia was dead. But those were extraordinary circumstances. And for the last goddamn time, *he felt fine!*

"Good to see you, Dr. Schuster," Tony said, interrupting Ben's thoughts. He looked at Ben and said, "Come on in."

Tony turned back to Anna. "We need Agent Benedict on the job. What are the chances he's going to have another meltdown?"

Anna glanced briefly at Ben and said, "I'm satisfied he's okay to work." She took a deep breath and added, "So long as he checks in with me every four hours."

"Checking in with her every four hours is going to interfere with me finding the girl," Ben countered.

"If you don't call the doctor, you don't work," Tony said flatly.

Ben knew when to cut his losses. He nodded once to show his acceptance. "So how are you going to use me as bait to find this girl?"

"The girl knows you and Dr. Schuster have been hanging around together. I figured we'd keep you and the doctor together at her place," Tony said. "We'll have MPD cops and ICE agents on hand but out of sight. That way, when the girl comes hunting you, we pick her up."

"I don't think that'll work," Nash said as he stepped into Tony's office.

"Why not?" Ben asked.

"Trisha Reynaldo might want to kill you and your girl, but she's not going to get caught doing it," Nash said.

Ben bit his tongue rather than correct Nash about Anna being "his girl" and avoided the odd look Tony sent his way.

"Trisha's not going to come anywhere near the doctor's place if there are police anywhere in the vicinity," Nash said to Tony. "She's done an amazing job of keeping herself under the radar."

"So what do you suggest?" Tony asked. He turned to Ben and said, "Where do you think she's hiding now?"

"If I had to guess, her Al Qaeda contact is keeping her under wraps somewhere in Columbia Heights." Ben hesitated, then said, "I have one more piece of information that might be useful."

Tony made a "go ahead" signal with his hand.

"I think whatever bioweapon is on its way here is going to end up in Georgetown."

"What makes you say that?" Nash asked.

"The One-Eight has been following MS around all over Georgetown this past week, hoping to intercept whatever it is they're bringing in. They think it's counterfeit money or weapons or drugs or something else they can steal and sell."

Tony crushed an empty Sprite can. "I really, really want to keep the One-Eight out of this."

"Put me back on the street," Ben said. "And I'll find the girl."

"All right," Tony said. "Take Dr. Schuster home first. Make sure someone from MPD is there before you leave."

Ben turned to Anna. "Let's go, Doc."

"Take good care of her," Tony said.

"Don't worry," Ben said. "I know just what to do with Dr. Schuster."

60

"I gotta admit, Doc, there's a certain symmetry to this—me wanting to work and you wanting me to stay at home," Ben said as he drove Anna from the ICE office downtown to her townhome in Georgetown.

"This is all my fault," Anna said, not bothering to hide the distress she felt. "I handled this badly."

"Yeah," Ben said. "It is and you did. You created this crisis of confidence my boss developed by sticking me in the hospital when there was no reason—"

"When a man tells me he wants to die, I can't stand by and do nothing!" Anna interrupted.

"I was upset," Ben retorted. "I thought my sister was dead."

"You thought you'd *killed* your sister," Anna shot back. "And it looked to me like you were going to make it up to her by killing yourself."

Ben remained silent, which left Anna nothing to fight against. She sighed heavily. "I thought you were suicidal. You had a gun. You were talking crazy. You didn't leave me any choice except to have you hospitalized to keep you from hurting yourself."

"I wouldn't have done it," Ben said sullenly.

"You say that now. You're sober now. You've stayed alive long enough to find out your sister wasn't killed by some gang kid, for which you blamed yourself."

"I would have gotten through it without your help. I have in the past. And I will in the future."

"I only acted in what I thought was your best interest."

"Someone who cared about me wouldn't have tied me down to a hospital bed," Ben said.

"If I'd done that to my sister," Anna said, turning bleak eyes in his direction, "she'd still be alive today."

"I'm not your sister."

"No, you're just the man I love."

Ben stared out the window.

Anna tightened her arms around her ribs protectively. "I take it you don't reciprocate my feelings."

He turned back to her, his blue eyes fierce. "Don't kid yourself, Doc. All we've got going is some really great sex. Whatever else I might have felt for you got stomped right out of me by those cops you had take me into custody. I can't forgive you for that."

Anna felt the tension vibrate between them. She knew she'd been right to do what she'd done. He seemed equally convinced she'd been wrong.

"I guess that's that," Anna said flatly. "If you don't mind a little advice—on my way out of your personal life—you might want to learn how to forgive. You can start by forgiving yourself for your part in your brother's death.

"Then you might want to forgive your mother for making the choice she did to split her children up at a time when she was grieving for a lost child and a broken marriage.

"Finally, you might want to forgive yourself. For taking innocent lives as a soldier. For failing to save your friend. And for letting your sister get hurt."

But most of all, she thought, *for taking the love I've offered and throwing it back in my face.*

Anna was gripping her hands tightly to keep from lashing out physically, when she was hurting so badly inside. "You aren't God, Agent Benedict. You're just one more flawed human being."

Ben stopped the car in front of Anna's townhome. He turned

to her, his mouth open to reply, but she didn't want to hear any more criticism of what she'd done. "Don't say anything."

"I was going to say the cops are in place." He pointed out the window to a car parked down the street.

She waited for him to say something personal. But it wasn't forthcoming. Ben obviously didn't share her feelings or even appreciate her efforts to help him cope with his illness. "Good-bye, Ben."

As she hurried up the front steps she heard him call after her, "Take care of yourself, Doc."

When she turned around, he was gone.

A plainclothes policeman stepped around the side of the building, lifted his jacket to show his badge, and said, "You okay, Dr. Schuster?"

"Yes, thank you," she said, managing a smile. "I'm fine."

Which was the biggest lie she'd told in a long, long time.

61

Aisha had eluded the police by exiting through the emergency room. She fled from the hospital to the closest bus stop, where a bus was just loading passengers. She did not see anyone coming after her as she stared out the back window of the bus.

She was sure the assassin would send the police to search for her where she lived, so she knew she could not go back there. She knew she should go to a public phone and call the number she had memorized to let Al Qaeda know she had been discovered, that continuing her assigned mission might cause it to fail.

But Aisha had no intention of doing that. If she told Al Qaeda the police were looking for her, they would never deliver the canister of biotoxins to her. Without the canister, she had no way to avenge her family's deaths.

Instead, she made her way back to Columbia Heights and Silvio's cousin's garage, where they'd agreed he would leave a message for her when the package arrived. She checked to make sure the police were not around before she approached the garage, knowing they would seek out Silvio because he had previously acted as a confidential informant. The police would expect him to know, or help them to find out, where she might have fled.

When she stepped out of the sunlight into the dark garage, Silvio glanced at his cousin, who was spray painting a '68 Chevy Camaro cherry red, then put a finger in front of his lips to warn her not to speak. He came to meet her and walked her out of the garage again, where she stood squinting in the alley until her eyes readjusted to the light.

"When is the canister coming?" she asked.

"It's here," Silvio said, looking around to make sure they weren't being observed.

"Where is it?"

"I hid it in plain sight. In my cousin's garage," he said with a grin.

"How did you manage that?"

"It's a fire extinguisher," he said. "I substituted it for the one he had on the wall."

"You idiot! What if your cousin has a fire?"

"Keep it down," Silvio said.

Aisha saw there were people passing by on the streets at either end of the short alley who might remember their argument if the police asked. "I want it now," she said. "Do you think you can get it out of there without your cousin seeing?"

"It would be better to wait until work is done for the day," he said. "Where can I meet you?"

"Why not give it to me right here, right now?" Aisha said. "You can put it in a backpack or something and sneak it out of the garage."

"The party isn't until tonight," Silvio said. "Why not leave it here until then?"

"What if something happens and I cannot get back here? Or your cousin has a fire," Aisha said contemptuously, "and tries to use it?"

"Where are you going to put it?" Silvio asked.

"Do not worry," Aisha said. "I will keep it somewhere safe." Although where, exactly, that was, she had no idea right now. She had a feeling of foreboding. Things had already started to go wrong. She would feel better with the canister in her possession.

"Fine. Wait here," Silvio said. "But don't blame me if I get caught sneaking out with it."

"You can explain to Al Qaeda what went wrong if you do," she threatened.

Aisha leaned against the back wall of the garage in the shadowed alley, waiting patiently, if anxiously, for Silvio's return, checking constantly for the cops she expected at any moment.

"Here," Silvio said, throwing a large backpack at her. "This is what it came in."

"Careful!" she cried, catching the backpack just before it hit the ground. She checked inside and saw a small red fire extinguisher. "Do you know what this is?"

"Of course," he said disdainfully. "It's a bomb. But it needs a detonator to blow up, which you're getting from someone else. There's no chance it'll go off, even if you drop it."

Aisha stared at Silvio in disbelief. He didn't know. Al Qaeda had kept him in the dark. Was she the only one who knew that what she carried in this backpack was a plague that would spread and kill many, many Americans?

She opened her mouth to tell Silvio the truth and snapped it shut again. He would want to warn his cousin, who would want to leave with his wife and three small children and perhaps his mother-in-law. And maybe his cousin would have a friend he would tell. Silvio might even decide to tell everyone in MS what was really going on, that if they didn't leave town, by the end of the week they would all be dead.

"Where are you headed now?" Silvio asked.

"It is better I do not tell you," Aisha replied. "That way, when the police ask, you will be able to tell them honestly, you do not know."

Aisha turned and walked away. Where to go, that was the question. Where to hide until tonight.

And then she had a brilliant idea.

62

Anna sat on the floor next to Penelope's basket, petting her cat as Penelope nursed her kittens. Penelope was purring, which Anna found soothing. Rocky lay dozing beside Anna, his chin on the edge of the basket, his nose no more than three inches from the cat's.

Anna had forgotten she still had Ben's dog. Which meant she was going to have to see him at least one more time, when he came to retrieve the rottweiler.

She hadn't expected to fall in love with Ben Benedict. Or to blurt out her feelings in the car. She wasn't dealing well with the pain of his rejection.

She shouldn't have been surprised. She'd known going in that Ben might not be well enough to love her back. But she hadn't been able to stop herself from caring. Now she was paying the price for her foolishness.

He wanted nothing to do with her.

All because she'd loved him enough—found the courage somewhere—to do what was medically best for him, knowing he would hate it and might never forgive her for it.

Anna glanced at the clock as she rose. Ben had dropped her off around 4:00 p.m. and she decided it was time for a long, hot, desperately needed bubble bath.

She was in the bathtub, the bubbles nearly gone, when she heard the phone ring. She reached for her watch, which she'd left on the edge of the tub. It was 4:35. She wondered if she had a patient in crisis and debated whether to try and get the call. She heard the answering machine pick up and then heard Henry's voice. He was sobbing.

Anna lurched from the tub and grabbed a towel on her way into the kitchen, where she kept the machine. She picked up the receiver.

"Henry? Is that you?" Anna said, trying to hold the phone against her ear with her shoulder as she wrapped the towel more firmly around her.

"Anna?"

"Henry? Your voice sounds funny. Are you all right?" Anna headed for the front door, ready to cross the hall dressed in no more than a large towel if Henry was in some kind of trouble at home.

"Anna, I'm scared."

"Henry, what's wrong? Where are you?"

"Anna, I'm in trouble. I was just hanging around with the One-Eight—"

"The *One-Eight?*" she interrupted, unable to keep the disapproval from her voice. "Are you at home? Should I come over?"

"I'm not home, Anna. Please don't be mad," Henry said. "I'm in—"

"Tell her what I said, nothing more!" an angry female voice interrupted.

As Anna listened to Henry recite words he'd obviously been told to speak, her knees buckled, and she sank to the kitchen floor with her back against the refrigerator. "Henry, tell me where you are," she said.

Anna heard the sound of a scuffle, then heard Henry scream in agony. "Henry! Where are you?" she cried.

Anna felt her blood run cold as a female voice she suddenly recognized said, "Your friend Henry is with me. If you want him to live, you will do exactly as I say."

63

Ben found himself thinking of Anna Schuster more than he wanted to after he dropped her off. He recalled the shadowed look in her eyes the first time he'd seen her. It was what had drawn him to her and made him so willing to trust her. She was someone who understood his suffering because she was suffering herself.

He'd admired her intelligence. Her compassion. And yes, her beauty. She was a stunning woman and an exciting sexual partner, which was what had tempted him to spend his nights with her when he knew better than to get involved.

And look how things had turned out.

He would never forget what she'd done to him. It was too monumental a betrayal.

It took guts for her to do what she did.

The problem was, he believed that in the same situation, she'd do it all over again. Even knowing how he felt.

She did it for your own good. You were talking crazy. You were out of your mind with pain and grief.

He was tempted to forgive her. To excuse her behavior because he could explain it rationally. But even if he excused her, how could he ever trust her again? No, he had to make a clean break.

His mind filled with images of Anna, naked in his arms. He remembered what it felt like to be deep inside her. He recalled the softness of her skin and the smell of her shampoo. The scent of her was in his nostrils even now.

Ben felt himself becoming aroused and swore. The woman had definitely gotten under his skin. If he kept his distance, he was sure his memories of her would fade.

Eventually.

The problem was, he had to stay in constant touch with her until he found the girl. And he had to see her again to get his dog. He imagined her petting the rottweiler, her fingers sifting through his fur, pushing it up, and then smoothing it down again.

He was hard as a goddamn rock.

Ben swore again. He glanced at the clock in his SUV. He'd spent the past three hours and fifty minutes driving around Columbia Heights in a fruitless search for Trisha Reynaldo. He'd noticed the increased ICE and MPD presence on the streets, but he hadn't heard anything over the police radio that suggested the public had any inkling of the biological terrorist attack that loomed.

It was so quiet on the streets of Columbia Heights that you could hear a mouse squeak. MS was conspicuously absent. The 1-8 was playing least in sight. Ben smelled a rat.

The increased ICE and MPD presence might be all the explanation he needed for the eerie silence. But knowing what he did about the impending attack, Ben was more than a little anxious.

Hell, he might as well make his 8:00 p.m. check-in call to Anna early and get it over with. He pressed the direct dial to Anna's home phone and listened to it ring. And ring. The call was picked up by Anna's answering machine, which told him she was unavailable and would return his call as soon as she returned.

"This is Ben. Give me a call on my cell when you get this message."

Ben snapped his phone closed irritably. If she was going to require him to check in, the least she could do was answer the phone.

He checked in with Harry and discovered that the MPD

hadn't been able to locate Trisha. He checked with Tony and was told that ICE hadn't found her, either.

He looked at the SUV clock, saw ten minutes had passed, and fumed. Anna should have seen the message light blinking by now and returned his call. After all, he was supposed to have called her right about now. He called her again, in case she'd been in the bathroom washing her hair or maybe had the hair dryer going and hadn't heard the phone.

The answering machine picked up again. "Anna, if you're there, answer the damn phone."

But she didn't pick up. Which scared him. Anna should be at home. Where she was safe. And protected by an around-the-clock police presence. Where the hell was she?

She wouldn't have missed talking with him. Not after everything she'd gone through to make sure he was on such a tight leash.

He keyed his police radio and contacted the MPD car sitting outside Anna's townhome. "Anything going on there?" he asked the cop who responded.

"It's been quiet," the cop replied. "Haven't seen the doctor or any sign of trouble since we came on duty."

Ben started to ask the cop to go up and knock on Anna's door. But with his luck, she'd be finishing up a shower and show up in a towel. He'd check on her himself.

He drove to Georgetown and parked right behind the unmarked police car, then went to the window and knocked. When it rolled down, he said, "Everything okay?"

"Nothing happening here."

"I'm going up to see the doc." He didn't hurry. He didn't want to feed his fear. But his heart was pounding when he knocked on Anna's door. It ratcheted up another notch when there was no response. He knocked louder and heard Rocky bark on the other side.

"Anna?" he called out as he pounded on the door. "Are you there?"

The door across the hall opened and a young black woman stepped out. "She went out."

"You must be Henry's mom," Ben said.

The woman smiled. "Yes, I am. I'm Elaine Fields. You must be Ben. Henry's told me about you. And of course, I've seen you coming and going this past week with Anna. If I may say so, you two look good together."

"Nice to meet you, Elaine," Ben said, shaking her extended hand. "According to the cops outside, Anna hasn't left her apartment. What makes you think she's gone?"

"I saw her leave through the basement as I was coming in."

"The basement? I thought this place only had one way in and out."

"There's an old passage underneath the building. It must have been a root cellar. It comes out in the alley."

"Why would she go out that way? I mean, the police out front are there to protect her."

Elaine shrugged.

"Do you have a key to Anna's apartment?" Ben asked.

"Of course. But I'm not sure I should let you in if Anna's not there."

"I think Anna may be in trouble. Would you get the key, please."

Elaine's brow furrowed a moment in thought before she turned and disappeared into her apartment. She returned with a key attached to a rabbit's foot keychain. "I hope I'm doing the right thing," she said, opening Anna's door.

Ben hurried inside, only to find the apartment empty save for his dog, who greeted him with a wagging tail, and Anna's cat, who ignored him. He looked for some disturbance, but except for a towel on the bed, everything was as neat as Anna always kept it. Rocky followed anxiously on his heels as he tore through the small apartment a second time. And found the tub still full of soapy water. That was odd.

And why would Anna go out the back way? What possible

reason could she have for avoiding the police, who were there to protect her?

Something was very wrong.

Ben saw the light flashing on Anna's answering machine and hit the button to listen to her messages.

"I don't think you should be doing that," Elaine said.

Ben thought she might be right when the first message on the tape turned out to be a patient. It was mercifully brief and was followed by a message from Anna's partner, Ike, the one she'd told him was her mentor, asking if he should find someone to cover her patients or whether she would be coming in to work.

Ben recognized the voice on the third message.

So did Elaine Fields. "That's Henry!"

Ben realized they were hearing both sides of the call, that Anna must not have cut off the recorder when she'd answered the call. Henry Fields was a hostage.

After Henry stopped speaking the Afghani girl got on the line and warned Anna not to call the police if she wanted to see Henry alive. She told Anna to come to a bus stop in Columbia Heights. There she would be called on the pay phone and told where to go.

Ben reached for his cell phone to call Harry and get him to send a black-and-white to the bus stop but hesitated when the next message began. It sent a chill skittering down his spine.

Trisha Reynaldo had suspected he would come to Anna's home when she disappeared. Had guessed he would check Anna's answering machine. So she'd left a message just for him.

"You know who this is. I have your woman. I will not kill her right away. I want you to wonder how she will die."

Ben felt his stomach turn over. He was afraid he knew exactly how Trisha would kill Anna. She might already have infected her.

"Oh, my God," Elaine said. "If that woman is going to kill Anna, what's happened to my son?"

"Go back home, Mrs. Fields, and stay there. I promise I'm going to find Henry and Anna."

Elaine Fields looked at him with terror in her dark brown eyes. They both knew how hollow his promise was. He'd said only that he would find Henry and Anna. He hadn't said he would bring them both back safe. Or even alive.

64

Ben felt sick to his stomach. His gut was telling him the truth, even if he'd been avoiding it all day like the plague. *Ha. Ha. Not the least bit funny, Benedict.* The world would be a lesser place without Annagreit Schuster. He would be a lesser man without her.

He realized, now that there was a chance he would never see Anna again, never have another chance to speak to her, that he cared for her far more than he'd allowed himself to admit. It didn't take much soul-searching to find the reason why he'd denied his feelings.

He'd seen how love played out with his parents and stepparents. And with Julia and Waverly. People who loved each other could hurt each other. There was pain at each betrayal. And the devastation of abandonment.

Now, when it might be too late, he could see Anna's "betrayal" as a sign of how much she loved him. She'd risked her career to stay with him. She'd risked their relationship to save him from himself.

And how had he repaid the amazing gift she'd given him?

By protecting himself. And hurting her.

He used Anna's phone to call Tony. "Trisha Reynaldo called Anna. The conversation was taped on Anna's answering machine. Trisha told Anna she was going to kill the kid across the hall, Henry Fields, if Anna didn't come to her. So she snuck out of here without alerting the police to what was going on.

"I could hear video games in the background when Trisha was on the phone. I think she's got Henry in Columbia Heights."

"Columbia Heights is a big place, with a lot of video arcades," Tony said. "Any suggestions where we should start looking?"

"Henry Fields was running around with the One-Eight. Start with every place they hang out. The One-Eight has been following MS around all week, so Henry might also have been snooping around an MS hangout. I'm headed to Columbia Heights right now," Ben said.

"I'll call in the troops—ICE and MPD," Tony said. "Wait till you have backup before you confront the girl if, or when, you find her, Agent Benedict. Do you hear me? Wait till you have backup!"

Ben disconnected the call without making any promises.

It wasn't hard to imagine Henry joining the 1-8 at Moe's, or Trisha going there instead of an MS hangout in order to fade into the landscape. But how had Trisha known about Henry's connection to Anna? Apparently Trisha Reynaldo had seen an opportunity to have her revenge and grabbed it.

But where would she take Henry from there? She might have flattered him into leaving the arcade with her peacefully, and it wasn't a stretch to think she had an accomplice to help her restrain the boy and hide him.

He worried about who that accomplice might be. The MS leader, Jorge Gonzalez, blamed Ben for killing his brother. Jorge wouldn't hesitate to kill Anna, especially once Trisha told Jorge about Anna's relationship with him.

Ben was sure of only one thing. The sooner he found Anna and Henry, the better chance he had of finding them alive.

Anna must have thought she'd be able to talk her way in and out of the situation. But she didn't know Trisha Reynaldo was not who she seemed. And that her intentions were entirely deadly.

Ben knew he was going to need special help to find Anna

and Henry. He looked down at the dog that hadn't left his side since he'd entered Anna's townhome.

He bent down and spoke to the powerful rottweiler, who stood easily on three legs, his brown eyes focused trustingly on Ben. "I need your help, Rocky," Ben said, rubbing the dog's ears and scratching under his chin.

Ben snapped a leash on the dog's new collar and led him outside. The cops who'd been watching Anna's apartment had been told to remain there, in case Anna returned. Ben waved to them as he opened the hatchback and gave Rocky's rump a shove as he leapt into the back of Ben's SUV.

By the time Ben was in the driver's seat, the bandaged dog had made his way forward and was sitting next to him in the passenger's seat.

Ben reached over to smooth the fur on the dog's back and said, "Let's go find Anna, Rocky."

The rottweiler barked at the mention of Anna's name. Anna, who'd convinced him to keep the dog. Who'd seen in the wounded animal a balm for the wounded man. Ever since he'd come to stay at Anna's, Rocky had never been far from Penelope—and Penelope had never been far from Anna, who never failed to praise and pet the dog. The animal had quickly become devoted to her.

Ben knew exactly how Rocky felt.

Before he'd left Anna's apartment, he'd asked Elaine Fields for one of Henry's dirty school uniform shirts. Then he'd snatched a pillowcase from Anna's side of the bed. He was gambling that Henry had been playing one of the video games at Moe's with the 1-8 when he'd been kidnapped by Trisha, and that they'd left Moe's on foot. Which was why he was bringing Rocky along to help with his search.

With any luck, Rocky would be able to track Henry and Anna in this urban landscape, where there were no footsteps in the sand.

65

Juan Alvarez, the 1-8 leader, confronted Ben the instant he stepped inside Moe's. "Where'd you get the deformed dog?"

Rocky growled at Juan and bared his teeth. Ben put a calming hand on Rocky's shoulder, but Juan eyed the dog warily and kept his distance.

"I'm looking for a couple of friends of mine," Ben said. "You seen Henry Fields today?"

"Don't know no—"

"Henry," Ben said impatiently. "Skinny black kid from Georgetown, braces on his teeth."

"Oh, him. Brat keeps following us around," Juan complained. "Can't get rid of him."

"So was he here today, or not?" Ben asked.

"Saw him. Don't know where he is now."

Ben had also brought a photograph of Anna with her twin sister that he'd taken out of the silver frame on her dresser. "Have you seen the woman in this picture?"

"Which one?" Juan said, smirking.

"The one on the left."

"She your bitch?" Juan asked.

Ben gritted his teeth and said, "Have you seen her?"

Rocky growled and took a step toward Juan.

Juan would lose face if he backed up for a dog, but he was clearly uncomfortable standing his ground. "No, man. I ain't seen her! Get that mutt out of here. He's probably got fleas."

"What he's got is a hard-on for you, Juan. I wouldn't move too quick, if you know what I mean."

Juan froze.

"We'll leave as soon as you tell me what I need to know," Ben said.

"What is that?"

"Who was Henry with when he left here?"

"That chick. The pretty one that caused all the trouble."

Ben felt his breath catch in his chest. "What was she doing in here?"

"Came to 'pologize. Said she didn't mean for no one to get hurt."

"Did you tell the cops she was here? I'm presuming they've been in here asking about her."

"Hell no, man. Didn't want no trouble."

"How did she end up with Henry?" Ben asked.

"She came in carrying this heavy backpack, and when she left, Henry offered to carry it for her."

Ben wondered whether the backpack had contained a fire extinguisher, and whether it was filled with a deadly cocktail. "Where'd they go?"

Juan pointed to the windows, which were blocked out by posters of video games—"Metal Gear," "Final Fantasy," "Call of Duty" and "Brothers in Arms." "How would I know?"

Ben turned to the crowd and raised his voice over the noise of the arcade games. "Anybody here see which way Trisha Reynaldo went when she left here with Henry Fields?"

Nobody spoke.

"This is a matter of life and death," Ben said. "Not that any of you gives a damn about some stupid kid, but I do. So help me out here."

One of the 1-8 boys working a nearby machine glanced at Juan as though for permission. Ben watched Juan nod before the kid said, "When I was coming in, they were headed south down the alley."

"Thanks," Ben said. He focused on Juan again and said, "No bullshit, this is life and death. You see the girl or Henry or the woman in this picture, call me."

He'd spent the past five months as Epifanio's friend, earning the 1-8's trust. It was time to see whether that effort would pay off.

66

Ben retrieved Henry's shirt from the car, then headed for the alley with Rocky. He let the dog smell the shirt, then began to walk south down the alley, waiting to see whether Rocky would pick up Henry's scent. If he did, Ben wondered whether he would follow it.

Ben wasn't counting entirely on the dog. He walked the alley as though it were a war zone, alert for any sight or sound that might tell him where his quarry was headed.

He felt a tug on the leash at the corner. Following Rocky as he turned east, Ben found himself walking in an industrial area of car painting and repair shops, garages, printers, shippers and movers. Most of the businesses were set up in small warehouses, any one of which would have made an ideal hiding place.

Ben took the picture of Anna and her sister out of his pocket, folded it so only Anna was visible, and began going door to door, asking if anyone had seen the woman in the picture. Unfortunately, if the warehouses had windows at all, they were usually up high. Still, he asked the men he found inside if they'd seen anyone coming or going along the alley. All to no avail.

At the sixth large building he came to, Rocky started pulling on the leash and sniffing at the doorsill. Ben saw a broken lock hanging open on the latch. He let go of Rocky's leash and retrieved his Glock before he opened the door, holding his weapon two-handed as he quickly stepped inside and to the left of the doorway.

While he waited for his eyes to adjust to the darkness, he could hear Rocky's claws on the cement floor, moving through what appeared to be some sort of storage warehouse filled with large, outdated appliances. Used refrigerators, stoves, washers and dryers were stacked nearly to the twenty-foot ceiling on wooden pallets, leaving narrow aisles clear.

Light came in from a ring of windows at the top of the building, but the stacked appliances blocked the light and cast the narrow lanes in shadows.

It was a perfect place for an ambush.

Ben moved slowly through the warehouse, expecting someone to shoot at him. His back itched. He could feel the sweat dripping between his shoulder blades, even though it was cold enough inside for him to see his breath. He waited for the trembling that had bothered him so much to start, but his hands remained steady on his Glock.

He heard Rocky bark once. Then he was silent.

Had someone killed his dog? Ben moved quickly but even more cautiously through rows of dented and rusted metal, every sense vigilant, ready for whatever enemy he encountered. Afraid that what he was going to find was a dead kid and a dead woman and a dead dog.

When he got to the back of the concrete building, Ben saw Rocky sitting in front of an ancient, rusted-out white Coldspot refrigerator on a low wooden pallet. The refrigerator was an antique, so old it had surely been made before the advent of magnetic seals that could be easily pushed open from the inside with a mere forty pounds of pressure. So old, it would be a deathtrap for anyone locked inside.

Ben ran to the refrigerator and yanked open the door. He gasped. Henry Fields was curled up against the back wall. He looked dead.

67

Ben nudged Rocky's nose aside with his hip as he reached in to see if he could feel a pulse. The boy's face was ashen and his lips were tinged with blue.

Henry opened his eyes and croaked, "Ben!"

Ben stumbled backward in surprise.

"You came! You came!" the boy cried as he reached out both arms to Ben.

Ben leaned down on one knee and pulled the boy out of the would-be coffin and into his arms. He couldn't believe he'd found Henry alive.

The boy slumped onto the concrete floor and started crying. The fresh tears mixed with dried tear tracks on the boy's cheeks. "I thought I was going to die in there."

"It's a miracle you didn't," Ben said.

"I found a hole where the metal rusted out in the back," Henry said. "I put my nose against it and I could breathe. But I had to bend my neck funny to get to it. Whenever I stopped there wasn't enough air. I don't know how much longer I could have kept it up. How did you find me?"

"Rocky did most of the work," Ben said.

The boy let go of Ben and hugged the dog, who whined when Henry began crying again. The kid seemed okay, but Ben knew he needed to get checked out by a doctor.

Ben called Tony and told him what he'd found.

"Was the weapon there?"

"I haven't seen it, but this is a big place."

"I'm sending a biohazard team to check out the kid and the warehouse. If necessary, they'll lock down the area. Hang around. You need to be checked for infection, too."

"I need to find Anna. I'll come in when I locate her."

He hung up before Tony could order him to wait. He knew he didn't have much time to question Henry before the biohazard team arrived, at which point he might find himself quarantined. So he had to ask his questions and run.

He put a comforting hand on Henry's shoulder and said, "Why did Trisha leave you in the refrigerator?"

"Anna talked her into it," Henry said. "Trisha was going to shoot me. She has a gun, Ben. Anna whispered to me that I shouldn't give up hope. That you'd come and find me."

The boy looked up at Ben as though he were a comic book hero come to life and said, "And you did find me. Just in the nick of time."

"How long have you been in there, Henry, do you think?"

Henry held up his arm, revealing a plastic watch featuring a cartoon character Ben didn't recognize. "Two hours and thirty-four minutes."

"What did Trisha plan to do with Anna?" Ben asked. "Where were they going?"

"She said Anna had to go with her to a party."

"A party?" Ben said, confused.

"In Georgetown. Anna said she'd go with her willingly, if she'd just leave me alive," Henry said. "Trisha told Anna to say good-bye to me, because she didn't have long to live. Why is Trisha mad at Anna?"

Because I care for Anna, Ben thought. That was all it had taken to earn the Afghani girl's hatred.

"Did Trisha have a backpack with her?" Ben asked.

"Yeah." Henry looked sheepish. "I saw her sitting in Moe's and one of the guys in the One-Eight dared me to talk to her. So I did. I don't know how your name came up, but I mentioned how I knew you and how you and Anna were, you know, kind of an item.

"She said she had to leave and asked me if I'd carry her backpack. I was kinda proud, you know, that she liked me. But when we left, this guy named Silvio showed up. That's when things went wrong."

Ben shook his head in disgust at the way he and Waverly had been duped. Silvio certainly fit the profile of someone Al Qaeda might use as an operative. He was a member of MS who'd come into the country illegally from El Salvador. But instead of deporting him when he was caught, Waverly had made him his CI. And given the fox free run of the chicken coop.

"I've called someone to take you to the hospital," Ben told Henry.

"I want to go home. My mom's a nurse. If I need to see a doctor, she can take me to the hospital."

"You can have the guys who show up call your mom and have her meet you at the hospital. If you're all right, she can take you home."

"What are you going to do?" Henry asked.

"I've still got to find Anna."

It didn't take long for the biohazard team Tony had sent to arrive on the scene. They were coming in the front door as Ben and Rocky headed out the back. Ben realized he hadn't told Tony about the party in Georgetown where Trisha was supposedly taking Anna. He debated whether to call his boss right back, but as he reached for his phone, Rocky jerked on the leash and headed on down the alley.

Ben followed him.

He felt his heart leap as Rocky began to pull harder on the leash. Maybe Trisha hadn't gone too far. Maybe she'd taken Anna to some MS hangout, and Anna was even now talking her way free. Anna was a pretty good talker.

Rocky stopped abruptly and sat down. Ben felt his heart sink. They were at a bus stop. He checked the route. It went through Georgetown.

68

Ben sat in a chair before the fire in his living room dressed in a tux, his elbows on his knees, Rocky lying at his patent-leather-shod feet. He'd spent a fruitless afternoon searching for Anna.

Word was that Henry was not infected with either anthrax or plague. No evidence of a biotoxin had been found on site. If Trisha had possessed such a weapon, it had been in a sealed container in the warehouse.

Nash sat across from Ben, a McClelland Scotch in hand. The sun had set, but twilight lingered along the horizon.

Ben had come home to change clothes so he wouldn't stand out at the Georgetown parties he would be attending that evening. Based on what Henry had said, he believed that one or more of the events was an Al Qaeda target.

He forced himself to sit quietly, resisting the urge to pace. In five more minutes, it would be time to go. He could keep himself still that long.

"MPD found the bus driver who picked up Trisha and Anna. He said they got off the bus somewhere in Georgetown," he told his older brother. "He can't remember exactly where. I know Trisha plans to show up at a party in Georgetown tonight. We just have no fucking idea which one."

"You have to appreciate the beauty of Al Qaeda's plan to use a fire extinguisher to spread the biotoxin," Nash said.

"How's that?"

"It would be impossible to get that sort of biotoxin into

food at a state dinner. So instead, Trisha works as kitchen help this afternoon at some catering operation—maybe at a hotel, maybe a smaller operation—for one of the many cocktail parties being held *before* the state dinner.

"She sets a small kitchen fire that she puts out with a fire extinguisher—which she's made sure is on the wall in place of the original extinguisher—thereby infecting all the food in the kitchen.

"Tonight, the caterer delivers the food to a cocktail party somewhere in town where Washington politicians are meeting and greeting. The guests enjoy the infected food. Then, lethally contagious, they head over to the state dinner at the White House."

"There's a state dinner tonight?" Ben asked.

Nash nodded.

"Can't President Taylor cancel the dinner?"

"It's the culmination of that peace summit here in Washington between the Israeli prime minister and the Syrian president," Nash said. "Canceling would create a lot of suspicion, even if we told the people at the very top why we're doing it. The populations of those two countries, who won't know the truth, are going to think the worst.

"Here's the icing on the cake," Nash continued. "Tomorrow, the various congressmen and senators who attended the state dinner tonight will join the rest of the House and Senate to vote on the financial package to support the Israeli-Syrian peace accord, thus spreading the infection to the country's entire leadership."

"How many pre-state-dinner parties do you suppose are being held tonight? Can we get to all of them?"

"I doubt it. They're all over the city, at hotels and in private homes."

"That's just great," Ben said in disgust.

"Al Qaeda may have told Trisha which hotel or private party she should infect, or may have given her several options in case there are difficulties with one choice or another. But if I were her, I know which party I'd choose."

Ben suddenly saw where Nash was headed. "Whichever one Mother or Dad is attending," he concluded. "That way she could accomplish her mission and at the same time keep her vow to harm me and mine. Of course, that presumes either Mother or Dad—or both—are attending one of those Georgetown parties tonight. And that Trisha Reynaldo has the resources to figure out where they'll be."

"I checked and they're both attending a party," Nash said. "Just not the same one."

Ben waited for Nash to elaborate.

"Mom and the senator will be at the Georgetown home of that ABC TV correspondent who's married to the Wall Street financial wizard. I can't remember her name."

"Jessica Waters," Ben said. "She's married to Holman Tracy. They only live a couple of blocks from here. And Dad?"

"He'll be at a party hosted by another Washington society favorite, that redheaded columnist for *The Washington Post,* Geraldine Hanson. I guess you know Patsy left him."

Ben's eyes widened. "Patsy told me she was going to Texas to spend time with her father. He's been sick."

"She took Camille with her and made arrangements for Amanda and Bethany to travel to Texas for the Christmas break."

"That doesn't mean she's left him."

"She bought one-way tickets," Nash said.

"How do you know all this when I don't?" Ben demanded. How had things between his father and stepmother gotten so bad that Patsy had left his father without him knowing about it?

"Dad's a mess," Nash said. "That bossy new executive administrative assistant to the president's chief of staff stopped me to tell me she was worried about him, now that his wife had left him." Nash held up his hands to show he'd had no part in it. "Don't ask me how she knew."

Ben couldn't believe he'd swallowed the lie Patsy had told

him about her travel to Texas. He'd seen that she was worried and upset, but he'd thought her concern was directed at her sick father. He'd never suspected the truth. "What happened to cause the rift, do you know?"

"Maybe Dad just took one longing look too many at Mother," Nash said quietly.

Ben didn't comment. He'd known there were problems with his father and Patsy's marriage. He'd ignored them, hoping that if he did, they would go away. He swallowed over the sudden lump in his throat. "Do you know if Dad and Patsy are getting a divorce?"

Nash shrugged. "Maybe they just need some time apart. At any rate, Dad's attending the Hanson party on his own."

Rocky whined in his sleep and Ben reached down to stroke the animal to quiet him, comforting both himself and the dog. At last he sat back up and said, "Okay. Presuming Trisha would go after Mother and Dad, how is she going to figure out which caterer to target?"

"Think about it," Nash said. "There are only a few Washington hostesses—maybe three or four—whose parties lure the really important politicians. Waters is one of those. Hanson is another. Ergo, their parties are two of the best targets for an attack."

"Fine. So we find out who the caterers are for their parties, find out who's had a fire and—"

"It isn't that simple," Nash interrupted.

"Why not?"

"We're behind the curve on this. The food has already been prepared and, in most cases, delivered wherever it's being served."

"Then people are already infected?"

Nash's eyes locked with Ben's. "I think we have to assume that."

"Are you telling me you think Anna's already been infected?"

"I'm sorry, Ben."

"Oh, shit."

The clock was running. He had less than forty-eight hours to find Anna and get treatment for her before symptoms appeared. Because after that, her chances of survival pretty much dropped to zero.

"I got her into this," Ben said to his brother. "And I'm going to get her out of it."

69

Anna was pretty sure she was going to die. Trisha and the young man named Silvio had brought her to a garage containing several cars in various stages of being painted. Trisha pointed a gun at her heart while Silvio tied her hands behind her. He tied her ankles with the same white rope.

"Could you please not tie that so tight?" Anna asked.

When Silvio started to loosen the rope, Trisha said, "Tighten it." When he did, she said, "Tighter."

Anna cried out as the rope cut into her flesh. "I came with you peacefully after you left Henry in that refrigerator," she said. "I rented an Escalade for you. You promised that would be the end of it."

The girl bared her teeth in a travesty of a smile. "I lied."

When Anna had arrived at the garage with Trisha, she'd been ushered inside by Silvio and told to sit on a stack of tires in the corner. Trisha had held a gun on Anna as Silvio drove away in the rented Escalade.

"Now what?" Anna had asked.

"We wait," Trisha said.

Silvio had returned a half hour later. Anna could see something heavy had been loaded in the back of the SUV because it rode lower to the ground.

Trisha turned to Silvio and said, "Put her in the car."

Anna thought she was going to be put in the back of the Escalade. Instead, Silvio opened the passenger door of a shiny red Camaro and gestured her inside. "My cousin just finished painting this baby." He smoothed the paint on the hood and said, "Fucker really knows his stuff."

Anna hopped awkwardly across the two or three feet that separated her from the Camaro, turned her back and sat down. Silvio shoved her feet inside and closed the door.

"All four windows are down, just like you asked," he said to Trisha.

Anna watched as Silvio opened the tailgate of the black Escalade, where she could see all the seats had been laid down to make a long bed. "Stuff's all been loaded," he said, pointing a thumb at the stacks of white plastic bags that lined three sides of the SUV.

As Silvio slammed the Escalade tailgate closed, he said, "I'm out of here. Good luck."

"What about your cousin?" Trisha asked.

"I made sure he won't be coming back to the garage for the rest of today."

Anna heard the waffled metal garage door behind her rattling down. Leaving her alone in the darkened garage with Trisha.

Her heart was pounding. In the moments before the late afternoon sunlight disappeared, she'd realized what was taking up most of the space in the bed of the Escalade: ammonium nitrate fertilizer.

The Escalade was a car bomb.

Anna started talking, knowing that her skill as a therapist was the only hope she had of talking the girl out of what she planned to do. "You don't want to kill a lot of innocent people, Trisha."

The girl said nothing. Anna turned her head enough to see that Trisha was struggling to get something out of a backpack. When the object was free, Anna saw it was a fire extinguisher.

"What's that for?" She was afraid the girl intended to set the garage on fire—and burn Anna alive—and wanted to be sure she wouldn't get burned herself.

Trisha held it up, staring at the canister with feral gray eyes. "This is what I will use to kill many Americans."

"A fire extinguisher?"

"This is not what it appears to be. Just as I am not what I appear to be."

"Who are you?" Anna asked.

"My name is Aisha Kamal. I am Afghani. My parents, my brothers, my husband, all were destroyed by Americans. Al Qaeda offered me the chance to have revenge. Today my dream of killing many infidels will come true."

"What's in the fire extinguisher?" Anna asked. "Something to set off all that ammonium nitrate?"

The young woman laughed, but it was a sinister sound. "This canister contains anthrax and plague. I would have used the white powder contained inside to put out a fire I started near food intended for your politicians."

Aisha frowned as she stared at the red metal container. "But the plan had to be changed. Another canister like this one was found in Texas. Al Qaeda was afraid the police would be waiting and watching for just such a fire."

"So you're going to blow up the canister with a car bomb, and spread the diseases that way," Anna deduced.

"Yes," Aisha said. "But not before I infect you. I want BENEDICT to find you alive. And watch you die. By the time he receives the letter I will send to him today, telling him where to find you, it will be too late for him to save your life."

When Aisha aimed the nozzle of the extinguisher inside the driver's side of the Camaro, Anna shoved herself through the open passenger window of the car.

But even as she did so, she knew her effort to escape the bioweapon was futile. She fell in a painful heap, hurting her shoulder when she landed on the cement garage floor. Staring up, she could see a powdery mist sifting out through the open window above her.

After the anthrax attacks in Washington in 2001, Anna had learned what she could about the disease. She knew she had about forty-eight hours to get treatment…or die.

Aisha was no longer carrying the canister when she came around the back of the Camaro to kick and shove Anna, urging her to her feet. She held a gun. "Get up!" the girl ordered. "Or I will shoot you where you sit."

Anna needed the girl's help getting to her feet. When she was upright, she leaned back against the Camaro breathing hard—and surely inhaling the biotoxin with every breath. "You weren't wearing anything to protect yourself when you sprayed me with that stuff. Doesn't that mean you'll die, too?"

"Of course. But not before I have wreaked vengeance for the wrongs done to those I loved."

Everything the girl had said suggested she'd be leaving Anna behind in the garage. Which meant there was still time for her to escape or, more realistically, to be rescued.

Unless plague killed faster than anthrax and she died of that before Ben found her.

Anna wasn't optimistic about her chances of escape, and even less of rescue. She'd been warned not to contact anyone or bring anyone with her, or Henry would be shot. Anna had believed the girl when she'd said someone was watching her.

Which was why she'd done exactly as she'd been told.

In retrospect, she should have called Ben. She should have known she would need help to rescue the boy. She'd been foolish. And stupid. And it was going to cost a lot of people their lives. Including her.

Anna knew she should try again to talk the girl out of her suicidal plan, but her throat and lungs were so constricted with fear, it was hard to speak.

As Anna watched, the girl attached something to the fire extinguisher. She had a horrible suspicion it was some kind of detonator.

The girl opened the hatch on the Escalade and said, "Get in."

"What?"

"You heard me. Get over here and climb in."

Anna stared at the girl, aghast. "I thought you were leaving me here."

"I have changed my mind," the girl said. "Your quick exit from the car tells me how capable you are of escape. I cannot take the chance that you will find a way out of here, or that help will find you in time to save your life. I want to be sure you die. I want to be sure I rob BENEDICT of what he loves."

Anna nearly blurted, *"He doesn't love me."* But the truth was, she thought perhaps he did, but was too afraid to admit it. And now it might be too late.

"You're wrong," she tried anyway. "I'm Agent Benedict's doctor."

Aisha raised a black brow. "Do not lie. I have seen how he looks at you. I want him to suffer. I want him to find pieces of you when this is all over."

Anna's heart skipped a beat. "Pieces of me?" She saw that sweat had beaded on Aisha's forehead and her upper lip. Her eyes looked wild.

"If he lives long enough," the girl said, turning fierce eyes toward Anna. She crossed the garage and grabbed Anna's arm, forcing her to hop awkwardly to the rear hatch of the Escalade. Then Aisha shoved her backward into the tiny space that was left in the center of the vehicle, wedging her in sideways between the bags of ammonium nitrate, so she could turn neither right nor left.

"The authorities will think this is only a car bomb, set by a suicide bomber," the girl said. "They will not know about the anthrax and plague. It will infect any survivors and the hospital workers and rescue workers and policemen who come to clean up the damage. And all of their families and their friends.

"Some will travel and carry the diseases with them. With luck, many thousands will die. Thousands of others will fear to leave their homes. My work will have been well done, and I can die satisfied that I have avenged my family."

Anna had counseled a former soldier who'd been the victim of a VBIED—vehicle borne IED—in Iraq. He'd actually been injured by a second VBIED, set off after rescue workers had arrived on the scene to care for victims of the previous bomb. This was the same idea, with the potential for equally lethal results.

"Some who survive the bomb will go to the dinner at the White House to tell the story," Aisha continued. "By the time anyone realizes what they are dealing with, a great many who supported the peace between Israel and Syria will have been infected."

Anna's eyes darted around, trying to estimate how much explosive power had been loaded into the car.

Aisha saw what she was doing and smiled maliciously. "You are surrounded by five hundred kilos of ammonium nitrate which I will set off with my cell phone." She reached up to shut the hatchback, but before she did, explained, "To do the most damage, I must be within forty meters of the house when the weapon explodes."

"Please don't do this," Anna pleaded. "Surely there's a better way to find justice for the harm done to you than to kill yourself and other innocent people."

"Justice?" Aisha spat. "Vengeance is what I seek."

Anna realized there was no reasoning with the girl. She was ready to die. And she didn't care how many Americans she took with her.

But Anna wasn't done arguing. "You have to listen to me."

"No, I don't." The girl climbed over Anna and stuffed a dirty rag in her mouth. She covered it with a piece of silver tape from a roll she grabbed from a nearby shelf.

"That should keep you quiet," the girl said. "I need to say my prayers. I want to praise Allah for all he has given me before I meet my family in Paradise."

70

Foster Benedict was surprised at how well his son looked, considering that forty-eight hours earlier Ben had been tied to a bed in the mental wing of a hospital.

Ben was perfectly groomed, but there were shadows in his eyes and a grimness to his mouth that told Foster his son had been pressed to the limits of his endurance. All right, pressed past those limits and destroyed. But somehow, he'd risen from the ashes like the proverbial phoenix.

For which, in good part, he thought the lady doctor might be responsible. He would have liked to thank her. If she could be found. If she were still alive.

"What have you found out about the delivery of the bio-weapon?" Foster asked his son.

"Nothing," Ben replied. "As of right now, there isn't a fire extinguisher left in a federal building in the city. No caterer of any note has reported a kitchen fire this afternoon in which an extinguisher was used to put out the blaze. We've got zip." He smiled crookedly and added, "But I wouldn't eat any hors d'oeuvres if I were you."

Foster chuckled, then sobered. "That means there will likely be an attack at one of the parties tonight. From the rumors you've picked up from the gangs, it'll be a party in Georgetown."

"I'll go you one better, Dad," Ben said. "It's going to be this party, which you're attending, or the one a couple of blocks from my home, which Mother is attending."

"You think that Afghani girl wants us both dead?"

"I do," Ben said fervently.

Foster thought of his ex-wife, who would likely attend the party with Ham but be left on her own once they arrived. "I don't like being apart from your mother on a night like this."

Ben shook his head. "You need to keep your distance, Dad."

"So at least one parent survives?" Foster said with a sardonic smile. "I've got news for you. I wouldn't want to live in a world without your mother in it."

Foster saw that his statement made his son look thoughtful. He wondered if Ben was reminded of Dr. Schuster.

"Have you heard anything from the kidnapped doctor?" he asked.

Ben shook his head. "The trail is cold. I'm betting Trisha will make Anna a part of whatever she's got planned tonight. She wants me to watch her die."

The bleak look in his son's eyes told Foster how much Ben cared for the kidnapped woman. "I'm sorry to make your job more difficult," he said. "But I can't just stand here and do nothing. I want to be with your mother."

"She isn't your wife anymore, Dad," Ben said in a harsh voice. "She isn't your responsibility. She's got a husband."

Foster wanted to retort, *"A husband who doesn't value her! A husband who leaves her alone too much. And there's the matter of a child she never told me about, a daughter, your sister. I don't want to die—or to have her die—without telling her I still love her. That I've never stopped loving her."*

Foster would have kept the silence he'd maintained for nineteen years, if Patsy hadn't left him. He and Patsy had spoken more than a few harsh words before his wife had finally left for Texas. He didn't think she was coming back.

He was sorry Patsy had been hurt, but he was glad to be free of a marriage where he'd felt guilty every day. He would never have kept looking at Abby with longing all these years if she hadn't returned his glances. But he'd never tested those looks by speaking what he felt. Maybe there was still a chance for the two of them to be together.

If she could be convinced to leave Ham.

Foster felt an ache in his chest and knew it for what it was. Despair. Abby would never leave Ham because a divorce would hurt Julia, especially as vulnerable as Julia was right now.

Foster's despair awakened the anger at Abby that always lurked beneath the surface. *You should have forgiven me. We would be together now, if you had. And how could you keep my daughter from me? I had a right to know about her.* He knew he was being a dog in the manger. Patsy had given him three amazing daughters whom he cherished. And telling Julia the truth now could only hurt and confuse her.

Loving Abby was like having a sore tooth that he couldn't leave alone. The best thing to do would be to pull it out and be rid of it.

Foster shook his head. If there was any chance at all that Abby was in danger tonight, he had to go to her.

"I'm headed for the party your mother's attending," he said to Ben. "Want to come along?"

71

"**A**nnagreit Schuster rented a black Escalade at 6:02 p.m. and had it delivered to her at a corner café in Georgetown. Your boss said you had the need to know."

Ben couldn't believe what the FBI special agent was telling him on his cell phone. Tony had brought the FBI into the search for Trisha Reynaldo earlier in the day and added Anna's name after she'd disappeared.

Because trucks used for VBIEDs were usually rented, the FBI had apparently done a search to see what had recently been rented and by whom and turned up Anna's name.

Ben turned to his father, who was driving them to the party his mother was attending at a mansion in Georgetown, and said, "Anna rented an Escalade this afternoon."

"SVBIED," his father said curtly.

"You thinking SVBIED?" the special agent on the phone asked Ben at almost the same moment.

Ben felt his stomach turn over as he realized what it meant to add the *S* to VBIED. *Suicide* vehicle borne improvised explosive device. "We weren't," he said as he glanced at his father. "But I guess we are now. How good are you guys at locating a car bomb in a situation like this?"

"Both the FBI and MPD are actively searching for the car, and ATF has bomb-sniffing dogs they're walking around the hotels in Georgetown, where a lot of tonight's parties are being held. But to be honest, there are too few men—and dogs—to do the job."

He gave Ben the license plate number for the Escalade but added, "Al Qaeda has probably changed the tag. Unfortunately, there are a lot of black SUVs in the District. Most likely the car we're looking for is in a garage somewhere and won't turn up until it's used to set off whatever explosives have been loaded into it."

"What about satellite imagery?" Ben asked the agent, knowing his father probably could have answered the question, but not sure whether he would. "Can you trace the Escalade from where it was rented, to the café, to wherever it is now?"

"Whoever set this up knew what they were doing. That whole area is tree-lined avenues," the special agent said in disgust. "There are still a lot of leaves on the trees and we've had cloud cover all afternoon.

"Al Qaeda might have changed the look of the vehicle before they drove it back into the open," the agent continued. "Or the car could be concealed somewhere in the neighborhood. It's going to be a bitch to find it."

"Are you going to block roads in and out of the neighborhood?" Ben asked, knowing he and his father hadn't encountered any MPD or FBI roadblocks during their drive across Georgetown.

The FBI agent snorted. "The kind of people who live in Georgetown aren't used to being told they can't come and go as they please. They're not going to accept just any old reason for being told to go home and stay there. And we don't want to create a panic. So far, we haven't been telling anybody what we're really looking for.

"In fact," the special agent concluded, "until you concurred with the SVBIED idea, I wasn't sure myself what we were dealing with here."

Ben swore under his breath. The whole situation was beyond his level of knowledge and expertise. He knew how to hunt down targets of opportunity. He knew how to kill, both up close and from a distance. But he knew little or nothing about the sort of real-life spycraft that seemed to be going on now.

"Keep me in the loop," he said to the FBI agent.

"My boss and your boss are on the same page. You'll know anything we find out soon as we know it," the agent assured him.

Ben shut his phone and slipped it back inside his tux jacket pocket, grateful for the interagency cooperation but wondering cynically how long it would last. He checked the 9mm Glock he was carrying concealed in a shoulder holster under his jacket.

They'd arrived at the site of the private party his mother was attending, where several young men in matching jackets, trousers and ties were waiting to park his father's Lincoln Navigator. Nearby, a couple of MPD officers stood, along with two men in dark suits seemingly talking to themselves, whom Ben presumed were FBI with earphones and mikes.

He searched the faces of the white, brown and black-skinned young men parking the guests' cars through narrowed eyes. Was one of them attached to Al Qaeda? Had Al Qaeda arranged to have someone on hand to make sure the Escalade was allowed to approach the house?

Ben looked from one end of the long block to the other and shook his head. There weren't even any orange-and-white plastic barricades to bar a terrorist from approaching with a car bomb. He knew the MPD officers and FBI special agents were armed, but he assumed whoever was driving the SVBIED would also be armed, probably with something infinitely more deadly.

Ben felt a chill of foreboding run down his spine.

"Do you think you can get Mother to go home?" he asked his dad as they headed inside.

"I don't know," his father said. "I'm sure as hell going to give it a try."

As the two of them separated to search out his mother, Ben surveyed the house. It had several brick stairs leading up to the front door, which meant the car couldn't easily be driven into the house. But as Oklahoma City had proved, a big enough bomb could do a lot of damage even if it remained outside the structure.

He also had to presume that the bioweapon would be part of this attack, that when the SVBIED exploded it would spread anthrax spores and plague into the atmosphere to infect Georgetown and the surrounding area.

The problem was, they didn't know for *sure* that any bio-weapon would be used in a car bomb attack. It might be difficult or impossible to quarantine everyone who'd be exposed to the deadly cocktail of diseases. Nor could they be sure that the rented car was going to be used for a bomb attack. Maybe it was simply being used as transportation to get Trisha—or someone else they didn't suspect—into a house where food could be infected with the bioweapon.

Although he felt frantic inside, Ben realized that his body had not been racked with tremors from PTSD for more than seventy-two hours. He smiled to himself. It was amazing how just knowing what had triggered the episodes of PTSD had helped him to avoid having them.

He felt a surprising pang of longing for Anna. He couldn't understand how he could care so much about someone he hadn't even known two weeks ago. He was worried. He didn't want to imagine where Anna might be right now. He refused to believe she was dead.

Trisha wanted to see him suffer. He had to believe the girl would arrange things so he would witness Anna's death. In which case, he would have a chance to save her.

Ben's lips firmed to a thin line. The violence he'd experienced over the past week had been terrible. He shrank from the thought of firing his weapon at another human being. But if Trisha Reynaldo gave him no choice, if shooting was necessary to save innocent lives from the acts of a dangerous Al Qaeda agent, he would do his duty.

Ben moved through the first floor of the three-story mansion, greeting the vice president, the speaker of the house and senators from Massachusetts and New York, all of whom he knew through parties his mother and Patsy had hosted. He was looking for any way the house might be vulnerable to a car bomb.

And found it.

At the back of the house, the Washington hostess had created a lovely garden room with French doors that led onto a slate patio. The backyard looked like some kind of enchanted forest, illuminated by enormous strings of white Christmas tree lights strung in the trees. A long, impressive lawn and fall garden ended in a six-foot-tall white board fence, which was all that separated the house from an alley behind it.

A car loaded with explosives could easily turn the fence into splinters and power on through the yard into the house through the French doors.

Ben made his way toward the alley, speaking to more guests he recognized, including an ABC TV political pundit and a famous comedian, who'd spilled out onto the lawn for private conversation or simply to escape the crush inside.

With cops guarding the front of the mansion, Ben felt more and more certain that any SVBIED attack would come from the alley. He wondered if MPD and the FBI had posted men back there, and decided to check. As he hurried toward the fence, a voice called out to him.

"Ben! Ben Benedict!"

Ben turned and saw his stepfather moving toward him with a drink in his hand. Ben met Ham halfway and said, "Where's Mother?"

The senator looked uncomfortable. He took a drink from the highball glass in his hand. From the way he had trouble getting the glass to his mouth, Ben saw he'd had more than a few. That was confirmed when Ham admitted, "Your mother and I have had an argument. A doozy. She's in the house."

"Mother's reasonable. Surely she won't stay mad long."

"She found out something." Ham looked sick. He staggered slightly and Ben reached out a hand to steady him.

"Look, Ham, why don't you take Mother home and—"

"Abby won't come near me. I'm not sure she's going to come home."

Ben wondered what Ham's transgression had been and thought immediately of the most obvious. The senator was a good-looking man, with a full head of silver hair, tall, with only a slight paunch that had come with age. His looks and power and wealth were a magnet for attractive women. Ben had never heard of any indiscretions, but that didn't mean the senator was an angel.

"Whatever you did, say you're sorry. Mom will forgive you."

Ham was shaking his head. "Not for this."

At that moment, Ben's cell phone rang. He let go of Ham to answer the phone.

"I figure I owe you one for Ricardo's little brother," the voice on the phone said. "I'm following this black Escalade and that girl you were looking for is driving it."

Ben gripped the phone as he listened to the 1-8 leader. Then he named the cross streets nearest where he was and asked, "How close is she, Juan?"

"Shit, man. She's right around the corner from you."

Ben turned to his stepfather and said, "Gather up everyone you see out here and tell them there's a fire in the house and they need to exit through the alley and head out to the corner."

"My car's out front," Ham said. "I'd rather go out that way."

"That way takes you back through the house," Ben said. "Do what I tell you, Ham. Gather up everybody out here and walk them down the alley to the corner."

Ham stared at him with eyes that saw too much. "It isn't a fire, is it? It's something else. Something a lot worse."

Ben didn't bother to confirm or deny. "Just go!" he ordered.

Ham hesitated another instant and looked to the upper floors of the house. "Your mother's inside. I need to go find her."

Ben felt his heart squeeze. "Dad's with her. He'll make sure she gets out."

His stepfather's eyes changed and Ben saw in them the ruthlessness for which Ham Hamilton was famous in the Senate. "Tell that bastard he can't have her. She's mine."

72

Nothing stayed a secret for long in Washington. Abby had heard rumors within a day that Patsy had left Foster and gone back to Texas. She was racked with guilt for her part in the difficulties between her ex-husband and his second wife. It was too bad Patsy had overheard her confession that Julia was Foster's child.

Personally, Abby liked Patsy Taggart Benedict. But she'd also been terribly jealous of her. It was hard not to feel glad she was gone. Which made her feel even more guilty.

She hadn't wanted to come to the Waters-Tracy party tonight. She would rather have spent the evening with Julia at the hospital. But her daughter was recovering well, and Ham had told her it was important for her to be there.

Her husband wanted to talk with a congressman who used his wife as a shield to keep from having to talk business at cocktail parties. Ham had asked Abby to distract the wife while he approached the congressman about appropriations for a military contract.

Abby never had a chance to serve her political purpose at the party. The hostess grabbed her arm and pulled her aside as she was coming in the door, telling Ham to help himself to a drink. Ham had protested, but Abby smiled at him and said, "I'll be with you in a moment, dear."

As Abby shed herself of her coat, Jessica Waters said, "You must be feeling terrible."

Abby felt a spurt of panic, wondering how her hostess had

discovered the secret she'd revealed to Foster and wondering what kind of personal—and perhaps political—repercussions the revelation might have. Was the ABC correspondent looking for some sort of exclusive?

Fortunately, Abby's panic kept her silent, because the hostess continued, "You must be devastated to learn your husband has a love child."

"What?"

Jessica Waters looked surprised, but also delighted to be the one revealing the news to Abby. "You haven't heard? The brazen woman announced it on one of those afternoon talk shows. It was taped at my network this afternoon for viewing tomorrow. I thought you would already have heard about it through the grapevine."

"What are you talking about?" Abby said, feeling faint.

"Your husband has a four-year-old son. From the pictures I saw, he's the spitting image of Ham. The woman worked in his office on the Hill. She's only thirty-one."

Abby put her hands to her cheeks to cool the sudden heat there. She thought back to Ham's behavior on their drive to the party, his unusual road rage when a driver had cut him off, how quickly he'd turned off the radio when she'd turned it on, his aborted attempts to speak.

And his irritable response when she'd asked if there was something bothering him.

He knew about the broadcast. And hadn't found the courage to tell her. She was hurt and humiliated that he'd been unfaithful. But she hated her husband for letting her come here knowing she might be ambushed with the news that he'd bedded another woman during their marriage and had an illegitimate son.

"Maybe you should sit down," Jessica said, urging Abby toward a chair.

She had to find Ham. She had to talk with him. But when she searched him out with her eyes, she saw he was deep in conversation with the speaker of the house. She couldn't bear the pity she was afraid she would find in the other woman's eyes.

Turning back to her hostess, Abby said, "I'd like to be alone for a while. Is there somewhere I could go? Upstairs, perhaps, where I can compose myself?"

"Of course, my dear," Jessica said. "Take the stairs to the third floor. There's a lovely bedroom up there. The stairs at that level are blocked off with a velvet rope. Just let yourself in and clip the rope closed again. That way you won't be disturbed."

"Thank you," Abby choked out.

Ham had found her upstairs. And confirmed the rumor.

She'd locked herself in the third floor bathroom, just in case her hostess sent someone upstairs to check on her. She'd been sitting on the toilet seat for the past thirty-five minutes trying to calm herself, without success.

Tears squeezed from beneath Abby's closed eyelids. She pressed a damp Kleenex to her runny nose. Her shoulders sagged. Like all marriages, hers had its ups and downs. She'd been certain Ham valued her as a good political wife. And he'd been a good and constant lover, even over the past five years when he must have been seeing that other woman.

How many others have there been?

That was the question that kept running through her mind. Exactly how gullible had she been? She'd left Foster for a single lapse in fidelity and married a man who'd kept a lover for years while he'd been bedding her.

How often had Ham cheated on her? With how many women? Was he seeing someone else right now? Was that why the woman had gone on the show, to protest her abandonment by her lover?

Her thoughts went round and round. She found no answers, because she wasn't posing her questions to the one person who could tell her what she wanted to know. Abby was honest enough with herself to admit she was afraid to ask Ham for the truth.

Would he lie to her? Would she know if he was lying?

The loud knock on the bathroom door frightened her, and she nearly fell off the toilet seat.

"Abby?"

She leapt to her feet, dabbed at the corners of her eyes with her fingertips, then wiped her nose with the Kleenex and dropped it in the trash. She took a deep breath and let it out. Then she opened the door.

73

Foster knew something was wrong when he asked Jessica Waters where he could find Mrs. Hamilton. The infamous Washington hostess hesitated, smiled, then said, "She went upstairs, to the third floor. To compose herself."

In Foster's experience, Abby didn't lose her composure in public, and only rarely in private. Something awful must have happened. He didn't ask what was wrong, simply turned and headed up the stairs.

He stepped over the velvet rope at the top of the stairs. The only closed door on the third floor led to the bathroom. He stood outside long enough to hear a woman sob, then sniff and blow her nose, before he knocked.

"Abby?" he called.

The noise stopped behind the door. Foster waited another thirty seconds before the door opened. Abby looked ravaged.

"Did you know about this?" she challenged.

"What's wrong?" he said. "What's happened?"

She opened her mouth but shut it again without speaking.

Foster turned as he heard someone pounding up the stairs. He was astonished to see Ham Hamilton taking the stairs two at a time. He stepped clumsily over the velvet rope at the top

"We need to get out of here," Ham said. "The house is being evacuated."

Foster reached for Abby's hand to lead her downstairs, but Ham pushed between them and grabbed it instead.

Abby snatched her hand away from her husband and snarled, "Don't touch me!"

Ham ignored her and grasped her wrist. "We can argue later. Right now, you need to come with me."

Abby fought her husband in earnest, trying to jerk free and reaching out to scratch his face with the fingernails of her other hand. Her eyes were narrowed and spittle flew from her mouth as she raged, "Let go of me. I despise you! I—"

Foster knew he had no business interfering between a husband and his wife. But with Abby so desperate to be free, he couldn't stand there and do nothing. He put a hand on Ham's shoulder.

And got more than he bargained for.

Ham let go of Abby and whirled on Foster, shoving his shoulders hard with the heels of both hands. "Get the fuck away from me and my wife! This is all your fault. We could be happy if you'd just leave Abby the hell alone."

"Stop manhandling her," Foster snarled.

"You had your chance and you blew it," Ham ranted. "Mind your own business! I can deal with my wife."

"*Deal* with me?" Abby retorted, her eyes blazing as her angry gaze shifted from one man to the other. "I want nothing to do with either one of you!"

She slipped past the two stunned men, struggled with the catch on the velvet rope at the top of the stairs, then grabbed the handrail to keep her balance as she fled.

Foster remembered what Ham had said as he'd come up the stairs and hurried after her. "Come on, you fool," he shouted back at Ham, who seemed rooted to the floor. "We need to get out of here!"

Abby had stopped dead in the middle of the empty living room, apparently unsure which way to go. "Where is everyone?"

Foster grabbed her hand and ran toward the garden room at the back of the house, figuring the attack would come from the front. "Come on. You heard Ham. We need to evacuate. This place is a target for terrorists."

"My car is out front," Abby said breathlessly.

Ham finally caught up to them and grabbed Abby's free hand. "Let go of my wife," he said, yanking Abby to a stop, so her arms were stretched wide between the two men, each pulling in the opposite direction.

Foster had turned back to confront Ham when he was distracted by movement to his right. He froze.

"Oh, shit," Ham said as he followed Foster's gaze.

Foster met Abby's eyes for what he thought would be the last time, willing her to see the love he felt for her, since there was no time to speak of it.

Then his gaze returned to the French doors, where a pair of headlights was coming straight at them out of the darkness.

74

Ben had stationed himself where he would have a shot at the driver if the Escalade crashed through the wooden fence. He was counting on the MPD officers and FBI agents to do the same if the attack came at the front of the mansion. He was expecting the driver of the SVBIED to be the Afghani girl. And he was scared shitless that his PTSD would show up at the wrong moment and he wouldn't be able to take the shot.

Ben could hear sirens in the distance. Whatever happened, backup and rescue services would be here shortly.

A few seconds later, the fence splintered with a *crack!* and Ben saw the nose of a black Escalade.

He wasn't more than twenty-five feet beyond the opening as the car scraped through the shattered fence. He could clearly see the driver's face.

And she could see him. Trisha Reynaldo was looking back at him, her lips pressed into a determined line, her eyes full of hate.

Ben took a shooting stance with his legs spread wide, his Glock steady in front of him, making it clear that if she continued driving forward, he would shoot her.

Ben heard his heart thudding in his ears. His hands trembled, but he realized it was from adrenaline, not panic. He held his breath as he took careful aim.

He waited as long as he dared. And then a little longer.

Stop the car. Stop. Don't make me do this.

Ben pulled the trigger twice before he threw himself out of the path of the vehicle, barely in time to avoid being struck.

He rolled as he fell and came up running toward the driver's side door. When he got close enough, he could see Trisha's body was slumped over in the seat. Ben was grateful the backyard was so long. The girl's foot must have relaxed on the accelerator, because the three-ton car and its heavy load quickly slowed.

Ben ran alongside until he could get the driver's side door open. He checked to make sure the Al Qaeda terrorist was no further threat. Then he stepped up onto the running board, turned off the ignition and shoved the vehicle into Park.

He didn't breathe a sigh of relief. He was too scared to breathe. All he could see in the back of the car were bags of ammonium nitrate. He saw a cell phone in the girl's hand and realized it must be the detonator for the IED. But if so, why hadn't she triggered the bomb? And then he had a horrible thought. Maybe someone was going to detonate the IED remotely. He backed away. The bomb squad could handle things from here.

Ben had already started to close the door when he heard a thump and muffled moan in the back of the van.

"Anna?" He was afraid to hope, but what else—who else— could it be?

Ben reached in and retrieved the keys from the ignition in case the hatchback was locked. He kept his Glock in one hand as he tried the hatchback with the other. It opened to the touch. The interior light came on as he lifted it, and he saw Anna lying between bags of ammonium nitrate.

She was wedged in tight. He looked to see if she was attached to anything explosive, but couldn't find any wires. When she tried to sit up, he saw she was tied hand and foot with white nylon rope. Dressed in a tux, he realized he had nothing to cut her free.

"Take it easy, baby," he said as he grabbed her ankles and

gently slid her toward him. When she was free, he lifted her onto his lap and pressed his cheek against hers. Then he carefully eased the silver tape off her lips and pulled a rag from her mouth.

She tried to speak, but her throat was apparently too dry.

"Let me get you inside and I can cut that rope off you."

"Ben," she rasped.

He grasped her chin and raised it so he could kiss her lips. "I've been so worried about you, baby. I was afraid I'd never see you again."

He tried to kiss her again and she turned her face away. "No, Ben."

He stiffened. She didn't want him. As he started to pull away, she leaned close and pressed her face against his chest. He was confused and said, "What's wrong?"

She leaned her head back and looked into his eyes. "You shouldn't have kissed me."

He gently brushed the hair back from her face and kissed her again. "Why not, sweetheart?"

"Because I've been infected with anthrax. And plague."

75

Ben and Anna were in quarantine at USAMRIID at Fort Detrick, Maryland. Ben was watching every sleeping breath in and out of Anna's chest. He'd insisted that he and Anna be quarantined together. He knew that these were the last days—the last hours—they would ever spend together.

He saw from the look on his father's face, through the glass wall separating them, that Foster had found out what Ben already knew. No matter what antibiotics were administered or how soon, everyone exposed to the anthrax-plague cocktail in Texas had died.

So far, the Al Qaeda bioweapon was 100 percent fatal.

Ben wasn't betting on his and Anna's chances of bucking the odds. They were going to die. The only question was how soon.

"What can I do to help?" his father said through the sound system that allowed them to talk to each other.

"Ask Mother to come in. There's something I need to tell her."

"I had an altercation with them, and your mother and I aren't speaking," his father said.

"Look, the two of you can hate each other the rest of your lives for all I care. But I don't have a lot of time. And there's something I need to say to both of you."

His father winced but said, "All right. I'll get her."

A moment later his mother was standing in front of the glass window. His father stood a few steps apart from and behind her. She pressed a hand against the glass and waited.

Ben put his hand next to hers against the glass. He didn't remember her hand being so small compared to his, but he'd left her household when he was only a child. Every memory of holding her hand was from a time when his hand was small, and hers had held his with a promise of safety.

A promise she hadn't kept. He removed his hand and turned his back on her, rubbing both hands together

"Foster said you had something important to say to us."

Ben took a deep breath and let it out. He could take his secret with him to his grave, but he thought he might sleep better through eternity if he got it off his conscience. He turned to his parents and said, "The day Darling fell, I was climbing the tree, and he followed me up."

He watched his mother swallow hard. "I knew that, Ben."

"How? I never told you I was up there, too."

"I was watching out the kitchen window. I saw you in the tree. I knew Darling was out there with you. Once you were up in the tree, there was no way you could have stopped him from climbing up after you. What happened was my fault. I should have come outside so I could keep an eye on you both. I just never thought—" She shrugged helplessly. "It wasn't your fault, Ben."

"Then why did you send me away?" Ben was surprised at the harshness of his voice.

She glanced at his father, then turned back to him and said, "I loved you so much, Ben. Of all my boys, you were the one closest to my heart. The night you were conceived…"

Ben watched his parents exchange pained glances.

"You were always special to me, Ben. It broke something inside me to send you away. But Foster and I had already agreed to split you boys up when Nash refused to go."

"It's my fault you didn't stay with your mother," his father said. "I was trying to get her to see how foolish it was to split up our family, but she…"

She hadn't taken his father back.

Ben's throat ached.

"I love you, Ben," his mother said. "Is there any chance you might be all right?"

"We'll know more tomorrow," Ben said evasively. "I have a favor to ask."

"Anything."

"Will you take care of my dog? And Anna's cat."

"We will," his father said.

Ben watched his parents exchange another poignant look. Anna coughed in her sleep.

Ben turned to look at her, then turned back to his parents and said, "Thanks." He reached up and turned off the sound system on his side of the glass wall and closed the blinds.

Then he walked back to the center of the quarantine room and drew the white plastic curtain that provided privacy around the two hospital beds that had been pushed together. Finally, he climbed onto the makeshift double bed and lay down beside Anna.

The longest anyone infected with the bioweapon had lived was 67 hours. Ben figured he had two and a half days left. Anna, he suspected, had slightly less than that.

She'd been frightened and exhausted when they'd arrived at the military facility, which had biosafety level-3 and -4 labs, and she'd almost immediately fallen asleep. Ben realized she was beginning to stir and leaned his head on his hand as he waited for her to open her eyes.

"Hi, there," he said, managing a smile as she looked up at him.

Her eyes darted around the curtained area before her gaze returned to rest on him. "Surgical scrubs?" she said as she tugged at the V in his hospital green shirt.

"They're a helluva lot better than that stupid gown they offered me first."

Anna looked down at the medical gown which was all she was wearing, then reached back and hurriedly drew the two sides together to cover her naked rear end.

Ben grinned. "I can't say I mind that you're wearing one, though."

Anna's face suddenly looked flushed. Ben hoped it was embarrassment and not fever.

"I was a little out of it when we got here," she said. "Where are we?"

"The bioweapons research facility at Fort Detrick, Maryland. They fixed up a safe room just for us."

Her eyes opened wide and he knew she was remembering what she'd told him about how Aisha Kamal had infected her.

"We've been quarantined," he said. "As far as anyone has been able to determine, you and I are the only ones infected with the bioweapon. Just in case, MPD picked up Silvio. He's in another room here at USAMRIID.

"A team from Homeland Security is decontaminating the garage where you were kept. They've got us here to make sure no one else gets infected. I have the sneaking suspicion we're also lab rats."

"You shouldn't have kissed me," she said as she raised her hand and caressed his cheek.

He leaned over and kissed her again. "I'd do it again."

"It was stupid," she said, sitting up and turning her back to him, giving him a view of the silky skin at her nape and the gentle curve of her spine. She suddenly seemed to remember that the hospital gown left her back bare and turned around to face him, drawing her legs up under her. She sat on the edge of the bed playing with the sheet she'd drawn over her lap. "What happens now?"

He shrugged. "They've shot us up with a buttload of antibiotics. All we have to do now is wait to get symptomatic." *And die.*

"How long will that take?"

"Couple of days," Ben said.

"I'm frightened," Anna admitted.

"Me, too," Ben said.

"I'm surprised to hear you admit it."

"Knowing you might die helps you cut through a lot of bullshit," he said.

"I can see how that might be true." Anna shot him a sideways look. She surveyed the makeshift plastic privacy curtain that surrounded the bed, arched a brow and asked, "Just how much privacy do we actually have?"

"What did you have in mind?"

Anna drew his head down and gave him a lingering kiss. "I want to make love," she murmured.

He pulled Anna close in his embrace and lowered his mouth to hers. When a woman had a dying wish, it was nice to be able to fulfill it.

76

How do you make love to a woman you love, if you know it's the last time you'll ever make love to her?

That was the question Ben posed to himself as his lips met Anna's in a tender kiss. He rubbed his lips across hers, teasing her plump lower lip with his teeth, aroused by the soft dampness of her mouth. Soon, they would both be deathly ill. Soon they would die. What he did now must last them for eternity.

"I love you," he murmured against her lips. He'd felt it for a long time and kept it to himself. Surely those were the words a woman most wanted to hear from a man she loved. And he knew Anna loved him. She'd said so. More importantly, she'd backed up those words by her actions.

To his surprise, Anna shoved hard at his shoulders and scooted up away from him, toward the rails at the head of the bed, until she was sitting upright. She met his gaze, her blue eyes glazed with pain, and said, "Don't."

He pushed himself upright the length of his arms to face her, wondering where he'd gone wrong. But how could it be wrong to tell her he loved her? "Was it something I said?" he asked wryly.

She didn't laugh. "You're only saying you love me because you think we're going to die. I don't want to diminish the respect and...caring...you feel for me by giving it a label it doesn't deserve."

Ben frowned and shifted to sit up, hanging his feet over the edge of the bed. He rubbed his nape and eyed her over his shoulder. This love business was a minefield. How was he supposed to convince her he was telling the truth, when the fact was, he would never have admitted how he felt except for the dire circumstances in which they found themselves?

He turned back to face her and said, "I meant what I said."

She didn't look convinced. She pursed her lips and crossed her arms protectively over her breasts.

He scratched at the couple days' growth of whiskers on his chin, buying time to decide what he should do next, what he should say. It was true he'd been posted to places where there weren't a lot of available women. But there had been opportunities over the years to make a more meaningful connection. He'd simply been afraid to fall in love. Afraid of being abandoned.

But that wasn't something you admitted out loud. Especially to a woman you loved and were trying to impress.

Anna laid a hand on his thigh and said, "It's all right, Ben. I should have let it go."

"I love you, Anna," he said, working to keep the frustration out of his voice. "What do I have to do to make you believe me?"

"I don't think you can," she said. "It doesn't matter, Ben. Really. Until we know we're going to live, nothing really matters, does it?"

Except he knew they were going to die. So everything that happened while they were still well enough to make rational choices mattered very much. "All right," he said. "Fine. You want to know how vulnerable I feel saying those words aloud? I'm scared shitless."

Her jaw dropped and he figured he'd gotten her attention. He reached out an arm and snagged her around the waist, pulling her close. He grasped a handful of her silky blond hair and arched her head back so he was looking down into her eyes.

"I love you so much that the thought of losing you makes my heart ache. I see your face and I can't catch my breath. I want to wake up every morning with you and make love to you every night. I want to have kids with you and grow old with you. And if that isn't eloquent enough for you, too damn bad."

He heard the beginning of a burbling laugh before he covered Anna's mouth with his own. He gently laid her head back on the pillow. It didn't matter if she believed the words he'd said. He'd show her that he loved her. He'd revere her with his hands. He'd cherish her with his body. He'd exalt her with his mouth. He'd honor her with his soul.

77

Anna sat up abruptly in bed. She'd woken herself up to stop a nightmare. *Nothing like a little PTSD to end a perfect day,* she thought ruefully. She looked at the clock and saw it was 2:08 a.m.

She glanced at Ben, who was still sound asleep despite the constant light in the room and the people in protective bio-hazard gear who came and went without regard to their need for sleep or their privacy.

She'd been dreaming about Trisha or Aisha or whatever her name was. In her dream, as in real life, the girl told Anna she was going to die, that once she was infected, the bioweapon would kill her.

Anna lay back down and spooned herself against Ben's back. She wondered if he knew they were going to die. She thought maybe he did. His lovemaking had been both achingly tender and raw with passion. Afterward, as they lay panting in each other's arms, he'd rasped those words again.

"I love you, Anna."

That was how she'd known for sure they were doomed.

She and Ben had known each other for barely two weeks. The only reason for him to make a declaration of love *now* was because he knew there would be no *later.*

The worst part was the waiting. Now that she'd rested, except for some scrapes and bruises, she felt perfectly fine. She wondered when the first symptoms would appear. And how fast things would go downhill after that.

She eased a hand over Ben's waist and felt him take it in his own. "You're awake," she said softly.

"Hard to sleep with all the activity around here." He turned over to face her, took her in his arms and said, "Nightmare?"

She nodded.

"Want to talk about it? I have it on good authority it'll make you feel better."

She smiled and shook her head. "I'm fine. Really. How about you? Any nightmares?"

"Strangely, no."

Anna thought it made perfect sense. If he knew he was dying, there was no reason to fear either the past or the future. But if Ben wanted to pretend they might live, she didn't mind pretending along with him.

He nuzzled her throat beneath her ear and murmured, "My family is going to show up here first thing in the morning."

"Why do you say that?" Anna asked.

"Just a hunch."

"Because we may be too sick to talk to them later?" Anna asked.

"Something like that. I'd like them all to meet you, if you don't mind."

"I don't mind. I wish I had some family for you to meet."

"Believe me," Ben said with a smile, "I've got enough family for both of us."

"I suppose we should try to get some sleep," Anna said.

"I'd rather make love with you again." Ben palmed her breast and teased the nipple with his teeth, causing her to catch her breath as a delightful frisson rolled down her spine.

Anna surrendered to the joy of loving Ben Benedict. It was not a bad way to spend what might be the last night of her life.

78

Ben stood in front of the glass wall the next morning with his arm around Anna. "I want you all to meet Anna Schuster." He wanted to add, "The woman I love," but the feelings he had for Anna were still too new and, under the circumstances, precious to be shared.

But if he didn't share them now, he might not have another chance. He pulled Anna snug against his hip, knowing that, in this instance, actions would speak more loudly than words.

"It's nice to meet you, Anna," Rhett said. He turned his attention to Ben and added, "The entire family, including Carter and Ryan, are here to see you. Except for Julia. She's still in the hospital, but out of intensive care. She sends her love."

Ben could see Carter standing behind Rhett, dressed in desert cammies. "How the hell did you manage to get here from Iraq?" he asked as Rhett pushed Carter forward.

"Compassionate leave." Carter flushed as he realized the message those words sent.

Ben shot Anna a reassuring look, then turned his attention to Ryan. "I can't believe you came," he said to the Black Sheep. "You're at West Point, too, aren't you?" Ben knew Ryan had made it into the military academy on his own merits. There was no free ride for the illegitimate son of a Medal of Honor recipient.

"Same class as Rhett," Ryan said. "Figured I might as well take advantage of the day off."

Ben snorted. Before he could make the snide remark on

the tip of his tongue, Anna said, "Thank you for coming, Ryan. It means a lot to Ben. To both of us."

"It's good to see you again, Doc," Nash said to Anna. "It looks like you managed to tame the tiger."

Ben smiled at his brother's jibe. Then he pointed a finger like a cocked gun at Nash and said, "Your turn is coming."

Patsy had apparently returned from Texas. The ABCs were with her. His stepmother and sisters had red-rimmed eyes that belied the smiles pasted on their faces.

Well, if they wanted to pretend, he could, too. "Hey, guys. It's good to see all of you again," he said in as cheerful a voice as he could muster. He pushed Anna a little bit forward and said, "Patsy, I want you to meet my girl."

He watched Anna's cheeks redden as she faced Patsy and said, "It's so nice to meet you, Mrs. Benedict."

Which was when Ben realized his father was missing from the crowd on the other side of the glass. "Where's Dad?" he asked.

"He was called away a few minutes ago," his mother replied.

At that moment, Ben's father strode in. The crowd parted as he walked right up to the glass and announced, "I have some good news and some bad news."

"Start with the good news," Ben said.

"I was able to get everyone except Julia here to bid you a final farewell."

Ben felt Anna's body tense, but she kept her gaze straight ahead. He cocked his head and frowned, surprised that his father had acknowledged in front of her the need for a "final farewell."

Ben felt Anna begin to tremble. He'd been hoping he could keep the truth from her. But if there was any doubt about the situation, his father's announcement had made their prognosis pretty plain.

"I'm not sure I want to hear the bad news," Ben muttered. He tightened his grip on Anna's waist in case she felt faint and said, "Go ahead."

"The bad news is that after all that work I did getting the entire family here, you aren't going to die. You aren't even going to get sick."

Ben heard Patsy gasp. His mother reeled. He saw Ham grab her shoulders to steady her and watched her lurch forward a step to free herself from his grasp. The ABCs stared at him in disbelief. Ryan snickered. Rhett glared at him.

"Is this supposed to be funny?" Ben said sharply. "Because it isn't. I know the statistics, Dad. In Tex—"

"In Texas," his father interrupted, "the bioweapon remained stable during dissemination. The batch in the fire extinguisher supposedly used to infect Anna was flawed. USAMRIID tested the stuff and found the excipient didn't attach properly."

It took a moment for Ben to grasp what his father was saying. He suddenly grabbed Anna and swung her in a circle that sent her feet flying off the ground. "We're not infected. We're going to live!"

Anna held on to his neck, laughing along with him.

Ben set Anna on the ground and stopped celebrating long enough to ask his father, "When do we get out of here?"

"They want to keep you at least seventy-two hours. Just in case," his father said.

"I thought you said the sample wasn't infectious," Ben countered.

"It won't kill you to stay here seventy-two hours," his father soothed.

Ben wasn't so sure. He glanced at Anna, who was refusing to meet his gaze. They'd been having sex like bunnies without using anything to prevent her from getting pregnant. And he'd been telling her as often as he could get the words out that he loved her. Now, he was going to have to live with the consequences of both those actions.

Ben wasn't at all surprised when Anna leaned close and whispered, "We have to talk. In private."

79

The instant they were alone, Anna offered Ben an "out." She suggested the promises of love he'd made while they were in quarantine, thinking they were going to die, had been offered under duress. And just like the three-day right of recision on a contract to buy a refrigerator he really didn't want, she wasn't going to hold him to it.

"That wouldn't be fair," she finished.

"What wouldn't be fair," Ben said, "is for you to walk away without giving me a chance to prove I meant what I said."

The lift of Anna's chin and the martial light in her blue eyes warned him that he was going to have a fight on his hands.

"We've barely spent a week in each other's company," she said.

"But what a week!" Ben replied with a grin.

"Be serious."

"I am serious, Anna," he said, sobering. "I've spent enough time with you to know I like what I see. I can understand you might doubt my feelings. All I ask is that you give us a chance."

She chewed on a hangnail as she thought it over. "All right," she said at last. "I'm willing. I just see one problem."

Ben tensed, wondering if she would set some condition on their relationship that would be impossible to overcome. "What's that?"

"We're going to have to get your dog his own basket. He's practically moved in with my cat."

Ben laughed as he picked her up and squeezed her tight. "I think that can be arranged."

ACKNOWLEDGMENTS

This book happened because I met a stranger on a plane. I was looking for an occupation for the hero of the first book of a brand-new series, and my new friend's husband just happened to be an ICE (Immigration and Customs Enforcement) agent. My hero quickly joined this updated branch of Homeland Security.

I want to thank Karen Goldsberry for her inspiration and support during the writing of this book. I'm grateful for the friendship of Sally Schoeneweiss, who listens with kind ears to my work in progress. A special thanks to Karna Small Bodman for advice on who's who in Washington. Any mistakes are mine.

Thanks to Liesa Malik and Pat Feliciano for locating information I couldn't find no matter how hard I looked.

I especially want to thank the sales force at Harlequin Books, who are so good about making sure my books get into the hands of readers. Kudos to Margaret O'Neill Marbury and Adam Wilson, who help me make my work the very best it can be. My thanks to Mary Helms, Amy Jones and Margie Miller for their parts in creating the stunning cover for *Outcast*.

There is no maintenance shed behind Lincoln Middle School. I've created problems with the magnetometer and MPD cop on duty at the school to suit my fictional novel.

Finally, I wish to thank the (anonymous) ICE agent who provided me with background information on ICE procedures.

Dear Readers,

Those of you who know my work must be wondering right now, "Which of those siblings in *Outcast* is Joan going to write about next?"

Since I've just finished a book featuring one of the Benedict brothers, I thought I'd head to Texas for the next book and write about one of the Taggart men. Or maybe not. Let me know whose story you'd like to see in print next.

By the way, Nash Benedict is featured in a story I wrote for the collection *Thriller 2,* edited by Clive Cussler, in stores in June.

If you're following my Bitter Creek series, be sure to watch for the paperback reprint of *A Stranger's Game*, in stores in August 2009, and be on the lookout for *Shattered*, the sequel to *A Stranger's Game*, coming soon from MIRA Books.

I love hearing your comments and suggestions. You can contact me at *www.joanjohnston.com*. Be sure to sign up on my mailing list if you'd like to receive an e-mail/postcard when the next book is in stores.

Happy reading,

Joan Johnston

MCN2624RR

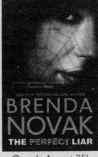
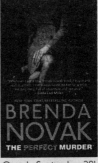

Bestselling Author

LAURA VAN WORMER

It's New York's most sought-after address. A boulevard lined
with majestic mansions and impressive apartments, it's where
passions and secrets collide, where love is destroyed,
then found again in the most unlikely place.

MICHAEL and CASSY COCHRAN—Television's perfect couple…but the
veneer is starting to crack.

SAM and HARRIET WYATT—A corporate secret could lead to them losing
everything they've achieved.

HOWARD STEWART—Perfect job, perfect wife—
both of which are perfect lies.

AMANDA MILLER—Wealth, fame and a lifetime of heartache. She's
given up on men—until she meets the one she can't resist.

Step onto Riverside Drive, where friends and neighbors
determine each other's destinies.

Available now, wherever books are sold!

MIRA®

MLVW2721

In 2009 Harlequin celebrates
60 years of pure reading pleasure!

We're marking this occasion by offering
16 **FREE** full books to download and read.

Visit
www.HarlequinCelebrates.com

to choose from a variety of
great romance stories
that are absolutely **FREE!**

(Total approximate retail value of $60)

We invite you to visit and share the Web site
with your friends, family
and anyone who enjoys reading.

REQUEST YOUR
FREE BOOKS!

2 FREE NOVELS
FROM THE ROMANCE/SUSPENSE
COLLECTION PLUS 2 FREE GIFTS!

YES! Please send me 2 FREE novels from the Romance/Suspense Collection and my 2 FREE gifts (gifts are worth about $10). After receiving them, if I don't wish to receive any more books, I can return the shipping statement marked "cancel." If I don't cancel, I will receive 4 brand-new novels every month and be billed just $5.74 per book in the U.S. or $6.24 per book in Canada. That's a savings of at least 28% off the cover price. It's quite a bargain! Shipping and handling is just 50¢ per book.* I understand that accepting the 2 free books and gifts places me under no obligation to buy anything. I can always return a shipment and cancel at any time. Even if I never buy another book from the Reader Service, the two free books and gifts are mine to keep forever.   185 MDN EYNQ 385 MDN EYN2

Name _____ (PLEASE PRINT) _____

Address _____ Apt. # _____

City _____ State/Prov. _____ Zip/Postal Code _____

Signature (if under 18, a parent or guardian must sign)

Mail to **The Reader Service:**
IN U.S.A.: P.O. Box 1867, Buffalo, NY 14240-1867
IN CANADA: P.O. Box 609, Fort Erie, Ontario L2A 5X3

Not valid to current subscribers of the Romance Collection,
the Suspense Collection or the Romance/Suspense Collection.

Want to try two free books from another line?
Call 1-800-873-8635 or visit www.morefreebooks.com.

* Terms and prices subject to change without notice. Prices do not include applicable taxes. Sales tax applicable in N.Y. Canadian residents will be charged applicable provincial taxes and GST. Offer not valid in Quebec. This offer is limited to one order per household. All orders subject to approval. Credit or debit balances in a customer's account(s) may be offset by any other outstanding balance owed by or to the customer. Please allow 4 to 6 weeks for delivery. Offer available while quantities last.

Your Privacy: Harlequin is committed to protecting your privacy. Our Privacy Policy is available online at www.eHarlequin.com or upon request from the Reader Service. From time to time we make our lists of customers available to reputable third parties who may have a product or service of interest to you. If you would prefer we not share your name and address, please check here. ☐

BOB09